ACCLAIM FOR

"Peeling back the curtain that shroud's life's messy corners, Catherine West has written a story that we all need. *Where Hope Begins* will take your breath and quite possibly your heart. West reminds us that even in the midst of heartbreak and loss, hope is never out of reach. *Where Hope Begins* will linger long after you close the last beautiful page."

Patti Callahan Henry

New York Times Bestselling Author

"Catherine West gracefully braids together grief, humor, and longing in her newest book. *Where Hope Begins* is a beautiful and heartrending story of a marriage and the two people who must decide if it is worth saving. A story for anyone who's had to start over—and those who wonder where others find the courage and strength to do so.

Lauren Denton

USA Today Bestselling Author of *The Hideaway*

"Emotionally gripping and stunningly honest, *Where Hope Begins* is a moving story that breaks the heart, then masterfully puts it back together, somehow fuller than it was before."

Katie Ganshert

Award-Winning Author of *No One Ever Asked*

"... chock full of raw emotion and beautiful prose ... wonderfully drawn characters and scenes pull the reader along on a rollercoaster ride of emotion."

RT Book Reviews
4^{1/2} Stars, Top Pick

"Catherine West's writing always pulls me deeply into the story, engaging my heart. In *Where Hope Begins*, the characters' struggles caused me to wonder, "What are they going to do?" and "What would I do if I were them?" West courageously wades into the turbulent waters of relationships—the struggles we all face. Rather than settling for easy or clichéd answers, she writes with realism, always choosing hope and grace.

Beth K. Vogt
Christy and Carol Award-winning author of
The Thatcher Sisters Series

"West's compelling and heart-wrenching, rising-from-the ashes novel realistically delves into the tough issues of suicide, anger, and guilt with a touch of grace and hope."

Library Journal
Starred Review for *Where Hope Begins*

"West is a good painter of atmosphere, making the foggy past ever so slightly sinister ... [she] manages the central tensions well."

Publisher's Weekly
Review for *The Things We Knew*

"A beautiful exploration of the bonds that tie us together as family and the secrets that sometimes unravel those threads. Catherine West builds a world worth entering and characters that linger long after the last page is turned.

Julie Cantrell
Review for *The Things We Knew*. *New York Times* and *USA TODAY* bestselling author of *The Feathered Bone* and *Perennials*

"In *The Things We Knew*, author Catherine West captures the nuances of deeply rooted familial pain and its impact on those in its wake. Intriguing setting, realistic characters with all-too-familiar tensions, and a tangle worth tracing to its source make *The Things We Knew* as satisfying as a Nantucket sunrise."

Cynthia Ruchti
Author of *As Waters Gone By* and *Song of Silence*

"West does an exquisite job depicting the complexity and messiness of overcoming trauma."

Publisher's Weekly
Starred Review for *The Memory of You*

BOOKS BY

catherine west

as the light fades

a novel

CATHERINE WEST

as the light fades
a novel

CATHERINE WEST

Published in association with Books & Such Literary Management, 52 Mission Circle, Suite 122, PMB 170 Santa Rosa, CA 95409-5370

Cover Design and Interior Layout | Yvonne Parks | PearCreative.ca

To contact the author | CatherineJWest.com

ISBN (Print): 978-1-09-145323-4

"Owning our story can be hard, but not nearly as difficult as spending our lives running from it."

BRENÉ BROWN

For all of us brave enough to own our stories, no matter the cost.

prologue

The man staring back at me looks old.

I painted his portrait once, which he wasn't very happy with. His hair was a deep brown; *raw umber*, I'd call it. Used that color a lot back in the day. Streaks of gray look out of place, like they're trying too hard to fit where they don't belong. And the part is combed on the wrong side.

Though my memory is fading, wrinkles I know weren't there before give new character and tell a thousand tales of a life well lived. Leathery skin pulls this way and that as he grimaces, equally perplexed by this new situation we find ourselves in. This place we're supposed to call home isn't. A long rectangular building that smells like a hospital on a good day and a sewer on a bad is filled with strangers who seem to know as little about themselves as we do. We're given barely edible food; watery eggs for breakfast, soup and sandwiches for lunch, and whatever mush they decide to throw together for dinner. Board games or cards for the ones who can still think over the endless blather of the television. Some just sit where they're put, suffering through endless days of doing nothing. Mindless routine for the mindless.

I suppose our surroundings are comfortable enough. I have my own room and a few things I still know are mine, like books, and photographs on the wall, but I've never liked change and I'm not about to embrace it now.

"You have no choice, old man."

His gravelly voice startles me. But he's right. I stare back at him and nod. Names come and go with increased frequency these days. I try to recall his before it slips away. But I don't need to remember it. It's the eyes that give it away.

Eyes the color of dark toffee, flecked with gold, a hint of green on a good day. Eyes that have seen the passage of time, held laughter and tears, watched over loved ones, and reluctantly let them go. Eyes that still twinkle with mischief and a resolute determination that says this is not the end.

The man gives a sudden smile, and recognition flips a switch.

I think it might be me.

one

Liz Carlisle never imagined she'd be back in this place. Certainly never dreamed she'd actually enjoy the simple act of walking the dogs around the Nantucket neighborhood she'd grown up in. Yet here she was.

Everything was different now. Renovations at Wyldewood, the rambling estate that Liz and her four siblings called home, were well underway. Her brother David and his wife Josslyn were overseeing the work on the house as well as running after their toddler twins, and her sister Lynette was still in Africa, so the task of trekking out with the family's two labs had fallen to her. Truthfully, any excuse to get away from the noisy house, now more of a construction zone than anything, was most welcome.

She studied the mottled branches above her as she waited for Diggory and Jasper to finish sniffing around the tree's roots. The leaves were showing off in a dazzling display of golds and reds, a shock of color that would inspire any artist. Not so long ago, Dad would have found joy in capturing the beauty of the scene on paper. These days he showed little interest in art. He showed little interest in anything.

Their father's slow decline was just one more thing she had no control over.

Liz sighed and breathed in the crisp air. Fall had taken its time this year, but today the salt-kissed island breeze held a chill that hinted of first fires and frosty mornings.

Could she survive winter on Nantucket?

The cold she could handle. She'd grown up with it. But the dreary, dull days, nowhere to go, no city lights, no nightlife . . . well, maybe she wouldn't miss that so much. She did miss her daily routine though. Rising at dawn to get in an hour at the gym before heading to work, being pulled along on the crowded sidewalks of the Financial District, the smell of smog and coffee and fresh bagels in the early morning air. The pinch of pride as she entered the shining glass building on Slate Street, riding the elevator up to the twenty-second floor to her corner office with a view of New York Harbor. Not that she'd ever really appreciated the view.

Liz shoved her hands deep in the pockets of her red leather jacket and put those thoughts away. That life was behind her. Time to move on.

She'd had little choice.

"Come on, guys." Liz urged the dogs forward and turned in time to see a black Jeep crest the top of the hill. Late afternoon sun filtered through the trees, and she squinted as the Jeep approached, weaving a little too dangerously for her liking. Her pulse picked up and set her on immediate alert. Somebody might have had a bit too much to drink this afternoon. Odd for an off-season Tuesday, but not unheard of.

The vehicle jerked left, veered across the road and back again.

Liz scanned the area for children or unsuspecting cyclists. Thankfully, the roads weren't that busy now, most of the island's summer residents and tourists having reluctantly made their way back to the mainland.

A striped cat suddenly scooted out from under the wild rose hedge to her left, and Liz held her breath. "Seriously?"

Sure enough, the small animal raced for the road, straight across the Jeep's path. Tires squealed and skidded, sending sand, crushed shells, and small stones every which way as the vehicle lurched off the road onto the nearest lawn, finally coming to a crunching stop at the base of an old black oak.

"Stay." Heart pounding, Liz hastily tied the dogs' leashes around a low hanging branch, not terribly confident of their obedience, but they were close to home. She raced down the hill, glanced back to see the two dogs settled under the tree, then pressed on toward the Jeep, hoping there wouldn't be blood. She hated blood.

There was no sign of the cat, so she assumed it was safe. The Jeep didn't look as bad as she feared. She hoped the driver was okay. Liz stepped over tire marks embedded in the grass and the bedraggled remains of what had been the last of summer's magnificent display of roses. Evy McIntyre's prize-winning roses, to be precise.

The door on the driver's side opened with a slow creak. Liz stopped a few feet away and watched a pair of skinny legs clad in tight jeans and clunky black boots emerge. And then a young girl stood before her.

A kid. Barely sixteen, if that.

Great.

Liz swallowed her first response and stepped closer. She gave the vehicle a cursory inspection and saw the airbag hadn't released. No blood on the kid. No bruises that she could see. "Are you all right?"

"Uh huh." The girl was a wisp of a thing, big dark eyes rimmed in heavy makeup and shoulder-length jet-black hair framed an almost ghostly-white face.

Liz stepped closer and put her game face on. "Have you been drinking? Drugs?"

The girl's eyes widened, her pale cheeks pinking. "What? No!"

"Are you old enough to be driving?" Liz had to ask. "Do you have a license?"

"What are you, a cop?" Defiance flashed in the dark eyes and Liz scowled. She had no time for teenagers, especially not ones looking for trouble.

"I'm a lawyer, and I can smell a lie a mile away. So think carefully and answer the question."

"Um . . ." The girl scuffed her boots on the grass and lowered her gaze.

Liz knew what was coming. "I'll take that as a no. Does this vehicle belong to you?"

"Not exactly." The teen twisted her neck from side to side, glanced at the front of the Jeep and then at the desecrated garden, turning back to Liz with a dramatic eye roll. "Well, that freakin' cat should have stayed put."

Before Liz could reply, the front door of the house flew open and Evy McIntyre stood on the wraparound porch of her impressive three-story home. It was one of the larger houses in the area. Evy came from old money and owned an art gallery in town where she showed, and sold, many of Liz's sister Lynette's paintings. Lynette and Evy had formed an unlikely friendship over the last year, but Liz hadn't seen much of the eccentric older woman since Lynnie left for Africa.

"What in heaven's name happened here?" Evy quickstepped it toward them in high heels, sequins on her teal blouse sparkling, a bright pink silk scarf flapping behind her. "Elizabeth?"

"Hi, Evy." Liz pulled her cell phone from the pocket of her jeans. "I was walking the dogs and this . . . happened. We should call the police. She doesn't have a license and the vehicle might be stolen."

"No, please, no cops!" The girl's eyes flared. "And it's not stolen."

Evy scanned the surrounding area and her garden, what was left of it, eyes widening at the sight of the crushed rose bushes. She took a slow breath and set a steely gaze on the girl. "Are you responsible for this tragedy, young lady?"

The girl stepped back a bit. "I guess."

"You guess. Are you hurt?"

"No."

"You, Elizabeth? She didn't run you over along with my poor roses?" Evy's thick eyelashes batted dramatically and Liz squelched a smile.

"Fortunately, I was on the other side of the street. She swerved to avoid a cat."

"Really?"

"Yes!" The girl nodded vehemently. "I swear that's what happened! I'm a good driver. I wouldn't—"

"You can't be a good driver if you don't have a license!" Liz sputtered. She caught herself before totally going off on the girl. She could see the kid was shaken and a little scared, despite her bravado. "Do you even have a learner's permit?"

"Uh . . ."

"Just as I thought. You know—"

"A moment, Elizabeth." Evy held up a hand to Liz, then turned back to the girl. "Name?"

"Mia Stone."

Liz gauged the fear in the teen's eyes. "Evy? Shall we call the police?" She waved her cell phone at the older woman.

"Please don't call the cops!" Tears formed and her bottom lip began to tremble. "I'll do whatever you want to make it up, pay you back, just . . . no cops."

"Are you kidding me?" Liz stared. She was a good little actress this one.

Evy tightened her lips, ignored Liz, and focused on the girl. "Young lady, you'd better come into the house. We will call your parents. And then I will determine your fate."

Oh, come on, Evy. She'd be making the kid hot chocolate in a few minutes. Liz stifled words she really wanted to say and put her phone away. "Evy, do you want me to stick around?" Liz didn't think the kid was capable of doing the older woman any harm, but these days one couldn't be too careful.

Evy simply smiled and shook her head. "We'll be fine. Thank you, Elizabeth." She ushered the girl toward the house without so much as a backward glance.

"You better call the cops on her," she huffed, half-tempted to do it anyway. But Evy wouldn't appreciate that, and the less involved Liz stayed the better. And maybe the kid deserved a break. Liz rolled her eyes. A few months ago that thought wouldn't have occurred to her. But these days she was more aware of the importance of second chances. So she left the girl's fate in Evy's hands, went to retrieve the dogs, and headed home.

———

Liz stepped over planks of new wood and two toolboxes on her way through the house to the kitchen. Wyldewood was a hive of activity, the construction crew making good headway on the renovations that would convert their childhood home into a B&B. In a way, she was sorry to see the transformation. But that was life. Things changed.

Her life certainly had.

She'd hoped to have a plan in place by now, to know what her next move would be. Maybe even a new job. Yet here it was, the last week of September, and she still didn't have a clue what the future held.

The crew was packing up for the day and she waved to a couple of the guys as they left. She found David and Josslyn in the kitchen, wrestling the twins, Brandon and Bethie, into the banquet eating area for supper.

David slid in beside Brandon and gave him a stern look. "Eat. No more fussing."

Liz could have sworn the almost three-year-old gave an eye roll. She grinned and took the plate Josslyn offered. Meatloaf, mashed potatoes with gravy and peas. That was a few extra pounds staring her in the face. "Thanks. Looks great." She longed for a slab of salmon or tuna with organic greens, but since she'd never mastered any culinary skills beyond ordering off the menu in her favorite restaurants, she couldn't complain. She grabbed a bottle of water and joined her family.

"How was your walk?" Josslyn asked as she cut Bethie's meatloaf.

"Interesting." Liz reached for the pepper mill and relayed the events of the past hour. "Evy was not amused, I can tell you. But at least the kid wasn't hurt."

"Who was she?" David shoveled food into his mouth, concern furrowing his brow. "Anyone we know?"

"Mia Stone? I didn't recognize her. Evy shooed me off, you know how she is. I don't think she was planning on calling the cops. I would've."

"Already got her tried and convicted, counselor?" David stilled his fork with a smile.

Liz shrugged. "If you can't do the time, don't do the crime."

David laughed and continued eating. "I know a Matt Stone. Doesn't have kids though."

"Well." Liz sighed. "I'd guess that young lady is going to be in a heap of trouble tonight, whoever she is."

Later, after they'd cleaned up and Josslyn hustled the twins upstairs for their bath, Liz retreated to the back porch. She liked it out here in the early evening. Liked watching the sun go down. Another anomaly she'd never imagined. Back in New York, she'd usually still be in the office at this hour, or just heading out for drinks or dinner.

David came outside carrying two mugs, sat beside her, and gave a long, tired-sounding sigh. "Coffee?"

"Thanks." Liz took the mug he offered, inhaled, and sipped with a satisfied smile. "Ah. You used the beans I bought."

David smothered a yawn, a deep chuckle on its heels. "How can you tell?"

Liz breathed in the welcome aroma. "I live in New York. I know my coffee."

"Lived." He turned his head, worried eyes settling on her. "Right?"

Liz stared back at him through the silence. "Yes, lived. Thanks for the reminder."

"Sorry." David blanched. "I just . . ."

"You worry. I know." Liz averted her gaze and studied the pink hue over the ocean. Not so long ago, she'd hated the sight of the sea. Hated this house, everything and everyone in it. Well, perhaps 'hated' was too strong a word. She'd lived here her whole life until she went to boarding school at fourteen. Now it seemed things had come full circle. Wyldewood had become her refuge.

"So. Made any plans yet?" David took on the tone that reminded her of their father.

The questions she wrestled with daily returned for another round.

Was she really ready to leave New York? Her career? The life she'd built there . . .

A life now in shambles.

"No plans." Liz drank too quickly, blinked moisture she'd blame on the temperature of the coffee if he noticed, and placed her mug on the wide arm of the bench. The once-dark teak had softened to gray, weathered with age. Liz ran a finger over the names carved into the wood so long ago and smiled at the memories. Though she and her four siblings hadn't been close in later years, their childhood had been filled with happy times.

A breeze cooled her heated face. Hard to believe summer had passed so quickly. A summer none of them would forget anytime soon. Decisions had been made, together, as a family. Liz couldn't remember the last time that had happened. Probably never.

The plan to convert their sprawling rundown home into a B&B had been forged, loans eventually secured, and construction was now underway. Which was all well and good, but she still had to live here.

She crossed her legs and faced David's questioning gaze. "To be honest, I'm not sure what to do next."

"Stay here. Start over here, on Nantucket." He smiled as though it was the simplest thing in the world.

Liz made a face. "And do what? I'm not sure there's a huge need for corporate lawyers on the island."

"Didn't you tell me you were considering taking a break from law? I mean, not that that kid could tell today."

"Very funny." Why in the world had she shared that thought with her brother? "Fine. I wouldn't mind taking a break, but I still need a job. I'm not about to join the construction crew."

"I'd actually pay to see that." David's laugh was wicked and Liz elbowed him.

"Don't hold your breath, big brother. Maybe I could see if Jed would hire me down at The Longshoreman. With Lynnie gone, he's probably in need of extra help." David laughed harder and Liz grinned. "I suppose you'd pay to see that too?"

"You waiting tables in that dump? Absolutely." He sobered and sipped from his mug. "Listen, Liz . . . I hate to be the bearer of bad news, but . . ."

His hesitation made her stomach churn. "What now? Is Lynette all right?" Anything could happen to her over in Africa. Or it could be their younger brother. She'd thought he was staying out of trouble now, but who knew. "Is it Gray?"

David held up a hand and shook his head. "Lynnie's fine. Gray's fine. It's just . . . I met with the architect this morning. He needs to get started on the second floor sooner. Like next week."

Liz took a breath. "The second floor. Where I'm currently living."

"Yeah."

"Great." She stared at her socked feet and picked dog hair off her jeans. Jasper and Diggory paced the porch and settled at the foot of the steps. Waves crashed against the cliffs below the garden, and a few gulls flew off into the darkening sky with mournful cries. "Well. I suppose I could go back to New York. I could find another job there." But the thought terrified her.

"And I'll repeat what I said last night," David growled. "Men like your ex don't give up. He'll track you down."

"If he wanted to track me down, he'd have done it already."

"Doesn't matter. If he makes any contact, I know what'll happen. You'll get sucked back in."

"I won't."

"Elizabeth." Her brother gave a low curse. "If I had a dollar for every time you've said that over the past couple years . . . Look, I'm not trying to be difficult, but come on. Is it worth the risk?"

Liz slipped her trembling hands beneath her legs. No, it wasn't worth the risk. Going back wasn't going forward. It was giving up.

At twenty-nine, she'd certainly expected to have her life in better order, maybe even be married. No kids, of course—she wouldn't go completely crazy. But a few months into their two-year relationship, the first time Laurence had shown his true colors, Liz discovered dreams didn't always come true.

She drank the remainder of her coffee and sighed. "I can't afford a place of my own here." Who was she kidding? She wouldn't be able to afford New York either.

David frowned. "I thought you had a good amount put away."

"Some. But Laurence still has a lot of my money." She hated talking about her ex-boyfriend. Hated even thinking about Laurence Broadhurst.

"How much money are we talking?"

"Enough, David." The actual amount filled her with self-loathing, and David's dark look did nothing to abate the feeling. She'd been paid well over the few years she'd served as legal counsel at Laurence's investment company. She did have a tidy amount tucked away, but the rest was in a joint investment account. She'd trusted Laurence, and that had been her biggest mistake.

"I never said I was smart." But she should have been. Instead of listening to logic, she'd been swayed by her heart and had to live with the consequences of that flawed decision.

"Okay." David groaned and shook his head. "And you're going to get it back how?"

Liz watched a line of ants disappear through a crack in the cement below her feet. Thunder rumbled overhead with the threat of rain. "I don't know yet. I don't suppose I could just ask for it." Legally, Laurence wasn't entitled to any of it. But she'd given it to him freely. A court case would be complicated, and costly.

David blew out a breath. "You could threaten to expose him. He owns the business. It's a big company. He's not going to want bad press."

It was something she had considered, but only briefly. "It's my word against his, Davy. I can't prove how many times he slammed me against the wall."

David hesitated, rubbed his jaw, and picked at a hole in his jeans just above the knee. "Gray has pictures." He spoke quietly, as though the words pained him.

Liz stiffened and a shiver shot through her.

An unwanted memory surfaced. Pictures. Spread out in front of her in a darkened room. Fear fierce and damning took hold that day, so many years ago, and the prickling on the back of her neck said it still held its ground.

"Liz?" David touched her arm and she startled. "Are you all right?"

She nodded. She had to get past this. It didn't matter. That part of her life was long buried. "Gray has pictures? Of me? How?"

Her brother met her eyes. "When you came home over the summer, that last time Laurence beat you up, Gray snapped a few shots. He was discreet about it, but he . . . we . . . thought you might need them one day."

"Look at yourself, Elizabeth! Is this what you call love? If it is, you've got a pretty warped idea of the concept." The words Gray spoke that awful night still rang in her head, still stung and brought a fresh wave of panic. She *had* believed Laurence loved her. The last incident had been the final tipping point. Prior to that, it was mostly verbal lashings, angry outbursts. Sometimes he got physical, but not always.

She accepted his tearful apologies, took the lavish gifts he offered, and pretended it was all right. Denied the truth to friends and family for far longer than she should have. She'd made up excuse after excuse.

Even told herself she deserved it.

But that night . . .

Fresh fear coiled tight and set her pulse racing. The very idea of confronting Laurence Broadhurst, the man she'd once thought hung the moon, was more than she could handle.

"It wouldn't be enough." Liz exhaled and glanced upward. "We couldn't prove it was him." Didn't want to try. They said healing would come in time, but she wasn't counting on it. "I've got enough in savings for now, until I make some final decisions."

"Okay. No pressure." He sent her a small smile. Liz understood his heart. David took his role as the oldest Carlisle sibling seriously, but with only two years between them, Liz knew she was the one he confided in. And he'd always looked out for her. Stuck up for her when the others teased her for always having her nose in a book, always studying, being the brainiac of the family. David had been there when she needed him. Until she'd finally pushed him away, afraid of what he'd do if he found out how bad things really were.

He had found out anyway, and their relationship had suffered for it.

"I'm sorry, Davy." She wiped her eyes. "This isn't easy. I'm walking away from everything I've worked so hard for. You know?"

"What was it worth if it didn't make you happy?"

The question wound around her like a scarf pulled too tight. What was happiness, really? Liz wasn't sure she'd ever found it. Wasn't sure she'd recognize it if it came up and kissed her full on the lips. Happiness, true love, romance . . . those were the things of fairytales, movies, and Nicholas Sparks novels. Real life was cut and dry. Work hard, have a little fun, no harm done, but in the end, nobody really wins. Happy endings didn't actually exist.

Childish laughter floated down from the windows above the porch.

David glanced at his watch. "They'll be coming down to say goodnight. But listen, earlier when I said I knew a Matt Stone? He's a friend of mine. He's got a place on his property he was talking about renting. I don't think it'll be too expensive."

"Oh." Liz sighed. Perhaps she could just move in with her father at the nursing home.

With everything going on at the house, moving Dad was the best decision, but also the hardest they'd had to make. They'd all wanted to keep him here as long as possible, but as nice as the idea was, his progressing Alzheimer's made the move the only logical choice. And not having Lynette around when it happened made for a far less dramatic transfer.

"Do you want his number?" David pressed. "Check the place out?"

"Who is this guy? You're sure that kid from this afternoon doesn't belong to him?"

"Nah. He doesn't have a family. Matt's from Boston. Used to come over for summers every year when we were kids. Moved over the beginning of summer. I thought he was only here for the season, but he told me he's teaching art at the high school now, so I guess it's permanent." David fished out his phone. "The place is out by Jetties Beach. Belonged to his grandparents. I haven't seen it in years, but he's a decent sort. I think it'd be worth having a look."

"A decent sort?" Liz scowled.

"You might have even met him. Yacht club crowd. Crewed with him a couple races." David smiled at her apprehension. "He's all right, Liz."

"Married?"

"No."

"David . . ."

He held up a hand. "From what I understand, the place is completely separate from the main house. You'd probably never see each other. I think it'd be okay."

"I don't know." She didn't need okay. She needed Fort Knox.

"I'll come with you to see it if you want."

Liz stretched her arms above her head and groaned. "I can go by myself." Not that she wanted to, but honestly. How long could she live constantly looking over her shoulder? "Text me the number. Since I'm soon to be homeless, I don't have much choice." David winced and she regretted her words. "Oh, relax, I won't pitch a fit. The renovations need to happen. I'll be all right."

"Hey, you two." Josslyn poked her head around the door as the twins charged across the porch. "We've come to say goodnight." Dressed in cozy pajamas, squeaky clean and beaming, their childhood innocence tugged at Liz's heart.

David put his phone away and picked up Brandon, while Bethie skipped over to Liz.

"Up, Iz." She raised chubby arms and looked up at Liz with an imploring gaze.

As usual, she couldn't resist Bethie's smile and lifted her into a hug, not even pulling back when her niece hugged her neck and planted a kiss on her cheek. She smelled like shampoo and Mr. Bubble. "Are you all ready for bed? Do you want me to read you a story?"

"Yay!" The little girl nodded enthusiastically. "*Cat in the Hat!*"

Liz followed them in, the sound of her own laughter ringing in her ears and surprising her. She'd better call this Matthew Stone, at least have a look at the house or apartment or whatever it was. And perhaps this was the push she needed. If she was going to start over, she had to take the first step.

"Auntie Iz?" Bethie snuggled against her and whispered in her ear as they approached the staircase.

"What, Bethie?" Liz whispered back, smoothing down the child's unruly blond curls.

Bethie giggled a bit, pressed her nose to Liz's and hugged her neck harder. "I love you, dat's all."

It was their favorite saying of late.

I love you, that's all.

Liz's eyes burned, but she nodded, smiled, and let a little hope in. "I love you too, Bethie."

Yes, she would survive this. She had to.

two

"Go away! I hate you!"

Matthew Stone leaned against the closed door of his niece's bedroom and dragged a hand down his face. "I can live with that, and you're still going to school tomorrow. Dinner is ready. You can come out and eat with me or stay in there until morning. Your call." He'd given Mia a day at home to cool off after yesterday's little joyride. He'd taught in the morning and then come home, and they'd argued for most of the afternoon. He wished now he'd sent her to school.

Back in June, moving to Nantucket seemed like the right decision, especially after the teaching job came up, but three months in, Mia was still miserable.

"I'll come out when I'm ready!"

Or hungry. Matt gave a silent nod and clenched his jaw.

He shoved his hands in the pockets of his jeans and strolled down the hall. The old wood floorboards creaked beneath his feet, the tired sound a match for his own exhaustion. Friends warned him living with a teenager wouldn't be a walk in the park. But he worked with adolescents, knew how to handle them. Still, the kids in the high school art class he taught seemed like angels compared to Mia. He'd had no idea parenting could be this difficult.

He lifted the lid of the Crockpot and stared at the beef stew he'd thrown together last night and turned on this morning. It smelled good, but he wasn't all that hungry. Yesterday's adventures with Mia had zapped his energy and his appetite, and he'd lost a few hours' sleep worrying about what could have happened to her in that Jeep. Thank God she hadn't been hurt. Or hurt anyone else. Matt shook his head. What was that saying his grandmother had been so fond of? *No use wearing yourself out over things you can't fix.*

Didn't mean he wouldn't try though.

As he straddled a stool at the counter, a bowl of stew in front of him, his cell buzzed. The knot in his stomach hardened. He was beginning to loathe that sound. He really wasn't up for another conversation with his sister.

Matt glanced at the number and exhaled. It wasn't Rachel.

Nicholas Cooper. Hesitation stayed his hand. Nick either wanted him to crew in his next race or it'd be a work-related call. Since Nick was managing the bank now, Matt hoped it was about the race.

"Hey, Nick." He pressed his cell to his ear and moved the spoon around the thick stew.

"Matt, glad I caught you. I'm just wrapping things up at the office, and we haven't heard from you yet."

Work related. "Yeah. Sorry about that." Matt jumped off the stool and crossed the small kitchen to the fridge, pulled a beer from the case of six he hadn't touched since he'd bought them on Saturday, and sat again.

The recent news of Anthony Cooper's cancer had rocked everyone, but from what Matt could tell, they were handling it pretty well. All things considered. Nick had stepped into his father's shoes quite neatly, taking over his position at the bank like he was born for it. Few people knew the truth. Nick's dream of becoming an architect was now on hold again.

"So about the loan. I said I'd have the money this week, Nick, but . . . something came up." A busted headlight and dented front fender on his Jeep, a broken fence, and a whole lot of damage to Evy McIntyre's front lawn. Not to mention the annihilation of her prized rose garden. Fortunately, the older woman hadn't called the cops. The threat had been enough though. By the time Matt arrived, his niece was fully expecting to be hauled off in handcuffs. And Matt vowed to never leave his car keys on the counter again.

"Matt, I can't give you another extension." Nick always managed to sound torn up when he was giving bad news. "I know you talked to Tucker Watts about this when I was away, and while I wish I could be more lenient—"

"I know." Matt let the spoon clatter against the side of his bowl and sighed. He rubbed his throbbing temple, hoping the headache he'd had all day would disappear.

When he'd first learned his grandparents had bequeathed their Nantucket home to him, he'd been thrilled. Then he'd come over, taken a look at the place, and realized it needed work. A lot of work. He should have sold it outright, but sentimentality got the better of him, and he decided to make the repairs and rent it out instead. But he'd needed a loan to do that. And it hadn't been rented long enough to make him any real money. "I'll get the money by the end of next week. Okay?"

"That'll work. You still don't want to sell?"

Matt shook his head. "Can't right now." Can't. Wouldn't.

Nick didn't press and Matt was grateful. Loud music blared from the room above him and a door slammed. Matt winced. Maybe things would be better tomorrow. Since school had started, he'd been called in to talk to the principal about Mia at least once a week, which was making a great impression on his new boss. But Matt wasn't the only one with problems.

"How's your dad, Nick?"

Nick's sharp inhale said things weren't good. "He's hanging in there, thanks for asking. We had to cut our trip short, and he was in the hospital for a while, but we've got homecare now. Still has some good days, but they're rare. Cancer sucks."

"That it does." Matt stared at the clock on the wall. "I'll be in next week, Nick." They said goodbye and he clicked off and pushed his bowl away. His hands circled the cold bottle of beer and he took a swig.

Days like this, he wished he were still back in Boston. He missed his friends, missed the O'Donohues, who were more family to him than his own. He hadn't planned on having Mia this long, but what choice did he have? He was all she had. He'd thought the move to Nantucket would be good for Mia. Give her a fresh start.

And here they were, still trying to get used to the new normal. He'd been amazed and thankful there'd been an opening at the high school for him, but Mia hated that he worked there. Not that they ever saw each other.

The salary was okay, but with having to pay back the bank loan, he'd be dipping into savings soon. Matt's stomach rumbled and reminded him to eat, so he forced down a few mouthfuls of stew and scanned his messages. Nothing new. He was going to have to let them know about that security job tomorrow. If only it didn't mean working nights and some weekends. The money would help, but he didn't like the thought of Mia being on her own. Didn't relish the thought of working two jobs either, but that was life. He would deal, and he wasn't in a position to say no. But he'd have to figure out what to do with Mia. Left to her own devices, there was no telling what the kid would get up to.

His cell rang again and startled him. A number came up he didn't recognize. Matt steadied his breathing, waited a minute for his pulse to slow down. "Matt Stone."

"Good evening, Mr. Stone. I hope I'm not disturbing you. I realize it's getting close to dinner time." The woman's cool, clipped tone did not belong to anyone he knew.

"Already had it. Who is this?"

"My name is Elizabeth Carlisle. My brother David gave me your number. He said you might have a place available to rent?"

Matt hesitated. He didn't want to sound too eager. "That's right." Actually, renting out the coach house had been Carlisle's idea. They'd been shooting the breeze over a beer last month, Matt had mentioned things were tight, and David remembered the coach house. Asked if Matt had ever thought of renting it out.

When Matt's grandparents had lived here, in their last years on the island, they'd had a live-in caregiver in there. It was small, but nice enough. He'd slapped on a fresh coat of paint, cleaned it from top to bottom. The place was in pretty good shape. He'd been meaning to list it, and if he couldn't get a full-time renter, he'd look into putting it on VRBO, but maybe now he wouldn't need to.

"David said you're near Jetties Beach?"

"Correct. It's not a big place. It was the original coach house. Been used for everything since then. But it was fully renovated a few years back, looks like new. One bedroom, eat-in-kitchen, bath and a good-sized living area. There's a path to the beach, and you've got ocean views."

"Okay."

She didn't sound impressed. Well, duh. He'd seen the Carlisle place. If that's where she was currently living, why would she be? Come to think of it, why would she want to live anywhere but there? As if to answer his question, a blood-curdling scream sailed into his ear.

"What was that?"

"Sorry. My nephew. Apparently the twins do not like bath time." She sighed and he heard the sound of a door closing. "Is it furnished?"

"Yep. Bedroom and living room. Kitchen table and chairs. But if you want it empty, that can be arranged." There were enough vacant rooms in the house to store stuff in.

"Furnished is fine. How much are you asking?"

He told her his price, low balling it, and waited through the silence.

"Well, it's a bit more than what I hoped, but may I come take a look?"

"Sure." If she'd been standing in front of him he might have hugged her. Though she did sound a tad on the frosty side. "Saturday morning okay? Around nine?" Mia would hopefully still be sleeping. He didn't want his niece scaring off a potential tenant. She agreed, he gave her directions, and they hung up.

A grin pushed across his mouth and Matt allowed it.

Maybe things would start to improve. Maybe he wouldn't have to regret his decision to move here after all. Maybe Mia would settle down and start respecting him.

And maybe it wouldn't snow in Siberia this winter.

"Who was on the phone?" Mia trudged into the kitchen, her eyes red and rimmed with smudged mascara.

Matt's heart clenched as he looked at his niece. "Somebody wanting to look at the coach house. I'm thinking of renting it, get some extra cash."

"Oh. Guy or girl?"

"A woman. Sister of a buddy of mine."

She looked skeptical. "You know her?"

"Nope. She used to live in New York."

Mia snorted. "Why the heck would she want to move to this rock?"

Matt inhaled and clenched his fingers. "I'm sure she has her reasons. Her family lives here."

"Sucks to suck." She opened the fridge, stuck her head in, and stayed there a while. Matt fought the urge to inform her she was wasting electricity. She emerged with a can of coke, a yogurt, and a bar of chocolate he didn't remember buying.

"I made stew."

"I don't eat meat. I keep telling you that."

"Sorry." Right. It was such a foreign concept to him that he kept forgetting. "But you can't have that for dinner."

She shot him a dark look. "What do you expect me to eat? Not the crap you make." She hoisted her slender frame onto one of the bar stools and popped the top on her soda. Dark hair hung around her pale face. If he remembered correctly, her natural color was closer to his own sandy brown.

"There's salad. Pasta. Make something healthy."

"Yogurt is healthy." She swung her legs back and forth and looked around the old kitchen with disdain. If they were going to stay, he should probably think about doing some upgrades in the main house. But right now he didn't have the cash. The wind had picked up, and rain started to hit the long windows.

"This house creeps me out. I bet it's haunted."

Matt shook his head. "It's big and it's old, but it's not haunted."

"Just because you don't believe in ghosts doesn't mean they don't exist." She twisted the small diamond stud in her nose and he clenched his jaw. That grossed him out big time, and she knew it.

"Cut it out, Mia."

She laughed and the gold stud above her top lip flashed. Why in the world would anyone want to pierce their lip? How unhealthy was that? One of these nights, he might give in to the strong temptation to sneak into her room and pull it out while she slept. Except she'd probably wake up, scream bloody murder, and accuse him of assault. Matt still wasn't used to this grown-up version of his niece. He wanted the little kid in pigtails back.

"We should have a séance."

"Are you kidding?"

"Why not?" She stirred her yogurt and plopped a spoonful in her mouth. Strawberry stuff dripped down her chin onto the countertop. He pushed a napkin toward her as a memory skipped across his mind. Mia at about a year old, in her high chair. He'd been trying to feed her, most of it ending up in her hair and on the floor. She'd been a messy eater back then too.

"Is having a séance against the law?"

"We're not having a séance."

"Oh, right. I forgot. God wouldn't like it."

Matt ran a hand down his face and prayed for patience. "No. Neither would I."

"You don't even go to church. What's the big deal?"

"That doesn't mean I don't believe. That I don't have a faith." He spun his bottle of beer around in a slow circle. He wasn't in the right frame of mind to discuss what he did and didn't believe with her.

"But you can drink, that's fine, I guess." She sat back a bit, her eyes glinting.

He knew when he was being baited. "In moderation, Mia."

"You shouldn't drink at all." Mia chomped on chocolate. "What if I got sick in the middle of the night and you were too drunk to drive me to the hospital?"

"Seriously?" Matt grinned. But he pushed the beer aside anyway. "Where do you come up with this stuff?"

She arched a thin black brow. "It could happen. My appendix could rupture, or I could have a heart attack or something."

"Mia, you're fifteen. I don't think you're going to have a heart attack."

"Kids drop dead all the time. Playing football or hockey or whatever. It could happen." She tapped black-painted fingernails on the red Formica countertop.

"Have you ever seen me drunk, Mia?" He grabbed a cloth from the sink and wiped up the mess she'd made.

She rolled her eyes. "No. But I haven't been around you that long."

"I think you've been around me long enough to know you won't. Okay?" Matt waited until she made eye contact again and offered a smile. He wasn't Joe Giovanni. Unfortunately, Mia's stepfather had done more damage than Matt could ever hope to repair. Earning his niece's trust was a tenuous task, one he wasn't sure he'd ever accomplish.

"Can I go out on Friday night?"

Matt gaped, propped his elbows, and rested his chin on his hands. "Were you physically present yesterday afternoon when you stole my Jeep, plowed through a fence, destroyed a garden, and rammed into Evy McIntyre's oak tree, or was that your evil twin?"

"Just kidding." Her grin came and went too soon. "Who would I be going out with anyway? I don't have any friends."

The sad statement settled over him. He'd been thinking the same, just hadn't wanted to say it. "So, about yesterday . . ."

"I don't get why she was so upset. It was just a few flowers." Mia huffed, like causing irreparable damage to someone else's property was something every kid did, no biggie. "It wasn't like I was on the main road that long. I stuck to the neighborhood roads. I would have been back before you finished your run if it wasn't for the cat."

Matt stared. "Mia. Do you get how lucky you are that Mrs. McIntyre didn't call the cops? You're not sixteen! You don't even have your learner's permit! What in the world were you thinking?"

"I just wanted to see what it was like."

Tension tightened his neck as he tamped his temper. "Well, now you know. You're grounded until further notice. And we're going to go see Mrs. McIntyre so you can apologize again and ask how you can make it up to her."

"What? I already called her. You heard me."

"You left a message on her voicemail. I want you to see her in person."

She muttered something under her breath he wouldn't ask her to repeat. "You suck. I wish I didn't have to live with you."

Matt went to the sink and poured out the rest of his beer. "At this moment, that makes two of us."

He didn't turn around until he heard the slamming of her bedroom door.

———

He was ready for Miss Carlisle too early on Saturday morning. The coach house smelled fresh and clean. New white lace curtains fluttered against the open window, and the sun shone against sparkling glass. He might suck at parenting, but he knew how to scrub dirt.

Matt strolled through the small house for the fourth time and stopped to fluff a pillow on the couch. The dark brown leather set was pretty new. She might like that.

If she wanted the place.

He left the door unlocked and went back to the main house. It was almost nine. As he walked through the back door toward the living room, a rap on the front door sounded. Matt nodded. Punctual. He approved.

He rubbed his jaw, realized he forgot to shave, and waited a moment, strangely nervous.

Then he blew out a breath and yanked open the door.

And sucked in air the next second.

The woman standing on his front step was not what he'd been expecting. He wasn't sure what he'd been expecting, but not this.

She was taller than he'd imagined, just a tad shorter than his six-foot frame, blond hair pulled off a finely sculpted face. She wore navy slacks, a white blouse, and a green cardigan, gold hoops in her ears, slender neck bare. The faintest hint of floral floated around him.

She took off her sunglasses, and eyes the color of a stormy sea studied him suspiciously. "Good morning. Mr. Stone?"

All he could do was nod, his lips inching upward. And that's a wow.

Matt cleared his throat and summoned maturity. "Hi, I'm Matt. You must be Miss Carlisle." He should probably stop staring. "Come on in."

She followed him inside, heels clicking on the wooden floor. He'd been up since the crack of dawn doing last minute and, possibly unnecessary, cleaning and dusting and polishing. The house was already clean—they mostly spent time in the kitchen and family room—but Matt hated dust.

"What a lovely place. I've always wondered what it was like in here." She glanced into the spacious living room they never used. "Your grandparents owned it, correct?"

"Yeah. They both passed away several years back, within months of each other, actually. Did you know them?"

"No." She shook her head. "I'm sorry. I'm sure my parents must have. David said you used to spend summers here when you were a kid. Did we ever meet? I wasn't one for the beach, though, and they had to force me to sail."

"Yeah?" So she wasn't the outdoorsy type. Shocker. "I don't recall, but it's possible. There were always so many kids around. Those summers seem like a lifetime ago." But they'd been some of the best times. "Anyway. My grandparents moved to the mainland in their later years for health reasons and decided to rent this place out."

"And now you're here." The way she said it almost made it sound like a good thing.

"We'll go out the back door to the coach house." He led her through the house quickly. "There's room for an extra car out here, and . . ." Matt stopped in his tracks when he reached the kitchen. "Hey, Mia." His heart began to beat a little faster. "You're up early."

"Uh huh." His niece sat at the counter in red and black-checkered pajama pants and his old Metallica sweatshirt he could have sworn he'd thrown out years ago. She stared down Elizabeth Carlisle in classic Mia fashion, sat back, and crossed her arms. "'Sup."

"It's you." Their guest seemed to stiffen slightly and Matt caught Mia's eye roll.

"It's me."

"You know each other?" What the heck? Matt looked from Mia to Miss Carlisle.

"Not exactly." Miss Carlisle sent him a cursory glance. "I happened to witness her unfortunate incident with Evy McIntyre's rose garden the other day. Your daughter is very lucky she wasn't hurt or didn't hurt somebody in the process."

"I see." A laugh scraped his throat. "Well, yes. My niece is very lucky. You, uh, weren't around when I got to Mrs. McIntyre's place." He'd definitely remember if she had been.

Miss Carlisle shook her head. "I made sure she was okay, then Evy came out and seemed to have it all under control."

"But you saw the cat," Mia said quietly. "Didn't you?"

"The cat?" Miss Carlisle frowned. "Oh, you mean the cat that ran in front of your car. Yes, I saw the cat. But that doesn't excuse the fact."

"See? I told you there was a cat!" Mia slammed her hand on the counter and grinned triumphantly.

"There was really a cat?" He couldn't help ask.

"Yes. But she was driving erratically before the cat scooted across the road. I thought it might have been a drunk driver."

Matt acknowledged a twinge of relief. So she hadn't been lying.

"I wasn't drunk!" Mia squeaked. "I hate alcohol."

"When have you even . . ." Matt swallowed the question. This was the weirdest conversation he'd had with a complete stranger in a stretch. "Anyway."

"Does she live here, with you?" Miss Carlisle was looking skeptical, and Matt shot Mia a silent warning. *Mess this up, and you're grounded for life.*

"Yes, Mia lives with me."

"Only because I have to." Mia scowled. "My mother got herself arrested and thrown in jail. My grandparents won't have anything to do with me, so I get the joy of living with Uncle Matt."

Way to go, Mia. Just lay it all out on the table. Matt tamped the urge to swat her one and somehow managed a thin smile.

"I'm sure he gets just as much joy out of the arrangement." Elizabeth Carlisle didn't miss a beat. "How old are you, Mia?"

"Almost sixteen. How olda you?"

Matt stifled a grin. Mia had only lived in Boston a short time, but she could put on a wicked good accent when she wanted to. But now wasn't exactly an appropriate moment. Which of course, was precisely her point.

"Okay, what say we move on?" Matt headed for the kitchen door and held it open. Miss Carlisle nodded, but didn't look convinced that being here was such a good idea.

They walked the few feet across the graveled courtyard until they reached the small cottage. The back lawn stretched to the left, running down to the wall at the edge of the cliff. Hydrangea bushes sported the last blue blooms of the season, and the flower bed running along the wood fence put on an acceptable show. The climbing rose did its own thing, still thick with pink in places. He'd been bored before school started, knew his way around the gardening shed from his years coming to the island as a kid, and he'd managed to bring the garden back to life.

The fresh coat of robin's egg blue he'd applied to the shingles last weekend and the two potted palms he'd purchased on a whim provided curb appeal, and the red front door made just the statement he wanted it to.

Elizabeth Carlisle smiled. Just a tiny smile that inched her lips upward ever so slightly, but it was enough to indicate appreciation.

"Sorry about Mia, she's kinda blunt." He needed to say something at least. "You, uh, didn't seem as shocked as she probably hoped you'd be."

She shrugged and tipped her head, inching her sunglasses downward. "I'm a lawyer, and I used to live in New York. Not much shocks me, I'm afraid. I'm sorry about her mother."

Matt suddenly felt a little lost as he looked into her eyes.

And he just wanted to tell her everything.

Get a grip, dude.

"Yeah. It's been rough. She's served almost nine months now. Mia's been through the wringer. But she's not really any trouble." That wasn't exactly a lie, was it? He fumbled with the handle on the front door.

"No loud music? You understand I'm looking for a place that's rather quiet. My house is in an uproar at the moment, and I'm afraid my nerves are completely shot."

"Join the club." Did he just say that? Matt exhaled and stepped into the small living room. She followed behind, pushed the front door all the way open, and left it that way.

"Oh." She nodded and took a stroll around, giving him a wide berth. She ran a finger across the mantel, inspected the spotless fireplace, tried windows and opened doors. "It's very clean. And bright. Quite cheery, actually."

"Is that a bad thing?" It sounded as though it might be. Matt rocked on the backs of his shoes and studied her.

"No, not at all. I'm just surprised. I have three brothers, and they're about as far from neat and tidy as you can get. David said you're single, so I expected . . ." She stopped, pressed her lips together, and flushed. She seemed confident enough, but he sensed a wariness about her that gave off warning signals.

He hooked his thumbs through the belt holes of his faded Nantucket reds. "I'm pretty regimented about certain things. I like to keep a clean house." With Mia around it was no easy feat.

"Well." She stepped back a bit. "So far so good." She marched toward the bedroom, and he waited while she looked around. He heard her flicking light switches and turning taps on and off. When she was done there, she found the kitchen. He'd worked on that this month. Replaced the counters, painted the cupboards, and shelled out for new stainless steel appliances.

"Is there a security system?" She was at the front door again, jiggling the handle and trying the deadbolt.

"Uh . . ." Matt wondered at the intent look on her face. "No security system." He'd never actually thought about it. His grandparents hadn't bothered with such things, and he figured the island was quiet enough. Most people around here didn't need to steal anything.

"Would you be opposed to my having one installed?" She shifted the black leather purse slung over her shoulder. "I could ask the contractor helping us at Wyldewood."

"Uh, sure." He almost grinned at the coincidence. "Actually, I start work with a security company next week. I could probably arrange for the installation."

"Really?" She looked confused. "David said you were a teacher."

"I am. I teach art at Nantucket High. But the salary isn't quite . . . anyway." He shut his mouth and folded his arms. "What do you think of the place?"

"It's lovely." She gave a wistful sigh. "The rent is fair, but I'm currently unemployed. I'm not sure what comes next for me, to be honest." A pained look crossed her face. "I'm not used to being without a job. And things here are expensive."

"Yeah, I hear that." Matt strode across the room to straighten a painting on the wall. "That's why I'm working two jobs. Except I have to work some nights and two weekends a month with the security company." Okay, why exactly was he telling her his business? A wild thought came out of left field. He shoved it off but it came back. Perhaps this could work in both their favors. He met her curious gaze and went for it. "This is pretty crazy, but . . . I could lower the rent some if you'd agree to keep an eye on my niece when I'm working nights."

Her blue eyes rounded and pink lips parted a little, but no words came. She tried again, then clamped her mouth again and shook her head. "It was nice meeting you, Mr. Stone."

Elizabeth Carlisle headed for the door, taking his hope for extra income right along with her.

"Wait! I mean . . . can we at least discuss it?" Yes, he sounded desperate. Well, he was.

"Mr. Stone." She sighed. "I'm not a nanny. I don't do kids. Little or big. Besides, your niece said she was almost sixteen. Surely she doesn't need *looking after?*"

She didn't know Mia.

Matt squared his shoulders and gave a nod. "I get it. It was a stupid idea. I just thought, well, I know your family, and you seemed to like the place . . . but, no worries. I'm sure you'll find something else."

She hesitated, her eyes clouding over. "I suspect you already know yours is one of the least expensive rentals on the island. You should be asking twice what you're offering me."

Matt groaned inwardly and stared at his shoes. David hadn't said much, but from what he'd surmised from their conversation, it sounded as though Elizabeth Carlisle could use a break.

"I like to be reasonable. There are enough folks out there happy to rip people off, I don't need to be one of them."

"How admirable." She sniffed and fiddled with a ring on her right hand. "You don't have any pets?"

"Not even a goldfish."

"What would you be expecting me to do, exactly, with your niece?"

"Do?" Matt frowned and she looked at him like he'd grown another head.

"Supervise her homework? Cook for her? Play Snap?"

"Uh, no. She can cook. I think. Basically, just that you'd be available if the need arose. Just so she, you know, knows there's an adult around."

"I don't know. It seems a lot to ask."

It did. Matt knew that and wasn't sure now why he'd done it. "I'm sure she'll be fine." He crossed his fingers behind his back. "I just need to know somebody's here when I'm not. To have someone to call if she needed anything." Like after she woke screaming from one of her frequent nightmares.

"I'll need to give it some thought. May I call you in a couple of days?"

"Sure." Matt walked her out and led her around the main house to where she'd parked the car. "Wow. I didn't think these old things still ran." The beige and faux-wood paneled Ford station wagon had certainly seen better days, but it wasn't unusual to see old cars here on the island.

"Runs better than you'd expect." She had her sunglasses back on and stuck out a slender hand. "Well, thank you. Goodbye, Mr. Stone."

The moment Matt clasped his hand around hers, a definite sizzle of attraction shook him to his senses.

Letting a woman like Elizabeth Carlisle live on his property was possibly the worst idea ever. Maybe she'd say she wasn't interested anyway. But he needed the money. "Thanks for coming, Miss Carlisle. I'll look forward to hearing from you." Matt stepped back and watched her drive off. Half of him hoped he'd see her again. The other half, the more sensible, cautious side, said it'd probably be a darn good thing if he didn't.

three

DRAKE

This room they say is mine is barely big enough to swing a cat in. The bed is comfortable, but I don't use it much. Sleep seems hard to come by these days. There's a desk with paper and pens I'm pulled toward at times. But all I do is doodle dizzy lines and circles and sometimes a shell. Although, I feel I was once capable of so much more.

The smell here is not familiar. Not home. I don't hear the ocean the way I did where I used to live. The windows won't open all the way, and it's hard to catch the breeze. I was never one for air-conditioning. I miss hearing the waves crashing against the rocks, *whoosh!* Miss sitting on the porch in my rocker. I think there were dogs, and a black cat that invariably found me the moment I sat and dug its claws in deep, purring with the satisfaction of its cruelty. I hate cats.

Soup for lunch. Hot and barely palatable; they're not much for salt around here. The rolls are on the stale side, rock hard, and I prove the point by throwing one across the room. They don't like that. I'm scolded like a child. It's rather amusing, truth be told, and I'm tempted to do it again. And then they bring out the pills.

Later, after I've pretended to nap and promised better behavior, I'm allowed to rejoin civilization, such as it is. The big nurse brings me to the large, bright room, where I see them waving at me. The man with the two tow-headed kids and the pretty wife. I wave back like I know them.

"Go visit with your family, Mr. Carlisle," Teresa says. Could be Teresa. Might be Sophia.

We go outside and sit on a weathered bench. A perfectly kept lawn leads down to a high wall. The sea stretches beyond it, but you have to strain to get a glimpse unless you're up on the porch. One day I'll ask if we can leave this place. Walk the beach perhaps. I'd like that.

The children fascinate me. Maybe two or three years old, and they seem to enjoy coming here, God knows why. Easy to please at that age. They chase each other across the lawn, chubby legs flying. Delightful squeals fill the air around us, but the man next to me shushes them, and the woman rushes after them to keep them safe. They can't escape the garden. I've tried.

I pat his knee to tell him it's okay, because I can't find the right words.

I wish I could remember their names. My leaky mind lets me down again. But their antics make me smile, and I'm glad they bring them. And the man . . . he said his name when they got here. What was it?

David.

"I don't want them being a nuisance." He offers me chocolate. No idea why, because I can't stand the stuff. But they all bring it. And I eat it anyway.

"Jefferson Starship." What in blazes does that mean? Sometimes the most ridiculous things come out of my mouth.

"Cool band." David grins, and I recognize the sparkle in his eyes. Reminds me of . . . her, I think. I see her long blond hair, so wavy and soft. I could run my fingers through it for hours. *Darling.* No, that wasn't her name. That was what she called me. And everyone she loved.

"Diana." I nod and smile as the little girl runs circles around the boy. Soon they tire of the game and race to where we sit. He gives them boxes with straws, and they scramble to find space on the bench. The girl makes herself at home on my lap, snuggles close, and presses a finger against my cheek.

"Hi, Pop-Pop."

"Diana." I smile back at her, knowing I'm wrong.

"That's Bethie, Dad. And this is Brandon." The man tousles the boy's hair. He also stares at me with big blue eyes that could have belonged to her.

"Bethie." It's a nice name I suppose. "Elizabeth." I remember now. She comes here too. All bluster and take-charge. I somehow know she got that from me.

"She's coming tomorrow. Tomorrow is Sunday." He rubs his nose with the tip of his finger. "She's not very happy with me at the moment. I had to tell her she has to move out. The renovations are ahead of schedule. We're gutting the second floor sooner than expected."

Renovations. Vague memories reveal plans and people coming and going and lots of arguing about it all until finally the decision was made. It's why I'm here, I recall. The noise and the mess. Safer for me, they said. Easier for them, no doubt.

"That's unfortunate." I've learned to play the game. "She'll be fine." Somehow I do know this.

He nods like he knows it too. "Hey, I talked to Lynnie last night. Remember, she's in Africa?"

"Yes." Of course I don't remember. I do know Africa is a faraway place with jungles and elephants and very hot sun. I was there once. Perhaps twice. My father's work took him there, although I don't know why. I think my parents lived in a big city in that country for a year or more. I visited from London, where they had me packed away in boarding school.

The noisy, foreign city streets were full of dust and dirt, and cars jammed the road, bicycles pushing past while people maneuvered around each other on the sidewalks. Whenever we ventured from our safe sprawling home outside the city limits, my mother was terrified I'd get lost. Being a cocky fifteen-year-old, I didn't share her fears. But now they have come true.

I am quite lost at times.

"Lynnie should come home." It seems to make sense. She might get lost too. And then what chance will I have of figuring out who she is?

"Well." He nods and wipes snot off his son's freckled nose. I'm assuming the child is his. The eyes, you see. "Soon. Lynnie will probably come home the end of October."

"Halloween." The word seems to fit with the last one.

"Yeah. Around there." He smiles too brightly, and I know I've done it again. Said the right thing without having a clue. It's quite a remarkable talent I seem to have acquired without even trying. "Maybe Ryan will come home too, I don't know."

"Ryan?" So many names. So much I can't remember. The pretty wife brings out the photo album. Again with the pictures. She's under the impression that somehow this will jog my memory. And in a way, it does. So I sit silent while she shows me the family they claim is mine.

David is the eldest, and she is Josslyn, his wife. Elizabeth comes next, the one who looks like her mother. Something in her eyes troubles me, a niggling I'm not sure about. There's Ryan, who is more like me, I think. Me and David. He's got a wide-open smile and sparkling eyes and holds a little black boy in his arms. I remember somehow he belongs to us too.

The one they call Gray grins up at me in living color and draws a chuckle. "That boy." I point and shake my head, and this makes them laugh. And then they show me Lynnie, who is the youngest, and for some reason my eyes smart. Is it possible to miss someone you don't really remember?

The small ones are off and running again, and the sun inches lower behind the clouds. They'll leave me soon, and I will be alone.

"This isn't home."

"I know. I'm sorry." David rests an arm around my shoulders and sighs deep. He is always kind and soft-spoken. I feel we haven't always seen eye-to-eye, although I don't know why. I remember being a father, the age he must be now, kids running around the place, but I don't remember enjoying it all that much. Not always. I preferred to be off on my own, up in my studio, away from the ruckus. Perhaps even in those early days I was creating my own trap-door to escape the happiness I knew I didn't deserve.

Worn wood floors, banging shutters, easels, and the strong scent of turpentine trip across my memory. I grasp for more details, but they fade too fast and a foul word flies out of my mouth.

David clears his throat, and Josslyn gets up to gather their things. And I know I've done something wrong.

"I get angry sometimes." I hate to admit it, but it's true. I've always had a temper. It was one of the things Diana loathed about me. *"Don't yell at me, Drake Carlisle or I promise you I'll pack my bags faster than you can stumble across the room!"*

"It's okay, Dad." David helps me up. "Almost dinner time. Wonder what it'll be tonight, huh?"

Oh, who cares.

Because it's not okay. Nothing about my being here is remotely okay.

I've made a lot of mistakes in my life.

Perhaps this place, this place where I am apparently destined to live out my final days or years—whichever God sees fit to grant, so far removed from everything I know and love, unable to think or speak or act appropriately anymore—perhaps this is all I deserve.

Liz drove to the nursing home on Sunday morning. The family had gone to church—had been going since Josslyn and the twins moved over—but Liz never went. Didn't see the point. Maybe one day she'd surprise them and go along. But not today.

Her father sat in a rocker facing the window. His graying hair was too long again, curling below his neck. White wicker creaked as he rocked back and forth, humming an old tune Liz recognized from days gone by.

The nursing home was a short drive from Matthew Stone's house. She'd passed it on the way. That would be one advantage if she decided to take the place. But she wasn't sure she would. The man seemed nice enough, but she wouldn't make the mistake of trusting him. And the whole kid thing was weird. Like she had time to look after a surly teenager.

Well, she did, but he didn't need to know that.

Liz clasped the canvas bag she'd brought along, filled with a few items Dad might enjoy, walked across the bright day room, nodded to a couple of the other residents, and slid into an empty chair beside her father's.

He turned and met her eyes, and Liz held her breath. This was the worst part. Not knowing if he'd recognize her. She'd learned to avoid greeting him first. It only seemed to confuse him and hurt more when he couldn't find the memories. So she offered a small smile and waited.

His weathered face crinkled and his lips parted in a familiar grin. "Hello, Bizzy-Lizzy."

Laughter caught in her throat at the childhood name, and she blinked sudden tears. "Hi, Dad."

He was dressed today. Some days he protested too much and preferred his pajamas. Today it seemed the staff had won. His paint-stained khakis had seen better days, and the white chambray shirt was tending toward gray, but he'd made the effort. That had to count for something. Except . . .

"No shoes, Dad?"

"Huh." He rubbed his scruff-covered chin and looked down, a chuckle rumbling through him. "Shoes. No. They left."

Liz patted his arm. "That's all right. Perhaps we'll find them in a bit. I thought we could walk outside."

His gaze veered upward to the window. "On a day like this? It's blustery. There's a storm coming in, girl."

The sun glared through clean glass, and Liz studied the clear blue sky, gathering her thoughts. She looked back at him and put on a bright smile. "I think we'll be okay. What do you say? Get some fresh air? Shall we go to your room and look for your shoes?"

"We mustn't stay out long." He heaved up and stood before her, hand outstretched. "Your mother and Cecily will have dinner on the table soon."

"I know." Liz stood, took her father's hand, and gave it a squeeze. "I'm sure they won't mind if we're a little late."

They walked around the carefully manicured grounds and eventually sat on a bench overlooking the ocean. This place was nice. Expensive, but Gray was making a huge comeback in the music world and was writing the checks to prove it. They were all eternally grateful for his generosity.

The garden area reminded her a little of Wyldewood, the way the house had looked when they were kids. Beautiful gardens and a spectacular view of the ocean. It was probably the reason Dad had settled in so easily. Perhaps he'd felt that too. Although, these days it was hard to tell what he felt. Or thought. In mid-stage Alzheimer's, Drake Carlisle's mind was fast becoming a jumbled maze of memory, harder to decipher each day.

Liz proffered his favorite Godiva chocolates, and he eyed the box with the glee of a child on Christmas morning. "These are the best kind, aren't they, Lynnie?"

Liz sighed. She wouldn't correct him. Soon he'd probably be calling her by her mother's name, and then Cecily's. The idea of Dad mistaking her for their former feisty housekeeper produced a grin. "So I looked at a place yesterday. It's not too far from here." She watched a group of squawking gulls land on the lawn nearby, and Matthew Stone's anxious face came to mind. He'd probably tried not to appear desperate, but it'd been obvious he wanted her to take the place. The little she'd seen of the main house gave no hint he might be strapped for cash, and his cool and calm demeanor would have fooled anyone. But Liz knew better. Appearances could be deceiving.

"Did you hear that your mother wants to paint the kitchen again?" Dad put down the box of chocolates and got to his feet, scouring the open sea. "Now, where are those boys? Out in that storm! Grayson's about to get himself grounded again."

He was lost in the past, no telling how long he'd stay.

"They'll be in soon, Dad." After a while, she gathered up their things and walked him inside. By the time she said goodbye, he'd gone silent, engrossed in an old movie playing on television. She spoke with the supervisor before she left, and got the weekly update. She'd chat with Dad's doctor next week, but by now they knew what to expect. There would be no improvement.

Liz took the long way home, driving slow. No job. No place to live. She tightened her hands on the steering wheel and shook her head. She needed to make some decisions. She'd never been one to have a bunch of girlfriends to call at all hours, but a friend or two to confide in, seek advice from, might be nice. But she had no-one. The crowd they ran with in New York were Laurence's friends. She doubted any of those women would give her the time of day now. She'd never really liked them anyhow. No. She was on her own. And for the first time in years, Liz recognized the odd sensation niggling her.

Loneliness.

four

Liz left the ATM on Monday afternoon and did some quick mental calculations as she marched down Main. She'd be okay for a few more months, but after that? All weekend she'd thought about the cute little cottage on Matthew Stone's property. She could imagine herself living there. It was furnished nicely. Not quite her style—she preferred modern design—but it would certainly do. If she agreed to his ridiculous suggestion, she'd be able to afford it. But somehow she hadn't been able to pick up the phone. But how bad could it be? She could handle a surly teenager, couldn't she?

She remembered that age all too well. And the memories were not pleasant.

As Liz passed Timeless, Evy McIntyre's gallery, she hesitated, seeing one of her sister's paintings in the window. The poignant Nantucket scene reminded Liz of many family times spent on that particular beach. Days when their chief concerns were whether they'd have enough marshmallows to roast and when the fireflies would appear. Even then, Liz remembered being on edge, wondering what people might think of her eccentric parents who laughed too loudly, partied too hard, and thumbed their nose at the highbrow society surrounding them.

She stood lost in her thoughts a moment too long, and soon Evy was waving her in. Liz sighed but stepped into the gallery anyway. She should at least say hello.

"Darling, so good to see you again. How are you?" Evy kissed her on both cheeks and stood back, scrutinizing Liz while adjusting her cats-eye spectacles.

"Oh, not too bad. Considering I'm still on this island." Liz took off her sunglasses and managed a smile. "How are you? So sorry about your garden."

Evy rolled her eyes. "Dreadful day that was. I'm just glad you weren't in the way, dear."

"Me too. I'm not sure what that kid was thinking."

"She wasn't thinking." Evy chuckled. "They never do at that age. Think they're invincible. Don't you remember? Surely you must have gotten into a few scrapes as a teen?"

"Me?" Liz shook her head. "I left the troublemaking up to my brothers. Well, mostly Gray. He got into enough trouble for the rest of us."

"I remember your parents complaining to me about him on more than one occasion. He's doing well now, isn't he?" The concern in Evy's eyes said she knew of Gray's struggles with addiction. It wasn't easy to hide anything in this small community. Of course, her brother's celebrity status didn't help. "Yes, he's doing well, thanks for asking." Enough small talk. "I noticed Lynnie's painting in the window and wondered . . ."

Evy's smile returned. "Oh, yes, we've had a few sales! That sister of yours is every bit as talented as your father. Yet she has her own unique style. It's quite perfect, isn't it?" Evy clapped her hands and marched across the pine floor, her long legs still shapely for someone of her age. Liz wasn't exactly sure what age that was, but she had to be in her sixties at least. Not that you'd know it, with her stylish bob, red streak and all. Her slender figure, careful makeup, and fashionable outfits would leave anyone guessing. Evy McIntyre wasn't aging without a fight. Liz admired that.

"I've been meaning to call about this, so I'm glad you're here," Evy said. "Can you hang on a moment while I write a check for Lynette?"

"Sure. Thanks." When they'd first met, Liz wasn't sure she liked the woman. She was brazen, blunt, and didn't suffer fools. Which gave them a few things in common, but Liz wasn't altogether comfortable with the way Evy seemed to see right through her. Still, Lynette had asked her to come in now and again, see how her paintings were doing, and collect any checks, so here she was. Evy was also one of the chief investors behind turning Wyldewood into a B&B. But there was something about her friendly demeanor, something inviting about her, that made Liz want to linger. "Lynette sends her love. She should be back near the end of October."

"And she'd better get to work right away." Evy's throaty chuckle reminded Liz of an old black and white film actress. "Mind you, we are coming into slow season. But I hope to do more business online this winter. That nice boy across the road gave me a brand new website. For a price, of course. Who knew a few taps of the keyboard could be so expensive? But never mind, it'll be worth it." Evy took a look around the empty gallery and nodded, turning back to Liz. "We're getting a lot of interest from the dealers who bought the last of your father's work. Would you want to sell any more?"

Liz strolled the gallery and studied some of the artwork on display. None of her siblings seemed willing to part with more of

Dad's paintings. Funnily enough, as time went on, neither was she. "I'll talk to the others again. There's just been so much happening this summer. And we've moved my father into the nursing home, and he's . . ." What? Not about to protest them making a profit from paintings he wouldn't remember.

"I understand. They'd be difficult to part with."

Liz was moved by the sympathy in the older woman's voice. Evy offered a kind smile and a small bottle of Perrier. Liz nodded her thanks. "Maybe once Lynnie gets home . . ."

"Of course. Just let me know. How is your father doing in his new surroundings? It can't have been an easy decision."

"It wasn't. He's settled in well. He has good days where he's not so agitated, but his memory is fading fast. I think it's the best place for him."

"And you? How are you doing?"

"Me?" Something about the way Evy posed the question made her want to pull up a chair and pour out her heart to the woman. Liz studied the varnished pine floor and the perfect pink polish on her toenails. Her weekly appointments at the salon were going to have to end. Another part of her life she had to let go. She took a swig of the fizzy water and shrugged. "I'm fine." Just need employment and a place to live, but other than that . . .

Evy arched thin eyebrows. "Really?"

Liz smiled. "Well. A bit out of sorts, not having a job, but I'm sure something will come up."

"I didn't realize you were looking for work." A twinge of interest sparked in Evy's eyes.

"I'm not exactly looking." Her own honesty took her by surprise. "I left my position in New York. I'm not going back to the city. Not right now anyway. I haven't really decided what to do next. Might take a break from law for a while." Liz wasn't sure now why she'd chosen the legal profession at all.

Evy played with the strand of colorful glass beads around her neck. "You know . . . this is rather providential. I happen to be in need of an assistant." Her sharp eyes looked Liz up and down, red lips pinched together. "You might just fit the bill. But I don't suppose you'd be interested. It's not as scintillating as the corporate world, that's for sure."

The woman could read her mind. "Actually, I'm rather enjoying being out of the corporate world. But, Evy." Liz smothered laughter. "Work here, in the art gallery, with you?"

Evy released a small sigh and rounded the desk at the back of the room. "I'm not getting any younger, Elizabeth. My doctor has instructed me to slow down. Not that I have the slightest intention of doing so, but if I can at least tell her I've hired an assistant, that might get her off my case."

"I hope it's nothing serious." Liz frowned. At Evy's age, it could be anything. Lynette would not be happy to hear her dear friend was ill.

Evy snorted. "Not at all. Slightly high blood pressure. A few aches and pains, nothing to worry about, really. But I do think some help might be a good thing. I've got a mountain of paperwork back there I've been putting off tackling, and two shows coming up before winter sets in. I can't offer a great salary I'm afraid, but it would be adequate, with benefits. Would you like to think about it?"

No. Liz dug her fingernails into her palms. No, she didn't want to think about it. At all. "I'll do it." She would? She wanted to sink through the floor, take back the words. What just happened? She'd never made a hasty decision in her life.

Evy gave a gravelly laugh that told Liz she looked as surprised as she felt. "Well, then." Her new boss held out a manicured hand, beaming. "Welcome aboard."

As they shook hands, the door chimed, and Liz turned to see Matthew Stone and his niece walk into the gallery. Not the person she wanted to see right now, and certainly not here. Unfortunately, there was nowhere to run, so she stood her ground and pretended it was the most normal thing in the world for them to run into each other in an art gallery.

"Afternoon, Mrs. McIntyre," He gave a cordial nod, one hand at Mia's elbow. "May we have a moment?"

"Mr. Stone. How nice to see you again. And if it isn't Maria Andretti." Evy stepped back, a slightly intimidating look taking over her features. "I'm just about to close up for the day, but do come in."

Liz tightened her grip on her bottle of water and looked on with interest. Mia rolled her eyes, lips curled downward. The black lipstick matched her nails. She wore ripped jeans, a very tight black, long-sleeved t-shirt that scooped too low, and shiny Doc Martens. Her wrists had several black leather, silver studded bracelets wrapped around them. The kid reminded her of some of the characters she'd seen in court back in her law school days. All headed for juvie.

"Afternoon, Miss Carlisle." Matthew nodded her way, and Mia cracked a wad of gum and gave the impression she'd rather be anywhere else in the world.

"Mr. Stone." She wasn't sure whether to stay or go, but something about this curious situation made her stay.

Evy tipped her head and tapped her fingernails on the granite counter-top as Mia approached, looking like she was coming to stand before a judge.

"Mrs. McIntyre, I'm sorry I ran down your fence last week, ran over your roses, and smashed into your tree. I'll work on your garden, my uncle will help me rebuild the fence, and I can plant new roses or whatever you want . . ." She sniffed and pushed a couple fingers through her hair. "But there's probably not a whole lot I can do about the tree."

Liz watched Matthew working to hold back laughter. It danced in his brown eyes when they flashed in her direction. He obviously adored his niece, miscreant that she appeared to be.

Evy gave a little cough and narrowed her eyes. "I'm sure the tree will survive. And I accept your apology, young lady. Thank you. I did receive the message you left for me on my phone the day after your unfortunate incident, but it's nice you came in person."

Albeit clearly under duress.

Matthew looked less amused now, and Mia shrugged. Evy leaned over the counter and even Liz felt the weight of her stare. "You may repair the fence and replant the rose bushes that are still intact with roots. I will show you what to do. The rest will have to be done in the spring. There isn't any point in planting new bushes with winter on the way. But, you know, I'm sure we can find a few jobs for you here at the gallery after school, to work off your debt. Would that suit?"

Mia gaped. So did Liz.

The girl's uncle gave a tight smile and sent Mia a look that said she had no choice. "That would suit just fine. When would you like her to start?"

Evy folded her arms with a smug smile. "You may report to my new assistant, Miss Carlisle, tomorrow afternoon. Come straight down after your last class, no dawdling."

Mia's surprised expression matched the one her uncle wore.

"You work here?" they asked in unison, sounding more shocked than Liz had been hearing herself agreeing to take the position.

"Apparently." Laughter bubbled up but she swallowed it. "I've just taken the position."

"Congrats." Matthew's grin made Liz smile.

"And how do you two know each other?" Definite interest gleamed in Evy's eyes, and Liz groaned inwardly. Lynette described her friend as a die-hard romantic who'd had a hand in pushing her sister and her boyfriend Nick together. Liz definitely didn't want the woman getting any ideas where Matthew Stone was concerned.

"We've just met, actually." Liz cleared her throat and gave Evy a none-of-your-business look. "I'll call you tonight to finalize our terms and hours, shall I?" She took a card from the stack on the counter.

Evy wore an amused expression. "Please do."

Liz headed for the door, but Matthew was beside her before she could reach it. "Hold up." His intent stare pinned her to the spot. "You didn't call me. About the coach house? Are you still thinking about it?"

No, no, no. "Yes." What was wrong with her today? "I mean, no. Not really. I . . ." Liz took a breath, appalled. She was never at a loss for words. "I mean, I don't know." She'd spent the weekend clearing out her room at Wyldewood. Contemplated putting up a camp bed in the study so she wouldn't have to move out. But the noise and the dust . . . even Josslyn was talking about taking the kids to her parents' on the mainland for a few weeks, until the worst of the demolition was over.

And she had a job now. Not that she expected the salary to be anywhere close to what she was used to making, but still . . . so it seemed she'd be stuck with the girl either way. "Can I have another day or two?" She wasn't sure why she was stalling.

"We've got someone else coming to look at it tomorrow," Mia put in, her stare dipping below zero. "They'll probably take it. Isn't that what you said, Uncle Matt?"

"Not exactly." He glared at Mia, and Liz tried not to smile. The kid was clearly lying through her teeth. And her uncle was not amused.

Liz waved a hand in hopes of putting out the impending fire. "I promise I'll make a decision by Wednesday. If you want to rent it to someone before that, fine."

"Okay." He gave an easy smile and elbowed his niece. She huffed and slammed out the door, and he gave a muted groan. "Sorry. Again."

"Sounds like you've got quite the handful there. How's your car?"

"Exhibit A." He nodded toward the door, and Liz spied the Jeep at the curb, the front fender bent out of shape, right headlamp smashed. "Could have been worse, right?"

"Yes. I'm very glad there were no other vehicles or people on the road." Liz swallowed and shook her head. "So Evy didn't get the police involved?"

"Thankfully not."

"You don't think she'll pull the same stunt again without repercussion?"

His dark look was answer enough. "I *am* punishing her. And, as you heard, she's going to make things right."

"Indeed. Well, then." Liz knew when to shut up. It wasn't her business.

He shoved his hands in the pockets of faded jeans, and she watched a vein pulse in his neck. A shadow of scruff skirted his jawline, light brown hair curling toward one thick brow as he assessed her with unsure eyes. "I'm doing the best I can."

"I'm sure you are." Now he was on the defensive, and Liz wanted to backpedal. "Teenagers are rarely angels, Mr. Stone. I'm sure your niece has her good days." Perhaps on Christmas or her birthday.

His expression softened. "We just heard on the weekend that her mom is up for parole. The hearing could be sometime this week."

"Oh." She'd almost forgotten about Mia's mother. "That would be good, wouldn't it?"

"I'm not sure." An air of hopelessness wove around him, and Liz found it hard not to be affected. She noticed Evy watching them and pushed the door open so they could make their way outside. "What did she do, if you don't mind my asking?"

"Embezzlement." His sigh was short and held a hint of judgment. "She was looking after an elderly woman, tucking away a bit here and there when she was given cash, then convinced the old lady to start signing checks over to her to deposit . . . until her charge's family got wind of it and the gig was up." He exhaled and pulled on a pair of shades. "Rachel's pulled a lot of crap, but this one tops all."

Liz had to agree. "Stealing from the geriatric population is rather frowned upon. First offense?"

He kicked the curb with the top of a beat-up sneaker and looked away. "She's done time before."

"How long did she get?"

"A year and six. She's served nine months, but apparently her good behavior has earned her an early hearing." He shrugged, fiddling with a set of keys. "I guess we'll see."

"Can we go already?" Mia shuffled back toward them. "Why is it freezing? It's not even October yet. This place really sucks."

"Mia, give me a break, huh?" Matthew spoke through clenched teeth. Liz felt sorry for the man. Still. That didn't mean she wanted to live beside them. "Have a nice night, Miss Carlisle. Call me when you've made your decision."

"I will." She watched them go, watched the way Mia slammed the car door, watched Matthew get in the Jeep, turn to her and say something, and the girl shake her head and slouch in her seat. When he turned his attention to starting the engine, Mia gave him the finger. Liz let out a low whistle.

Teenager or not, that young lady was a piece of work.

Matthew Stone was in way over his head.

The sad thing was, she suspected he knew it.

five

Later that night, Liz put clean plates away and scanned the kitchen for anything else to do while Josslyn finished sweeping.

"I don't think we'll ever see the end of this dust." Her sister-in-law shook her head, dumped the dustpan, and put the broom back on the hook behind the door.

Liz took the whistling kettle off the stove and fixed two mugs of tea. She joined Josslyn at the banquet and watched her inhale the spicy aroma of jasmine green tea.

"Thanks, Liz. This is absolutely needed right now."

"No problem." Liz sipped carefully, put down the mug, and managed a smile. She usually preferred a glass of wine to unwind at night, but tea was fine. Probably better for her anyway. Her brother was upstairs putting the twins to bed, allowing his wife a bit of quiet time. Liz looked around the yellow kitchen, memories dancing.

Mom and Cecily always made a good team. Cecily, who'd been cooking and cleaning for them before Liz was born, knew how to give Diana just enough work to make her feel useful, but not enough to make her feel overwhelmed. Their mother was no Betty Crocker, but she always insisted on being involved. At least once a month they'd pick at an inedible casserole or a burnt loaf of bread. All of Cecily's careful instruction never did much good.

With Dad in the nursing home and the work going on here, Cecily had gone back to looking after her grandson after school. But she still dropped by a few times a week to see how they were doing, brought food, and often took the twins to the park with her grandson.

"How's it going to work, you guys being here once they start demolishing the kitchen?"

"I'm told our new wing will be ready by then." The first thing they'd agreed to do was to build David and Josslyn's living quarters. This meant closing off a couple of rooms at the back of the house, putting in a new staircase that connected to two upstairs bedrooms, and they would put in a new bathroom. It all sounded rather complicated, but so far Liz was impressed with the speed of the construction crew. "They're saying the next couple weeks for sure. I suppose if it isn't ready, the kids and I could spend some time with my folks. Been thinking about heading over for a bit anyway, just for a break. But I hate to leave David on his own."

"I'm sure David will manage." Liz studied the pretty woman sitting across the table. She didn't know Josslyn all that well. They'd had a better relationship in the early days, when they all lived in New York, before the twins came along. Liz would go to their place for dinner on occasion, sometimes spend the night. But then she met Laurence, and he was all-consuming. David didn't like him. After a few attempts to get them all together, she'd given up. And the twins took up most of David and Josslyn's time anyway. Liz found it better to steer clear. But perhaps she should make more of an effort with Josslyn. It might be nice to have a friend.

"How are you doing, Liz?" Josslyn's eyes were kind, the question sincere. "I know we haven't had much chance to talk with everything going on. But I wanted to say I'm sorry, you know, for everything you went through with Laurence."

The awful weight of regret and leftover fear pressed down once more. Liz blinked and looked away. "Thanks." She stared at all the old magnets her mother used to collect still stuck on the fridge and wondered what would become of them. Wondered what her mother would have said about Liz's involvement with a man like Laurence Broadhurst. Well, she knew the answer to that. "I'm just glad to be out of that situation. Glad to be home." She actually meant it. Perhaps for the first time.

"Such as it is." Josslyn smiled. "I'm sorry it's such bedlam. Probably not what you need right now."

Liz shrugged. "I suppose I'll have to take Matthew Stone's place." There wasn't a choice, really. Other rentals she'd seen online were beyond her means. She'd done the math again that evening. She could afford it. And even if she'd had a place to sleep here, stepping around drills and hammers and tripping over electrical cords and toolboxes every few minutes seemed silly. "It's a nice little cottage, and he's giving me a good deal. Except . . ." Liz sighed and pulled fingers through her hair. "He's got this niece. Remember the kid I told you about the other day? The one driving the Jeep?" She told Josslyn about Mia in a few short sentences, watching concern creep across her sister-in-law's face.

"That poor kid. Can you imagine what she's gone through, having a mother in jail? No wonder she has an attitude."

Liz raised a brow. She hadn't thought of it that way. Maybe Josslyn was right. Still. "Josslyn, feeling sorry for her is fine, but you haven't met her. She's got trouble written all over her. I'd rather not spend any more time with her than I have to."

"Maybe she needs a friend, Liz." Josslyn's smile said she knew exactly what Liz would think about that.

"Please." Liz groaned and drank some more tea. "I'm sure she's got plenty of friends. But I need a place to live, and I need that job. I just wish both options didn't involve a juvenile delinquent."

"Mmm." Josslyn nodded, studied her wedding rings, then looked up at Liz, serious. "Sometimes we're placed in the strangest of circumstances for the most important reasons."

Matt sat on the deck with his coffee and watched the waves. The sunset was spectacular tonight. He reached for the expensive camera on the table beside his chair, a prized possession that he'd probably paid too much for, and snapped a few shots. So many different hues striping the sky. The scene before him looked like a painting and brought a measure of much-needed peace. He had to believe they'd get through this. Even on the crazy days. Even when Mia gave him that *I hate you* look that spoke louder than words and pierced his heart. He knew deep down she didn't mean it. They just didn't know each other all that well yet.

Mia had been six when Rachel married Joe Giovanni, just turned seven when they'd moved to Arizona. Matt hadn't seen a whole lot of them since then. He'd been busy with his first teaching job in Boston, jumped into that life, and avoided family functions at every opportunity. Not that Rachel and Mia would have been at any.

If he'd known just how bad things had been . . .

His cell phone rang and he put the camera down. Matt glanced at the number and groaned inwardly. So much for finding peace.

Matt considered letting it go to voicemail, but guilt got to him and he put the phone to his ear. "Evening, Mother."

"Matthew, dear. I've been trying to reach you for days. Have you been ignoring my calls?"

He leaned back in his chair and closed his eyes. That would be a yes. "Now what possible reason would I have for not wanting to talk to you?"

"I can think of several, but never mind." She sniffed and he heard ice clinking. He imagined her wandering the large pristine kitchen in their Beacon Hill townhouse, Dad probably out at some boring faculty function at the university, and, come to think of it . . .

"What are you doing home on a weeknight? You are in Boston, right?" Between her numerous charities and his father's speaking engagements, his parents were rarely home for dinner.

"Matthew." His mother's sigh was a little on the shaky side, and he sat up, apprehension tightening across his shoulders.

"What's wrong, Ma?"

"We need to talk."

"I gathered that. You called me. So talk." Matt clenched his jaw and chided himself. Despite their strained relationship, she was still his mother. "Sorry. I'm just tired. What's going on?" More clinking and a few sniffles. She was worrying him now. "Mom?"

"We'd like to take some time away from the city. Your father suggested we come over."

Laughter shot out of him. An unbidden reflex, like the way his leg kicked when the doctor tapped his knee. Matt got to his feet, made sure the patio door was closed. Mia was inside watching a movie. She didn't need to hear this conversation. And he didn't need her to hear it. "You're joking. My father hasn't taken a vacation in years. And I seriously doubt he wants to spend any time with me."

His mother let out her classic sigh. He could picture her pinched expression, the look that screamed displeasure. The one she frequently wore around him. "Don't be so dramatic. You saw each other last Christmas."

"And spoke for a whopping two minutes. Brought a tear to my eye."

"Stop it, Matthew. I need you to listen to me."

"I'm listening, but I'm having a little trouble comprehending," he growled, exhaustion biting. The past few nights of little sleep were bearing down. Mia had been up with nightmares three times last night. He was seriously contemplating professional help. Neither of them could carry on like this.

"We're coming to the island for a visit. We've already made the arrangements."

He stopped in his tracks, his entire body rigid. "That's impossible. You can't."

"Of course we can." She made it sound like the simplest thing in the world. "You've got plenty of room in that old house. The sea air will do us both good."

His parents really wanted to come here? What the heck was going on?

Growing up, it never occurred to him that having parents he rarely spent time with, who showed little involvement in his schooling or life in general, wasn't normal. Not until he was ten years old and, by chance or providence, met Patrick O'Donohue on the soccer field.

Matt couldn't remember the details now, but somehow they'd wound up on the same team and become friends almost at once. Patrick's large boisterous family had taken Matt in as one of their own from the moment he walked into the crowded kitchen of their two-story walk-up in the South End. The full to bursting home was always filled with warmth and laughter and jokes and hugs—

things he was not familiar with. He lived with untouchable antiques, pristine rooms, and the unspoken rule of be seen but never heard.

Matt slumped into the Adirondack chair he'd vacated a moment ago and watched the sun sink low. In a few moments it'd be dark. Nights were always the worst. Nothing to do but stare at the stars and wish for a less complicated life.

"You hate Nantucket." He couldn't remember the last time his parents had been here. From around the time he was nine, he and Rachel were sent every summer. They spent at least a month on the island with their grandparents, and he'd looked forward to the trip each year. Rachel, two years younger, grew tired of the visits when she got older. She wanted to go off to camp with her friends, while Matt always wished he could stay longer. By the time he turned thirteen—thanks to his sailing prowess, which impressed his parents, added to the fact that they wouldn't have to deal with him at home—he was spending his entire vacation here. Sometimes Pat and a couple of his brothers would come too. Those had been the best times. "You seriously want to come to Nantucket? Summer's over. Nights are starting to nip."

"Matthew, I can't get into this over the telephone. I don't want to argue. We're scheduled to arrive on Friday. Can you meet us at the ferry?"

He blinked and stared at his socked feet. A cool breeze came up, made him shiver. "Mia's living with me. Did you forget about that?"

The frosty silence that followed told him all he needed to know.

"Mother, did you hear me?" He pressed fingers against forehead and waited.

"Yes. I heard you." Her usually stiff and in-complete-control tone cracked just a tad. "We didn't know if she'd still be there."

"I'm her legal guardian. Where did you think she'd be living?"

"So, Rachel . . .?"

Matt searched for the right words, but there were none. "Is still in jail, yeah. But apparently there's a parole hearing soon."

Another long, uncomfortable silence spoke volumes. "I see," she said at last. "And if she is released?"

"Great question." Matt sat forward and rubbed his head. He'd been pondering the dilemma since Rachel had called him early Saturday morning. She was over-excited, expecting too much, expecting Mia to be overjoyed at the possibility of living with her again. "I don't have an answer."

"You sound exhausted, Matthew. I told you taking on that girl would be too much."

He bit back a word she wouldn't want to hear and glared at the darkening sky. "I'm fine. And 'that girl' is your granddaughter."

"Really? I'd forgotten." Phyllis Stone's classic cutting sarcasm rang in his ear. "So are you telling me we're not welcome? That you don't want us to come?"

If only he could.

Matt ran a hand down his face and kicked his heels together. "Mia's been through a lot. I'm not sure you and Dad showing up right now is best."

"We would really like to come."

"He knows Mia's here?" This was the most bizarre conversation he'd had with his mother, ever.

"Yes, he knows. Look . . ." Her tired-sounding sigh shook him a little. "I can't explain right now. Let's just say some things have happened recently, and your father is making some changes. We want to come to Nantucket. To see you. And meet our granddaughter."

His eyes smarted and blurred his vision. He wanted so badly to grab hold of those words, pull them in tight, and truly believe them. But years of rejection and hostility still sat front and center and snatched hope away.

Matt blinked and gave his head a shake. "Why now? You never gave a crap before. She's almost sixteen years old. And he has never, not once, laid eyes on her."

She clucked her tongue, a habit she only resorted to when tamping down anger. "You know the history between your sister and us, so why even go there?"

"Because it's relevant. What am I supposed to tell Mia?"

"Tell her that her grandparents are coming to visit. Simple."

"Right." Matt shook his head. There was nothing remotely simple about it, and she knew it.

"I still don't understand why you left Boston and moved to Nantucket. Do you really think that was a wise decision? Why didn't you just sell that old, drafty place?"

Matt leaned over his knees and took a deep breath. His mother had a way of getting right to the root of the matter and goring it out. "As I explained, I thought coming here would be good for Mia. Give her a fresh start."

"You gave us the impression you'd be there just for the summer."

"I decided to stay."

"Apparently. And have you visited your sister lately?"

Matt sighed and wished this wasn't so hard. "I went over a few weeks ago. She's doing okay."

"I'll never understand it." Her voice got shrill and sang with stress. "Stealing from an old woman! It's despicable."

"So you've said." A million times. "Like I told you, when Rach and Joe split and she and Mia came back to Boston, I really thought she'd changed. It seemed like she'd cleaned herself up. She took some first aid courses, was talking about enrolling at a community college for nursing." Matt watched as a few stars began to brighten the blackening sky. "Seemed like she'd stay clean this time."

"It always comes back to that, doesn't it?" his mother asked quietly. "Is that why she stole that money? To buy drugs?"

"I'm assuming. Hoping she'll kick it for good this time. But once she gets out . . ."

"You can't save her, Matthew."

He closed his eyes against the pointed words. "I never said I could. Look, despite what you think, being here is better for Mia. She was getting into trouble back home and—"

"So you're saying she's a problem child?"

He clenched his jaw. "No, she's not a problem child. She just has problems."

"And with all your parenting experience, you're fully equipped to handle them."

Old anger tightened his chest. "And you wonder why we never talk." Matt gripped the arm of the chair. "Oh, don't let me interrupt. Please, Mother, tell me how disappointed you are that I'm thirty-three years old, still single, and don't have the slightest intention of settling down and giving you grandchildren." He wouldn't bother adding the *why would I even want to give you grandchildren when you don't even know the one you've got* comment.

"There's no need to be snippy. How is Mia, really?"

"Like you care?"

"That's not fair, Matthew. You know I try."

He snorted. "You try? Sure. You send money. But you wouldn't recognize her if she passed you on the street. Probably wouldn't recognize your own daughter anymore either." Acid burned his stomach, and he quelled the urge to cut the conversation short and run to the bathroom.

"I couldn't go against your father's wishes at the time. And Rachel didn't want to see us."

"Can't imagine why."

"As I've said, I don't want to argue with you. We'll talk more when we get there. You can be as nasty as you want."

"You're serious about coming?" Panic rose. What was her motivation? A few possibilities raced through his mind, none of them good. One of them was sick. Or they were splitting up. Or . . . maybe they finally had had a change of heart. But he wasn't about to drag Mia into this without finding out first. "Look, if it's that important to you, I can come over to Boston and we can talk about introducing you to Mia. I can meet you for lunch. But you can't just show up here."

"Of course we can. You're worrying for nothing. I'll email you our travel itinerary. I know that house has five bedrooms, but if it's too much trouble for you, we can book a hotel room. But we are coming, and that's all there is to it. I'll see you on Friday, dear." She clicked off.

Matt gave a frustrated yell, dropped the phone onto his lap, and raked fingers through his hair. His heart beat so wildly he wondered if he might pass out. He took a few deep breaths and tried to calm down.

Why, oh, why couldn't he just have a normal family?

"I can't do this. This is too much." Maybe God would do him a favor and she'd call back to say they weren't coming after all.

Miracles still happened. Once in a while, anyway.

But . . . maybe things *would* be different this time. Matt knew better than to cling to false hope. He'd done that one too many times. Thinking his parents would ever change was about as futile as trying to convince Mia that there was nothing wrong with a nice juicy steak every so often.

Mia.

Matt groaned again. She said very little about her grandparents. Which wasn't surprising, considering their rejection of her. Phyllis and Harrison Stone were a breed unto their own. He had no idea what Rachel might have told her daughter about their parents over the years, although he could imagine. And now, apparently, he'd be having that conversation with Mia.

Why, why, why?

Because you're a putz, Stone. A big old pushover. Always trying to do the right thing. Always cleaning up other people's messes. Helping them live their lives while yours passes you by.

"Yeah, I know. I'm an idiot." Maybe they should get a dog. Then at least he wouldn't have to talk to himself. His cell rang again and Matt groaned aloud. That was *it!* "Oh, come on, Mother! Haven't you done enough damage for one night?"

"Mr. Stone?" A younger woman's voice on the other end jolted him into a sitting position.

He glanced at the screen. "Miss Carlisle." He scrubbed his face. "Sorry about that. I thought you were my mother. No offense."

"Okay." She cleared her throat. "Well, none taken." There was a distinct pause, and he wondered if she might have deemed him a complete knucklehead and hung up. "Are you all right?" she finally asked.

He emitted a short laugh, the tight band across his back easing a bit. "Talking to my mother ranks right up there with being forced to spend an afternoon in a shopping mall with my niece."

"Not a big shopper then?"

"I'd rather have a root canal."

She laughed, and he heard dogs barking in the background. Although he'd been a kid the last time he'd been over there, he could picture the old Carlisle house with its many rooms and passages, and memories crept in unwanted. How sad that he'd spent his entire life wishing to be part of other peoples' families.

"It's funny." She gave a muted sigh. "Before I called you I was just thinking it'd be nice if my own mother was still here to talk to."

He flinched and rubbed his jaw. "Feel free to borrow mine anytime. Although I doubt she'd give the kind of motherly advice yours might have."

"Mine was hardly perfect. But I do miss her. Well, anyway . . ." She lapsed into silence again.

Matt stared at the dark ocean and wondered how much he should be telling her. Especially if she was still contemplating moving in next door. "Aside from throwing my mother your way, is there anything else I can do for you, Miss Carlisle?"

More laughter produced a grin from him. He really needed to get a life.

"Actually, yes. I'm calling back about the coach house. Is this a bad time to talk?"

"Uh, no. It's great." Matt felt like he was in free fall, no idea when the ground would rise up to meet him and send him flying. "You're interested then?"

"I am. If I can, I'd like to move in as soon as possible. Do you have a lease agreement drawn up? I'll need to review it, and of course we will have to discuss the situation regarding your niece, as I'm still not sure about that request, and I'd really rather—"

"Miss Carlisle?" A totally uncharacteristic chuckle snuck out of him. "Take a breath."

"Sorry." Her low feminine laugh soothed him in a way he didn't understand. Didn't exactly appreciate either. "Perhaps we can meet tomorrow, at the gallery," she said, more composed. "Will you be coming to pick Mia up when she's through?"

He blanked, then suddenly remembered their conversation with Evy McIntyre that afternoon. Mia would be helping at the gallery after school tomorrow. "Yes, right. Okay. Tomorrow it is."

They hung up, and he sat back with a satisfied smile. The day hadn't been a total disaster after all. Now all he had to do was break the news to Mia that she was about to meet the grandparents who had banished her mother from their lives before his niece was born.

six

Liz sat at a desk behind the counter at the far end of the gallery on Tuesday afternoon, inputting figures into a spreadsheet. She checked the time again, and glanced at Evy a little warily. Mia Stone should have walked through the door at three-thirty on the dot. And now it was almost four. And the gallery had customers.

Evy dealt with the mainland visitors smoothly, made two sales—sizeable ones—placed one painting on hold, and sent them all away happy and smiling.

Liz saved the document she was working on and waited until the door clicked closed. "She didn't call."

"Oh, I'm well aware." Evy waved a manicured hand in her direction, not seeming the least bit bothered. "I didn't expect her to. And the fact that she is not here tells me we're going to have more on our hands than we bargained for."

Liz stared. "You still want her to work for you?"

Evy gave a thin smile. "We had a deal. Our young friend may need a reminder that she is indeed in my debt. And should I decide to press charges . . . You're the lawyer. What do you think I could do with destruction of property, severe emotional trauma?"

Liz stifled a grin at Evy's stricken expression. "I'm not sure she'd care. From what I've seen of the girl so far, I doubt Mia Stone cares much about anything, except maybe herself."

"Hmm. Sad, isn't it?" Evy's sigh was wistful.

Liz felt the weight of her own words. Not so long ago, some could have said the same about her. She'd run as far from family as she could and built a life around the things that mattered to her. Things she'd convinced herself were far more important than the siblings she'd grown up with. Then her perfect world came crashing down, and she wasn't sure what mattered anymore.

"It's quiet now," Evy mused, picking up a roll of bubble wrap. "Why don't you go take a walk, check out a few stores. If she's in town, she won't be that hard to find."

"Me?" Liz shook her head. "No, thanks." An altercation with a surly teen was the last thing she needed today. But Evy raised a brow, and Liz knew she wouldn't win this one.

"Fine. I'll go. But short of dragging her here, if she won't come, I'm not sure what you think I can do."

"Oh, something tells me you can be quite persuasive when you need to be." Evy's tone held a hint of hesitation. "Don't be too hard on her."

Liz pulled on her jacket. Who knew Evy McIntyre would be a pushover when it came to kids? She left the gallery with an unexpected smile on her face.

Her first day at Timeless hadn't been terrible. She enjoyed the pristine surroundings, even enjoyed interacting with a few customers. She imagined most visitors to the gallery would be tourists, and they would be few and far between in the coming weeks. She was already making a preliminary list of innovative ideas to keep the place busy during winter.

She popped into a few of the stores, but no sign of Mia. She'd probably gone straight home and was curled in bed listening to music or watching Netflix, ignoring the world. As she walked toward the coffee shop she often saw kids congregating at after school, Liz caught sight of the girl on the bench on the opposite side of the road.

Mia leaned over her knees, cell phone pressed to her ear, dark hair falling forward. Even from this distance Liz could see the bright pink stripes. Those definitely hadn't been there yesterday.

Liz crossed the cobblestoned road quickly, slowed her pace when she got close enough to hear the girl crying. She took a breath and waited. Mia dropped her phone, swore, picked it up off the ground, and glared at it.

Liz approached the bench and sat on the end of it. "I assume that phone you were just using has a clock on it?"

Mia snapped her head up, wiped her eyes, and sent Liz a look that could have scalded milk. "I know I'm late. Something came up." She reached for the pink earbuds that sat around her neck and plugged them into her ears. Her ripped jeans, black boots, and baggy red-plaid flannel shirt were not exactly appropriate attire for the gallery.

Liz sighed, her patience already frayed. She plucked one earbud from the girl's ear and met the angry red-rimmed brown eyes flashing her way. "Look, Evy was expecting you, and you didn't show. You're getting a huge break, you know. Do you have any idea how much trouble you could be in right now? Driving without a license, destruction of property—oh, let's not forget driving a stolen vehicle, even if it does belong to your uncle. I wouldn't be surprised if all that fun landed you a little stint in a correction center someplace, should Mrs. McIntyre decide to press charges."

Mia stiffened, folded her arms, and stared straight ahead in stony silence. Her bottom lip quivered, and two tears slipped slowly down her cheeks. Liz blew air through pursed lips, battling defeat as she watched Mia battle emotion. Remorse pinched. Liz didn't have the first clue about teenagers. Maybe threatening wasn't the way to go.

"Mia? Are you all right?"

"Do I look all right?"

"You want to talk about it?"

Mia grabbed her backpack, fumbled through it, and pulled out a tissue. Blew her nose, got to her feet, and marched off in the direction of the gallery.

Okay, then. Apparently not.

Liz scrambled to her feet and followed the girl down the street.

Evy greeted Mia and hustled her off to a back room to put her to work. For the next two hours, Liz monitored the girl as she swept furiously, put boxes up on shelves, and systematically completed all the chores on Evy's long list.

Evy used the rest of the time to go through locking up procedures with Liz, making sure she familiarized herself with the alarm system the combination to the safe, then ceremoniously presented her with her own set of keys.

Liz eyed the keys dubiously. "I'm not sure I'm going to be working here that long."

Evy gave the throaty chuckle Liz was already getting used to. "As long as you are, I'd rather you had these." She sent a pointed look toward the back room. "At the moment, I think it's wise that we both know where things are, don't you?"

A smile tickled Liz's lips. "So you're not as trusting as I thought."

"Oh, I'm willing to give her my trust." Evy lowered her voice. "But she will have to earn it. And she's not off to the best start. Any idea why she was so upset?"

Liz shook her head. "Not a clue. She wouldn't talk to me."

"Not surprising. At that age, they don't share much. Well, at least you got her here."

Liz tidied up the front desk while Evy retreated to her office to close out her files for the day. At five-thirty the front door buzzed, and Matthew Stone walked through it looking windblown and worried. He nodded her way and swept a gaze around the empty gallery, no doubt wondering what they'd done with his wayward niece.

"She's tied to a chair in the back room."

He whipped his head around, his eyes wide. "She's where?"

Liz laughed, but the haggard look he wore chased off humor. "I'm kidding. She's finishing up in back there. You want me to get her for you?"

He shrugged, raked fingers through messy hair. Hesitation hovered on his face, feet planted to the floor. His khaki pants and blue cotton shirt sported a few splotches of red paint. "Was she okay?" His voice held a slight tremor.

Liz left the desk, stood a few feet away, and decided to be honest. "Well, she didn't show up when she was supposed to. I went to look for her and found her on Main. She was clearly upset but wouldn't talk to me. So to answer your question, no, I don't think she is."

He sighed like he'd expected as much. "Her mother's parole hearing was today."

Ah. That explained it. Liz offered what she hoped was a comforting smile. "I'm so sorry. She was denied?"

"No. Granted." He set his jaw, his eyes stormy. "My buddy Pat called Mia when he couldn't reach me. I was teaching an afterschool class, so I couldn't take the call." His stricken look said it all. "I wanted her to hear it from me."

"So she's getting out. That's good, isn't it?"

He scrubbed his jaw. "Mia's relationship with her mother is complicated."

"I'm sorry." Liz didn't know what else to say. She knew all about complicated family relationships. She wished she hadn't been so hard on the girl.

"And on top of all that, my parents have decided to visit. They'll be here on Friday."

"Is that what was going on when I called the other night and you thought it was your mother?"

"Yep. That's what was going on."

"You don't sound happy about their visit." Actually he sounded like he'd been sentenced to take his sister's place in prison.

"No?" Matthew gave a short laugh. "It's a long and extremely screwed up story. My parents and I don't get along. And they've never met Mia. So there's that."

"They what?" Liz tried to hide her surprise, but the crooked smile he wore told her she hadn't managed it.

"Told you it was screwed up."

"Oh, boy." Liz fiddled with the pearls around her neck. And she thought her family had issues. "You do have your hands full."

The door to the back room crashed open. "Finally! You were supposed to be here fifteen minutes ago." Mia flounced into the main room of the gallery, backpack slung over one shoulder. "I did everything on the list." She stared Liz down. "Where's the old broad?"

"Mia." Her uncle growled a warning and cleared his throat.

"What? I just wanted to tell her I was done. So we're even."

"Uh . . . Mia?" Liz pushed hair behind her ears and narrowed her eyes. "That wasn't the arrangement. You're to come every day after school until Evy says otherwise. And she may need you on some Saturdays."

Mia's mouth hung open, and Liz almost flinched as she caught sight of the stud in her tongue. "What? No freaking way! That's crap!"

"Yo." Matthew put a hand on Mia's arm and studied her with a stern expression. "That's enough."

Mia curled her lips and spat a word Liz would have been grounded for using at that age. Matthew shook his head, took a step back, and tipped his head toward the door. "Go wait in the car."

"I'm thirsty. I want a soda. Can I have some money?" Mia twisted the stud in her nose and actually smiled.

"Car. Now."

Mia stormed out of the gallery, and the bell on the front door jangled violently. They both jumped.

"Bet you're real happy you took this job, huh?" He tried out a grin that didn't go far, and Liz suddenly wanted to hug him. She shook off that flagrant thought and put some space between them, retreating to tidy papers and cards on the counter.

"You'd better go. I wouldn't trust her to wait for you. She's probably halfway through town by now."

He rolled his eyes but looked out the window all the same. "Nah. She's in the car."

Liz looked toward the vehicle and saw Mia sitting in it. "So she is."

"She blows hot air most of the time. She listens. Eventually."

It was more than that. Liz had already gauged the extent of Matthew's love for his niece. Now she was beginning to suspect the unruly girl might have more feelings for her uncle than she cared to admit.

"Here it is." He pulled out a sheet of paper from the beat-up brown satchel he carried over his shoulder and handed it to her. "Lease. I didn't forget. You can start moving in whenever you're ready."

Liz met his eyes and hesitated. He smiled, a real smile this time, warm and sincere, but shadowed in sorrow. She felt sorry for him.

Matthew Stone was a man in turmoil, yet he seemed kind and clearly wanted to do right by his niece. She wondered why Mia was with him, where her father was, why she didn't know her grandparents. Not that it mattered. She wasn't about to get involved.

But if she lived next door . . .

Alarm pealed through her, sending all sorts of second thoughts her way. She had a million reasons why she should tell him she'd changed her mind. Mia, for one. She wasn't at all sure she had the stamina to deal with a messed-up kid like that. And what if she wasn't ready to be on her own again? What if leaving Wyldewood and the safety net being with family provided turned out to be a catastrophic mistake?

Matthew rubbed his jaw, clearly unnerved by her silence. "You having second thoughts?"

"No." Liz sighed and scanned the lease. Standard stuff. A flash of the small living room with ocean views, sun streaming through clean windows, produced a smile, and she looked up to find him watching her.

His forehead furrowed, shadows moving through his eyes. He raised a dark brow in question, and for a brief moment she considered backing out. Her instincts weren't always good when it came to men, but somehow she felt she could trust this one. Past experience told her not to be so stupid. Trusting men was what got her into trouble. No. She'd have to keep things cordial but businesslike. No feeling sorry for the man. Or his niece. She had enough to worry about anyway. But if she signed the papers she held, finding a new place to live would be off the list.

"No second thoughts," she said firmly, and her heart jumped a little when he smiled in relief.

seven

Matt drove aimlessly while Mia sat in sullen silence. Music blared from her earbuds, and he tried not to worry about her going prematurely deaf. She refused to look at him, staring out the salt-splattered window of the Jeep, slapping out a beat on her knees.

He'd been trying to find the right words since he'd talked to Pat on the way to pick her up from the gallery. The anger on his niece's face made his heart hurt. He wanted to see her smile again, hear her laugh. When she was little, he could make her laugh at anything. While his buddies were out partying, Matt preferred to stay home and babysit. Once he graduated high school, he officially moved into the O'Donohues' basement apartment where Rachel and Mia were living. He helped out as much as he could between his classes at the community college. Rachel was already on the downward spiral again.

By the time Joe Giovanni entered their lives, Matt's love for his niece was fierce, and he fought hard to convince his sister she was making a huge mistake. The man creeped him out big time. Matt knew Giovanni was bad news, but he couldn't prove it. His gut told him his family would be in trouble if Rachel didn't heed his warning. But like always, Rachel only thought about herself, and she married the guy without telling any of them.

The day they left Boston for Arizona, Mia watching him from the back window of the beat up, dirt-splattered truck, tears rolling down her face, Matt's heart was shredded. He'd tried to keep in touch as much as he could, tried to visit, but getting across the country wasn't easy or cheap, and eventually the visits grew few and far between. And then around Thanksgiving last year Rachel showed up on his doorstep without warning, Mia in tow. The happy little girl he remembered had grown into a surly, angry teenager, with a story behind those flashing eyes he wasn't sure he wanted to know.

Matt slowed and turned down Broad, found a parking spot near The Juice Bar and pulled into it.

Mia turned his way with a sour look. "What are we doing?"

"Getting ice cream." He took the keys from the ignition and opened his door.

"What about dinner?"

"You got a problem with ice cream for dinner now? Didn't used to." He grinned as memory flashed.

"I made you dinner, Uncle Matty!" Mia, five years old, rushed him the moment he walked through the door of the small two-bedroom apartment the three of them had recently moved into. He'd been teaching for a year. Rachel was working too, trying to stay sober.

Matt swept Mia up and planted a kiss on her nose.

"You made me dinner? Well, aren't you just the best little girl in the world." He breathed in her wide smile and felt the day's stress slip away. A kid in his art class had committed suicide last night. The other kids were devastated, naturally, and the staff had spent most of the day dealing with crying girls and angry young men. "What're we having?"

Mia giggled and pressed her nose to his. "Guess."

"Hmm. Steak and mashed potatoes?"

"Nope!"

"Green eggs and ham?"

"Nope!" She giggled and wriggled in his arms. Matt hugged her tight and shrugged.

"I give up. Tell me."

"Ice cream!

"Ice cream for dinner?" He tried to look as shocked as possible, and she laughed in delight.

"Isn't that the best idea ever?"

"It certainly is." He kissed her forehead and set her down. "Best ever."

Matt shook off the memory and tried to smile like he meant it, but it was a weak effort. "You coming?"

"Seriously?" Mia's dark eyebrows shot skyward. He wondered whether she had the same memories. Whether she remembered much about the years they'd spent together. He'd been her world then, she his. And all he wanted to do right now was turn back the clock.

"Let's go." Matt waited while she got out, locked the Jeep, and jogged toward the shop, Mia clomping along behind muttering something about him being the weirdest guy on the planet.

Ice cream in hand, they walked down South Beach Street and headed toward Children's Beach. He made short work of his butter pecan waffle cone, but Mia was still working on her banana split.

"Now you want to walk on the beach?" She cut her eyes and shoveled a spoonful of whipped cream into her mouth. "It's too cold."

"It's fine." He pulled on the thick Red Sox sweatshirt he'd brought with him and nodded her way. "You warm enough?" She'd put on a denim jacket when they left the Jeep.

"Whatever." She kicked at a small rock and twirled her spoon. "Gonna be dark soon. I'll just wait here."

"Won't be dark for a half hour. C'mon. I want to talk to you." Matt headed down the stairs, exhaled, and summoned courage. This was a conversation he didn't want to have. For so many reasons. And she probably felt the same. In fact, he wouldn't be surprised to look back and find her still standing on the steps. But he heard her behind him a moment later, huffing and sighing like walking along a beach eating ice cream on a school night was possibly the worst punishment in the world.

After a few more minutes, Matt stopped walking, found an old overturned log, and sat down. He dangled his hands over his knees, watched the boats bobbing as the sun dipped low, and searched the sky to spot the first stars. Normally he'd have his camera, but this wasn't the time to take pictures. "Sit, Mia. It's sand. It won't kill you. There's room here if you want."

She gave a painful sigh and lowered herself onto the log. "I know what you're going to say. I already heard, from Uncle Pat."

Matt nodded slow, a lump forming in his throat. "I know. I'm sorry about that. He couldn't reach me and thought he was doing me a favor by telling you. But I wish he hadn't."

"I would have found out eventually." Head low, she picked up handfuls of sand and let it trail through her fingers. He studied the pink streaks in her hair, still tempted to ask her what that was about, but when he'd first seen them this morning, he'd promised himself not to make a scene. Pink streaks weren't the worst she could do. It was hardly the hill to die on.

Matt placed a hand on her shoulder and let out a breath. "I didn't mean I'd have kept it from you. I meant I wanted to be the one to tell you."

She shrugged off his hand. "Well, you weren't."

Guilt hit hard but he ignored it. No point dwelling on things he couldn't fix. "He probably told you that your mom will be staying in Boston. She'll go to a halfway house at first, make sure she's still getting treatment and counseling." Matt blinked and waited until he felt he could control the tremor in his tone. "I've arranged for you to call her tomorrow afternoon. And we can figure out when to go over to visit."

"I don't want to talk to her." Mia shifted and turned her head away. Her shoulders shook a little, and he knew she was fighting tears. "And I don't want to visit."

He'd expected as much. "Mia, I know you're angry. But you've only seen her twice since we moved here. I know—"

"You don't know!" Mia glared at him, fury ripping across her face. "You don't know anything! You don't know what it was like for me, having to leave and go live with him. You don't know about the things he did . . . you don't know how he treated my mom and me, and you don't know how glad I was when we moved back to Boston last year." She gulped a sob and shook her head.

He waited, letting her continue.

"She promised she was gonna get clean, and she was really trying! And then she ruined it all! She had a good job, and she screwed it up, and now I have to live here on this stupid island, go to a stupid dinky school where I have no friends and everyone looks at me funny because I have a mom in jail! You have no idea how that feels, Uncle Matt, so don't even pretend you do!" Mia pushed to her feet and stormed off down the beach.

"Great." Matt raised shaking hands and pulled fingers through his hair.

The things he did . . .

Mia's voice echoed on the wind.

Matt exhaled and allowed reality to sink in. He couldn't stomach contemplating the abuse Mia had suffered at the hands of her stepfather. When they'd first come back, he'd had suspicions, but Rachel would clam up when he pressed. This was the first time Mia had brought it up, and he knew he couldn't force more from her tonight.

The wind picked up strength as the sky faded into dusky gray. They'd have to head back soon. And he hadn't even broached the subject of his parents' impending arrival.

"Mia." He got closer and she turned and walked the other way. Matt's long legs had no trouble catching her. "Mia, wait." He put a hand around her wrist and pulled her to a stop.

"What?" She shook her head. "What do you want from me? Am I supposed to be happy about her getting out? Supposed to say I can't wait to see her? Pretend everything's fine when it's not, like you do?"

Ouch. She did have a knack for shooting straight from the hip.

Matt let her go. "Okay, Mia. Tell me what you want. If you don't want to be here, do you want to move back to Boston?"

She huffed and blessed him with an eye-roll. "Where would I live? With her?"

Good point, kid. Now they were getting somewhere. "I guess if you're not living with me, that would be an option eventually."

"Well, that would be freaking awesome. I don't get why we had to leave Boston. We could have done fine."

"You know why we left. I thought coming here would be good for you. For both of us. But if you really hate it that much, we can talk about a new plan."

She shook her head in stony silence.

"What? You want to stay here then?" Matt rubbed the back of his neck, wishing there were a magic pill for patience.

"I'd rather stay here than live with my mom."

Matt sighed at the sad truth. "I hope you won't always feel that way, Mia. I hope your mom stays clean this time. And I hope that one day you have a chance at a real relationship. Look . . ." He took a breath and scratched his jaw. "I know I'm not the easiest guy in the world to live with, but I want to do right by you. I don't want to make things harder on you."

"I know." Tears shimmered in her eyes. "I just miss my friends."

"Your drug-using, shoplifting, loser friends?" The words were out before he could rethink them. He shoved his hands in the pockets of his jeans and bit his lip.

"They were still my friends."

There was no sense in arguing "Okay. Anyway. Maybe you can just think about it. About visiting her. We could go over in a couple weeks, see how she's doing."

"I just told you—"

Matt inhaled and nodded. "The thing is, your mom wants to see you. She's asked if we would visit once she gets out and settled." He had to be honest. "And I think she is hoping you might want to move back, eventually, to live with her. Thoughts?"

The word she answered him with was not what he wanted to hear. Her language was another issued he'd have to deal with. Just not tonight. "Are you deaf? How many times do I have to say I don't want to? Tell her no." Mia drew a circle in the sand with the top of her boot. "I mean, you're not exactly a rave, ya know, but at least you're around most the time. At least you care about me. Even though it's super annoying."

Matt tried not to grin. "Well, you have your finer moments too, kid." He watched the circular motion of her boot. "I don't want to tell her you don't want to see her, Mia. Will you think about it? I'll go with you. We wouldn't have to stay long."

"Why does she even care?" She finally met his eyes, and he saw the truth in them. And he hated that she felt that way toward Rachel, but right now he couldn't blame her.

"You're going to have to forgive her sometime."

"Whatever. Are we done?"

"Sure. I guess we're done."

Oh, and by the way, your grandparents are coming to visit.

Mia started walking back down the beach before he could get the words out. He let her get ahead of him and took the time to gather his thoughts. Tried not to call himself the coward he was. But maybe it'd be better to tell her about his parents' visit tomorrow. She'd had enough for one night.

They both had.

eight

Thursday rolled in with wind and rain. The storm bolstered Matt's hope for ferry cancelations. Despite his wishful thinking, the weather service said by morning it would be all over, with a pleasant forecast for the weekend. His parents would arrive tomorrow, and there wasn't a thing he could do about it.

Mia had to be told.

"Hey." He wandered into the living room after supper and sank into a leather recliner, swiveled to face her and nodded toward the television. "Mia, shut that off a minute. I need to tell you something."

She gave a *what now* expression, but he caught the fear in her eyes. "Is it about my mom again?"

"No. Not about your mom." He wondered when she'd stop walking through life waiting for the other shoe to drop. But for now, there wasn't much he could do to fix that.

"Then what?" Huddled under an old afghan, she twirled a strand of shocking pink hair around her finger and studied him through bleary eyes. She still hadn't slept a full night since being in his care. "You already grounded me, made me work for the old lady and the snooty b—"

"Mia." Matt held up a hand, closed his eyes a moment, then shot her a tired smile. "Not tonight, please."

She sighed, crossed her arms, and shut her mouth. Matt drummed his fingers on the arms of the chair and nodded. "Thank you. Okay, first off, Miss Carlisle took the coach house. She's moving in on the weekend."

"Fandangtastic." Her sarcasm swept around the room. Matt shook his head at her surly expression. What would it take to make her smile again?

"Ya know, this might come as a shock, Mia, but I'm not here to please you. Money's a little tight. I need to rent the place out, and the lady needs a place to live. And you need someone close by when I have to work nights."

"What?" Mia shot up. "No freaking way is she gonna come in here and tell me what to do!"

"No. She's not." Matt sat forward, ignoring his throbbing temples. "But I am telling you what to do. Like it or not, kid, I'm the one in charge around here. And I think it's worked out okay so far, but you gotta stop pushing me. I'm not out to get you. But I'm not putting up with your crap, and I don't expect Miss Carlisle to either. Got that?"

"Whatever." Mia punched a pillow, sniffed, and swiped a hand across her eyes. He never knew for sure when he was being played. And that annoyed the heck out of him.

"Are you done?" She tossed the clicker between her hands.

"Your grandparents are coming to visit." He sat back and waited for the explosion.

It didn't come.

She simply stared through soulful eyes that told him nothing. "Why?"

Why, indeed.

The simple word sang the song he'd memorized years ago. But he'd never been able to figure out answers to the questions it asked. "I'm not real sure, Mia."

"That's lame. How can you not know? What'd they say?"

"Not much. Your grandmother called a few days ago, said they needed to get away, that they were coming to the island."

"When?" Her eyes got a bit rounder.

"Tomorrow." Matt breathed it out and willed the tension in his temples to dissipate. "I wasn't sure how to tell you," he rushed on before she started in. "With the news about your mom, you were upset enough already so . . . I figured I'd wait."

"Do they know about what happened, that she went to jail? Do they know I'm here?"

"They know." Matt rubbed his chin. "They want to meet you."

"After fifteen years? Whatever." She stated the obvious with lack of emotion that really didn't surprise him. "My mom told me they don't really talk to you either. What'd you do that was so bad?"

"More like what I didn't do." Matt leaned back and focused on the photos that sat on the fireplace mantel. Nan's photos that he'd found packed in one of the boxes he'd opened the first weekend back here.

Pictures that told stories of happier times. Him and Rachel goofing around on the beach, playing tag with the waves. Photos of him with Patrick sailing in their first regatta. The four of them, Rachel, Nan, Pop, and him, arms around each other, grinning like fools at something Pop had probably said just before the picture was taken.

He missed his grandparents something fierce. Wished Mia had known them. Wished hers were half as good as his had been. But wishes were as useless as a camera without film.

"I guess you're gonna tell me to behave."

Mia's voice pulled him back to the moment, and Matt blinked at her. Then he chuckled, his mood lifting a little. "Would it do any good?"

"Probs not." She cracked a wad of gum and shot him what could have passed as a wink. "Well, between this and Miss Cranky Pants moving in, my weekend just got real exciting."

"Let's try out a little respect, okay? Is that too much to ask?"

"I dunno. You don't exactly have the best manners either, even if you are a Brahmin from Beacon Hill."

"Ha." He smiled at her use of the word most of his buddies used to describe Boston's elite, and wagged a finger. "None of that around your grandparents."

Her grin told him he could count on it. "So what's the deal with you and them? I know my mom got pregnant with me and they kicked her out. What happened with you?"

"It's kind of complicated."

"No duh. Everything with you is complicated." She tossed him a rare smile. "You know, if you'd lighten up once in a while, you might actually get a girl to stick around for more than a date or two."

Heat crept up the back of his neck, but she had a point. It wasn't that he couldn't get a date. He just didn't much care how they went. "Since when is my love life any of your business?"

"What love life?"

"True enough." Matt chuckled, worked the kinks out of his neck, and nodded. "Look, about my folks. We don't tend to agree on much, Mia. My father is an a—ah, let's just say, opinionated and . . . well, it is what it is. I have no idea why they're coming, and I'm not exactly over the moon about it. So fasten your seatbelt, kid. It's gonna be a bumpy ride."

"Can't wait." She yawned, stretched her arms above her head, and shivered a bit as a bolt of lightning flashed across the window. "Dang storms. Power's not gonna go out is it?"

"We have candles and battery-powered lights if it does."

"I hate the dark."

"Never would have guessed." He grinned, and she stuck her tongue out. Mia slept with the light on all night. He had the Nantucket Energy bills to prove it.

"I got my reasons."

"It's okay, Mia." He said it slow, gentle, and a flicker of sadness moved into her eyes.

"Uncle Matt?"

"Yeah?"

"He doesn't know where I am, does he?"

A thudding began in his chest, fear sneaking up around him before he had a chance to recognize it. "Who?"

"Joe." She shrugged and looked away, but he saw her shivering.

Matt moved onto the couch and put his hands on her drawn up knees before she could protest. "Mia. Look at me."

Tear-filled eyes turned his way. "What?" she whispered, the word trembling off her tongue.

Matt thumbed a tear from her cheek. He would still give her the world if he could. If she'd let him. Once upon a time, he'd told her dreams came true. Told her she was a princess, that she could be whatever she wanted to be and she'd be great at it.

He'd known what had been taken from her not long after they had shown up at his apartment after leaving Arizona. He let them stay of course. What else could he do? Mia was shut down, angry, tearful, and confused. He'd tried to talk to Rachel about his niece, but she refused to get into it with him. Said they were going to make a fresh start, the both of them. Mia was fine.

His niece was about as far from fine as her drug-addicted mother.

It had been obvious Rachel was still using the minute she walked in the door. He saw it in her eyes, her skin, her thin frame and shaky hands. All the promises she'd made over the years, every time they'd talked and she swore she was clean . . . all lies. He'd been so angry he almost kicked them out then and there. But he couldn't. And she made more promises she never intended to keep.

Things were good for a while. Until they weren't. The first night Rachel left, no explanation, gone God knows where, doing God knows what, Matt realized he was on his own. And Mia woke up screaming. The moment he'd flicked on the bedroom light, rushed to her side and tried to offer the comfort of a hug, he'd known.

He rubbed the spot on his cheek where she'd slapped him that night, and the memory of her thrashing in the bed, struggling to get away before she realized it was him, choked him as though it had happened yesterday.

Matt still couldn't fathom what kind of monster would want to touch a child. Countless sleepless nights over the past year brought no clarity. Much as he tried to avoid dwelling on it, much as Mia tried to hide from it, the ugly truth lived with them and made its presence known when he was least expecting it.

If he ever laid eyes on Joe Giovanni again, God forgive him, the man was as good as dead.

Matt met Mia's troubled gaze, pushed her hair back a bit so he could see her face. "Nobody's going to hurt you here. You're safe. I promise."

"Do you really have to work nights at that security job?"

Matt mentally kicked himself. Why hadn't he thought this through? Of course Mia wouldn't want to be on her own at night.

Even with Miss Carlisle in the coach house, she'd still be alone in the house. Maybe his parents being here would actually be a good thing.

"For now, I guess. I don't know. I'll have to see what I can do, Mia." Maybe he'd install an alarm system in the main house when they put in the one for the coach house.

She wiped her eyes and almost smiled. "I know it bugs you when you have to get up nights. Sorry. It's just . . ."

"It's okay." He knew. Matt's eyes landed on a sketch pad half hidden under the blanket. He pulled it out without asking permission. "Where'd you get this?"

"It's mine." Mia grabbed for it too quickly, and he held it out of reach.

"Looks like one of mine. I bought a couple the other day. One went missing." He flipped it open and his heart stilled. The first few pages were filled with pencil sketches. So perfect and intricate in every detail. The beach. The house. There was even one of him, snapping a shot with his camera. He met Mia's eyes and smiled. "You've been holding out on me."

"Whatever. They're just dumb drawings." She made another grab for the book, but he held it tight against his chest.

"Are you kidding me? Mia, these are amazing. How long have you been drawing like this?"

"Since forever." Her cheeks pinked a little. Matt handed back the book.

"Why aren't you taking art at school?"

She shrugged, running a finger over the spirals that held the pages together.

"Because I'm teaching it?" He waited, half dreading the answer.

"No. Not cause you're teaching it." Mia sniffed and glanced away. "I'm just . . . I don't know. I'm not that good."

Why couldn't she see the talent she had? The shading, perspective, light, everything was spot on. Matt shook his head. "I think those drawings are pretty great, Mia. And I'd love to have you in my class. Seriously. Will you think about it?"

"Maybe." A shutter banged against the side of the house and she jumped. Tears flooded her eyes again. "I wish I wasn't so freaking scared of everything," she whispered.

"Come on." Matt pulled her into his arms and held tight, waiting for the moment she would push away and tell him she wasn't a kid anymore. But she sank against him with a cry that almost shouted relief and finally let go of the barrage of emotion she'd been wrestling with long before the moment he'd walked into the room of the precinct the day Rachel had been arrested.

"Yeah. That's good. You let that out." He patted her back, stroked her head, and let her get it out. She'd probably claim to hate him again in five minutes, but for right now, he'd take this moment.

nine

"I don't understand why she couldn't be here to meet us." Phyllis Stone wiped down the kitchen counter, folded the tablecloth she'd insisted they use on the patio table where he'd suggested they have a late lunch.

It was going on four in the afternoon, his parents had only been here a couple hours, and Matt was exhausted. "As I explained, Mia has an after-school job at the art gallery. She'll be here for dinner." He'd gone a bit overboard—bought a tenderloin, a small quiche for Mia, a couple of expensive bottles of wine, and even made a chocolate cake last night. One day he might get rid of the inherent need to please his parents, but today apparently wasn't going to be that day.

"Why does she need an afterschool job at her age?" Phyllis sniffed and smoothed her blond hair, cut in a neat bob, the style she'd worn all his life and probably most of hers. Matt sighed and stretched out his legs under the kitchen table. His father had retreated upstairs for a nap. Matt couldn't remember his father ever taking a nap.

They both seemed tense, uncharacteristically subdued, and strangely preoccupied.

"I had an afterschool job at her age," he reminded her. He wouldn't tell her the real reason Mia was working at the gallery.

She laughed and put a hand behind her neck. "Stocking shelves at that awful corner store. I remember. You didn't need it."

Oh, yes he did.

Gerald Casey, Patrick's maternal grandfather, went out of his way to make sure the neighborhood boys stayed out of trouble. When he wasn't coaching baseball, he was behind the counter of his popular variety store, giving Matt and Patrick every job under the sun. They made twenty bucks a week and spent most of it on candy and baseball cards. But there were life lessons learned under the watchful eye of the crusty Vietnam vet, and Matt soon realized that if you wanted to get anywhere in this world, you needed to work at it. Life was not as easy as his parents made it seem. Most people couldn't just write checks to make their problems go away.

"Is there any tea?" She had her back to him, searching the cupboards.

"I'll get it. You take a load off." Matt rose, found the box of Darjeeling he'd purchased yesterday, her favorite, and went about making it. He grabbed a soda from the fridge for himself, found a mug that didn't have a chip in it, and soon sat at the table opposite his mother.

He studied her face for answers. She looked a little tired, less pulled together than usual. "So what's up with this impromptu visit?" He couldn't stifle the question another minute. He'd been on edge since they arrived, and now he had to know.

"Do we need a reason to visit our son?"

"Uh, when visiting your son is something you never do, yeah, it would seem so."

She stirred a little sugar into her tea and caught him watching her. She blinked and quickly looked away, but Matt swore he caught a flash of moisture in her eyes. His heart beat a little faster, and he fiddled with the leather strap of his watch. "You okay, Ma?"

"I'd be better if you'd speak the way you were brought up to." She took a sip, her expression neutral again. He couldn't stop a grin. His relationship with the O'Donohue family would always rankle her. Yet they'd done more for him and Rachel than his parents ever had.

But even their kindness couldn't save Rachel in the end.

"You, uh, you and Dad, you're not getting divorced or anything are you?" Not that it would shock him. His parents had never displayed open affection toward each other, and they rarely traveled together, but he'd always liked to believe they were happy in their own way.

Surprise widened her eyes. "Why would you think that?"

Matt shrugged. He probably didn't need to expound on his reasons. "Dad looks tired." It had been months since he'd seen them, but both his parents looked like they'd aged. His gut hadn't stopped churning since he watched them step off the ferry. Aside from stilted conversation over lunch, which Matt carried most of, neither of them had said much.

"We're not getting any younger." She flashed a smile and sipped her tea. "Smells wonderful in here, Matthew. Is that a cake I spy over there? Chocolate ganache? Your father's favorite, if I'm not mistaken."

Changing the subject. One of her favorite tactics when she didn't like the way a conversation was going. Matt shrugged and wound his thumbs together. She wasn't going to be forthcoming, that much was clear. He could continue his interrogation, but the shadows under her eyes made him zip it. "Yeah, well. Thought we'd have a nice dinner. Which reminds me, I should get the vegetables peeled." He pushed to his feet, eager to be free of the frustration he felt whenever he tried to talk to his mother.

Her sigh said she felt the same. "Perhaps I'll take a walk on the beach then."

"Put on a jacket. Wind's come up." She wouldn't offer to help with the cooking. She'd never cooked a day in her life, and they'd always counted that a very good thing.

A couple hours later, Matt began to panic. Dinner was ready. His parents were waiting.

And Mia was late.

Part of him wondered if she'd show up at all.

Matt checked his watch for the fourth time. The three of them sat in the living room, his mother toying with her glass of chardonnay, Dad draining his second scotch. It was going to be a long night.

Just as he was about to try her cell again, the front door flew open. Mia burst into the room, Elizabeth Carlisle hovering behind her looking a little frazzled.

"Don't start. I know I'm late! The stupid bus broke down!" Mia dropped her backpack to the floor and bent to untie the laces of her clunky boots. Matt inhaled, slowly got to his feet, and glanced at his parents.

They sat rigid in their seats. His mother took a generous sip and placed her glass on the side table, smoothed down her gray slacks, and stared at Mia with a tight smile. Dad also put down his glass, adjusted black-framed glasses, and leaned forward slightly, his head tipped the way it did when he wanted to say something but didn't quite know how.

Matt had half-expected him to appear in his usual professor attire of bow-tie and tweeds, and had been relieved to see his father adopting a slightly more casual mode of corduroys and open-necked starched shirt, classic light blue. He now ran a finger under the collar of his shirt, his eyes fixed on his granddaughter.

"Sorry to intrude." Miss Carlisle side-stepped Mia, obviously aware of the awkward moment. In fact, she looked like she'd rather be anywhere else. Matt could relate. "I saw Mia walking home, so I offered a ride. And could I just drop off a few things this evening? I'll be quick."

Matt stared at her wide, questioning eyes in silence. Lucid thought returned in a slow trickle, and he gave his head a shake. "Oh, sure."

His parents were on their feet now, waiting expectantly. Matt glanced from them to her and caught the bemused look she flashed him. Way to come across as a total idiot.

"Uh, Mom, Dad. This is Elizabeth Carlisle. She's renting the coach house." Had he told them he'd rented the place out? From the startled expression on his mother's face, that'd be a no.

"Harrison Stone." Dad stepped forward with his congenial smile that always made Matt a tad uncomfortable. Mom took her turn, and, fortunately, didn't try to initiate conversation.

"Pleasure to meet you both. Well, I'll let myself out. Enjoy your evening." She nodded in his direction, then neatly extricated herself from the tension-filled room.

A little air left his lungs. Matt wished he could follow her, offer to help. He'd dropped the key and her copy of the signed lease over to the gallery yesterday, so he didn't have that excuse. And he couldn't leave Mia anyway. The poor kid looked ready to hurl.

Today she was dressed more appropriately, her jeans newish and not ripped, and she wore a white blouse with a black vest overtop. Her makeup wasn't too overdone. He vaguely wondered if Evy had asked her to tone it down. Matt made a mental note to thank the woman.

Still, she was just a kid, and she had to be feeling the weight of his parents' stares as much as he was. There weren't many things worse than being placed under Harrison Stone's microscope.

Mia shuffled closer to him, chewed on a fingernail, and waited. Matt put an arm around her shoulders. Didn't know why, really, but he suddenly felt a fierce desire to protect her. To his surprise, she didn't shrug him off.

"Well. You must be Mia." His mother came forward first, hesitated a few feet away, and nodded, as though she'd just unlocked a great secret. "Yes."

Uh huh. No . . . kidding. Mia swallowed a small cough. Matt knew what she was thinking, and if he was right, they were riding the same train of thought. He almost grinned.

Just don't say it out loud, kid.

Mia studied his parents in silence. Matt wondered what she saw beyond the expensive clothes and jewelry, the stiff way they held themselves, the faint interest in their eyes. He wondered because he wasn't sure what else there was. Whether she would ever be anything more to them than an embarrassment, proof of their failure to instill moral values in their daughter.

"You look just like your mother." Dad peered at her, rubbing his chin between his thumb and forefinger.

"Yeah, I've heard that."

He felt Mia stiffen as her grandparents approached, and she sent him a sidelong look. He hoped they wouldn't try to hug her. Then again, he couldn't remember the last time they'd hugged him, so that probably wouldn't happen. Matt mulled over his father's words. He hadn't thought much on it before, but now he saw Rachel in Mia's eyes, her nose, her smile—when she chose to give it.

Nobody moved. The moment inched toward painful, and Matt cleared his throat. "Well, dinner's ready. Mia, do you need to go wash up?"

"Sure." She flashed him an almost grateful smile.

Matt nodded and pushed his fingers through his hair as she skipped out of the room and thumped up the stairs. He settled a wary gaze on his parents. "You ready to eat?" He supposed under normal circumstances, he should have asked if they were okay. But this night was far from normal, and frankly, he didn't really care.

"That would be fine, Matthew." His father straightened, fiddled with the sleeves of his shirt, rolled them up meticulously, then actually offered a smile. "Can I help?"

"Help?" Matt lifted a brow, not sure he'd heard correctly. The back of his neck was too warm. He hadn't bothered to dress for dinner, as was their custom. Figured his old jeans and red Henley would do. He crossed the room and cracked a window, cool air flooding in. "Sure, I guess. There's a bottle of red on the kitchen counter, want to open that?"

"Consider it done." And with that, his father strode toward the kitchen, looking uncharacteristically cheerful. Matt followed, his mother behind him.

"What can I do?" Mom sounded on the verge of tears. She retrieved the white wine from the fridge and refilled her glass with an unsteady hand.

"Well . . ." He grabbed some paper towels and cleaned up the few drops on the floor. "Would you set the table? Everything is still in the same drawers. If you remember."

Her laughter seemed a little on the shaky side. "I think I can manage that." Her smile bothered him. He so rarely saw it. "And while you're dishing up, perhaps you can tell us who Miss Carlisle is and why in the world she's moving into your coach house."

ten

DRAKE

She's here again. The pretty one. Can't remember her name, although I think I said it earlier, when she arrived. They told me this morning it was Sunday, and she always comes on Sunday. We sit in the day room, where they have the television turned so loud nobody can hear themselves think.

Ha.

Considering the nut-jobs around here, that's probably a jolly good thing.

"Did you have a good week, Dad? How was your lunch today?" Always full of questions, this one. She's agitated, winding her blond hair around her fingers the way her mother used to do. Her blue eyes search my face, pierce through me, and I have to smile. She's so much like her.

"Diana." I say it loud, this little victory. This snatch of memory that will be gone in another instant. "Your mother. You look just like her."

She stares at me like I've stood up, hand over heart, and recited the Pledge of Allegiance. Which I never bothered to remember even when I had a mind that worked. My British pride wouldn't allow it.

"Dad . . . thank you." She smiles and wipes tears. Thank you? Seems a silly thing to say. I must find a reply, but nothing comes. I glare at the television and take a gander around to see if there's anything I could throw at it. That might shut it up.

"Shall we go for a walk? It's warm today. Would you like that?" Pretty asks. "It's still light out. We can watch the sun go down." She puts a hand on my arm, hesitantly, like she's not sure I'll allow it. Some days I do hate to be touched.

"Excellent." My old body creaks as I push up and fumble with the zip on my heavy cardigan. She steps back and waits for me to accomplish the tedious task. Knows better than to try to help me.

We amble out to the expansive patio and I breathe in sea air. Whoopee! Watching the sun go down on another day ranks right up there with forcing my way through the slop they serve up at this place and dare call edible. "Cecily can bring dinner." Confound the woman. For all her faults, she sure knew how to cook. Why don't they hire her here?

"Oh." Pretty wears a look of surprise. "Well, I can ask her to bring you something next time she visits." She laughs a little, and I stare at the flawless features, blue eyes, and nary a hair out of place, searching for the name that won't come.

"Liz." I clap my hands together and she jumps.

"Yes?" She's always looking at me like she's never sure what I'll do next. Which I suppose is perfectly appropriate. Her guess is as good as mine.

"Your name. You're Elizabeth."

"Yes, that's right." She smiles smugly. "I am your eldest and most intelligent daughter." She pulls a green wool jacket around slender shoulders and we walk a little further. "Shall we sit for a bit? You're not cold are you?"

"Hell no. Hot as a furnace in there." I plop down on the bench, stretch my legs, and study the brown slippers somebody put on my feet. The leather is cracked and faded. Rather like me. The thought produces a chuckle that rumbles through me like the mail truck that chugs up the driveway every morning. And there is usually an envelope or postcard for me.

From Lynette.

They tell me, remind me over and over, that she is my daughter. She signs her name, Lynnie, in big, bold letters. Probably thinks she's making it easy to remember. The loopy writing regales me with descriptive stories about elephants and giraffes and orphan children I couldn't care less about. I like it when she sends the pictures though. She looks like this one too, all blond haired beauty and quiet elegance, but I think I remember she smiles more.

This one, not so much.

"I moved into my new place this weekend." She . . . Liz . . . sits beside me and studies her fingernails. They are rounded and painted a pretty shell pink. She likes color. Greens and blues and sometimes red. My hands suddenly itch for a paintbrush. Why?

"A place. Good." Whether it's good or not is beside the point. Doesn't matter to me. "What kind of place?"

"Oh. It's a cottage. It's quite nice, really. I think I'll be okay there." She speaks softly, like she's trying to convince herself. "Although, I'm not sure what's going on next door. Strange family, if you ask me."

"Not like ours." I have no idea why that pops out of my mouth, but it makes her laugh. Sudden, girlish laughter that makes me stare at her in surprise. But then I laugh too. It feels good, sitting here together, laughing.

"No, ours is perfect." She laughs louder, like what she's just said is the funniest thing in the world.

"Perfectly perfect." I like repeating words, putting them together. It helps me remember what they mean. Something tells me our family is far from perfect, but what does it matter now?

"I thought I'd go over next Saturday, to New York. I've booked a flight." Liz leans back and shades her eyes from the sun. "Evy doesn't need me at the gallery. I'd like to pick up the rest of my things. From Laurence's place. I'm not sure if he'll be there, but . . . it'll be okay."

I sit straighter, laughter fading as a chill races through me. That name. It makes me feel . . . what? Anger. I grip her arm and she whips her head around.

"Ow! What is it, Dad?"

"Nonsense." It's not what I mean. Not what I want to tell her.

Frustration kicks at my inability to voice my thoughts. A vague flash of memory tells me this is wrong, what she wants to do, going to see that man. This Laurence. I reach for the reason why, but then it's gone, and I release my grip on her. And the only words I can think to say would have made my very proper English mother scold me from here to kingdom come.

She doesn't laugh, but she does smile. A sad sort of smile that squeezes my heart too tight. "Well, I suppose you're right there." Her knowing look says that somehow, she understands. And I have to be satisfied with that.

———

"I can do this." Liz niggled her lip and stood on the busy Manhattan sidewalk on Saturday afternoon, staring at the building she'd called home just a few months ago. Her palms were sweating. All she had to do was walk through those glass doors and get on the elevator. Back to the place she'd lived for almost two years. With the man she thought might one day become her husband. Until one night, about six months after she moved in, he snapped.

She couldn't remember why now. Laurence never really needed a reason. She could say the wrong thing, laugh at something he didn't find amusing, look at him the wrong way, it didn't matter. Once his eyes narrowed and he stared in that cold, calculating way that warned of hell heading straight for her, there was no logic in it. Nothing she could say or do to stop the demon from overtaking him.

And yet she stayed.

And hated herself a little more each day.

She knew the dangers of self-deprecation. Her counselor consistently warned her away from unhealthy thoughts and gently pushed her toward a place of forgiveness. But Liz wasn't sure she'd ever get there. Most days it was easier to ignore the healing work she still had ahead of her.

She jumped as someone jostled by in their hurry to get wherever they were going. Heart pounding, she swallowed all reservations and entered the building.

Of course it would be okay. She'd heard from Susan, her former secretary and friend when it suited, that Laurence was planning to be on the Cape this weekend. His parents owned a monstrosity of a home in one of the area's most exclusive neighborhoods. They traveled frequently and were rarely there. Laurence was happy to put it to good use. She recalled many weekend events and parties they'd hosted together. She'd been younger and more naïve then. Actually believed she belonged there. Imagined welcoming the rich and famous crowd he ran with into her home, once she became Mrs. Laurence Broadhurst.

Now the very idea conjured up nothing but nausea.

Liz removed her sunglasses, walked through the foyer, past the concierge who tipped his head her way as though she still belonged there, and headed toward the elevators.

And then she saw him.

Laurence. Coming out of the stairwell from the parking lot, engaged in deep conversation with a slender brunette, hands linked, heads almost touching.

Liz froze, unable to move, even though she knew she must. For a split-second, the world stopped spinning. And she thought he might have seen her.

She backed up, slid on her shades, and slammed against the marble wall in the corner of the lobby. She held her breath as they approached, thinking he would stop at any moment. But they kept walking. Right past her.

He moved with brash confidence. She used to love that. The easy way he talked, the long stride, the stylish clothes—today he was in casual attire, in madras shorts and a white polo pulled tight over sculpted muscles he toned to exhaustion daily. His dark hair was combed back, smooth jaw sporting just a touch of stubble, giving him that sexy bad-boy look he worked to full advantage. He flashed a smile at the woman as she laughed, and Liz was momentarily disarmed.

Tempted to call out, let him know that she was here.

For an alarming moment, she imagined being back in his arms, running her hands over the rippling muscles of his back. Saw herself swept off her feet, his mouth close to hers, whispering words he knew she needed to hear. Telling her she was beautiful. Beyond perfection. His and his alone. Then he would kiss her. Kiss her so deeply and fully that her entire being quivered and cried out for more. It never took long for him to convince her to put down whatever she was doing and retreat down the hall. The good moments between them always convinced her things would get better. Things would not be this way forever. Even when his gentle touch turned rough and his words grew venomous, she told herself he didn't mean it.

He always apologized. Tearfully. With presents and promises.

And she would always forgive him. Feeling dirty and used up and completely unable to do anything about it.

Her heart clenched and she brought a fist to her mouth. What was wrong with her? What did she think she was doing, coming here?

She watched them exit the building, let out her breath in a low exhale, took off her shades and wiped her eyes.

This was probably the stupidest thing she'd done since the last time she'd let him lead her down the hall, knowing they'd both had too much to drink. Knowing his mood was foul with talks of a company takeover. Knowing that no matter how hard she tried, how much she tried to distract him, sooner or later he'd turn, and she would be at his mercy, begging him to stop.

He never stopped.

Liz moved toward the elevator, and a hand clamped down on her shoulder.

"Fancy meeting you here."

No. Oh, no.

Liz stifled a scream, jerked out of his grasp, and whirled to face him. Forced herself to meet his eyes and sucked in a shaky breath as she clenched her hands at her sides. "I came for the rest of my things." Things she was so desperate to have that she'd put herself in the most dangerous position.

"Really?" He narrowed his eyes, leaning in a little. She could smell the faint hint of toffee on his breath. His one weakness when it came to sweets. "Were you planning on breaking and entering, Lizzie? I've had the locks changed."

Of course he had. Sweat slid down her spine, but she pushed her shoulders back. "You can't keep my things, Laurence. That stuff belongs to me."

"Ah. Well. Since your boxes are still in my apartment, I suppose, technically, they belong to me."

She wouldn't argue the legalities. Liz took a step back and tried to smile. "Perhaps we could be civil about this."

A familiar glint crept into his eyes. "Of course. Why would I want to keep your things?" He sounded perfectly amenable, although she suspected a silent rage seethed on the inside. "Everything is boxed up in the spare room. All you had to do was ask. I'll have them shipped over, shall I? To your parents' home on the island? That is where you're living, isn't it?"

Liz shook her head, her hands starting to shake. "I'll call your secretary with an address." And it wouldn't be one on Nantucket. She attempted to side-step him, but he blocked her path, his smile gone.

"No need to lie about it. I know where you are." His voice chilled her and made her wish she'd never come. "Leaving me was the biggest mistake you ever made. You know that, don't you?" Cold eyes pierced her as he stood in silence.

Say something! Everything in her wanted to scream every single evil thought she'd ever had about him. Wanted to list each and every reason why she should have left him long ago. But Liz could only stand mute, pinned under his glare. Finally, he stepped away, putting much-needed space between them.

"Just remember, Lizzie, anything you say against me is simply the word of a jilted lover. Nobody will ever believe you. And if you ever try to take me down, I will find you." He grabbed her wrist and squeezed. Hard. "I will always find you."

eleven

Liz jumped as a sudden gust of wind rushed through the open windows of the cottage on Sunday afternoon and slammed a door shut. She almost dropped the box of dishes she was carrying in from the car. She'd been back on the island since yesterday evening and still didn't feel safe. Still couldn't breathe properly, her nerves frayed, her heart rate through the roof. She'd barely slept; saw Laurence around every corner, waiting for her.

Instinct almost made her head home, straight to Wyldewood, when she got off the ferry last night instead of here to her own place. It was too new here. Too foreign. But she didn't want to deal with David's questions, so she'd returned to the coach house, pushed a heavy chair against the front door, and slept with the light on all night.

David was helping with the rest of her move today. He'd been busy last weekend, so she'd only brought clothes and a few boxes, enough to manage for the week until he could bring the rest in his truck.

He probably knew she'd gone to New York. He'd called her cell a couple of times yesterday, and she let it go to voicemail. The way he unloaded the back of his truck in stormy silence, giving her the eye every once in a while, said he was biding his time, probably trying to figure out how to ask without yelling.

Because she'd promised her brother she wouldn't go back without him.

And she shouldn't have.

When she replayed those few minutes after seeing Laurence and the woman he was with, she wished she had walked straight up to them, demanded he let her into the apartment, and given that girl fair warning about the man Laurence really was. But she was weak. She'd lost her nerve the minute she laid eyes on him, allowed fear to paralyze her into silence.

Liz lifted white china plates and placed them in the cupboard of her kitchen.

Her kitchen.

When she'd lived with Laurence, they'd barely used the pristine long room at the front of the penthouse, all cold steel, and white granite. Laurence was very particular about his food, and she quickly learned that the better option was to go out to his favorite restaurants. Or accept the too frequent impromptu visits from his overbearing British mother and let her do the cooking when she was in town.

Perspiration pricked the back of her neck, and Liz reined in her thoughts. She needed to stop thinking about Laurence Broadhurst. She ran a hand over the smooth, white-and-gold flecked quartz counter and imagined a few weeks from now, this place would feel very much like home. At least she hoped it would.

David strode into the kitchen carrying two overflowing grocery bags. "I put your suitcases in the bedroom. Joss packed some food for you, said if you want to join us for meals, you're welcome any time."

She tried to put on a smile. "Thanks. But I'm perfectly capable—"

"Of taking care of yourself. We know." David unpacked the bags, letting her place the items in the fridge and cupboards. Then he let out a long breath and turned her way. "You went to New York, didn't you?"

Liz backed up and folded her arms. "Yes."

"Without me."

"Obviously." She rolled her eyes and left the room.

"I can't believe you would do that!" He barreled after her. "Why would you put yourself in danger like that? You know what that guy is capable of, Liz! I honestly don't get—" David almost smashed into her as Liz stopped mid-stride. Matthew Stone stood in the middle of her living room.

He pushed a hand through his hair and looked a little uncomfortable. "Sorry. I knocked but . . . the door was open. I wondered if you needed any help."

David snorted. "She doesn't need any help. Liz prefers to do things all on her own."

"Shut up, David."

"Whatever, Liz." She watched his anger fade as a smile took over his features. Of all of them, he was the quickest to forget and forgive. "Couple more boxes in the truck, then I think we're done." He moved past them, leaving Liz to study her new landlord.

He looked like he'd just come up from the beach. A ripped t-shirt and board shorts that had definitely seen better days gave him the look of the younger guys who took to the waves on boards and spent their nights hanging out in bars. But from what she'd seen of him so far, he didn't seem that type.

"Surfing?"

"Nah. Went for a run." He swung a pair of sneakers from their laces to prove the point.

"Ah." He was a sporty one apparently. Sailing. Running. Liz liked her yoga, and the past few years she'd taken up taekwondo. It was a release for her, and she'd been surprised at how much she enjoyed it. "I'm not much of a runner." Well, that wasn't exactly true. She was good at running from the past.

She fiddled with her watch and swept her gaze over the pile of boxes in the living room. She'd forgotten how much stuff she'd accumulated since college. When she moved in with Laurence, she'd left a lot of her childhood belongings at home. David seized the opportunity to get rid of it all, hauling it down from the attic, and now her life sat around them, neatly taped and piled in dated boxes, her mother's bold script slashed across each one of them.

And she didn't know where to begin.

"This is it." David added two more boxes to the pile and straightened. "I gotta get back. The kids are in fine form today; Joss needs a break. You call me later, Liz. I mean it."

"Thanks for bringing my stuff over." She stepped around the boxes and saw her brother to the door. She smiled sweetly and ignored his dark look. "I'm okay, let it go."

"We'll talk." He nodded toward Matthew, skipped down the three front steps, and hopped into his truck.

Liz let a little tension out of her shoulders and fiddled with the switches on the wall. "Which one works the fan again? I can't remember." Into the first few days of October and the weather was warmer than September had been. She'd enjoy it while it lasted. Winter winds on Nantucket were not pleasant.

Matthew strode to where she stood, shot out a long, tanned arm, and flicked the middle switch. The blades of the fan began to turn, sending welcome cool air around the room.

"Ah, that's good. Feels like summer again today, doesn't it?" She sent him a tentative smile and twisted her hands together a little nervously. "Thanks for checking in, but I'm fine. Honestly, I don't even know where I want to put things yet, so . . ."

"You sure?" He nodded toward the pile of paintings stacked against one wall. "Those your dad's?" He was flipping through them before she could answer. "Wow. He was incredible. I'd forgotten."

Liz watched with guarded interest as the man admired her father's artwork. "Those are the ones I'd like to keep. We all picked out our favorites once we decided to renovate. We'll hang a few back up at Wyldewood once things are up and running, but . . ." She shook her head, thinking of the cluttered art studio they'd decided to keep in what was now the private section of Wyldewood, where David and Josslyn would live. "There are so many."

"Are you going to sell them?" He straightened, leveling his gaze.

Liz shrugged. "We really should. Evy wants us to, of course. It's just . . . my dad has Alzheimer's. His paintings are all we're going to have left."

Matthew raked fingers through his already mussed hair, apparently a habit of his when he didn't know what to say. "I'm sorry."

"Yes." She glanced around the crowded room and wondered when it would feel like home. Whatever that felt like. Wyldewood was the only real home she'd ever known. She realized now how much she'd taken that for granted.

"I'm pretty handy with a hammer. I can get those hung in no time."

Liz hesitated. She wanted to be alone right now. To lock the door and do this by herself. But there was something about his easy manner that coaxed her to let her guard down a little. "You wouldn't by any chance be avoiding going back to your own house, would you?"

"Ha." His grin stretched his cheeks in a most appealing way. "Mia went to the movies with some friends about an hour ago.

Sitting around sipping tea and making small talk with my parents on a Sunday afternoon isn't exactly my idea of a good time."

"Well, if putting up paintings is your idea of a good time, be my guest." She wasn't going to refuse the help. The last time she'd tried her hand at a hammer, it hadn't gone so well. The memory of her bruised, black finger made her shudder. "Now, let me think." She picked up a beach scene and pondered it. "Where should this one go?"

He had a good eye. Within an hour, paintings were hung, furniture moved around, and the comfortable living room beginning to look a little lived in. The pale green paint on the walls was even growing on her.

Liz found some water bottles in the grocery items from Josslyn and handed one to him. They stood on the patio and she watched the waves, tried to push thoughts of yesterday out of her mind, but her pulse still hadn't quite returned to normal.

"You okay?" He leaned against the wooden railing and looked her over like he knew all her secrets. Good thing he didn't.

"Moving is a little exhausting." She brushed dirt off her t-shirt. She probably looked a mess. Not that it mattered.

"Yeah." He nodded agreement. "I didn't have much to bring over from Boston, but opening the house up again . . . my grandparents still had a ton of stuff stored here. Not sure what to do with half of it."

"Perhaps your parents could help?" They seemed the type to know a thing or two about antiques. "Or talk to Evy. She'd know who to send you to."

"I bet. Maybe I'll do that." He drank deeply from the plastic bottle. "So how do you like working at the gallery?"

Liz shrugged. Actually, she didn't hate it. "It's a salary. Not what I'm used to doing, but so far so good. Evy's all right."

"Seems to be. She's giving Mia a break, that's for sure." He seemed to hesitate, then smiled. "Hey, thanks for giving her a ride the other night."

"Oh, no problem. How did it go?" Liz tried not to appear too interested, "Mia meeting your parents."

He shrugged, the breeze playing with his hair. "It went. It was pretty awkward. I don't think they knew what to say. But Mia can hold her own. Dinner was kind of boring the first night. She was unusually quiet. I was a bit disappointed." His eyes danced with good-natured humor, and Liz couldn't help laughing.

"Maybe she was nervous. I'm sure she'll be back to her old self before you know it."

"No doubt. She's not one for holding back her thoughts."

"Yes, I'm well aware. I wish I'd had a bit more gumption at that age." Where had that thought come from?

"Really? You don't strike me as having been shy a day in your life."

"Well, not shy exactly." Just stupid. Liz brushed hair out of her eyes, eager to end this strange conversation. He didn't need to know the mistakes of her past. "Your niece is independent, and she's not afraid to speak her mind. In my opinion, those are good traits. Perhaps she just needs to learn to harness them, point them in the right direction."

"Well, Miss Carlisle, if you have any suggestions on how we help her do that, I'd love to hear them." His smile was broad and Liz looked away. Time for him to leave. She left the patio and walked through the living room.

"Thanks for your help." She hovered near the front door and hoped she didn't seem rude. "Um, do you have a date yet, for them to install the alarm system?"

He shook his head. "Sorry, with everything going on, I forgot about it. I'll arrange it on Monday. I'll call to see what fits with your schedule."

"Just let me know when and I'll be here." And make it fast.

"Okay." He got that look again, like he knew her deepest thoughts. And fears. "So I saw your light on pretty late last night. Did you fall asleep and forget to turn it off?"

"Oh, gosh." She hoped her cheeks weren't blistering. "Yes, I suppose I must have. I'm so sorry. I hope it didn't bother you."

"I was up." He gave that nonchalant shrug again. "Mia and I seem to share the insomnia gene. Our lights are usually on at all hours too."

Evading the truth. That would be her first assumption if they were in the courtroom. She saw the confirmation in his eyes. "Good to know."

"Okay, well. I'll be right over there." He tipped his head with that half-smile. "If you need anything, just yell."

Liz swallowed and sincerely hoped she would not have to do that. "Thank you, Mr. Stone."

"Please. It's Matt. Mr. Stone is sitting in my living room." He scrunched his nose. "Actually most people call him Professor, but that's beside the point."

"Yes." Liz fiddled with an earring and sighed. She might as well tell him. "Your father. He's a prof at Harvard, right?"

Surprise lit the man's face in an appealing way. "Yeah, why?"

"A friend took one of his classes. I sat in on one once."

"Small world." He leaned forward with a skeptical expression. "So how boring was the old dinosaur?"

A smile tugged her lips. She could learn to like this guy. "He was . . . interesting." She'd heard a few less than complimentary comments about the professor, but his son didn't need to know that.

"All right, Matt. You've done enough around here. You'd better head back or they'll think I've kidnapped you."

"Right." That grin again. "Thanks for letting me hide out here a bit, Elizabeth."

"You can call me Liz if you want, everyone does."

"I don't know. You seem more suited to Elizabeth, in my opinion."

"I've always found the shortening of names to be highly annoying." Liz laughed and pushed the door wider. "Have a good evening, Matthew."

"You too, Elizabeth." He laughed, gave a short nod, and then he was gone.

But her smile stayed.

Despite the anxiety she'd felt all night and this morning, the day was ending on a good note. She would move on. Forget Laurence Broadhurst and the damage he'd done. Somehow, she would build a new life, here on Nantucket. And somehow, God help her, she'd learn how to be happy.

twelve

Letters to Dad

Hi, Dad.

The movie sucked. Waste of nine bucks I could have spent on art supplies. Nine bucks! For almost three hours of garbage. Sheesh. I told Uncle Matt I was going with friends. I don't actually have any. I went by myself, just to get out of here.

When I got off the bus this afternoon, I watched the way the light bounces off the glass of the windows of the house. I haven't quite figured out how to capture light yet. But I will.

Uncle Matt saw my sketchbook the other night. He got this weird look, like he couldn't believe what he was seeing. He said my drawings were amazing. They're okay, I guess. I wouldn't call them amazing. He's way better than me, but I think he likes photography more than drawing and painting. We went for a walk on the beach this morning, and he took a ton of pictures of stupid stuff like shells and driftwood. We saw seals though. I think they're cute. I wonder if you were an artist too or if I get it from Uncle Matt. Definitely not from Mom. She can't even draw stick figures.

Oh, we have a new neighbor now. Well, she's living in the coach house, but I guess that makes us neighbors even though the coach house is part of this property. Liz Carlisle. She's a lawyer, go figure, but she's not doing that now. She's working at the art gallery in town, with Mrs. McIntyre. I have to work there too, long story. She's kind of hard to get a bead on, (Miss Carlisle), and I'm usually pretty good at reading people. If I had to put money on it, I'd say she's hiding some pretty dark secrets. Well, I guess I know all about that.

I thought we'd be long gone back to Boston by now, but Uncle Matt decided to stay. Have you ever been to Nantucket? It's boring as stink, but it's not so bad. Of course, I act like I hate it. Because I pretty much do. But sometimes, like when the sun hits the water just before it goes down and throws a million different lines of yellows and oranges and scarlet pinks further than your eye can see, it's pretty cool. Uncle Matt really likes it here. Takes him back to his childhood, he says. He and my mom used to come stay with their grandparents here when he was a kid. The house is so dang old I can't believe it hasn't fallen down already. Every time I walk up the stairs I fear for my life.

"Mia, take those darn boots off, ya sound like an elephant!" Uncle Matt yells that at least twice a day. Usually I remember to take them off at the door. Sometimes I don't.

Speaking of elephants . . .

There's been a big one sitting on its keister in the middle of the room ever since Phyllis and Harrison Stone showed up last week.

That elephant would be me. And my dear mama, Rachel.

They haven't said word one about her yet.

It's weird, ya know? Seeing these people you're related to, knowing they don't know the slightest thing about you. Knowing you wouldn't know them from Adam if you passed each other on the street. I always thought how cool it'd be if I came from a big family. I remember going over to Uncle Pat's when I was little. He's not my real uncle, that's just what I ended up calling him because he's Uncle Matt's best friend and we saw them all the time. We lived with them too, when I was a baby. They had an apartment in their basement. I don't remember that though. I remember it was fun at their house, always so many people around, kids to play with. But then Mom met Joe and we took off to Arizona. And after that, I never had a real family. Joe doesn't count. He was never family. He was never anything.

It kind of sucks in a way, not having a brother or sister. But a lot of my life has sucked. Big time.

So now I have grandparents. Well, such as they are. We haven't said more than a few words to each other. Dinner the first night was super awkward. Seemed like they didn't really know what to say. How's school, what am I taking, what things do I like to do, those kinds of boring questions that they probably don't really want to know the answers to anyway. I guess when you're a highbrow, you just know how to keep up conversation and act interested. Uncle Matt kept giving me the stink eye, like he was afraid I'd pop out with a cuss word or something. During those lame lulls in conversation, it was so tempting.

Did you come from a big family? Maybe you even have one now. I guess I'll never find out, but wherever you are, *whoever* you are, I hope you love your life. It's a really hard thing not to.

Also, my mom is getting out of jail.

———

Sunday night Matt couldn't stand it any longer. Once Mia ventured upstairs saying she had homework, he found his folks in the living room. His mother sat on an overstuffed lounger by the window, reading on her iPad, and Dad was thumbing through a book on yachting. Matt cleared his throat and decided not to debate that one. Far as he knew, Dad had never sailed a day in his life.

"So." He sank into the recliner and let the old leather ease his sore muscles. Gramps' favorite chair, and Matt wouldn't be parting with it anytime soon. "What's up with the two of you? Why the impromptu trip over? You were so eager to get here, but outside of asking about the weather and a compliment on my chocolate cake, neither of you seem to have much to say."

Mom uncrossed her legs, closed her iPad, and straightened her pale yellow cardigan. She flashed his father a look that Matt had no idea how to interpret. He'd never cracked the code of their silent language.

Dad put his book down, took off his glasses, rubbed his nose, and let out a sigh that somehow scaled the wall between them. "I suppose we do owe you an explanation." He fiddled with the brown buttons of his thick navy sweater, glanced at his watch, and raised his eyes to the ceiling. Music filtered through the floorboards above them. Not as loud as usual, and Matt supposed he should be thankful. He hoped Mia was doing her homework.

"I don't want to be disturbed," Dad said quietly.

Matt got up and shut the double doors, his heart pounding harder. Mia wouldn't come down unless she needed food, and she wouldn't have to come in here to get to the kitchen anyway. "Okay. What's going on?" He sat again, tapping his foot against the worn rug.

"I've resigned." Dad sat forward, hands splayed, like he was trying to explain something to his students and they weren't getting it. Actually, it didn't look like he was getting it either.

"Resigned? As in you quit your job?" The job that had meant more than anything in the world to his father for longer than Matt could remember.

"Yes." Mom's sigh was heavy as she pushed her hair back into place. "Yes, Matthew. Your father has left the university."

Matt scratched his chin. "Why, exactly?" The esteemed Professor Stone was one of Harvard's elite. He ran the History Department like a Brigadier General. People lined up to get into his lectures. Matt never understood the fascination himself; the Greeks, Ancient Rome, The Golden Age . . . but apparently a lot of people loved it. And in that world, his father was Zeus.

Mom laughed a little awkwardly and reached for the bottle of wine on the table beside her chair. "It appears that your father is a bit of a male chauvinist pig, if you can imagine." She topped up her chardonnay and took a sip. "Telling young women that they should stay in the kitchen where they belong, barefoot and pregnant no less, seems to be frowned upon by the administration."

"Now, Phyllis." Dad narrowed his eyes and put on his black-rimmed spectacles. "That is not what I said, and you know it."

"You may as well have." She waved a dismissive hand, her mouth pinched in a thin line. "It's how it was construed."

"I don't care how it was construed!" Dad snapped. "It was misconstrued! I'm innocent. I can't just be kicked to the curb like this! Tossed out like a stack of old newspapers! I have tenure, I have—"

"Harrison, they don't give a rat's ass what you have!" Mom hissed. "There have been enough complaints over the years, Lord knows. It's a wonder this has taken so long. We're not living in the 1950's, darling. This is the 'Me Too' era, and they've got you by the—"

"Wait, whoa! Time out." Matt put up a hand and stared them down. "Complaints? What happened, exactly? Did you resign or were you fired?"

"It was 'strongly suggested' that I resign," Dad growled. "In the interest of all concerned, I agreed."

Matt let out a slow breath. Oh, this had to be bad. Really bad.

Dad stood and strode across the rug. Adjusted the photos on the mantel. Brushed fluff off his sweater. Walked the room with hunched shoulders, his usual swagger gone. Eventually he sat down again. Finally, he met Matt's eyes, massaged his jaw, and nodded. "Three female students threatened to file a sexual harassment case against me."

Matt pressed his head into the back of his chair, folded his arms, and waited until he could trust himself to speak. He glanced at his mother, watched the way her hand trembled as she grasped the stem of her wine glass, and wondered how much she was drinking these days. He turned back to his father. "Three. Sexual harassment. Complaints." He took a deep inhale and let it out as slowly as he could. "What did you do, exactly?"

"I don't know. Stop saying exactly. I don't know, *exactly*. I make comments. You know."

"No, I don't know."

"You father is a flirt, Matthew. An incorrigible flirt. And, let's be frank, sometimes he can be a bit of a pig. Years ago he got away with it and nobody said anything. But the days of the Old Boys' Club have passed us by, and now it is time to pay the piper."

"Oh, shut up, woman!" Dad's face got beet red, and Mom sat back with a smug smile.

"Did you . . ." Matt had no idea how to say it. "How far did this go?"

"Now look!" Dad pointed a thin finger at him, brown eyes blazing. "I am a man of integrity! I don't care what they said about me. Yes, in hindsight, my comments were derogatory. My behavior may have been demeaning. Yes, perhaps I do have antiquated views and voice them when I should keep my mouth shut, but never, not once, have I ever laid a hand on any woman who was not my wife. And that is the honest to God truth."

Mom gave a quick nod. "It's true. The girls said it was all verbal. If it were anything more, we wouldn't be sitting here right now, I can tell you that."

Dad kneaded his brow. "Well, I'm sorry for all of it. But I am still without a job."

"I suppose this is where we should be thanking my parents." Mom sniffed and fiddled with the rings on her finger. "We shall hardly be destitute, dear. You don't have to work another day in your life if you don't want to. You've never really needed to."

"All well and good for you to sit on your family's pots of gold, darling wife. I didn't earn that money."

"You've not complained whilst spending it," she retorted.

Matt sighed and pinched the bridge of his nose. He swore he could physically feel his blood pressure rising. He was twelve years old again, getting ready to creep out the back door and catch the T to Pat's house, unable to stand the sniping a minute longer. Why his parents hadn't divorced eons ago was one of life's great mysteries.

"Okay, so you're unemployed. I still don't get why you're here."

They both looked at him like he was stupid.

"The scandal, Matthew!" his mother cried. "Honestly. Use your brain. Can you imagine what our friends are saying about us? About this whole horrid situation? It's too much. I had to leave a DAR meeting last week because of it. Vicious women spreading lies! You have no idea."

He truly didn't. Matt gave a slow nod and closed his eyes a minute. Now he was getting a full-blown headache. "So basically, the two of you are hiding out here until this whole nasty business blows over?"

"Precisely, darling." Mom rewarded his genius with a rare, winning smile. Matt suddenly felt very, very tired. His mind moved rapid-fire over the numerous other options available to them. A round the world cruise. A villa in the south of France. London. Paris. But no, here they were, on Nantucket. In his home.

"And this would be for how long?"

"Oh, at least until after the holidays." She drained her glass and stared at his father. "Don't you think, dear?"

"I don't care. I just do what I'm told." Dad had picked up the book again, appearing quite enthralled by its pages. "Do you know my one big regret in life, Matthew?"

"No idea, Dad." Seriously?

Dad clapped the book shut with a harrumph. "We never went sailing. You and I. Never did a lot of things. I was always too busy, wasn't I? Ah, well. Bit late in the season for sailing now, I suppose. Although, I'm sure there are those who might think my sinking to the depths of the vast Atlantic would be the perfect solution to this grand debacle."

"Sheesh, Dad," Matt muttered, raking fingers through his hair.

"Oh, don't listen to him! Harrison, you are widely exaggerating as usual, and quite frankly, it's getting tiresome."

"Mm." Dad got to his feet with a blustery cough. "As are you, my dear. As are you." He slashed his arm through the air in great flourish and drew himself up. "I am taking my leave. Goodnight."

He left the room in a hurry. Matt opened his mouth, shut it again, and sat back.

"Oh, just say it," Mom spat.

Matt shook his head. "I'm not real sure what to say."

"Well, that's a first."

He took a moment. Finally let out his breath and looked at his mother. "You okay? This is kind of a big deal."

"Of course I'm okay." Her shaky smile contradicted that. "I'm not going to leave him, if that's what you're thinking."

"I'm . . . okay . . . why not?"

"Because I love him, God help me. And I believe he can change. And if he can't . . . well, I suppose then I'll have a decision to make."

Matt let out a long sigh and voiced his thoughts. "Why didn't you just take a cruise or something? Why come here?" *Why bring me into it?* Matt felt a little bad for that, but really . . .

"I considered everything." She picked up her iPad again. "Suggested several other options, as a matter of fact. Italy. Ireland. He does love Ireland. But your father didn't want to go anywhere. He's been quite down in the mouth over the whole thing, as he should be. He insisted on coming here. I never thought he liked the place all that much. But here we are." She pasted on a smile, as though being on Nantucket was the best thing in the world, and resumed her reading.

Matt mulled that over. The faintest flicker of hope sparked again. They had come, knowing Mia was here. With all the bitter past between them. They had come. Was it possible for their relationship to change after all this time? He stared at the ceiling and willed that hope away. He'd been disappointed before.

A door closed upstairs. His father's footfalls told him it was the smaller room on the other side of his bedroom. Not the guestroom with the queen bed he'd made up for them. And with that definitive click, Matt realized his parents were sleeping in separate rooms.

thirteen

Liz kept an eye on Mia as the girl swept the floor of the empty gallery on Tuesday afternoon. Watched the way she paused in front of each painting, stood back a little, tilted her head this way and that.

Interesting.

Lynnie and Dad would do the same thing. Whenever her family had visited the mainland, no matter where they landed, there would always be a mandatory few hours spent at some art gallery or museum. Liz enjoyed the museums best, but the boys would be bored out of their minds. Lynnie and Dad loved scrutinizing each piece of art and discussing it in great detail. Liz glanced at Evy and found her also watching the girl.

"Well, I'll be darned," the older woman said softly.

"She could be looking for dust."

Evy chuckled and shook her head. "I don't think so."

Mia resumed her sweeping, but her gaze kept returning to the painting on the wall. One of Lynnie's. A beach scene with Wyldewood in the background. Actually, that particular painting was a favorite of Liz's. A pinch of pride at Mia's appreciation of the piece took her by surprise.

"Are you going to say anything?"

"Not just yet." Evy picked up a pile of papers and headed for the back room. Liz rolled her eyes. Evy thrived on being mysterious. She returned with her handbag over one shoulder. "Well, I'm off to that blasted doctor's appointment. Goodnight, Liz. Goodnight, Mia."

Mia was absorbed in the painting again. Evy walked across the gallery and stood behind the girl. "Sucks you right in, doesn't it?" Mia jumped a foot, and Liz grinned at Evy's raspy laugh.

"I was just looking," the girl mumbled.

"No." Evy shook her head with a knowing smile. "You were appreciating. As one with any knowledge of fine art would be expected to do." Mia shrugged and shuffled off with the broom, her cheeks a little flushed. "See you tomorrow, darlings." Evy sent Liz a smile and flounced out.

As the door to the gallery opened and closed, Liz caught a glimpse of three girls and a taller boy out on the sidewalk. She checked her watch. Mia was due to leave in about five minutes.

Mia returned, shot a look at the door, and then hovered at the desk. "Got anything else for me to do?"

Liz raised a brow. The girl had grudgingly worked through Evy's to-do lists since starting at the gallery, mumbling complaints under her breath all the while. Today she was asking for more work? Something was up.

"Did you turn the answering machine on?"

"Yeah."

"Done the bathroom?"

"Yep." Mia scratched chipped black polish on her fingernails and shifted from one foot to the other. Her attire was a little more presentable—jeans with a white long-sleeved cotton blouse with a plaid waistcoat overtop—but the clunky boots still bothered Liz. And those awful piercings gave her the shivers. At least the girl didn't interact with the customers.

"Well, good." Liz shut down her computer. "Looks like you have some friends waiting for you. You can go. I'll lock up and put the alarm on."

"They're not my friends." Mia looked toward the door again. Liz began to get the picture. Something about this situation put her on alert.

"Is your uncle picking you up today?"

"No." Mia fiddled with the black leather bracelets around her wrist. "He had a meeting, then he's working. I'm supposta take the bus." Liz registered a faint look of fear in her eyes. She'd forgotten Matthew had mentioned he'd be working tonight.

Mia clearly did not want to go out there by herself. Liz put some files away and locked the drawers on the front desk, and contemplated the matter. She really didn't want to get involved in the kid's high school drama.

"I guess I'll go then." Mia shuffled toward the door like she was heading for a firing squad. Liz sighed.

"Mia."

The girl turned expectantly. "What?"

"I'm pretty much ready to go. You can ride with me if you want. I have to stop by Wyldewood first though."

"What's Wyldewood?"

Mia's look of confusion made Liz grin. "Sorry. That's the name of my family's house. Where I used to live. I need to go walk our dogs."

"Oh. Okay." Mia shifted her backpack to her other shoulder.

Once the alarm began to beep, Liz pushed open the front door, let Mia go first, then locked up. The girl walked quickly past the group of kids.

"Hey, Mia," a girl with long blond hair called. "How's your little job? Community service or what?"

"Mia, how's your mom?" another yelled. "Still in the slammer?"

Mia kept her head down and kept walking. Liz figured she didn't actually care where she was going. And she was headed in the opposite direction to where Liz had parked.

"Hey, Mia, wait up!" The tall boy jogged past Liz. Liz quickened her pace. By the time the boy reached Mia, she'd slowed a bit.

"Leave me alone, Chris," Liz heard her say.

"Look, don't worry about Summer and those girls. They're idiots."

Liz nodded in silent affirmation. Whoever this Chris was, he was no dummy. Maybe.

"Whatever." Mia stopped, swung a look over her shoulder at Liz. "Where the heck is your car anyway?"

"Other way." Liz stood beside them and looked the boy up and down. Good looking kid. White Vineyard Vines button-down over jeans, and deck shoes. Yacht club. Money. Probably here because he got expelled from some elite prep school on the mainland. She stuck out a hand. "Elizabeth Carlisle."

"Christopher Cooper." He shook her hand with confidence and a smile that seemed familiar.

"Which Coopers?"

"Anthony Cooper is my uncle. He's, um . . . sick. My parents are here for . . . well, a while, I guess. To help." He shrugged, clearly uncomfortable discussing family business with strangers.

"Ah." She nodded. "Well, we would normally be neighbors if Wyldewood wasn't under construction. My sister Lynette is dating your cousin, Nick. Well, I think they're still together. She's traveling at the moment." She really needed to make more of an effort to get in touch with Lynnie.

"Oh, they're still together." Chris rolled his eyes and snorted. "He never shuts up about her. Holy cow. When is she coming home? Better be soon or he's gonna throw himself off a cliff."

Liz laughed at the teen's exaggeration. "I certainly hope it won't come to that." She swiveled and took a gander up the street. The girls were nowhere in sight. She wasn't altogether sure whether Mia wanted to talk to Chris Cooper or not, so she decided not to put her in that position. She caught Mia's eye. "We'll just head back this way, shall we? I'm parked near Mitchell's."

"Okay." Mia side-stepped her, staring at the ground as she walked.

Chris shoved his book bag over one shoulder and matched Mia's stride. "So, um, were we going to talk about that social studies assignment?"

Liz held back a bit.

"Whatever."

"Well, since we only have a week, I thought . . ."

"Can you just text me later? I'll check my schedule. Maybe we can work on it tomorrow, at school."

"Sure." The wind picked up and blew through his blond hair. Liz wondered what Mia was thinking. He pulled out an iPhone and slowed down. "Can you give me your number?"

Liz stopped at her car as Mia rattled off her number. "We're right here. It was nice to meet you, Chris. Say hello to Nick for me?"

He gave her a genuine, friendly smile. "I will. Nice meeting you too, Miss Carlisle." He pocketed his phone and looked at Mia. "Talk to you later, okay?"

"Mm-yup." Mia scrambled to get into the car without a backward glance. Chris grinned, gave his head a half shake, and walked away.

Liz let out her breath, dumped her bag in the back, and got in. She started the engine and turned to Mia. "Nick Cooper's cousin. Small world. He seems nice."

"He's a rich highbrow. I know the type."

Liz fiddled with the a/c and debated her response. "Just because his parents might be wealthy doesn't mean—"

"Whatever." Mia pulled earbuds from her backpack and plugged them into her phone. "That's your sister? Lynette Carlisle? She did the paintings in the gallery?"

"That's right."

A hint of awe shimmered in the girl's dark eyes. "Sweet."

"She's not on island right now. But maybe you can meet her when she gets home." Really? Now she was inviting the kid to meet her family? She'd definitely been out of New York too long.

"That's okay." Mia lowered her head and pressed some buttons on her phone.

"You know, Mia—"

"I don't want to talk."

Liz nodded. "Okay. No talking then." She pulled out of the parking space and turned up the radio. What was the point in trying to be nice? This was exactly why she was never having kids. Ever.

Mia snapped her head up a short while later, when Liz pulled up outside Wyldewood. "Whoa. You grew up here?"

"Yup." Liz supposed the large, gray, cedar-shingled house with its long windows, green shutters, and wraparound porch looked impressive if you weren't used to it. Of course, it looked more impressive without scaffolding everywhere and the piles of dirt, bricks, and wood all over the beat-up lawn.

"It's way bigger than our place."

"It is." Liz nodded. "But my family is converting it into a B&B. So everything's a little different now." That was understating it.

"Come on." She and Mia walked across the front yard. "Watch your step there." They made it to the far side of the house without incident. Liz knocked, then pushed open the front door of the new extension David and Josslyn had just moved into days ago. The sound of total bedlam reached her ears, and she smiled at Mia's raised eyebrows. The dogs were barking and the kids yelling, and they all came charging in their direction the moment she called out a hesitant hello.

"STAY!" Liz stepped in front of Mia and put up a hand. Diggory and Jasper screeched to a halt on the new terracotta tiles, tails wagging, tongues lolling. But the twins paid no mind and launched their little bodies at her with an exuberance she could hardly ignore. Liz crouched to hug her niece and nephew and shot a side look at Mia, who was hovering by the front door. "You okay with dogs? And kids?"

"I guess." She didn't look too concerned. Liz stood and pointed at the dogs. "This is Diggory, that's Jasper. They're very friendly." To prove the point, they both lolloped toward Mia, licking her hands when she attempted to pet them.

"Do the kids have names or just the dogs?" A giggle shot out of Mia. Liz startled at the sound. She wouldn't have believed it if she hadn't been standing beside her.

"Um, yes. Of course." Mia had made a joke. Miracles still happened. "Brandon and Bethie. Guys, this is Mia." Upon hearing her name, Bethie demanded to be picked up, and Liz held the child close as she watched Mia holding out her hands for the dogs to inspect and giving one a scratch behind the ears.

Brandon ventured over and began to instruct Mia how to pet Jasper by taking her hand and smacking it on the big dog's head. "Dis way. See?"

Mia's face lit with laughter. "Maybe not. How about like this?" She showed him how to be more gentle, stroking the dog's head, explaining things in a quiet voice, the surly expression Liz had grown used to completely gone.

"Hey." David walked toward them with a grin.

"Hey." Liz leaned into his side hug, still mesmerized by the normally surly teen's transformation.

"Who's this?" David whispered.

"Matt Stone's niece. Mia. I'm giving her a ride home."

"The juvenile delinquent?" David raised a brow.

"Shh." Liz couldn't stop a grin.

"Well, come on through. Cecily's here. She brought dinner, praise the Lord. We're just about to eat."

In the bright new kitchen, Josslyn and Cecily were serving up a baked ham and the gooiest, most amazing looking mac and cheese Liz had seen in a long while. She'd probably gain several pounds just by staring at it. But she inhaled deeply anyway. When was the last time she'd worked out? She made a mental note to start her exercise routine again.

"Girl!" Cecily turned from the stove, put down her serving spoon, and crossed the room in a hurry. Liz squeaked as Cecily pulled her into a smothering hug. "You look good. Are you good?" She stepped back and gave Liz the once over.

"I'm good, Ce-ce." Not about to fall apart or whatever scenario you're imagining right now. "Is that your famous mac and cheese I smell?"

"Sure is. Now you come on and sit. We'll get some extra plates." Liz rolled her eyes at Cecily's insistence. You couldn't go a minute without the woman wanting to feed you.

"Actually, I just came to walk the dogs. And I have to get Mia home." And get herself out of this kitchen before she ate everything in sight. She introduced Mia to Cecily and Josslyn. David poured iced tea and settled the twins into booster seats.

"I took the dogs out earlier," he said. "I had some time. Sorry. I should have called."

"Oh, well." Liz glanced at Mia. The girl was already beside the twins, entertaining them by racing her fingers across the table.

"We could stay," Mia suggested brightly. "I can text my uncle. He won't care, he's already at work."

Liz tried not to gape. "Won't your grandparents be expecting you for dinner?"

Mia shrugged. She didn't have to say more. Liz knew she probably didn't want to be alone with the older couple she barely knew. She couldn't blame the girl. And that macaroni and cheese was calling her name too loudly. "All right. But call him now."

A few moments later, they sat around the kitchen table, and Mia passed Liz her phone. "He wants to talk to you."

Liz tried not to sigh. This was a bad idea. But Cecily and Josslyn were so insistent, and Mia seemed to want to stay. "Hello, Matthew."

"Elizabeth. So, you're where, exactly?"

"At Wyldewood. I was just coming to walk the dogs, but they want us to stay for dinner."

"The dogs want you to stay for dinner?"

"Yes. I mean no, I . . ." Liz frowned. The man was laughing. Loudly.

"You're sure Mia's okay?"

"Actually, she's rather in her element. I'm still absorbing it." Liz spoke quietly, but Mia wasn't paying her any mind anyway. She was too busy helping Josslyn feed the twins.

"Saving her from the wolves then, are you?"

"What?"

Matthew chuckled. "Saving her from enduring a meal with my parents. Alone. I'll call my mom and explain. Tell the kid she owes me."

"Will do." Liz clicked off, put Mia's phone on the table, and found Cecily watching her. The older woman's eyes widened, but she stayed quiet. "We're good. Your uncle said you owe him one."

A grin scooted over Mia's mouth and Liz smiled.

"Okay, then. Mia, have some ham." David pushed the heaping plate of pink meat toward the girl.

"Um . . ." She scrunched up her nose. "I'll just have the pasta. And coleslaw."

"You what?" Cecily shook her head, her mouth turning downward in disapproval. "Don't tell me you're one of those vegetarianites. You can't exist on no meat, child. You skinny enough as is."

"I don't eat meat. And I'm fine," Mia countered, her eyes flashing.

Liz smothered a snort by shoving a piece of ham in her mouth. David cleared his throat, his mouth twitching with laughter, and Josslyn took a long drink of iced tea.

"Mmm, girl." Cecily sat forward, wagging her fork. "See, you don't know me yet, Miss Mia, but I've been dealing with children like you for years. Two of them sitting right here. And they know better than to say no to Cecily. Isn't that right, David James?"

"Yes, ma'am." David was close to erupting into laughter, and Liz elbowed him.

"You allergic to meat, honey?" Cecily continued.

"No." Mia seemed to shrink a little under Cecily's stern gaze. "I just don't eat it."

"You protesting the killing of animals by not eating them?"

"Not exactly." Mia twirled her fork in a huge mound of mac and cheese. Liz thought she saw a slight grin come and go.

"Religious reasons?"

"No. Ma'am."

Cecily nodded and slipped a slice of ham onto Mia's plate. "Well, then." She pushed the plate a little closer to Mia, a smug smile set in place. "You eat that up and tell me if that isn't the best piece of ham you ever had in your life. Then we'll talk."

Mia stayed quiet while the rest of them talked about the renovations, what was going on with Liz's siblings, and her dad. When they finished the meal, Liz did notice Mia's plate was cleaned.

Later, while Mia helped Josslyn put the twins to bed, Liz sat with Cecily and David in the small but cheery new living room. "This looks great." She looked around, seeing familiar artwork on the walls, their mother's photographs on the table by the window. They had agreed to keep much of the original furniture to use in the main rooms of the guest house, along with the baby grand, grandfather clock, and many antique pieces their guests would be able to admire.

David handed them coffee and flopped onto the sofa with a weary sigh. "Good to be moved in. Thanks for helping out today, Ce-ce. Joss needed the break."

Cecily sipped and sent her trademark smile his way. "Happy to do it, you know that." She trained her gaze on Liz. "So, how are you? Like your new place?"

"It's pretty nice. You guys should come over sometime." Liz yawned and set her mug down on the coffee table. She still hadn't had a good night's sleep since seeing Laurence.

"I'll bring you some food." Cecily knew the extent of Liz's culinary skills. "Heard you're working at the gallery where Lynnie shows her stuff. You like it?"

"Sure. It's slowing down a bit, but I have some ideas for Evy that I think she'll go for." She'd been meaning to write up a plan and print it out. Maybe she'd get to that tonight.

Cecily angled her head, studying her. "You really are starting over, aren't you?"

Liz flushed under her knowing look and simply shrugged. Was she? Some days it still felt like running away.

"So." David put his mug down. "Tell us about your little trip to New York."

Cecily sucked her teeth and sat back. Liz shifted in her seat, her stomach tightening. If she could rewind time, she'd never have done it. She'd gained nothing and lost a few hundred bucks in airfare, not to mention a whole lot of sleep since that day. "It was no big deal. I just thought I could go and get my stuff back and . . ."

"No big deal?" Disapproval rumbled in Cecily's chest. "Honey, that man near knocked you senseless. You got no business going over there by yourself and you know it."

"Well, I did. And I saw him. And it was fine." Liz bit her lip and groaned inwardly.

"You saw him?!" David and Cecily spoke in unison.

She shook her head and glared. "Nothing happened. He was in the lobby. With some girl. He wouldn't let me up to the apartment. Said he'll send my stuff over here."

"Liz, for crying out loud!" David sat forward.

She held up a hand. "Look, I wasn't alone with him. Not exactly. Nothing. Happened."

"Why would you put yourself in that situation? What if you'd gotten in and he'd been in the apartment?"

"Well, that didn't happen!"

"You didn't even tell us you were going!" So much for David letting it go.

"David, take a breath. Honey, we're just concerned." Cecily reached over and patted Liz's arm.

"I know." Tears smarted, and Liz looked at the floor. Counted all the colors in the rug and told herself for the thousandth time that week how stupid she was. "It was a bad decision. But I just wanted my stuff back. I won't go again, I promise."

"You can't, Liz. Seriously. The dude is dangerous." David's tone held a warning Liz knew better than to ignore. "You can't have anything over there important enough to risk your life over."

If he only knew.

She nodded and looked at both of them. "I said I promise. Okay?" They didn't look completely satisfied, but it would have to do. Mia and Josslyn returned, and Liz got to her feet. "We should get going. Thanks for dinner."

"Yeah. Thanks." Mia looked from Josslyn to Cecily, clearly not sure who to thank.

Josslyn placed a hand on the girl's shoulder. "You're welcome, Mia. It was so nice to meet you. And I'll call you about babysitting."

Mia nodded with a shy smile, and Liz stared. "Babysitting?"

"Sure." Josslyn nodded enthusiastically. "Well, more like a mother's helper. I can hardly manage the two of them, and I wouldn't expect Mia to. But we talked about her coming over sometimes to play with the twins while I get some things done around here."

"Oh-kay." Liz kept her game face on. This had been the strangest day. When they were finally in the car, she let out her breath, stared out the windshield into the black night, and wondered what to say to this mysterious young girl.

"You have a cool family." Mia raked her fingers through her hair and sent Liz an unexpected smile that changed her face entirely.

Liz eased out the driveway onto the main road and nodded. "Yes. I guess I do."

"And you never told me Gray Carlisle was your brother. He's like . . . ah-mazing!"

Liz couldn't contain her laughter a moment longer. "Oh, he's amazing all right." So Mia Stone was a normal fifteen-year-old girl after all. Who knew.

fourteen

Evy closed the gallery early on Thursday, so Liz took the opportunity to drive to Bartlett's Farm, where they sold the best produce and pretty much everything else an aspiring chef might need. She'd been spending some time on Pinterest lately, picking out recipes she thought she could make without burning down the coach house.

As she unloaded the grocery bags from her car, she heard the crunching of gravel and turned to see Phyllis Stone smiling at her.

"May I give you a hand?" the older woman asked.

"Oh, thank you, no, I can manage." Liz fumbled with a couple of bags and dropped her keys.

Phyllis bent to pick them up with a laugh. "Let me at least open the door for you."

Once they'd unloaded the bags in the kitchen, Phyllis surveyed the kitchen with a smile. "Well, this looks lovely. Matthew said he'd done some work, but I didn't expect everything to be new."

Liz let her wander around the place while she put things away.

She came back into the kitchen as Liz was pondering the ingredients she'd laid out for her dinner. Liz tried to get a clear impression of the woman. Certainly well put together, in casual slacks, white blouse, and pink cashmere cardigan. Smooth blond hair, possibly dyed or at least highlighted, no hints of gray. She was maybe around the age her mother would have been now, early sixties. She held herself with a self-assured air, but as Liz looked closer, she saw tension lines and shadows under the woman's eyes that told another story.

"What are you making?" Matthew's mother relaxed a little and her smile came out.

"Good question." Liz laughed. "I'm not much of a cook I'm afraid. But I thought perhaps I could try following a recipe. Grilled chicken with asparagus and couscous. Sounds simple enough."

Phyllis made a face and waved a manicured hand. "Darling, don't ask me. I can barely boil water. Although, I have taken a few cooking classes with a friend lately. Don't tell the boys. I'm waiting for the right night to surprise them. If I have the nerve."

Liz smiled. She liked this woman. "Would you like a drink, Mrs. Stone? Tea or coffee? Maybe a glass of wine? You can keep me company while I figure this out, if you'd like."

"Well, that would be lovely." She pulled out a chair and sat down. "But you must call me Phyllis. And I've got my phone handy. I can call my friend if we get into trouble with the recipe."

———

Liz relaxed at her kitchen table that night, a satisfied smile set in place. She'd managed to create a decent meal without anything exploding or burning to a crisp. Phyllis had called her friend anyway, just to be sure Liz was preparing the chicken correctly. Salmonella, she'd warned, one couldn't be too careful. Miracle of miracles, it had turned out okay, and Liz enjoyed a perfectly grilled chicken breast, crispy asparagus with a bit of crumbled bacon, a spicy couscous, and a glass of chilled chardonnay to wash it down.

"Anything's possible when you put your mind to it, Elizabeth." She spoke the words her mother would so often say, then shook her head. Didn't they say talking to yourself was the first sign of insanity? A rap on her front door startled her out of her thoughts and jacked her pulse. Perhaps it was just Phyllis, come to see how things had turned out.

Liz walked through the living room, willing her heart to slow down. She hoped they'd hurry up about installing that alarm. She was getting tired of lugging that big chair around every night before bed. They'd been scheduled to come this week but another job had delayed them. She peered out the window first, then undid the bolt and opened the door.

"Good evening, Matthew."

He stood at the bottom of the two steps, three large boxes beside him. His smile flashed under the porch lamp. "Elizabeth. Sorry to disturb. David dropped these off earlier. Said they were delivered to the house for you today."

Liz studied the boxes and recognized Laurence's handwriting. A shiver of fear raced down her back. She let out a measured breath and gave a slow nod. "Okay. Thanks."

He heaved one upward. "They're kind of heavy. Let me bring them in for you."

"Thank you." She instructed him to set them in the living room, pressed herself against the open front door. This was it then. The last of her things. She no longer had any ties to Laurence Broadhurst. Except for the nightmares. And the money he still had. There was probably little she could do about either.

"You okay there?" He looked concerned, and Liz forced a feeble laugh.

"Of course. Thanks for bringing them over."

"No problem. Wow, it smells good in here. I didn't interrupt your dinner, did I?" He studied her through steady eyes, his smile hesitant.

"No, I just finished." Liz couldn't stop a smile. "Would you believe it's the first meal I've cooked that wasn't a total disaster? Your mother helped me."

"My mother?" His brows shot skyward. "Are you sure about that?"

"Quite. We figured it out together. She's very nice."

"*My* mother? The woman you met in my living room the night they arrived?"

"The very one. We had a nice chat. I gave her a glass of wine."

"That'd do it." A grin came and went. "What exactly did you talk about?"

"Oh, gosh, I don't know. Cooking mostly, and how we hate it. She knew my parents. Said she and your dad even went to a couple parties at Wyldewood when you were younger."

"No kidding." He gave a long whistle. Disbelief crowded his eyes. "Somehow I'm having trouble picturing that."

"I didn't have trouble picturing it at all."

Matthew shrugged. "Stranger things, I guess. Hey, thanks for taking Mia with you the other day. I think she had fun. She's going over there to help with the kids tomorrow afternoon."

"Really? That's good." Was it? She supposed it was. Truth be told, she was pleased she'd offered to take Mia with her. It certainly got the girl's mind off that unpleasant encounter with her schoolmates that afternoon. Liz stepped away from the front door as the ocean breeze kissed her face. "Did you know she's being bullied?" The question shot out before she thought it through.

"Bullied?" Matthew scratched the stubble on his chin. "That's a heavy accusation. What makes you say that?"

Great. What was she doing sticking her nose where it didn't belong? "Well, I don't know for sure. Sit for a minute?" She pointed him toward the living room. "Do you want a glass of wine? I've got some open."

"Nah, I'm good." He sat heavily, watching her through worried eyes.

Liz positioned herself in a wingback chair, indicating the sofa. "It's really none of my business, but . . . that afternoon, when I offered Mia a ride, there were some girls loitering outside the gallery. Mia was clearly uncomfortable and didn't want to leave alone. They made some unkind comments when we walked by. About her mother."

He pushed fingers through his dark hair and shook his head. "I can imagine."

"Well. I'm glad I was there to give her a ride." Liz knew what it was like to be different.

She could still remember the girls at her school giving her side looks and whispering behind their hands when her parents showed up for events. Her mother in her flamboyant outfits, looking like a throwback flower child from the '60's, her father half-sloshed, loud and exuberant. Mia Stone walked a hard road. "So she didn't mention it to you?"

He leaned back against the thick cushions and gave a half-hearted laugh. "Mia doesn't say much about how she's really feeling. With the exception of my rules and my cooking of course. She has no problem expressing herself on those matters."

Liz wound her fingers together and met his gaze. "She handled it well. Ignored them actually. I was tempted to give them a piece of my mind."

"You didn't?" Another grin came and went.

"No, I didn't. This time."

"Probably wise. Well, good for her. I'm glad she didn't retaliate."

"Girls can be pretty horrible. I was picked on in high school. It's no fun."

He shot her a surprised look. "Really? You? That's hard to believe."

Why couldn't she keep her mouth shut around this man?

"It's true. I wasn't always a high-powered, cocky lawyer." Liz pushed the old memories aside. "Anyway, I tried to make sure she was okay. She wouldn't talk about it afterward."

"Mia's not much of a talker. You might have noticed." His eyes crinkled as he smiled, and Liz found herself smiling back.

"The age, maybe. I think she had a good time at David's. She seemed to anyway."

"She did ask me if I knew your brother Gray. Think I earned a few points when I said I did. Had no clue she was a fan."

"Right?" Liz suppressed an eye roll. "It's a rare breed of teenage girl who doesn't succumb to the magical charm my brother seems to weave over his followers."

"I think the Gray Carlisle charm works on any girl regardless of age, from what I've heard." Matthew laughed, light dancing in his eyes. "How's he doing anyway?"

Liz glanced at her phone. She really needed to call Gray soon. Get a full update. "I think he's doing well. Back in the recording studio from what I hear." She hesitated, pondering the thoughts that had been pricking her conscience all week. "So, I wanted to ask, is Mia artistic by any chance?"

"Artistic?" He stared, like she'd suddenly uncovered a secret he'd been hiding. "Why do you ask?"

"Because Evy and I caught her studying a painting the other day. Not just looking at it, but you know . . ."

"Walking into it."

"You do know." Of course he did. Liz wanted to kick herself for forgetting he was an art teacher, which meant he was probably an artist too. She hoped that didn't make him as loopy as Lynnie and Dad.

"I didn't know about her artistic talent until recently," he told her. "Found a sketchbook of hers and couldn't believe what I was seeing. She's really good. She'd kill me if she knew I said anything to you."

"So she's not taking art in school?"

"Nah." He knuckled his chin. "Been figuring out a way to get her to do it, short of forcing it on her, which probably wouldn't go over well."

"No, I doubt it would." Liz thought a moment. "What about a community project she'd have to get involved in? They still do that kind of thing?"

"Sure." His face lit. "That's not a bad idea."

She could see his mind going a mile a minute already and wondered what he'd come up with. "So she takes after you, huh?"

"I guess there must be something in the genes." She could have sworn he flushed under her stare. "Though I'm more into photography these days."

Photography. The word still evoked that nails-on-a-chalkboard shudder. She clenched her jaw and managed a smile. "I'm not."

"Okay." Matthew sat forward a bit and rubbed a tear in his jeans at the knee. She watched a few threads come loose. He raised his eyes to hers and blinked a couple times, getting that look again, like he wanted to say something but wasn't sure he should. "Some days I think Mia would be better off someplace else. With a real family."

Oh. His words sagged with sorrow. Pain shone from his eyes. She was all too familiar with those feelings of helplessness.

Liz nodded and pushed her hair behind her ear. "You know . . ." She studied one of her father's paintings on the wall and lost herself in the past for a moment. "I hated my family. Well, not hated. They were just . . . different. My parents drank a lot. They were always having crazy parties, saying completely inappropriate things. Let us kids run wild most of the time. If it wasn't for Cecily, we'd probably all have gotten in far more trouble than we actually did."

"Cecily?" He relaxed a little, his smile encouraging.

"Cecily was our housekeeper. She was the one who kept us in line, while my mom wanted to be everybody's best friend. Cecily's really like family. Mia met her the other night."

"Nice." He appeared captivated by the glimpse into her childhood.

"Well, anyway. I used to complain to Cecily about my parents. The way they carried on was embarrassing." Liz crossed her legs and felt the burn of memory. "But she'd say 'you can't pick your family, honey, because the good Lord done it for you. And one day they might be exactly what you need.'" She sniffed, feeling silly about the emotion the past still provoked. "For years I thought those words were about as far from the truth as she could get. I was pretty sure I would never need my family. When I left Nantucket, I never thought I'd be back. Never wanted to live here again. I was done with crazy."

"I know the feeling." His thin smile piqued her interest.

"Well." She nodded, blew out a breath, and clutched her elbows. "Crazy has a way of catching up with you wherever you go, I guess."

"Too true." He tipped his head in the direction of the main house. "Got all kinds of crazy going on over there."

"Honestly?"

"Like you wouldn't believe." The expression on his face told her whatever it was, it wasn't good. "Still trying to figure out which end is up with my parents."

"I'm sorry." She could see the seriousness of it in his eyes. "I suppose what I'm trying to say is . . ." Liz went on before she lost her nerve. "Cecily was right. I need a place to call home. I do need my family. I think we all do, eventually, don't you?"

"Maybe." Matthew let go slow laughter and shook his head. "Right now I'll take your word for it. Because at the moment, I'm wishing my parents were anywhere but here."

Liz stood with a smile. "I'm sure it'll get better."

"Oh, I'm sure. When hell freezes over." He followed her to the door. "But thanks for the chat."

"Anytime." Really? She wanted to smack herself. "I probably didn't help much."

"Don't sell yourself short." Matthew clapped his hands together. "All right. Well. Have a good night."

"Um, I was wondering . . . with your parents here . . ." Liz hesitated, but had to ask. "Do you still need me to be around for Mia at night? Will that change things? I don't want you feeling I'm not earning my keep."

"Oh." Matthew frowned and shook his head. "Don't worry about it. My folks are apparently going to be here for longer than I thought but, well, I told Mia to still call you while I'm at work if she needs anything. Is that okay? It's just, she doesn't know them, and—"

"She doesn't really know me either."

"True." He gave a small smile that tugged her heart a little. "But I think both Mia and I are more comfortable with this option."

"Okay." Liz shrugged. She wouldn't push it, but she hoped Mia wouldn't actually call her in the middle of the night anytime soon.

He said goodnight, and Liz watched him jog across the courtyard, closed and locked the front door, then turned toward the three boxes. Looming, threatening, daring her to open them. She knew she had to open them, eventually, but somehow couldn't bring herself to do it.

Crazy had a way of catching up with her all right.

And here it was again.

Sitting in taped up cardboard boxes in her living room.

fifteen

DRAKE

"Come on, Mr. Carlisle. You're gonna like this." The big nurse takes me into the day room after lunch. Instead of the usual tomblike atmosphere, the place is swarming with activity. Easels are set up in a few spots around the room. And there are kids everywhere. Well. High schoolers, I suppose, by the looks of them. Hooligans. For some reason, I remember what they're like at that age.

They're talking to the residents. A couple of the girls are sitting with the ladies, knitting and crocheting. A few tables are set up, and kids are playing cards and chess with the old coots. There's music coming from somewhere. Everyone seems happy, smiling and laughing like it's Christmas.

And I'm confused. Maybe it is.

Too many people. Too much noise.

"What day is it?" I lose track too easily.

"Tuesday afternoon. Come on now, what would you like to do? Play cards?"

"Uh, no thank you." I swivel on my slippers and barrel into Theresa or whatever her name is. She places her hands on my shoulders and turns me back around.

"Don't be silly. Look, there's paints over there. You like painting, don't you?"

Do I?

The smell in the air is familiar, and my brain stretches to name it. Turpentine. Oils.

Heaven.

"Sir?"

"What?" I jump as a man comes up beside me, and my sharp response startles him. But he smiles anyway. He's youngish. About the same age as my son. The one that visits. David. I think. I notice his eyes right off. Deep brown flecked with gold. They complement the color of his wavy hair and the sun-kissed streaks.

"Sorry, didn't mean to sneak up on you. I'm Matt Stone. I teach at the high school. Thanks for letting the kids come hang out here this afternoon."

Is that what they're doing? Hanging out? "I don't own the place."

He laughs like he's not sure whether he should. Then he points across the room. "Want to try a little painting? Oils or acrylics, I brought both."

"Humph." He looks like he's giving me the greatest present in the world. "I don't know." I scratch my head and take a few steps toward the unoccupied easel. There's a young girl sitting on the window seat, staring at all of us like we're from another planet.

Got that right, kid.

She's trying to look bored, but I see her eyes. And they're taking it all in. She's a sideline sitter who secretly wants to get in the game.

So I'll call her bluff. She stiffens slightly when I shuffle over and stand in front of her.

"Who are you?" My voice sounds far more intimidating than it used to. More like a bark. But I don't scare her. She stares right back at me, unflinching. I'm impressed.

"Mia." She pushes straight dark hair behind her ears, and my eyes are drawn to the bright pink streaks.

"Nice hair."

She grins. "Thanks. Yours is cool too."

That makes me snort. I refuse to let them cut it, and have it tied in a ponytail. I usually forget about it until I try to lie down and feel the bump at the back of my head. Maybe I'll get it cut after all. Someday.

I run my hands down the beige shirt they put me in this morning over my favorite pair of pants. Soft brown ones, holes starting in the knees. I have new clothes. I just don't like wearing them.

"You know how to paint, Mia?"

"Mia's a great artist." The man has been hovering, and he pipes up with that information too quickly. The kid gives him an award-worthy glower that makes me grin. But she gets to her feet and clomps over to the easel anyway. Looks like she's been shopping at the Army/Navy Surplus on Broad Street.

"I paint some," she says quietly. "Not that great though."

"Nah. Me either." For some reason that sounds funny. But if there's one thing this sad excuse for a brain knows, it's that when someone tells you they're *not that good*, they probably are.

She picks up a brush and stares at the empty canvas. Tips her head this way and that, then looks at me sideways. "You like the ocean?"

"Love it." I venture closer. When she hands me a brush, my fingers curl around it, and it feels like home. She nods and makes the first stroke. A bold streak of cobalt blue in exactly the right spot, and I see at once where she's going. My hand itches to join the dance, and I dip the brush into a splotch of deepest sea-foam green.

And so we begin.

Matt stood to the side of the room and watched the activity, pleased he'd managed to pull it all together. The idea had come to him after his conversation with Elizabeth last week, and he'd approached the principal to discuss it—bringing Mia's freshman class to the nursing home one afternoon a week. A few phone calls were made, the day set, and here they were. And by all accounts, he'd say the event was a success.

He watched his niece with a lump in his throat. The way she was interacting with the older man, chatting—well, now they were laughing about something—made his heart soar. He hadn't seen her smile like that since she'd come to live with him. Who knew all it would take was a paint palette and an old dude with dementia.

One of the caregivers nodded his way, pointing to her watch. It was time to go. He began to move around the room, letting the kids know they needed to start packing up. Out of the corner of his eye, he caught the tall, blond kid making his way over to Mia. What was his name? Cooper. Nick's nephew or cousin or something. He was a decent kid, taking transfer credits while his family was on the island to help with Nick's dad. He sucked at art though. Matt didn't know he and Mia were friends. That was interesting.

A few kids had gathered around the easel where Mia and the old man were still painting. Matt helped put a few board games away, then crossed the room.

He stared at the painting in progress and sucked in a breath.

Mia glanced his way, her eyes shining. He gave a nod and a brief smile. She'd be totally embarrassed if he made a big deal about what he saw in front of him. But, wow. The two of them were creating something that, when finished, should be hanging in Evy McIntyre's gallery.

An angry ocean tossed a small yacht upon the waves, surf rushing and crashing against rocks, storm clouds rolling in from the west. He could almost taste the salt on his tongue.

"What's all this?"

Matt startled at the voice beside him. Turned and found Elizabeth Carlisle staring at him, surprise smacked across her face. "Huh?" He scratched his head, words eluding him. What was she doing here?

"What's going on, Matthew?" A funny sort of smile inched her lips upward as she pointed toward the small crowd of kids and the old dude. "My dad is painting?"

"Your . . . dad?" Suddenly it all made sense. He stared at the painting, the old man, and then Elizabeth. "That's your dad? Drake Carlisle?"

"Last time I checked. He doesn't always remember that's who he is, but yes."

"Well, I'll be darned."

"Mr. Stone, the bus is here." A kid tapped him on the arm and Matt nodded, clapped his hands together, and got the group's attention.

"Okay, guys, say your goodbyes, and file out quietly. The bus is waiting."

"So . . . this is your community service project?" She moved past the kids and walked to where her father stood. Mia's eyes about bugged out of her head when she caught sight of her. Matt almost laughed out loud at her confused expression. He could relate.

"Hello, Mia," she said quietly, assessing the half-finished painting. "Did the two of you do this?"

Mr. Carlisle scratched his nose with the tip of his brush. "She's pretty good, eh?"

"Indeed. How are you, Dad?" Elizabeth leaned over to kiss his cheek.

"Whoa, what?!" Mia stepped backward in a hurry.

Matt grinned. "You've just been painting with one of the country's greatest artists. How does that feel?"

Mia's face darkened to match the storm she and Drake Carlisle had created. She fired the death stare, turned on the heel of her boot, pushed past the other kids, and marched out of the room.

Great. Matt sighed and crossed his arms. Here we go again.

"I had a kid like that. A few of them. I think." Mr. Carlisle laughed happily as he put paints away and handed the box to Matt. "They get better with age."

Matt pressed the box back toward him. "You keep these. In case you feel like doing some more work on this."

"Righty-ho!" The man's face lit with a grin, and Matt smiled.

Elizabeth took her father by the arm. "Come on, we need to get you ready for dinner. I left work early today, thought I'd sit with you tonight. Is that okay?"

"Sit where you like, missy." He untangled himself from her and bent to pick at a blue spot of paint on his pants.

She gave an eye-roll. "Well. Looks like this was a good idea, Matthew. Maybe you can tell me more about it later." Drake was hightailing it to the door. "Gotta go, he's probably going to try to escape on the bus."

Matt watched her run from the room, still a bit bewildered. Well, well, well. Drake Carlisle. He hadn't expected this. At all.

sixteen

Matt arrived home later that afternoon to find his mother in the kitchen, her hands deep in dough. He scanned the room and gave a low whistle. He'd wager she'd used every appliance, dish, and pot he owned. "Mother. What are you doing?"

She turned his way with a smile and blew a bit of flour off her nose. "Hello, darling. How was your day?"

Matt raised a brow and went for a beer. He definitely needed to sit down. Never in his life had he experienced this particular scenario. Dreamed about it, wished for it, but not once, to the best of his recollection, had his mother ever been standing in the kitchen when he'd returned home from school, let alone asked him how his day was. "My day was fine. Is Mia home yet?"

"I don't think so." She returned to whatever was happening in that bowl. "I didn't hear her come in, anyway."

The gallery had closed a half hour ago. He'd stopped by to get her, but she'd refused a ride, said she'd rather take the bus. She was probably off someplace sulking. Hopefully she'd show up at some point. "Could you, um, tell me what you're doing?"

"Pizza!" His mother pulled her hands from the large, brown, ceramic bowl, washed them at the sink, and covered the bowl with a dishcloth. "There. We'll let that sit a bit, and I'll roll it out around six. What time do you think Mia might be home?"

Pizza. Matt pulled at the collar of his shirt and glanced at his watch. "She should be home soon. Since when do you know how to make pizza?"

She laughed, patted her hair down, and pulled the apron from around her waist. She wore a baggy white cotton blouse over dark blue jeans. Matt blinked. Had he ever seen her wear jeans? And . . . slippers? "Where's Dad?"

"Oh, who knows. Probably walking the beach. Sulking." She busied herself finding a glass and the half-empty bottle of wine, gave herself a generous pour, and sat opposite him at the table. "Isn't the internet amazing? I even found a video on YouTube that showed me exactly how to make the dough. And I've prepared all the toppings. I went to Bartlett's this morning. Found some wonderful fresh mozzarella. That place is still fantastic, isn't it? Oh, your fridge is a little full."

"Okay." Matt suspected his expression conveyed his bemusement, and his mother confirmed it with the scowl she tossed him.

"I *can* cook, you know."

"Mother!" Laughter shot from him. "I'm thirty-two years old and I cannot remember you ever cooking a meal a day in my life. Remember that time you decided you'd make Christmas cookies? I don't think they were supposed to be black and bricklike."

She pursed her lips and wiped a few patches of flour off her arms. "I've been taking lessons. At the community center."

Matt floundered for a reply and took a swig from the bottle in his hand instead. "The community center?"

"Patricia took me." She smiled sweetly, as though it were the simplest thing in the world.

"Patricia?"

"O'Donohue, dear. Don't be dense."

"Trish O'Donohue? Patrick's mother?"

"How many Patricia O'Donohues do you know, Matthew?"

"Are you kidding me?" His mother had loathed the O'Donohues. Okay, maybe loathed wasn't exactly being fair. She'd certainly never exhibited any great pleasure over his friendship with Patrick and all the time he spent with the large Irish family. His parents had attended one Christmas party at the O'Donohues' when Matt was around twelve. He'd begged them to come, mostly to get Pat's mother off his back about it. They'd stayed an hour, looking extremely uncomfortable the entire time. After that, he didn't bother hoping their two families would ever be friends.

"Since when do you even talk to Patricia O'Donohue, Mother?"

"Oh." She sipped and smiled again. "That's a funny story."

"I'll bet."

"After your father 'retired'"—she made air quotes and he tried not to grin—"he drove me crazy being around the house all the time. You know what he's like. No hobbies. Work was everything to him. So I started finding more things to do. I began volunteering at the Children's Hospital. I sit on the Board, but you know I'd never actually . . . anyway. I ran into Patricia at the hospital. She volunteers too. Isn't that a coincidence? We had coffee, and I suppose it went from there. Did you know she sings in the choir at her church? And she . . . oh, I need to roll out the dough." She popped out of her seat and strode to the counter. Matt watched her lift the dough from the bowl and cut it into sections. "Rolling pin?"

"Uh . . ." Did he even have one? He went to the drawers and wracked his brain as to where his grandmother had kept the darn thing. And pizza pans. No doubt she'd ask for those next. If he couldn't find any, he'd run to the store. Because that was a whole lot better than contemplating the alien invasion that had clearly occurred at some point and replaced his mother with this semi-domesticated woman he barely recognized.

"So, Mom. I heard you were over at Elizabeth's the other night." Ah. Way in the back of the cupboard he pulled out a couple of well-used pizza pans.

"Oh, yes! She's a delightful girl, isn't she?"

Matt put the pans on the counter, straightened, and stared at her. Something in her tone and smug smile set off a warning. "Mother."

"What, darling? I'm just saying she's a lovely girl. Perhaps you should get to know her a little better."

He bit back a grin, strode across the room, and put his hands on her shoulders. "And perhaps you should mind your own business."

She arched a thin brow. "Perhaps." Her smile popped out again. "Isn't this nice, Matthew? Being able to visit, spending time together. I have missed you, you know."

He got that knot in his stomach again and wished for the thousandth time that he didn't feel things so deeply. But she was right. Even when he didn't want her to be. "Yeah." He leaned in and kissed her cheek before he could stop himself. "It's nice, Ma. It's real nice."

———

"Mia! Come out of there, please." Matt leaned against the bathroom door and squeezed his eyes shut. She'd slammed through the house fifteen minutes ago, refused dinner, raced up here, and locked herself in the bathroom.

"Leave me alone! I told you, I'm not hungry!"

"I don't care. You're coming downstairs, and you're having dinner with us. Your grandmother made a vegetarian pizza just for you, and you're going to eat it if I have to break this door down and carry you to the table." So he wouldn't be winning any awards for best parenting style anytime soon.

Something clattered to the floor and he heard her swear. "Mia?"

"What?" Her reply was muffled, like she'd shoved a facecloth in her mouth.

Matt's heart rate picked up. "Can you open the door, please?" He jiggled the handle and she shrieked.

"Go. AWAY! I need some privacy. I got my period!"

Matt leaned over his knees and wondered how people did this. "Okay. I'm leaving. But please come downstairs when you're done. I mean it."

"Fine."

"Everything okay up there?" Mom asked when he returned to the table.

"She's in a mood. It happens. A lot." Matt shrugged and picked up his pizza. Took a bite. "Hey, this is actually good."

"Don't talk with your mouth full." But she smiled just the same.

"We'll make a chef out of you yet, dear," Dad remarked drolly, like he didn't believe it for a moment.

Mom cut into her pizza with a knife and fork, cut his father with her eyes. "At least I am trying to do things with my life. What do you do? Sit around all day reading and doing God knows what on that computer."

"I am writing." Dad took a long drink. "I am writing a book and you know that."

"A book? What are you writing about, Dad?" Matt asked. Did he really want to know?

"The rise and fall of the Roman Empire and what today's cultures can learn from it. And no, I don't have a title."

"Wasting your time," Mom muttered.

"I am not wasting my time, and as for what I do on my computer—" Dad bit off his words as Mia skulked into the room and sat down.

"Mia. Have some pizza, dear?" Mom stood and removed the foil from Mia's pizza, gave her a slice, and sat down again. Matt held his breath while Mia stared at the colorful triangle on her plate. She raised red-rimmed eyes and stared at her grandmother.

"You made this?"

"I did." Mom sat back proudly, her smile genuine. Matt fought to stay silent as Mia bit into her pizza.

"Good." She mumbled something else and proceeded to demolish the rest of it and helped herself to more. Okay then. Matt breathed relief, resumed his meal, grabbed the salad bowl and the dressing. He wouldn't get into it with Mia. Not now at least.

"Well, Mia, how was school today?" Mom asked after a while, her voice too bright. Matt stifled a groan. Oh, that was so not the question.

"Stupid." Mia shot him a glare that made him want to shoot one right back.

"How can school be stupid?" Dad pushed his empty plate away and peered down the table. "Don't you enjoy your classes?"

"Some. But we have a dumb art teacher who drags us to dumb places."

"Really?" Matt watched his father's eyebrows inch upward. "That does sound terrible. What kind of teacher would do that?"

Matt cleared his throat. "Me, Dad. I'm the dumb art teacher. I teach art. Remember?"

Mia snorted and Matt worked to check his frustration. Why he expected his father to have the faintest clue . . .

"I'm well aware, Matthew," his father said quietly. "I was trying to be funny."

"Right." The pizza sat heavy in his stomach, and Matt reached for his water glass. "Mia's class did a little community service today, spent some time at an old folks' home."

"Total set up," Mia growled.

Set up? Matt clenched his fingers and held her angry gaze. "I had no clue Drake Carlisle was a resident there. Believe me or not, I had nothing to do with that."

"Drake Carlisle?" Mom perked up. "I have a couple of his paintings. You remember the Carlisles, don't you, Harrison? We went to their house a few times when we used to come over in the summers, years ago now, but at any rate. As it turns out, Elizabeth is their daughter."

His father reached for another slice. "The pretty one next door?"

There was no hope. "That would be her." Matt smiled anyway. "Drake's got Alzheimer's though. But he can still paint. He and Mia—"

"Stop!" Mia's anger filled the room. It'd been building for a while. Matt had sensed that sooner or later something would set her off.

"Mia, don't." Matt knew his warning would be ignored, but he should at least try to prevent the impending explosion.

"Don't tell me what to do! I hate you right now!"

Before Matt could respond, his father spoke. "Lower your voice, young lady. Show some respect for your elders." Dad set a stern look on Mia, and Matt wished he could clap a hand over his father's mouth.

"Excuse me?" Mia pushed her chair back and stood. "I don't have to listen to you."

"My God, you're so like your mother! Sit—" His father cut off his words, his face ashen.

The room fell silent.

Matt watched Mia's eyes fill with tears, his stomach churning.

"I'm done." Mia picked up her plate, and stormed out of the room.

Dad blinked and shook his head. "I'm sorry. I don't know where that came from."

"Oh, heaven help us." Mom breathed a sigh and poured another glass of wine.

"Really, Dad?" Matt put his head in his hands. It wouldn't do any good to rush after her. She wouldn't talk to him tonight. He knew enough now to sense when to approach Mia after a meltdown.

A heaviness smothered the room. Dad picked bits of pepper off his uneaten pizza, Mom rubbed a thumb and forefinger up and down the stem of her wine glass, creating a supremely annoying squeaking noise.

"She's right, you know." Matt waited until they both looked his way. "You can't barge into her life like you've always been there. You can't tell her what to do."

"I know. I apologize." Dad did look contrite. "But she is so much like Rachel." He gave a beleaguered sigh. "Sometimes it feels like yesterday."

"How do you manage her?" Mom asked warily. "She's so . . ."

"She's had a rough go, Mom." Matt kept his voice low on the off chance Mia was lurking, but he'd heard her bedroom door close a few moments ago. "She's fifteen, and she's never really lived in a stable environment. She doesn't trust anybody. If you were expecting to waltz in here and establish a relationship overnight, it's not going to happen."

His mother pinched her lips together and stayed silent.

"A child needs discipline, structure. What does she intend to do with her life?" Dad gave the look Matt had always hated. His steady gaze scrutinized, measured, and came up wanting. And Matt couldn't take a minute more.

"I don't know, Dad. I think just making it through the day is a pretty big deal right now. And what she needs most of all? Love. That's what she needs. But I'm not sure you know the first thing about that." He stood and marched from the room and headed for the back door. The plates needed clearing and the kitchen was a mess, but Matt didn't care. They could deal with it.

seventeen

Thump. Thump, thump. Thump, thump, thump. Thump.

Liz looked up from her laptop and frowned. The incessant noise had been bothering her for the last fifteen minutes. She hadn't heard it when she'd gotten back from the nursing home. She'd made her supper, pasta with tomato sauce and bell peppers tonight, pondered the surprise of seeing Mia and Matthew Stone in her father's environment, and eventually decided it was probably a good thing. He'd certainly seemed happy at dinner. Ate everything without a fuss, and even commented that the stew was edible.

She'd made her coffee, settled on the sofa the living room, and then the noise started. At first, she'd thought it was the wind banging a shutter, but she'd scoured the cottage and found nothing. Sat down again and went back to what she was working on—Liz's Life Plan. Pathetic as it was.

Thump, thump, thump, thump. It had to be coming from outside. Liz grabbed a sweater, slipped into a pair of loafers, and unbolted the front door. Across the dark courtyard, behind the main house, sat a garage. Light shone through the slats of the window that faced her. She ventured into the cool night and followed the sound.

The side door to the old structure was open, giving her full view inside. Back toward the corner of the cluttered room, a punching bag hung on a rusted chain. Matthew Stone danced around it, gloves on, pounding the thing as though his life depended on it. The guy had a pretty mean right hook. His jaw clenched as he concentrated on his punches, his dark hair stuck to his forehead, eyes flashing. Muscular arms dealt their blows with deft precision, a thin cotton tank top plastered to his chest.

There was no denying it. Matthew Stone was an extremely attractive man. Much as she'd told herself that didn't matter as she'd signed the lease, moved in, perhaps she'd been wrong. Because the familiar feeling that curled in her stomach and sent heat rushing through her was dangerous. She recognized it for what it was. Desire. A longing to be held, touched, needed. Her old enemy, back again.

Liz pressed her hands around her hips, inhaled, and took a step backward. But the thumping had stopped, and she'd been spotted.

"Elizabeth?" Matthew moved away from the bag, hands in mid-air, waiting, she supposed, for some explanation as to why she stood there staring at him as if she'd never seen a man before.

"Sorry. I just . . . didn't know what the noise was."

"Oh. Well, I'm sorry if I disturbed you." He ripped the Velcro tab off one protective glove with his teeth, pulled it off, and went to work on the other. He tossed them aside and reached for a towel and a water bottle.

"It's okay. I wasn't doing anything important. Just attempting to figure out my life, and that never goes well." She stayed in the doorway, but his pained expression stirred curiosity. "Are you all right?"

He gave a half laugh and leaned over his knees a moment before nailing her with his eyes. "You ever feel like you're doing everything you possibly can to make it all work, but it's falling down faster than you can put it back together?"

She took a tentative step forward. "All the time, actually."

He wiped his flushed face with the light blue towel. "Mia thought I set her up. Taking her class to the old folks' home today, having her paint with your old man. Truth is, I didn't have a clue he was Drake Carlisle until you walked in. But I don't expect she'll believe that."

"I see." Liz had wondered at the girl's abrupt departure that afternoon, but had been too busy with Dad to give it much thought. "So you're taking out your frustration on the punching bag."

"A stress reliever. I'm not really much of a fighter."

"Living with a teenager must be stressful." Especially when that teenager was Mia Stone.

"Add my parents to the mix and it's a wonder I'm in here and not at a firing range."

Liz smiled. "Then perhaps it's just as well Nantucket doesn't have a firing range." She wondered what he'd think if he knew she'd been considering purchasing a firearm. She'd never been a fan of guns, but since her run-in with Laurence . . . it might not be a bad idea.

Liz pushed aside anxiety and wandered around the garage, trailing her hand over dusty boxes. Bicycles lay stacked against a folded ping-pong table, beach umbrellas and chairs piled in another corner, a rusty lawnmower lay on its side. "I bet there's a lot of history in here."

"I guess so. Never thought of it that way." He scanned the room, his eyes coming back to rest on her.

"Looks like you've a chore ahead, if you plan to go through all this anytime soon."

Matt grunted. "So much junk. My grandparents threw everything in here when they moved back to the mainland and rented the place out. I don't think it was ever used for cars. Just a place to store the stuff they didn't want. It was all locked up when I got here. So nobody could steal anything worth taking, I guess."

She walked back to where he stood, heaviness descending again. "I imagine someone like Mia likes to keep her feelings pretty tightly locked up too. So nobody can steal anything worth taking."

His eyes held hers for a long moment. One corner of his mouth lifted in a half smile. "Are you comparing my niece to a garage?"

Liz smiled back and shook her head. "All I'm saying is, she might have good reason for acting the way she does. She doesn't like to draw attention to herself. This afternoon, she let her guard down, she had fun, she showed off her talent, and people noticed. And she didn't like that. Maybe she doesn't like to be noticed, doesn't like to admit she's actually good at something?"

"She draws enough attention to herself at school. You want to know how many times I've been called in to talk to the principal since she started? And how do you explain the piercings, the hair, the makeup? Everything she does screams 'look at me'!'"

Liz took a slow, measured breath. "Or 'help me.'"

Matthew's eyes flared. "Wow." He finished his water in two deep gulps and crunched the plastic bottle in his hand. "I've been trying to figure her out for months, you just meet her and what, a week or two later, you nail it?"

"I wouldn't say I've nailed it. I'd say there may be more to her attitude and smart mouth than she's willing to talk about. She can hide behind all that makes her Mia, the hair and makeup and the don't give a crap persona, but sooner or later, that thing she's running from? It'll catch up with her." Wind rattled the old windows around them, and Liz shivered.

"Speaking from experience?" Matthew moved toward her.

She shrugged, her heart pounding at the idea of actually confiding in him. "Maybe."

"Want to talk about it?" His eyes stayed on her, his face serious, unspoken questions floating like the dust in the beam of light from the hanging bulb above them.

Hesitation hitched the words in her throat until at last, she shook her head. "No."

His lips parted in a smile. "Well. If you ever do . . ."

"Thanks." She was trembling. He was a foot away; she could feel the heat from his body and his breath as he spoke. It was too easy to get lost in those searching eyes. Too easy to forget that they barely knew each other, that she couldn't give him what he might want. That she would never give any part of herself up to a man again.

"Are you okay, Elizabeth?" He touched her, his fingers briefly brushing across her hand. She pulled her hand away in automatic reflex. Her muscles tensed, and her brain kicked into high gear.

Matthew stepped back, understanding creasing his forehead. "Sorry."

"I should . . ." Go. Run. Get out of here. But she couldn't move. All she could do was stand there and stare at him. That unflinching gaze of his sucked her in. Told her she didn't need to be afraid, he could be trusted. Attraction woke again and almost pushed aside fear.

"It's all right," he said quietly. "There's nothing to be afraid of." Like he could read the inner workings of her mind. The tenuous moment stretched the silence between them. She fought sudden confusion and found reality again.

"The alarm. I wanted to ask when it was being installed." Good. Get them back on safe ground.

"Right." He nodded. "I'm sorry it's taken so long. I'll make sure it's on the schedule tomorrow."

"Thank you. Well, goodnight then." Liz turned and pushed through the door before he could say anything else. Because if he'd come any closer, he might have seen the longing in her eyes. Might have picked up on her fluttering heart and traitorous mind. Might have known that, God help her, she had wanted him to move closer. Wanted him to kiss her. Wanted . . .

"Elizabeth?" His voice stopped her as she crunched across the crushed shells of the courtyard.

She drew in a breath and slowly turned to face him. "What?"

He lifted his shoulders and let them fall. "I didn't mean to frighten you in there. I mean I . . . I let my emotions charge ahead sometimes. I like you, and I like talking to you, but I know—"

"No. You don't know." Liz held up a hand. "Let's just leave it that."

"Okay then." He shrugged. "If that's what you want."

"It is."

He looked away for a moment, then captured her eyes again. "I understand we don't know each other well yet, but I'd like us to be friends. What do you think?

No. Never. Not happening. Liz folded her arms and opened her mouth. "Of course."

"Good." His smile shone through the semi-darkness and somehow breathed light into her shattered soul. "Sleep well, Elizabeth."

Liz sighed as she watched him jog back to the house. That was a joke. She hadn't slept well in years. And becoming 'friends' with a nice guy like Matthew Stone? That was probably the stupidest thing she'd ever thought about doing.

Well. Not the stupidest. Not by a long shot.

"You are a complete idiot, Elizabeth," she muttered as she marched up the steps to the cottage and locked the door firmly behind her.

Later that evening, her nerves still singing like livewire, she sat cross-legged in the living room, staring at the boxes in front of her.

"You're being utterly ridiculous." If she didn't stop talking to herself soon, she'd end up as Dad's roommate, like it or not. She retrieved a pair of scissors from a kitchen drawer and marched back to the boxes, slit open the packing tape on all three, and sat back on her haunches.

The first box was mostly office stuff, tax receipts and other items from her desk. The second, memorabilia from her time with Laurence. Why had she kept all this stuff? Menus, postcards from places they visited, friends' wedding invitations and ceremony orders-of-service. Liz scowled at the contents and pushed the box aside. She'd toss all that out. Burn it. The last box . . . she knew before she flipped the lid . . . would contain her photo albums and jewelry box—an elaborate mahogany piece, a gift from her parents on her twenty-first birthday. And in that jewelry box, an envelope that contained photographs she hadn't looked at in years. Photographs she wished she hadn't kept.

Photographs she wished had never been taken.

A handwritten note lay on top of the albums and screamed through the silence.

Overwhelming fear fell over her, tears stung her eyes, but she reached for the note anyway, already knowing what it would say.

Ah, Lizzie,

> *I did enjoy looking at all your photos of days gone by. Quite the collection, I must say. Especially the ones hidden at the bottom of your jewelry box. Ones I expect you don't ever want anyone to see. My, my, my. What a naughty girl you*

were. I always suspected you had another side to you. Shame you never really let me see it.

I do miss you.

L

Liz stared at the note for a long while. Fumbled through things with trembling hands, found the old mahogany jewelry box, and carefully laid it on the floor in front of her.

There, beneath the top drawer, was the white envelope. The photographs would be inside.

Scott Howarth. Liz studied the name written in white chalk on the blackboard at the front of the classroom. Their new art teacher. She glanced around the room at her classmates. The sophomore girls were ogling the man as though they had never seen one before. The boys looked bored. She wasn't sure how she ended up in this class, really. Her guidance counselor suggested she take it for extra credit, and after all, she was Drake Carlisle's daughter. She must have some artistic ability. Liz was pretty sure she didn't, but here she sat anyway.

She sighed, determined to make the most of it, and took another look at their new teacher. She'd heard he was young, and that was true. He'd come over from England. This was probably his first teaching job. He was tall, good looking, with a head of thick dirty-blond hair. He probably worked out, judging by the biceps bulging under his navy shirt. When he turned to face the class, his eyes landed on her. Cobalt blue eyes that glinted with a hint of mystery.

"Good morning, miscreants." His grin reached right through her. "My name is Scott Howarth, and I bring you greetings from the other side of the pond. This is my first time in America, and I am extremely happy to be here." Liz straightened in her chair, soaked in the lovely British accent he spoke with as he rattled off the names on the register, and jumped when she heard her own. "Elizabeth Carlisle?"

"Here." Slowly she raised her right arm until his eyes locked with hers.

"Hello, Elizabeth," he said softly. And it was at that precise moment she fell completely in love.

———————

Liz picked up the envelope, her throat burning. How many years had it been? How was it possible to still feel such shame and guilt, to feel like it happened yesterday? If she closed her eyes, she'd be back in the school's art studio. See him drawing the blinds, locking the door, and crossing the room with that smile that melted every inch of her body and made her want to do . . . everything. At seventeen, she didn't care that it was wrong. Didn't care what might happen if they were caught. All she cared about was being loved.

She flipped the envelope and froze.

The seal had been ripped.

And the envelope was empty.

eighteen

MIA

Letters to Dad.

Hi, Dad,

I should have written before now. This week totally sucked. Thank God tomorrow's Friday.

I guess you should know I have a really bad temper. Sometimes I feel like I just want to explode. And this week I really could have. But I don't want to get in more trouble, so I . . .

Mia put down her pen, pulled up the sleeve of her sweatshirt and scratched the bits of dried blood on her arm. Her stomach clenched as she stared at the thin cuts. So many times she'd tried to stop. Told herself she'd never do it again. But when that anger hit, the feeling was so overwhelming, so all-consuming, there wasn't anything she could do to stop it.

The backs of her eyes burned. What was the use in thinking about it? She was such a loser. She pulled her sleeve down, sniffed, and picked up her pen again.

. . . Anyway. So Tuesday wasn't a good day. We had to go to this old folks' home and do stuff with the residents. I mean, I guess the idea was pretty cool. The old people really seemed to be getting into it. Some of the kids played cards with them or just talked. Uncle Matt brought along some easels so some of them could draw or paint. And I ended up painting with this old dude. Who was totally amazing. Turns out he was Drake Carlisle. Ever heard of him? He's a really famous artist here on the island. Used to be anyway. He's pretty loopy now. I had no idea who he was, and I'm pretty sure Uncle Matt set the whole thing up. When it was time to leave, everyone was staring and looking at our painting, saying how good it was, and it was so embarrassing . . .

A knock on the door startled her, and Mia snapped her head up. She shut her journal, shoved it under the covers, and opened her laptop. "What?"

Uncle Matt poked his head around the door. "Can I come in?"

"You will anyhow." She gave the dramatic sigh he hated and tried to ignore the way her heart lifted at the sight of him. She loathed that feeling. Because she couldn't let herself get sucked in, couldn't trust him again. He'd already let her down, walked out of her life once.

Uncle Matt crossed the room and perched on the end of her bed. His hair was damp and messy, and he smelled like soap, fresh and clean. The scent took her back to the bathroom of her childhood.

Something about that smell always made her feel safe. *He* had always made her feel safe.

She rubbed her eyes and looked away. She'd been pretty much ignoring him since Tuesday, and he'd given her space. What she'd said about getting her period had been genius. She'd file that away for future use. Last night she'd pretended to have a headache and stayed in her room. But the anguished look on his face now made her feel sorry for him. "Say what you want to say."

"I didn't set that up on Tuesday, Mia. I swear it. I had no idea that guy was Drake Carlisle until Elizabeth showed up."

She wound her thumbs and finally met his eyes. Eyes that had told her a million times how much he cared. Even after all the years apart, she knew he still did. Her uncle was either a real sucker for punishment or he really was one of the good guys.

"You just happened to see my sketchbook last week and all of a sudden I'm painting with one of the best artists in the country? Awful convenient."

A pained look passed over his face. "I know it looks that way. And yeah, I was hoping you'd enjoy the painting. Because you're good. You have a gift, and I want to encourage that. But I didn't know who he was. Really. Sometimes . . ." He hesitated, like he wasn't sure whether to say any more. "Sometimes things happen the way they're meant to."

"Right. Like karma." She threw that in on purpose.

"Something like that."

Mia shook her head. Uncle Matt didn't go to church, but she knew he believed in God, that it was important to him.

When she was around ten, back in Arizona, Mom had tried church for a while. Tried to get clean again that year. They'd made friends with a family in the apartment across the hall. Yvonne Jones. Mia remembered her as an overweight, smiley woman, always giving great big long hugs, which annoyed her at the time. Her three kids were loud and funny, and Mia got close with them, especially Sierra who'd been the same age. Yvonne and Mom talked long into the night while the kids played or watched cartoons, then Mia and Sierra whispered together in the big bed when they were supposed to be sleeping.

Eventually, Mom gave in to Yvonne's invitations, and they visited her church. To Mia's great surprise, her mother said she'd liked it and wanted to keep going. Which was cool with Mia because she kind of liked it too. Until Joe got sick of them not being around every Sunday to wait on him, knocked Mom around, and told her they couldn't go anymore. Yvonne and the kids moved away a few months later, and that was the end of it.

"Okay, karma, God, whatever." She managed a small smile. "Maybe I overreacted."

"You?" His grin popped out. "Never."

"Whatever. Let's just forget it."

"So you're talking to me again?"

"Probably." He made a big show of looking all relieved, and she tossed a stuffed animal at him. "Don't be so lame."

"I'll try." He stretched his arms over his head. "You, uh, you doing okay in school? Haven't heard from the principal lately."

She huffed and scowled when he looked her way. "I'm doing okay."

"Good. Making friends?"

"Some." As if.

"Okay. Well, you know. If anyone ever gives you any trouble, you can talk to me."

"I said I'm good." She answered too quickly and saw the way he picked up on that. He was too smart.

Mia scanned the room that had been hers since the beginning of summer. It was the smallest room in the house, with two dormer windows overlooking the ocean. The curtains were flowery and faded and matched the poufy chair in the corner. There was an old desk complete with an ancient typewriter that didn't work but was kind of cool. The worn rug might have been red-toned once, but now seemed a sorry mix of grays and browns with one or two splotches of magenta that somehow managed to escape the sun's rays. There wasn't a built-in closet. Just a hulking wardrobe that took up space at the far end of the room. The dark wood was worn and scratched but still smelled good, and each time she opened it, Mia held her breath a little and looked for Narnia.

Uncle Matt followed her eyes with a quiet smile. "You sure you don't want to take down that wallpaper?" He scrunched his nose at the pink roses climbing up and down the walls. The yellowed paper peeled in places and had probably been put up years before she'd even existed.

"Maybe. It's kinda gross."

"We could paint the walls. Whatever color you want. Within reason of course."

"So not black?" Mia leaned back against her pillows and allowed a smile. It felt good to smile.

"Let's go for something a little more cheerful. I'll pick up some paint sample books tomorrow. Yeah?"

"Okay." She pushed her hair behind her ears and studied him. "How long are they staying?"

"Your grandparents?" He raised his eyebrows and scratched the stubble on his chin. "God only knows. Look, I'm sorry about that, at dinner the other night. My dad. He . . ." Uncle Matt's words got lost in the thickening air, and Mia tapped her nails on the top of her laptop. Rain began to tap the windows, and she listened to the wind's song for a moment.

"He hates me."

"He doesn't hate you. He doesn't know you, Mia." Her uncle moved up the bed a little, his eyes sad. "You know that things between them and your mom weren't great. She was . . ." He flashed a grin. "A little hard to handle."

"Like me?" Mia crossed her arms.

"Way worse than you."

"Was it just because she got pregnant?" That never made sense to her. Not really. "I mean, kids get pregnant all the time. It's not that big a deal." She watched him clench and release his fingers a couple times. He stared at her, like he was trying to come up with the right thing to say.

"Mia, back when you were born, the friends my parents had, the school we went to . . . kids didn't get pregnant. Rachel was the first. It was a scandal. People talked. The church—"

"What church?"

"The church we attended at the time." He pushed back on the bed and sighed deep. "It doesn't matter. Anyway, the thing is, it was hard. They blamed Rachel for the way everyone ostracized them. Blamed her for getting pregnant, for not . . ." He clamped his mouth shut and stared at his hands. When he looked up again, his eyes shone too brightly. "None of it was your fault. You know that, right? She tried to be a good mom to you. I promise you that. At the beginning. She really loved you, kid. She does love you."

Mia's throat burned and she bit down hard on her bottom lip. It was all bull. Moms that really love their kids didn't run off with drug addicts. Don't let guys . . . "Uncle Matt?"

"Yeah?"

"Do you know who my father was?"

The question filled the room with more tension than she knew what to do with. She'd wanted to ask it for months. Almost from the first day he'd taken custody of her. But every time she thought she was ready, she lost her nerve.

"Do I . . .wow." He scrubbed a hand over his face and stared at her through wide eyes. "Have you talked to your mom about this?"

"I tried. A couple times. All she says is that he didn't care. About her or me. I'm not sure she even knows who he is. Maybe she just slept around with a bunch of guys. I wouldn't put it past her."

"Mia . . ." He laced his fingers together. Shrugged and looked sad. "I'm sorry. I don't know. I don't have the answer to your question. That's the truth."

Disappointment pushed her shoulders down but Mia sighed and managed a smile. "That's okay. I mean, I'm just curious. I don't actually want to meet him or anything." In her dreams, she did. In her dreams, he turned out to be the nicest guy in the world. An international businessman who never knew he had a kid. Or a soldier, serving on foreign soil, a hero. In her dreams, the men she conjured up were always kind and funny and smart, and would never in a million years do a thing to hurt her. And they'd kill anyone who tried.

Kind of like Uncle Matt.

"Do you think my grandparents know?"

He flashed her the look she knew pretty well by now. The one that said let it go already.

"I don't know, Mia. They might. But—"

"I know. Don't ask."

"Maybe at some point. When you know each other a little better, huh?"

"Do you think they'll ever talk to my mom again?"

"I'd like to think so. I hope so."

"What can I do to make them like me?" She looked away fast. She hadn't meant to ask that. Ever. Uncle Matt placed a hand on her shoulder and she heard his sigh, long, and deep and filled with a thousand sorrows. Finally, she forced her eyes back to his. "Not that I care."

"No." His smile came and went. "But if you did, I'd say just be yourself. Tell them stuff, share a little. Don't clam up when they ask you a question. Respect them for who they are and where they're at right now. But if they say anything, anything that hurts you or confuses you, you come to me, okay? I mean it. I won't put up with that."

She swiped a hand across her eyes. Dang him, why'd he have to be so nice? "Thanks, Uncle Matt."

"You gotta have my back too, though," he put in. "Don't let them talk crap about me."

"Why would they?" Mia laughed a little, couldn't help it. "You're like this perfect person. Everybody likes you. You've probably never done a thing wrong in your life."

"Ha." He stood and stretched his arms above his head. "I think they'd beg to differ on that one." He bent to touch the floor and popped back up again. She watched him study the poster of Gray Carlisle she'd taped on the wall earlier in the week. "Where'd you get this?"

Mia shrugged, tried not to smile, and made like it wasn't a big deal. "Liz brought it into work. He signed it for me."

"So I see." Uncle Matt turned toward her, his eyes doing that funny crinkly thing they did when he thought too hard. "Elizabeth really brought you that?"

"I know. I was kinda shocked too. I didn't think she liked me all that much."

"She likes you fine, Mia."

"She tell you that?" Mia narrowed her eyes. "When you were in the garage together on Tuesday night?" His face darkened and she gave a snort. "Relax. I wasn't spying on you. I got up to go to the bathroom and saw the two of you walking out the door. I don't actually care what you do, you know."

"Yeah, you do." His smile said he saw right through that. "She wanted to ask me about the alarm for the cottage. That's all."

"Uh huh. You still haven't done that?"

"Had to reschedule it. Then I forgot. But it's done now." Uncle Matt sighed. "So I gotta work tomorrow night. Um, I told Elizabeth. So you can call her if . . . you need someone."

Mia swallowed, her stomach clenching. "I don't need anyone."

He nodded slow, shoved his hands in the pockets of his hoodie. "Well. If you did, call her. Don't wake up your grandparents."

"As if."

"Done your homework?"

Mia flipped open her laptop with a grin. "Soon as you stop yammering and get outta here, I can finish it."

He backed off, his eyes lighting the way they did whenever he tried not to laugh. "Point taken. So. Are we good?"

"'Suppose so." She tugged at a strand of hair. "You gonna make us go back to that place again? The old folks' home?"

"You want to?"

"Maybe. It wasn't terrible."

"Good." He strode to the door and glanced over his shoulder. "Same time next week."

Mia groaned loud, rolled her eyes, waited until he shut the door behind him, then smiled wide.

nineteen

Liz locked the gallery and walked toward her car on Friday afternoon, more than ready for the weekend. Mia hadn't been able to come today. Doctor or dentist or something Matthew said. She hadn't paid that much attention. Her cell phone rang as she unlocked the car door. She slid into her vehicle, scanned the name, and took the call with a grin. "Well, if it isn't my famous little brother back from the dead."

Gray's gravely chuckle made her smile. "Not dead. Just busy. Studio time. Wedding plans. And a three-year-old who thinks she's ten. I can't keep up."

Liz leaned against her seat and smiled. "You sound happy, Gray."

"Insane people usually do." He laughed again. "Anyway, I was just calling to check up on you."

She gave a short laugh. "There's a switch."

"Right? So? How's life on the island?"

"Oh. You know." She filled him in on her move, the job with Evy, the renovations to Wyldewood, and Dad. "So we're managing. He's settled in well. And I guess I'm . . . I'm okay."

"Good. No news from the creep then?"

"No news." Liz shut her eyes. David had told Gray all about her going to New York alone, and she'd gotten an earful from him as well. She wasn't sure what her next step would be where Laurence was concerned. But she had to take one. Had to get those pictures back. "Heard from Lynnie lately?"

"Actually . . ." He paused, and Liz sat up a little, trepidation tingling. "She's sitting right beside me."

"What?!" Liz jerked up, banging her knee on the steering wheel.

"Hi, Liz!" Her sister's voice breezed through the phone, followed by the giggle Liz hadn't realized how much she'd missed until that moment.

"Lynette! You're back in the States? Are you coming home?"

"Yes, and yes. My flight got in this morning. I'm catching the ferry tomorrow. Nick's going to meet me."

"Why does nobody in this family tell me anything?" Liz grumbled, ignoring her sister's laughter.

"I didn't decide until this week. It just seemed like the right time. Nick's dad is, well, he's not doing so great and . . . I need to be there for Nick."

"Okay." Liz breathed in and tried to tick off all the questions in her head. "The house is a mess. I'm not sure there's a room ready yet."

"I know, David told me. I'm going to stay at Nick's. They've got plenty of room. That way I can help with everything too."

"Of course." She made a mental note to call Nick later, offer to, well . . . take them out for dinner or something.

"I can't wait to get home," Lynette rushed on, all enthusiasm and energy. "How's Dad doing?"

"He's good. Seems to have settled well." Liz hesitated. "He's losing a lot though. So don't be surprised if . . ." Somehow she couldn't say it. She heard Lynnie's intake of breath and swallowed a lump in her throat.

"He might not know me, you mean."

"He might. He still has some good days."

"All right. I'll be prepared. How are the dogs?"

Liz laughed and felt a little sorrow slip away. "The dogs are fine. I'm sure they'll be happy to have you home."

"I'll come see you when I get in. David said you're renting someone's coach house?"

"Yes. Is Ryan with you?"

"No. He's going to stay another month. I think they want to come home for Christmas though. And for—" Liz heard Lynnie's squeak of protest and Gray muttering something about her big mouth.

"Liz?" Her brother was back on the line.

"Still here, Gray."

"We set a date. For the wedding."

"Oh, finally." Liz studied the roof of her car, counting the mold spots. "So when is it?"

"We thought New Year's Eve. Well, Tori thought. I'm just going along with whatever she wants. I would've married her months ago in the courthouse, but she wants this girlie wedding. You know, twinkly lights, and flowers, all that fussy stuff. And I think I have to wear a suit."

A grin tickled the corners of her mouth. "Good Lord, you might even have to cut your hair."

"And shave."

"Tragic." Last time she'd seen her brother, he'd been sporting one of those awful goatee things and one of those awful man buns.

It wasn't his best look. She wouldn't be sorry to see the back end of either, and neither would Tori by the sounds of it.

"Well, all right. So where is this momentous event going to take place?"

"Um . . ." He cleared his throat. "We thought Wyldewood?"

Laughter tumbled out of her until she wiped her eyes. "Gray. You have no idea what the place looks like right now! There's no way. Sorry. It's really not possible. If you want to get married here, there are other options. Why not The Wauwinet or Cliffside? Any number of nice hotels would be more than happy to host your wedding."

"We tried a few. They're either closed for the season or already booked. Some could do other dates, but Tori really has her heart set on New Year's Eve."

"Seriously? Did you tell them it was for Gray Carlisle?"

"No, Liz." He gave a small groan. "I didn't, because we want to keep this quiet. Private. Friends and family only. Which is why the house would be perfect."

"Would be if it wasn't being ripped apart." Liz sat forward and rubbed her eyes. "Why not New York? Or New Jersey if you must. I'm sure there are at least one or two nice places there."

Gray made a growly noise. "We just want a small thing. I don't want press. Bigger places will be harder to secure. Besides, Wyldewood is home. It's where we fell in love again."

Liz made a gagging sound. "And if it snows? No flights. No ferries. Nobody will be able to get here. *You* won't be able to get here."

"Ah, there's my sister, the positive thinker. We'll come early. It'll be fine. I've already put in my order for clear skies."

"Because you're so tight with the Almighty?"

"Have a little faith, Liz."

"Now you sound like Lynnie." Liz watched an old man and his dog cross the street. How on earth would they cope with Dad at the wedding? "You seriously think we can hold a wedding at Wyldewood, in less than two months?" She did some quick calculations and shook her head. "Are you on drugs again?"

"You're hilarious." She could feel Gray's glare through the phone. "Hire more people. Bring in another construction company if you have to. I'll pay for it. I'm making money again, you know."

"So you keep reminding us all." As much as she wanted to see Gray and Tori tie the knot, what he was proposing was simply impossible. "David will never agree. He hates to be told what to do, and he doesn't like working under pressure."

"He's already agreed," Gray said smugly.

"Oh, for Pete's sake." Liz muttered under her breath and wondered for the umpteenth time how she'd ended up in a family of lunatics.

"Come on, Liz, you're the most organized one out of all of us. I know you planned your fair share of frou-frou events when you were with Broadhurst. Can't you work a miracle or something? Lynnie can help."

"We can do it, Liz!" Lynette yelled in the background. "Everyone will help!"

"Wait. Are you asking me to plan your wedding?" Liz closed her eyes. This couldn't be happening.

"Liz, hi!" Tori was on the phone now. "Look, I know we don't know each other that well yet, but honestly, we need your help. You know Nantucket. You have connections. Gray and I would be so honored if you'd agree to help plan the wedding."

Wonderful. Liz bit her lip and wrestled with her options. "Victoria, I am most certain your fiancé can afford to hire a wedding planner."

"But we don't want a wedding planner. We want you."

"Say yes, Elizabeth." Gray was back on. "I'll throw in a couple bottles of Cristal for your troubles."

"No."

"A trip to Bermuda? Hawaii?"

He was unbelievable. And she knew he wouldn't stop until she agreed. "This is madness."

"Naturally." Gray laughed. "We're Carlisles. Did you really expect anything less?"

A little past eleven-thirty that night, Liz sat cross-legged on the couch, scrolled through Pinterest, and munched on popcorn. Back in New York, she'd probably be at some over-priced restaurant sipping on after-dinner drinks and making plans to hit up the newest nightclub. She hadn't realized how much she'd missed the peace and quiet of the island until it was all she had.

A storm had rolled in earlier, thunder and lightning making sleep impossible. Rain pelted the roof at sporadic junctures. After hanging up with Gray, she'd driven straight to Wyldewood and demanded to know what in blue blazes David was thinking, agreeing to have Gray and Tori's wedding at the house. He hadn't been able to come up with a good answer and looked completely flummoxed by the entire prospect. Josslyn simply shook her head. Gray had no doubt worked his magic and bamboozled their brother into agreeing before giving him a chance to think about it.

"Madness." She slipped an elastic off her wrist, tied her hair up, and took another handful of popcorn. As she glanced across the room, she saw the lights of the upper level of the main house were still on. A figure stood in one of the windows. She knew Matthew was working. Was it Mia? A moment later her cell buzzed with a text.

Mia. *You awake?*

Liz frowned, her heart picking up speed. *I am. Stupid storm. Me too. Kinda scary, right?*

Oh, boy. Well. She couldn't argue with that. She typed quickly before she changed her mind. *Want some popcorn?*

She waited for a response. Wondered if she'd get one. But then: *Be right there.*

A couple minutes later, Liz disarmed her new alarm system, threw open her front door, and found the girl on the front step. Mia was huddled under an umbrella, wearing an oversized Boston Red Sox sweatshirt, checkered pajama pants, and a pair of Uggs. She put her umbrella down and stepped inside while Liz bolted the door shut. "You okay?"

"I couldn't sleep and saw your light on." Mia's voice trembled a little and she rubbed red-rimmed eyes. "Actually, I was asleep, but I woke up. I hate storms."

"Me too." Liz nodded and pointed to the couch. "Take off your boots and sit. Do you like hot milk and honey?"

Mia stared. "I don't know. Never had it."

"Really? My mother used to make it for me all the time when I couldn't sleep. It's delicious."

Mia screwed up her nose. "Sounds disgusting."

Liz grinned. "Wait and see. Put the television on if you want. I'll be back in a minute."

Later, they sat on the couch, and Mia sipped from an old Harvard mug, licked her lips, and presented Liz with a half-smile. "Not bad."

"Told you." Liz blew on hers, took a small sip, and set it down on the coffee table. "So guess who's getting married?" She filled Mia in on Gray's news and watched the girl's dark eyes widen with every word.

"So, he's like, coming here? For his wedding?"

"That's the plan." Liz couldn't help laughing. "Honestly, I don't know what you kids see in him. He's really not that special."

Mia's mouth fell open. "Seriously? He's . . . he's . . . oh my gosh." She gave up the power of speech and simply shook her head.

Liz rolled her eyes. "The thing is, I have no idea how we're going to make this work. You've seen the mess at Wyldewood, and they're insisting on having it there. Not that we could find another location at this point. So I've been looking at some pictures. I guess you're not really interested in weddings at your age but . . ." She showed Mia the ideas she'd pinned anyway. The girl scanned through Liz's newly created wedding-board and gave a huff.

"Don't you think it's dumb, the fairytale wedding dream and all that? Some of the girls at school sometimes, they talk like having a wedding is the most important thing in the world. Spending all that money, all that fuss for one day. It just seems so . . . fake. I mean, as if it's going to last." Mia sucked her teeth and took another drink. "Look how many people get divorced, right? It's ridiculous to spend all that money on a day that means nothing."

"Well." Liz drew in a breath and fiddled with the ring she wore on her right hand. A brilliant cut sapphire that Laurence had given her two Christmases ago. She thought he'd been about to propose, but he'd quickly set her straight. Oh no, she'd be getting the Hope Diamond when that happened. She didn't know why she still wore the ring, except for the fact that she liked it. But maybe it was time to get rid of it. She'd probably get a good amount for it. "I happen to agree with everything you just said."

Mia sat back and stared. "Really?"

A smile slipped out before she could stop it. "Yeah, sad as it is." Liz scrolled through a few more photos. "But not every marriage ends in divorce. I know plenty of happy couples." One or two at least.

"What about you?" Mia asked. "Ever been married?"

"I have not. Don't think that's in the cards for me."

"Too much trouble, huh?"

"Something like that." Liz laughed and wondered what the girl's childhood had been like. "I suppose if the right man came along, I might consider it. But then, how do you really know if he's the right man?"

"Exactly!" Mia clapped her hands together. "My stepfather was the biggest loser on the face of the earth. But my mom thought he was all that. Married him, and off we went to Arizona. Boring as stink out there, by the way. Unless you like hot weather and cactus."

"Mm." Liz realized she was seeing Mia for the first time without makeup. She took in the pale skin, wide eyes with thick eyelashes, and finely sculpted jawline. She was a pretty girl. In a couple of years, she'd be a knockout. Liz wondered if she'd ever believe that. "I was in Scottsdale for a conference once. I thought it was quite nice."

"Right. Probably at the Fairmont, weren't ya?"

"I think so. How long did you live in Arizona?"

"Too long. We left Boston when I was seven. Came back last year. I was glad. My mom seemed happy too, for a while. To get away from him, you know? But then she . . . well. Same old same old. She's been on and off drugs my whole life. Don't know why I expected anything different." She reached for the laptop and pointed at the screen. "I like the way they have the lights strung here. If you had a big room with beams, you could do that easy enough."

"Right. It gives a nice ambiance, doesn't it? Let's pin that one." Liz swallowed sorrow and sipped from her mug. "So you didn't like your stepfather much?"

"Like him? There was nothing to like. He beat my mom all the time, and he . . ." Mia's eyes shone too brightly as she shook her head in slow motion. "I hate his guts. I hope he's dead."

She shouldn't have asked. Oh Lord, she shouldn't have asked.

"I'm sorry." Liz tried to recover from Mia's truth-telling. Tried to extricate the awful lump in her throat and the strange emotion that made her just want to give the kid a hug and tell her it was all going to be okay.

Wow, seriously? Where did that come from? She didn't have a maternal bone in her body. She was a lawyer. She'd heard enough unhappy childhood stories. Life was terribly unfair sometimes. And some kids got a raw deal. But somehow, tonight, Mia's story seemed different. And it made her feel things she'd long since convinced herself incapable of.

They watched a movie. Liz didn't pay attention to any of it, and by the time it was over, Mia was curled up under a blanket, sound asleep. Liz let out a long sigh and rubbed her tired eyes. Rain still pounded the roof. She couldn't very well wake the girl and put her back on the path to the house. She reached for her phone and scanned through her contacts until she found Matthew's number. Considered a text, but then stood and walked across the room while it rang through.

"Elizabeth? What's wrong? Did Mia call you?" He was on full alert, sounding far more awake than she was at one in the morning.

"Everything's okay." She tried to sound calm, but her mind was filled with images she didn't want to think about. "She's here. I guess the storm woke her. I was awake anyway. It's fine. Anyway, she's sound asleep on my couch. I don't want to wake her. I just wanted to let you know, so you didn't get home later and freak out."

"Ah." A sound got stuck in his throat, and he didn't say anything for a minute. "She doesn't do so well in storms. Which kind of sucks considering where we live."

"No kidding. We do get some doozies. My brothers would make fun of Lynnie and me. We'd always hide under the covers and wait for it to be over."

"You don't like to watch the lightning?" His voice slowed and he sounded a little less tense. She hadn't meant to scare him, but she couldn't very well not let him know where his niece was.

"Not me. Gray's the lightning chaser in our crazy clan. Speaking of, guess what he sprang on me today?" She curled into a chair and told him her tale of woe, not at all surprised when his soft laughter flooded through her.

"He knew you wouldn't turn down the challenge."

"You think?" Liz smiled and closed her eyes with a sleepy yawn. "It'll be the best darn wedding Nantucket has ever seen, even if I have to move hell and high water to do it."

"I have complete faith in you, Elizabeth. Hey, this could even be a new career for you. You will be the ultimate wedding planner."

"I hate weddings."

"Of course you do." He chuckled, and she heard the scrape of a chair and the thud of boots. He was probably walking around whatever building he was watching tonight. "Show me an unattached person who doesn't."

"Right? I always retreat to the ladies' room when the bride gets ready to throw the bouquet."

"Good call. I hang out near the bar and try to avoid unnecessary conversation with over-eager women."

She laughed. "Well, this shouldn't be quite as bad as some I've attended. Gray said he wanted to keep it low key. Ironically, my brother wouldn't know low key if it came up and kissed him."

"That's why you're in charge."

"An excellent point." Liz yawned again. "Well, I'll let you go. Enjoy the rest of your shift."

"What, you don't want to stay up and talk to me for three more hours?"

"Sure. I'll just sit here and you can listen to me snoring in about two minutes."

"I doubt you snore."

"Hanging up now, Matthew."

"Probably a good idea. Goodnight, Elizabeth. Sleep well."

Oh, that was debatable. But she put herself to bed anyway, closed her eyes, and found herself imagining what Matthew Stone would look like in a suit.

twenty

Matthew rose with the sun on Sunday morning, pulled on shorts and a t-shirt, and jogged down to the beach. He ran for longer than usual, sneakers sinking into wet sand, heart pounding as he pushed himself beyond his limit. Finally, he slowed, leaned over his knees, and took a few deep breaths. He'd come home after his shift yesterday and crashed. Mia had woken him at one point to see if he wanted food. He hadn't emerged until dinner and couldn't even remember what they'd eaten. He wasn't cut out for this line of work.

He inhaled salty air, walked back toward the steps that led up to the house, and wondered what Elizabeth was doing today. He found his thoughts focusing on her more often than he liked. In the weeks they'd known each other, she'd somehow managed to infiltrate that high wall around his heart. He enjoyed talking to her. Enjoyed being around her. Not that they'd spent a whole lot of time together. The few chats they'd shared didn't exactly count as anything close to a date.

When was the last time he'd been on one of those?

And if he asked her out? Matt grinned and wiped sweat off his brow with the bottom of his shirt. Elizabeth Carlisle would turn him down quicker than the loan officer at the bank. Nah. He had enough to worry about without putting a woman in the mix. Albeit an extremely attractive and interesting one. Of course, there were her issues to consider. Her wariness, the need for the alarm system, the distrust he saw in her eyes. He couldn't help wonder what kind of past relationships she'd had. His head told him he was better off not knowing, better to steer clear. But he had a sinking feeling his heart had other ideas.

"Matthew? What on earth are you doing? You'll catch your death!"

Speaking of women he didn't understand.

His mother stood at the top of the steps, huddled in an argyle blanket she'd pulled off the couch in the sunroom.

"Coming." He took the stairs two at a time, pausing at the top to give her a smile. It wasn't all that bad, having them around. He hadn't thought he'd missed his parents. Missed the relationship they'd once had. But now that they were here . . . "It's going to get a lot colder than this in the next few weeks, you know." They'd probably be on their way back to Boston before Thanksgiving anyway. Inside, Matt grabbed his sweatpants from the chair where he'd left them, pulled them on, and strode to the kitchen to get water. He stopped in his tracks. The mouth-watering smell of bacon wrapped around him. His dad was at the stove. Cooking.

Sunday breakfast.

A fleeting image of the four of them—him, Rachel, and Mom and Dad—sitting around the table, laughing about something Dad had said, flickered in the recesses of his memory. It was their tradition. Every Sunday, they'd eat breakfast together before going to church. He'd forgotten that.

Mia glanced his way from where she stood setting the table, bare feet poking out under black skinny jeans, an oversized sweatshirt covering the rest of her.

"What are you doing up?" He couldn't help ask.

"They woke me." She actually grinned like that was a good thing. Coffee. He needed coffee.

"Well, do you want to change first? Shower?" Mom hovered, holding a mug of steaming coffee toward him.

"Uh . . . no. I'll just take that." Matt took the mug she offered, shook his head, and swept away the cobwebs in his mind. He sank into his chair at the table and stared at Mia. She shrugged and gave him a *don't ask me* look.

Dad served up fried eggs and bacon and pancakes. The four of them ate mostly in silence, his mother remarking on the weather and when it might snow, Dad grunting some tacit reply. It was hardly the happy family routine from his childhood. Then again, they hadn't been a happy family for a lot of years.

Matt suddenly dropped his fork and stared at Mia. "You're eating bacon."

She raised her eyes mid-bite, crunched the whole slice up in her mouth, and swallowed with a smile. "So?"

"You don't eat meat." Matt blinked. It wasn't even ten in the morning. Could this day get any weirder?

"Meh." She shrugged and popped another piece into her mouth. "Changed my mind."

"Apparently." Matt reached for the coffee pot. He needed more. And then some.

"I've got homework." Mia was the first to finish, pushing back her chair.

"Plate in the sink, please," Matt muttered.

She raised a brow that said she'd been going to do that, stood with her empty plate, started toward the sink, then turned back toward them, her eyes fixed on her grandfather. "Thanks. That was really good."

Matt watched color creep into his father's cheeks. They hadn't spoken of Dad's outburst that awful night. Easier not to, he supposed. And from the looks of things, Mia was ready to move on.

Dad cleared his throat, took off his glasses, and blinked at his granddaughter. "You're very welcome, Mia."

She nodded, loaded her plate into the dishwasher, and scooted out of the room.

Mom poured more coffee, and Matt concentrated on the clock on the wall.

"Matthew, we've been talking." His mother's voice cut through the silence, and Matt swallowed a groan.

"About?" He faced them, mentally ticking off any number of directions the conversation could go.

"Why are you working two jobs?" she asked quietly, clear eyes studying him. "Why are you renting out the coach house? Are you really that strapped for cash?"

He inhaled, propped his elbows, and steeled himself for the impending conversation. "Well." Matt let out his breath. "Actually, yes. As you may know, Mother, living on Nantucket is not cheap. I inherited the house, yes, but that's put me in a whole new tax bracket, and my salary doesn't match it. I had to take out a loan to make some repairs to the main house and then the coach house before I leased the place. So I'm still paying that off. And it's not just me anymore. I have Mia to support."

"You have a trust fund." Dad sat back, folded his arms, and stared him down. Even he was beginning to look like he might belong on the island. He'd done away with his starched button-downs, opting for more casual polo-neck shirts and a navy cable-knit sweater that made him look far less formidable.

"The last time we had this conversation I told you I didn't want it." Matt sat back, clenched his fists, and stared out the window at a collection of clouds moving slowly across the gray sky. "That hasn't changed."

"The last time we had this conversation you were twenty-one, and you were not the sole guardian of a teenage girl," Mom reminded him astutely.

"She's not lacking for anything." It was hard not to resent the insinuation. "There's food on the table. She's in school. She's . . ." His heart rate sped up and he drew in a breath. "She's fine."

"Is she?"

"I just said, she's fine." He lowered his voice. "She's got some issues, for sure, but so would you if you'd gone through what she has. I love my sister, don't get me wrong, but Rachel's got a lot to answer for. A lot." He dragged a hand down his face. He needed to shut up. It wouldn't do any good to dredge up the past. To give them all the details. And he was pretty sure Mia wouldn't want him telling them anything.

Unspoken words passed between them in a glance he couldn't interpret. Mom fiddled with the gold buttons on her wool cardigan, brushed back her hair, and gave a small sigh. Dad looked like he had a bad case of indigestion.

"Better tell him, Phyllis."

"Tell me what?" Matt straightened.

Mom met his eyes with a pained expression. "The other night, when Mia was so upset . . . remember?"

"She's upset pretty much every night, Mom," he growled. "Which night?"

"Tuesday, I think? The day you took the kids to the old folks home?"

"Yeah, okay."

"Well, it's just . . . that I . . ." she blinked, her eyes unusually moist. "I found a razor blade on the bathroom floor that night. It had blood on it."

"A razor blade?" Matt shook his head. "You mean a disposable razor?"

"No." Mom sighed and glanced at his father again. "Just a blade."

"Was it yours?" He swung his gaze to his father. But he knew Dad was using the bathroom on the other side of the house.

"Sorry." Dad raised a hand. "I use an electric razor anyway."

If there was a razor blade on the floor of the bathroom he shared with Mia . . . he scrambled to think of any other possible reason for her discovery. There wasn't one. Could he insist on denying the very thing they were trying to tell him?

"Do you think Mia is capable of hurting herself?" Dad asked in a low voice, glancing toward the door.

"Hurting herself?" A buzzing sound started in Matt's ears.

"Cutting, Matthew. You know when—"

"I know what cutting is, Dad. I teach high school." They couldn't be right . . . Matt took a shaky breath and lowered his head. If Mia were cutting, he'd know. Wouldn't he?

He raised his head to meet their worried faces, his vision blurring. "No. I think you're wrong. There must be another explanation." Had to be.

"I know it's not a possibility you want to contemplate, Matthew," his mother interjected, "but when I worked with Big Brothers, we—"

"Stop!" Matt slammed a hand on the table and shot to his feet. "Mia isn't one of your charities, Mother. And you can't come into my life now and act like concerned parents, okay? You're a few years too late. You can't throw money at us and make it all better!"

"Matthew." Dad leaned forward in that annoying way when he wanted to get a point across. "Calm down and try out a little civility. We're just trying to help."

"Help?" Matt placed his palms on the table and stared him down. "You? You want to help? I can't handle the irony of that statement. I don't even know what to say to you." His breath raged along with his feelings, so many years of bottled emotions begging for release.

Dad cleared his throat. "Despite what you may think of me, I have been convicted of no crime." The pointed words were a direct hit. A subtle attack on Rachel.

"This isn't about you, Harrison." Mom put a hand on Dad's arm. "Matthew, we've been here a few weeks now, and whether you believe it or not, we are concerned. You're clearly exhausted, and Mia is . . . well, frankly, I think she's got more problems than any of us know how to deal with. I don't sleep all that well myself these days, so I've heard her up during the night. Heard you get up to go to her and try and calm her down. How long do you think you can carry on like this?"

He sat in silence, his chest tight, emotions raging. It was a question he'd been asking for a while now. But he hadn't done a thing about it. Hadn't talked to Mia. Hadn't made an appointment with the therapist in town his doctor had recommended.

"Have you considered professional help?" Mom's voice cut into his thoughts again. "Counseling?"

"Of course I have. I'm not a complete idiot." Matt ran his tongue across his dry lips. Blew out a breath and went to the sink where he filled a glass with water and drank deeply. Dad was right. He had to calm down. Slowly he walked back to the table and sat.

"I'm sorry." He worked to keep his voice level, his feelings in check. "But I'm finding it a little hard to wrap my head around this conversation. I'm not used to having parents who actually give a crap."

His mother sighed and wiped her eyes. "I'm not sure that's entirely fair. I know we've had our differences, and I know you think the way we handled things with your sister was wrong—"

"Wrong?" He scoffed. "That's the understatement of the century! The day Rachel told you she was pregnant you decided her fate! You kicked her out of your home. There was no discussion. No leniency. One strike, you're out. That's how things work in this family. She was barely sixteen years old, Mom!"

"We're well aware, Matthew," Dad growled. "But you don't have all the facts."

"What are you talking about?"

Mom shot his father a furtive glance. "You're right, Matthew. The way we handled the situation with your sister was wrong. And we can't change that. But what about our relationship with you? You pushed us away. You moved in with Patrick's family once you graduated high school, you refused our financial help, and you rarely talked to us. For years. You have some responsibility in this."

"I was angry!" As if that explained it all. "What did you think would happen to Rachel? If it hadn't been for Pat's family, she would have ended up in a shelter! She was a kid and she made a mistake. She wasn't ready to have a child. Would you have wanted her to have an abortion?"

"Of course not. But she had other options. We begged her to consider adoption. Your father had arranged for her to go away, to a nice home out on the west coast. We thought it was settled, but then she changed her mind. Insisted on keeping the baby."

Matt blinked moisture and shoved down a lump in his throat. "She didn't tell me that."

"I suspect there are many things your sister didn't tell you," Dad said quietly. "We couldn't get her to see reason after that. We told her we didn't approve, that she was doing the wrong thing. Things were said between us that shouldn't have been. She packed her bags and left. We didn't kick her out, as you've been led to believe. It was her choice."

"I tried to talk sense into her over those next few months," Mom said. "You know I came to see her at the O'Donohues', several times. You saw me." She gave a shaky sigh. "But she refused to come home. Refused our help. And later, after Mia was born, when she started up with the drugs again . . . that was the end of it."

His father shook his head. "She soundly rejected the suggestion of rehab. You must remember that? It was almost like she was determined to destroy her life at that point." Dad coughed, pushed fingers through his hair, and settled his gaze on Matthew. "We offered to take Mia. I was willing to send Rachel anywhere she wanted to go. There were any number of private schools we would have sent her to. She could have gone on to any college. She was bright you know, she could have gotten in anywhere, had she set her mind to it."

"You what?" Matt scrubbed his face, frantic for a breath. "You . . . were willing . . . to raise Mia? Really?" It was all too much. Too late. Yet, he knew they were telling the truth.

His father heaved a sigh, studied the table, then looked up. "I believe it was at that point your sister told us to go to hell. To stay out of her life and never contact her again. Something to that effect." Dad waved a hand. "So there you have it. The ugly truth. Like it or not, that's what happened. Slightly different from the version you've been led to believe, I assume."

"All these years, why didn't you say anything?" Matt could barely get his voice above a whisper. "Why didn't you tell me what really happened?"

"Because it was done and we didn't see the point," Dad barked. "And we didn't want to sully your relationship with your sister. She needed you."

Needed him? Had Rachel ever really needed him? When Mia was born, Patrick's parents had stepped in, helping her with the baby as much as they could. Rachel worked as a check-out girl in the nearby Stop 'n' Shop. Tried to take a few classes at night to complete her GED. Almost got it too. She started using again shortly after Mia's first birthday.

Matt sat with his head in his hands and took deep breaths. At last he raised his eyes to meet their worried faces. "It didn't matter in the end." He choked the words out. "I couldn't help her."

Mom reached out to clasp his wrist. "You're helping her now. You're taking care of her daughter. And we want to help you. Can we at least try to make amends? Will you give us that chance?"

Matt swallowed and rammed his fingers through his hair. "I'm not the one you need to be having this conversation with."

"What do you want from us?" Dad asked wearily. "We've told you our side. We've said we want to help. You. And Mia. Why is nothing ever good enough? Do you want us to leave? Go back to Boston? We can certainly do that."

"Be my guest," Matt snarled. What was the use? Reconciliation after all this time was too ridiculous to pin any hope on. "I'll drive you to the ferry."

"For heaven's sake, you two." Mom raised her hands. "This isn't going to solve a thing. Now, Matthew, the ball is in your court. We do want to help. We'd love to stay longer, perhaps through the holidays, and pitch in around here. But if you'd prefer we left, well, we'll abide by your wishes."

"That'd be a first," he muttered, squeezing his eyes shut a moment. He was going to have a monster of a headache by the time this little chat was over. He looked at his mother and dealt with a sharp blow of regret. The tears in her eyes told him he'd gone too far. She never cried. Not in front of anyone. He could count the times on one hand.

"We're sorry," she whispered, taking a deep breath. "I suppose it was silly to assume we could come over here and pick up like nothing ever happened. A second chance is clearly too much to ask for."

Got that right. Matt exhaled. His mother was the master of manipulation. And he was always the first to get sucked in. Which was precisely why he'd spent the better part of the last ten years avoiding his parents. And was that any way to live? Maybe they *were* sorry. Maybe this time she actually meant it.

"You really want to stay?" He aimed the question at his father because he was easier to read. Dad didn't hide behind carefully constructed words or body language.

"If you will let us, yes." Shadows sat beneath his eyes, and his jowl sagged a little. Matt noticed a few more gray hairs around his temple. Wondered whether it was possible for his father to finally loosen up a little and live a life that might make him happy. Because for all his acclaim and accolades and awards, Matt had never believed Harrison Stone to be a happy man.

Matt stared at the scratch marks on the old oak table and struggled for words. "Why?" It was all he could say.

"You see?" Dad huffed. "Stubborn. That's what you are, boy. Stubborn as a mule."

"Really? Now where in the world would I get that from?"

"Stop!" Mom glared at them. "Yes, we've made mistakes. Awful mistakes. With Rachel, and with you, Matthew. But we've nothing to hold us in Boston. We've got plenty of money, more than we need. Is it so unreasonable to think we might want to spend time with our family?"

A harsh laugh escaped before he could stop it. "Um, yes." Oh, he so needed to get out of here. To end this farcical moment in time that would mean next to nothing by day's end. "And what about the two of you?" he asked, some hesitation hitching in his throat. "It's obvious you're not exactly basking in matrimonial harmony. We don't need any added tension around here."

Dad responded with a sigh, and Mom pinched her lips together. Their eyes met and she gave him a timid look. "Perhaps this would be a good place for us to work on that." Matt wasn't convinced of the sincerity of the suggestion, but it was better than nothing.

"Perhaps you're right, dear." Dad placed a hand on the table, palm up. His mother slipped hers into it. And they smiled.

"Okay, fine. You can stay." He shook his head, already regretting his words. "But if this goes south and you being here makes things more difficult, you go. No arguing."

"Very well." His father nodded somberly and Mom shrugged, looking a little put out. As if she would ever cause any trouble. "And would you please consider taking your money?" Dad pressed. "It's just sitting there. You could pay off that loan. Save the rest for Mia if you want, but you don't need to be working two jobs. Not when Mia clearly needs you at home. Surely you can see the sense in that?"

Matt stared at his father a long moment. He could see the sense in it all right. If he stood on tiptoe and looked over the top of his pride. "I'll think about it. I need to go shower." He got to his feet, heard Mia clomping down the stairs. The next moment, she popped her head around the doorframe.

"Can I go to Wyldewood this afternoon? They want me to watch the twins while they talk wedding stuff."

"Homework?" He prayed she hadn't been eavesdropping on the entire conversation.

"Done. Well, I have a chapter left to read, but I can do that while they're napping." Mia smiled sweetly. "You said I should get out of the house more."

"Fine. You can go." He'd half a mind to ask if he could go too.

"Cool. Can you drive me? Liz is already there. She said she'd come get me, but I figured you didn't have anything to do. You could maybe go down on their beach if you wanted, to take pictures."

Mind reader. A little tension slipped away. "You're good, you know that?" He strode to where she stood and pulled her in for a hug. She made a shrieking noise, but didn't pull away. "I'll drive you, but I gotta shower first."

"Yeah, you better. You stink." Mia pushed him off and went to the fridge. "Any more bacon?"

"I think we can rustle some up." Dad was on his feet at once. Mom too, going for more coffee. At least it wasn't wine.

"Mia," Dad said as he took out another package of bacon. "I was wondering; do you know how to play chess? Your great-grandfather had a wonderful board in the living room, and I'm just itching for a game."

Matt rolled his eyes. "Mia doesn't play chess, and I'm sure she has no desire to learn."

"Actually, Uncle Matt, I do know how. Uncle Pat taught me when I was little. I haven't played in a while, but I'm sure I can remember." Her smug smile made his heart lurch a little. Dad's chuckle ran around the room and tugged the knot in his stomach a little tighter.

He was living in the Twilight Zone.

"Knock yourselves out. I'll be down in a bit."

twenty-one

Liz sat cross-legged on the floor of David and Josslyn's living-room on Sunday. She'd arrived around ten, and they'd been talking for two hours, trying to make plans, while the twins raced around, screaming like little banshees. She'd finally made the suggestion of calling Mia to see if she could come watch them for a bit so they could actually think in peace and quiet. She glanced at her watch. Mia should be here any minute. If not, she'd take the two little hellions upstairs and lock them in their room.

"How many people do you think they're planning on inviting, Lynnie?" Her younger sister had nearly knocked her over when she'd seen her yesterday. Liz had brushed off her enthusiasm, but was more relieved than she'd admit to have Lynette back safe and sound.

Snuggled in the crook of Nick's arm, her blond hair still a mass of curls and tangles, she wore a golden glow and a peaceful expression that said her time in Africa had been well spent. Her sister scrunched her nose at the question.

"Hard to say for sure. I think they're talking between fifty and sixty. I don't know if they've gotten that far yet. And I'm so jet-lagged that really, anything they said went in one ear and out the other."

"I'm not sure we can blame that entirely on the jet-lag." Liz tapped her finger against the side of her cheek and grinned as Lynette stuck out her tongue. She studied her laptop and added another line to the do-to list. "I'll have to pin them down on numbers. Invitations need to go out ASAP so we know how many are coming. And where will people stay?" She shook her head, appalled all over again at the ludicrousness of the entire thing. "So let's assume eighty people at the most? Hopefully less. Do you think we could have the living room space ready to set up tables, David? We'll have to do things inside. I think it'd be too cold to use tents outdoors, even with heating."

"I went to an outside event last winter," Nick said, his fingers trailing through Lynette's hair. "The tents were warm, with a sub-floor and everything. It was just like being indoors. I can make some inquiries." Lynette beamed up at him and Nick leaned in for a kiss. Liz bit her tongue, tempted to tell them to get a room.

"Wonderful. Tents – Nick." She tapped over the keys again.

"Oh, wait. I think that was in October." Nick corrected himself with a chuckle. "Probably wouldn't work at the end of December."

Liz shot him a look and raised her eyes heavenward. "Not helpful, Nick." She frowned at the document she was working on. "No, there's no way we can be outside. We don't want everyone to freeze." Her cell phone buzzed on the floor beside her and she glanced down. A chill raced through her as she saw Laurence's number on the screen. What on earth?

"Liz?" David's voice pulled her gaze back up.

"What?"

"If we hire the extra crew like Gray suggested, I'm pretty sure we can have the living room ready. I'll call some guys tomorrow."

"Okay." Her phone buzzed again with a text message. Sweat slid down her spine and fear dried her throat. No, no, no. She couldn't handle this. Not now.

"Don't look so worried," Lynette said with a smile. "We'll make it work."

"And if we can't?" The twins made another noisy pass through, and Liz tamped her temper. "Okay. What about food? Do they want caterers?"

"I can do the food." Cecily charged into the room from whatever she'd been doing in the kitchen. She'd come to see Lynnie first thing this morning, but as usual, put herself to work. Liz wondered if the woman ever slept.

"Ce-ce, you can't. It's too much," Liz said. "Gray can pay for catering."

"That boy loves my cooking," Cecily insisted, her eyes shining. "We could serve buffet style. I bet he'd love some barbequed ribs and chicken, baked beans . . ."

"Sounds good to me." David grinned and rubbed his stomach.

Liz shook her head. Might as well stick a pig on a spit while they were at it. She wouldn't suggest it. "I'll talk to Gray and Tori about food."

Cecily put her hands on her hips with a triumphant smile. "I can get the church ladies to help. If that's what Gray and Victoria want. It'll save some money for sure. And my sister makes the best cakes on the island. I'll give you her card."

"Fine. We'll see." Liz ducked as a teddy bear flew through the air, straight for her head. She snaked out an arm and grabbed Brandon as he raced past with a shriek. "Cut it out! Now!" Her nephew's little face crumpled, and he burst into loud, startled tears.

"Liz, seriously?" David got to his feet amidst Brandon's screams. Bethie started crying too, and Josslyn picked up her daughter just as Mia appeared, her uncle right behind her.

"We knocked but nobody answered."

"I'm not surprised," Liz huffed. "I can't hear myself think in here."

"Chill out," David growled, rocking back and forth with Brandon, who was still screaming.

"Um . . ." Matthew cleared his throat and followed Mia into the room a little hesitantly.

"Hey, Matt! Good to see you, man." Nick got to his feet, greeted them, and introduced Lynette.

Liz took the opportunity to scan her messages and wished she hadn't. She looked up again and found Matthew glancing her way. A hesitant smile pulled his lips apart. "What time should I pick Mia up?"

"Can we call you?" Josslyn handed Bethie to Mia, sounding completely frazzled. "Or someone can drop her home. Liz?"

"Mm. Sure." Five text messages. He wanted to meet. To talk. The thought made want to vomit.

"I can come back." Matthew patted a large black bag he had hoisted over one shoulder. "Actually, I was wondering if you'd mind if I walked the beach. Took some pictures."

"Oh, are you a photographer?" Lynette brightened and Liz groaned. She could see where this was going.

Matthew shook his head. "Just a hobby."

"He's really good," Mia piped up. "He's just being modest. He entered a show over the summer and won first place."

"Sweet." Nick grinned. "Ever shot a wedding?"

Lynette clapped her hands. "Yes! Perfect. What are you doing New Year's Eve?"

"Um . . ." Matthew's brow furrowed as he shrugged, glancing at Liz again.

"He's busy," Liz snapped. "I'm sure Gray will have his own—hey!" Brandon had been released to the floor again, found his teddy bear, and whacked her over the head with it. Liz squelched a yell. "Enough! David, can't you . . ." She clamped her mouth shut.

"Calm down." David glared at her, moving his son away from Liz.

Liz lifted her hands. "You're spoiling them! We're trying to have a conversation and they're running around like little hooligans!" Brandon started howling again.

"Liz, they're just babies." Lynnie went to Brandon and picked him up, soothing him with soft words and a kiss.

"Give me a break." Liz shook her head. Her phone buzzed again and she grabbed it, got to her feet, and stared at Lynette in frustration. "Right. Well, since you seem to have all the answers, as usual, why don't you plan this stupid wedding, Lynnie? I'm sure it'll be perfect with you in charge." Anger tightened her chest, and she stalked past Mia and Matthew, ignoring the startled looks on their faces. Let them think what they liked. Perhaps it was about time they met the real Liz anyway.

Liz grabbed her windbreaker, whistled for the dogs, and headed for the beach. She needed space. Needed air. Needed a drink.

Needed to throw her phone in the water.

Because right now she wanted nothing better than to call Laurence Broadhurst back and tell him exactly where he could go and how long he could stay there.

Diggory and Jasper raced over the sand after seagulls and Liz slowed her pace. She had to think. Breathe. Make her brain work logically. The texts were meant to taunt her. To incite a reaction. She would not respond. But Laurence had something she needed. She wanted those pictures back. Of course, he knew that. She'd have to negotiate somehow without getting caught in his web. She'd need to be clever. Because he was too calculating, too dangerous. And she'd been fooled before.

She stared at the numbers on her phone but couldn't bring her shaking hands to press the buttons. A seagull screeched as it flew past, and Liz jumped, dropped her phone, and swore.

"Hey." Matthew was beside her, bending and reaching for her phone, picking it up to pass it back to her before she could take her next breath.

"Thank you." Liz pulled air into her lungs and tried to control her trembling.

He met her eyes and studied her in silence. "I won't ask if you're okay, because you're obviously not and you'll probably try to convince me you're fine." A soft smile played over his face. "So I'll just say if you need to talk, I'm here."

A half-laugh, half-cry caught in her throat, embarrassment prickling her cheeks. She turned and began walking down the beach. He fell into step beside her with a low chuckle. Liz stopped short. "What's so funny?"

"Oh, nothing. I was just thinking it sounds as though you've had about as crappy a day as me so far." His open gaze did something to her soul. Spoke into hers somehow and said he was a man who could be trusted. A man who would not hurt her. Who would listen and not judge. Who might even take care of her if she'd let him. And yet . . . fear warned her not to get too close.

"Sorry to hear that." She pushed her hair back and tried to smile. "I guess I got a little carried away in there. My sister brings out the worst in me." Where did that come from?

"Really?"

Liz shoved her hands in the pockets of her windbreaker and sighed. "I don't know. I always feel like she's . . ." What? "I feel like she can do no wrong, and I'm always the mean big sister." Because that didn't sound childish at all.

"I doubt anyone thinks that," he replied with a laugh. "Sibling relationships are rarely uncomplicated." He set his bag down and pulled out a camera. Focused on the ocean and snapped a few shots. Liz shivered at the sound. It still had the power to draw her right back into the school's art studio, the room dark, the door locked. Even after all these years, she could still hear his voice, coaxing her to undo another button on her blouse. And then another. Not that she'd needed much coaxing once his hands had finally found their way beneath her blouse, his mouth close to hers, whispering promises she was stupid enough to believe.

"Tell me about it." She tried not to sound on the edge of a nervous breakdown. "And I'm blessed with four of them." She took a few steps sideways. "I feel like I've spent my life trying to get away from all this. And now I'm right back in the middle of it."

Click, click, click. "I always wanted a big family," Matthew's quiet voice wrapped around her. "I ended up getting one in a way, by default. My best friend back in Boston, Pat O'Donohue. Six of them all together, and his parents kind of adopted me into the clan. You wanna talk crazy, you should see the lot of them all in one room." He faced her, pointed the camera her way.

Liz's hand shot out before she could stop it.

"Easy." Matthew stepped back, lowering the camera, a thousand questions standing in his eyes. Her cell buzzed from her pocket, a reminder that she'd never be free from past mistakes. Not really.

Answer me, Liz, or I swear I'll . . . She could almost hear Laurence's voice, threatening, that hard stare piercing her. Could feel his hand sliding up her arm, across her shoulder and around her neck, pressing down with the hint of heightened pressure until she gave in. Gave him what he wanted. And hated herself for letting a man wield his power over her again.

"Elizabeth?" Matthew narrowed his eyes as her cell buzzed again. "Somebody's being awful persistent."

"I know. My ex." She laughed and tried to pretend it was nothing.

"You don't want to talk to him."

Genius. "I . . . can't." Her heart raced harder and, suddenly, she needed to run. She took off at a clip, running down the beach, not caring if Matthew followed or not.

twenty-two

Salt spray stuck to her cheeks and joined the tears that streamed down her face. Her breath came hard and fast, and eventually she slowed, her white KEDs filled with cold, wet sand. She sank down, dumped the sand out of her sneakers, and put them back on. Then she pulled her knees up and buried her face in her arms. How long had it been since she'd really cried? Allowed herself to grieve for the horrors she'd gone through as a young girl, and then the nightmare she'd lived more recently. She'd forced it all from her mind, believing it was the easier way. The safer way. Forget it ever happened. Move on.

But she hadn't given herself any time to heal.

The sessions she'd had with the therapist in town told her that. The pain that surfaced was too much, too suffocating. After enduring a few weeks, she hadn't gone back.

She sensed Matthew's presence beside her. Heard him sink to the sand, his steady breathing somehow slowing hers. And before she could raise her head to warn him away, he'd wrapped an arm around her shoulders. A moment later she felt the vibration of her phone again. And again. She shuddered and kept her face down, another sob sticking in her throat.

"Give it to me."

She obeyed in silence and watched as he turned it off and passed it back to her.

"You and I, we're not that different, you know." His voice thrummed around her, winding its way in, lifting her chin and forcing her to look at him.

"How's that?" She sniffed and wiped her eyes.

Sunlight sparkled off the sea and shimmered in his eyes. "We like to pretend we can handle things we've got no business trying to. Not on our own."

"You think?" Liz managed a smile. "And you thought I was the perceptive one."

He lifted a shoulder, a half-grin fading too fast. "I don't know exactly what you've been through. I can guess, and I'd probably be right. But I do know if you answer those messages, if you call him back, you'll give in. Because you're not as strong as you think you are."

Liz nodded, staring at the blank screen on her phone. "I thought he would leave me alone," she whispered. "I thought once I left him, left New York, it would be over. I need it to be over." She swung her gaze toward him, eyes burning.

Matthew cupped her face, the unexpected gesture warm and comforting. He wiped her tears with the base of his thumbs. "I'm sorry you've been hurt, Elizabeth."

"Thank you." She could barely get the words out. "Some would say I deserved what I got. Deserved the abuse because I let it happen. I didn't stop it. I didn't get help. I stayed."

His ragged sigh and the spark of anger in his eyes said enough. "Whatever he did to you, you did not deserve it. Nobody deserves that." Under normal circumstances, his closeness would have alarmed her. But it didn't. He didn't. He made her feel safe. And she didn't know what to do with that.

"Of course I know that. I'm a smart, educated woman. I should know better. I should have walked away the first time he hurt me. Any woman in her right mind would have. But I didn't." She released a shuddering sigh. "There is something seriously wrong with my head."

Matthew gave a slow smile. "It's not always that simple. And there's nothing wrong with you." He drew back, stretched his legs out, and clasped his hands together.

Liz missed his touch the moment it was gone. She lowered her gaze and bit her bottom lip. This was ridiculous. She barely knew him. The last thing she needed right now was to complicate her life with another relationship that would only end in disaster. Whatever these crazy feelings were that stirred whenever she was around this man, they needed to stop.

"Wouldn't it be nice if life were easy?" She wound her thumbs and watched the waves roll in. For a few moments, the sound of the sea was all she heard.

"Sure. But it's not." Matthew spoke again, drawing her eyes back to his. "And sometimes it's harder than we ever imagined." He played with the camera strap around his neck. "My sister was in an abusive relationship. For years. I begged her not to marry the guy, but . . . Rach rarely took advice from anyone, especially me. They got married and moved across the country. Mia was just a little kid. By the time she and Mia came back to Boston last year, the damage had been done. And Mia . . . probably got the worst of it." He stopped his words and looked away, digging his shoes into the sand.

Nausea balled in her throat as Liz realized the implications of what he'd said. "Oh, Matthew, no." She remembered Mia talking about her stepfather the night she'd come over. Liz closed her eyes against the thoughts. "Did he . . .?"

"I think so." He looked at her again, his eyes shimmering with moisture. "She hasn't said. But my gut tells me it's true. All the signs are there. I've just been pushing it away. Hoping it didn't happen. I'm pretty good at pushing away the past too." His smile was sad. "But then this morning . . ." He inhaled and let out a shaky sigh. "My parents sat me down for a chat. My mother found a razor-blade in the bathroom. They think . . . we think . . ."

"She's cutting?" Liz put a hand on his arm. She'd wondered as much. Wondered at the extent of Mia's issues, her attitude, her fears. "I've seen it before in a few families. One kid was doing it because they thought it was cool, but the others . . . they did it to escape the pain."

"I don't know what to do," he said hoarsely. "I'm a teacher. We're trained, told how to handle this kind of situation if we suspect a student to be self-harming. But when it's family . . ." He groaned and ground out a curse. "I haven't seen any evidence, marks or anything."

"Hmm. And you don't think it strange that she always wears long sleeves?"

"Does she?"

Typical man. Liz gave a sad smile. "Yes, from what I've seen. Even when we had that warm spell a couple weeks back. Evy and I remarked on it. She could also be doing it on her legs. The inside thigh, where nobody sees."

He gave another low groan. "How do I deal with this?"

"Well." Liz thought for a moment. Who was she to give anyone advice about emotional trauma? She'd spent half her life running from it. "I think you have to deal with it the same way you would if it was a student. Obviously she needs professional help. You know that."

"Yes."

"And most of all, she needs to know she's safe. That's she's loved. And you're already doing that." She squeezed his arm, and he turned her way again, pain simmering in his eyes.

"I'm trying. She doesn't make it easy."

Liz laughed and shook her head. "Maybe not, but you're doing it anyway. You adore her. I could see that the very first day we met. She's a lucky girl." Liz swallowed her words. "I mean . . . all kids should have an uncle like you." Right. That'd work.

"Huh." A sudden smile lit his eyes and chased off the sadness. "I need to talk to her for sure, but I'm scared of setting her back. She's been pretty good attitude-wise lately. She's even opening up a bit with my folks, which I never thought would happen. I think you've played a part in that."

"Me?"

"I know you guys talk at the gallery. You go out of your way to be nice to her, Elizabeth. She trusts you. She would never have called you the other night if she didn't."

Tears pricked and Liz blinked them away. "Matthew, I'm really not a nice person. What you witnessed in there this afternoon? That's pretty much the real me."

He nudged her shoulder. "Maybe you're not giving yourself a chance because you're too afraid of being hurt."

"Maybe you have no idea what you're talking about," she muttered, not really meaning it.

He leaned in a little, his lips perilously close to hers. "I think I might be right where you're concerned." Was he actually going to kiss her?

"Don't . . ." Oh, she couldn't. Couldn't let this happen. Wouldn't.

"Don't what?" He sat back again, eyes narrowing in confusion.

"Um, nothing." Way to be a complete idiot. She wanted to hightail it back to the house as fast as possible, yet she sat there, staring at him, wishing for things she didn't deserve.

He brushed hair off his forehead and produced a smile that threatened to split her heart in two. "You can trust me, Elizabeth. I hope you know that."

She nodded, aching now with the need for connection. To simply be held in a man's arms, no strings, no expectations. But if she shared those thoughts, it would end. This strange friendship between them. Because the physical desire would overtake everything and ruin it all. Just like it always did.

Liz scrambled to her feet. "I should get back. You can stay. Do . . . whatever you do with that thing."

He rose with a slow chuckle, and the spell she'd fallen under was broken. "Are you going to be okay?"

Her hand felt for her phone and her heart clenched. "Eventually, sure. Today? Not so much."

His sigh said he understood her perfectly. "This moving on thing isn't for sissies."

"Got that right." She smiled, curiosity poking her. "Is that why you moved to Nantucket? To get away from something?"

Matthew pushed sand around with the top of his deck shoe, eyes focused on the frigate far out to sea. "Sort of. Both our lives got turned upside down with Rachel's arrest. Rachel asked me to become Mia's legal guardian after her sentencing. There was no one else. Mia was getting in trouble, a lot. We were having a hard time adjusting to living together. And my girlfriend didn't appreciate a sullen teenager giving her the evil eye every time she came over."

"Ouch." Liz made a face and he laughed.

"Sadly, I didn't miss her much after we broke up. I doubt it would have lasted even without Mia in the picture. But yeah, I guess you could say I came here to get away. To start over. I just hope I don't end up regretting it."

"I know what you mean. Starting over is . . . well, kind of terrifying. And I think I'll steer clear of romantic relationships from now on."

He looked surprised. "Not even if the right guy came along?"

"I don't believe there is such a thing as 'the right guy,'" she scoffed. "Besides which, I'm not datable." They really didn't need to go further with this conversation. Liz began a slow walk back toward the house

The barest of smiles raced over his mouth. "Explain."

Well, if he really wanted to know. "I have trust issues."

He grinned again. "That's a given. And you've said you're kind of a witch. Anything else?"

Oh, he made her laugh. "I have expensive taste."

"Okay. Not shocked."

"I don't like flowers and sappy cards that really don't say anything."

"Blech." His horrified expression made her giggle.

"I'm not all that fond of children." Okay, she threw that in to put him off. "And I have a brown belt in taekwondo."

"Seriously?" His grin faded.

"Yep. And I don't have any friends. Oh, and I hate having my picture taken. So don't ask. Ever."

"I think I need to write all this down." Humor jumped in his eyes. "Okay, so definitely not dateable. But you're wrong about the friends."

"No." She gave her head a firm shake. "Not a one. Promise."

"I'm your friend."

Oh.

Her eyes began to burn again and Liz pushed back annoying emotion. "You might live to regret that." She sighed and pulled fingers through her windblown hair. "Matthew, I'm an emotional train wreck waiting to happen. The last thing I want is to inflict my crazy on anyone, nice guy or not." She watched his eyes shift slightly, processing her words.

"I think you're a very smart woman, Elizabeth." He hesitated and then gave her that smile again, the one she was starting to look forward to seeing whenever he was near. "Would it be all right if I call you sometime and ask if you're up for a drink or a cup of coffee? With your friend. Who happens to think you're pretty great, by the way, and would very much like to learn more about you and all your issues."

She arched a brow and let go a long whistle. "I think you might be a little crazy too."

He chuckled and lifted his arms above his head in a noisy stretch. "Probably why we seem to get along so well."

"I suppose coffee with a friend couldn't hurt." Liz allowed a smile and felt a little of the day's anxiety float away. "Matthew . . . thanks for being one of the good guys."

His eyes crinkled with laughter. "We're a dying breed."

"That you are." She turned on her heel and swung her sneakers by the laces, a feeling she hardly recognized warming her all the way through. "You've got my number then, friend." She picked up her paced and headed toward home.

"Elizabeth?"

She could hear the smile in his voice, but she looked back over her shoulder anyway. "What?"

"Keep your phone on."

twenty-three

DRAKE

They told me at breakfast that those kids were coming back today. I scarf down my lunch, prowl the day room, and wait for the bus to pull up. The others that live here look comatose. Sitting around in wheelchairs or on the couches, some calling out incomprehensible words like their lives depend on it. Some days I think this place is hell.

I don't want to be here. I don't belong here.

Or maybe I do.

Last night I dreamed I was back home. Must have been home, because the rooms were familiar and I knew every inch of them. And the smell of the sea was all around. A beautiful woman with long blond hair sat in the room that looks out at the ocean, several small children running around her. The boys whooping and hollering, chasing each other in some game, a little girl in her lap pointing at a picture book, another girl sprawled on the couch, her nose in a thick book. Something by Dickens. And where am I? Just watching.

I try to speak, but they don't hear me. Or don't want to hear me. One of the boys races past my legs and I reach for him, but then he's gone. They're all gone. And I'm left sitting up in bed, sweat on my brow.

Alone.

I catch a glimpse of the yellow bus snaking up the driveway and my heart jumps. "Bus is here!" A couple of the old farts look up and grunt, but nobody seems to care. Perhaps I shouldn't either. I find a chair in the corner and flop into it, playing with the frayed end of my untucked shirt. I remember last time we painted. Could have been last week or yesterday, I don't know. But I do recall the sensation, the victory in accomplishing something I thought I'd forgotten.

My hands itch to hold a paintbrush again. Colors fly across my mind like a scarlet sunset settling over the calm sea after a long, hot day.

Soon they're piling into the room, all grins and loud exuberance of youth. I reach back into memory and try to find some for myself. But nothing comes, so I sit in silence and watch them set up tables and easels. There she is, the girl. I remember her. The one with the gift.

She stands in front of me with an expectant look on her face. "Hey, Mr. Carlisle."

"Hey yourself." I don't know why I say that. It's something the young man who looks after me here says. He yammers on about his girl and his kid while he washes me and helps me dress. What's his name? Garth or Gregory or who the heck knows. I focus on the girl and those pink streaks in her dark hair. I peer a little closer and tap the side of my nose. "What is that?"

She grins and twists the diamond stud sticking out of her right nostril. "Just a piercing."

I widen my eyes. "Horrendous." That makes her laugh.

A tall boy with blond hair and sparkling eyes hovers near the girl. I sweep my gaze over him and frown. Hmm.

"Easel's all set for you, Mia," the boy says with a goofy grin. And she rolls her eyes at me, confirming my suspicion. But I watch the way her cheeks pink up a little, and I think she kind of likes him too.

"Mia." I get to my feet, grateful for the flash of clarity as I suddenly know that this is what she's called. "What shall we create today?"

"Something with light," she muses, assessing the canvas with careful eyes. "I'm having trouble with that, you know? Capturing it."

I do know. "You have to let it come to you," I tell her, opening the box of paints and sorting through the tubes. My hands seem to know what they're doing even if my mind doesn't. "If you force it, it will run away. You can't fake it. Some things you have to wait longer for."

"Huh." She nods, all serious, like what I've just said makes all the sense in the world. I have no idea if it does or it doesn't.

I glare at the tall kid. "You, boy, what's your name?"

"Chris Cooper, sir."

Something flickers in the dark part of my mind. "Cooper." I sigh and the thought slides away. "We need water."

"Yes, sir." He shuffles off happily enough, and I shoot the girl a wink.

"Today, young lady, we are going to capture the light. Are you ready?"

Mia followed the old guy's brush strokes and hoped nobody would notice how bad her hands were shaking. Because this? This was the most freaking amazing thing she'd ever done in her whole life. And not that she wanted to boast or anything, but she was good. She'd no idea how easy it would be until she started doing it.

"Yes." He stood back and nodded his head a bit, scrutinizing what she'd accomplished so far. The idea of painting Wyldewood came unexpectedly, but she could easily envision the early morning sun shooting off the long glass windows.

He knew the curve of the driveway, painted bushes and trees the way Mia imagined they'd looked before there were ladders and trucks and crap all over the front yard. It was too hot in the room, the heat turned up high for the old folks, and she longed to take off her sweater. But she couldn't, so she suffered through and hoped they'd take a break soon. Drawing and painting usually took her mind off things, steadied her and gave life a little hope. Today her arms were itchy. She was nervous, afraid somebody would say something, call her out for the fraud she was, say maybe she wasn't good at all.

"You have it, you know," he said quietly.

Mia met his eyes, and something about the way he looked at her made her want to cry. Stupid. She put her brush down and scratched her arm. "Thanks." That was dumb, but she couldn't think of anything else to say.

"Gotta use the can." Mr. Carlisle sauntered off, and Mia watched him go with a grin. She began tidying up their workspace, conscious of Chris Cooper making his way across the room. He stopped in front of the easel and gave a low whistle.

"That's so good."

Mia shrugged and swirled a paintbrush in a small jar of turpentine. "He did most of it."

"No he didn't. I was watching." Chris smiled when she turned to face him. What was his deal anyway? "So I was wondering. Would you maybe want to go out sometime?"

"With you?" She blinked and tried to ignore the way her heart picked up.

He made a show of looking around them and grinned. "Well, yeah."

"Oh." Great. Now what? "I don't date." That would do it.

"You don't like guys?"

She rolled her eyes. "I like guys fine. I just don't trust them."

"Aha." He grinned as though he'd discovered the answer to a great mystery.

"What 'aha'? It's true."

"Well, then I'm sorry to hear it." He shook his head. "Do you drink coffee? Soda?"

"No." She pulled off the paint-splatted apron she'd put on earlier and scrunched it between her hands.

"Ice cream?" He raised a brow. "Everybody likes ice cream."

Well, she couldn't argue with that. "I guess."

"Great! So how about we hit up The Juice Bar after school?"

"Can't. I work at the gallery in town after school, every day." Didn't get paid a dime for it though. Slave labor.

"Shoot, I forgot. That's the place Lynette has her paintings. Are you going to show your work there too?" He sounded interested and she scowled, wishing Mr. Carlisle would come back.

"Am I what?" Mia stared and forced a smile. "No."

"You totally should. You'd probably give Lynnie a run for the money." He tipped his head toward the painting they'd done that day. Mia watched late afternoon light dance in his eyes and felt something shift. He was definitely cute. And nice. But that didn't mean she'd be spending any time with him.

"Who's giving me a run for the money?"

Mia jumped at the sound of Lynette Carlisle's voice, and Chris laughed. Her smile squeezed Mia's heart a little tighter. Liz was right behind her, not looking nearly as happy.

Lynette stopped short at the easel, stepped back a little, then looked at Mia. "Did my Dad do that?"

Mia nodded, but Chris cleared his throat. "Actually, Mia did most of it. It's really good, right?"

"It is." Lynette nodded. "You're very talented, Mia. Isn't she, Liz?"

"Hmm?" Liz looked distracted as she flashed a tight smile. "Sure. Yes, it's great."

A blush warmed her cheeks, and Mia floundered for something to say. Her uncle was on the opposite side of the room, his back to them. She caught Liz scanning the room and noticed the way she looked back at them in a hurry when she realized Mia was watching her.

"Where is my dad anyway?" Liz asked.

"He went to the bathroom."

And on cue, Mr. Carlisle magically appeared in the doorway and strode toward them. She silently thanked him for the intervention. She didn't know what to say in front of Lynette. Liz's sister was nice enough, but Mia found herself in awe of her talent, embarrassed that Lynette would give her any praise at all.

"Oh, look at that masterpiece!" Mr. Carlisle declared. "Who did that?"

Laughter snuck out of her, unexpected and definitely unwanted. Lynette and Chris laughed too, and Lynette kissed her father's bristly cheek.

"Hi, Daddy."

He startled a little and looked at her in silence. "Hello. Are you with this bunch?"

"Dad, it's us," Liz interjected. "Lynette and Liz. Your daughters."

"Whatever you say." Mr. Carlisle stepped away from them and studied the painting again. "Yes. That looks just about right."

Hurt flared in Lynette's eyes, but she quickly blinked it away. "Did you have a nice time today?"

"I suppose so." He swung his gaze to Mia. "Did we have a nice time?"

"It was great." Mia nodded and tried to dislodge the disturbing rock in her throat. The other kids were starting to pack up, and Uncle Matt told everyone it was time to go. He indicated to her to wrap it up. "Well, we need to get going."

"Nice to see you again, Mia. You know, if you ever want to come over to the house, you're welcome to use the art studio. It's practically the only room they're not smashing to bits." Lynette laughed, and Liz looked like she'd swallowed a lemon.

"You can thank me for that." Liz sounded annoyed. "I had to beg the architects to work around it. I was actually going to suggest the same, Mia. I'll see what you're up to next time I'm heading over to Wyldewood, shall I?"

"Uh, sure." Mia shrugged, raising a brow when Chris caught her eye. Seemed like Liz didn't care for her younger sister all that much.

Lynette touched her shoulder and smiled. "You guys better go. Looks like everyone's heading out. Nice to see you again." She turned her attention to her father. "Okay, Dad, shall we head back to your room for a bit? It'll be dinner time soon, but I brought some pictures to show you. Remember I said I would?"

"Of course I don't remember."

Mia bit her lip to stop a grin, and started putting paints in the box Chris held. Mr. Carlisle tapped her head, and she almost dropped them all. "You come back soon, young lady. That's an order."

"Yes, sir." Mia watched him go, sorry for Lynette. He clearly didn't know who she was today. But at least she had a dad.

"I suppose I'll go with them." Liz sighed and shook her head. "Not that I'm needed any longer." She marched off and Mia glanced at Chris.

"Is she always that fun to be around?" he asked.

"Liz is all right once you get to know her, really." For some weird reason, she felt like she needed to defend her. Maybe she'd inhaled too much turpentine. "What are you grinning at?" Chris was looking at her in a goofy way that made her want to punch him.

"Nothing. You just look happy."

"So? Is that not allowed?" What the heck was he talking about?

"Oh, it's very much allowed." His grin widened as he hoisted the box to one shoulder and flicked his hair out of one eye. "And just so you know, I will ask you out again. I don't give up that easily." He started to walk away, and Mia gave a loud sigh.

"Chris?"

"Ye-ah?" He made a slow turn, hope in his eyes.

Mia put a hand on her hip and pressed her lips together. "I don't give in that easily. Just so you know."

His resounding chuckle bounced off the walls and sang to her heart long after he'd left the room. Mia gathered up her things, ignored her uncle's questioning look, ignored the other girls' glares and whispered words behind hands, and ignored the longing to chase Chris Cooper down and say yes. Yes, she'd go out. Yes, to ice cream. Yes to being with someone who didn't make her afraid all the time.

But what was the point? He'd find out who she really was sooner or later and kick her to the curb with the rest of the garbage. Right where she belonged.

twenty-four

Matthew cleaned the kitchen that Saturday morning with only the radio for company. His parents had gone off for the weekend. He grinned, remembering the blush in Mom's cheeks this morning when they'd told him they were heading to The Wauwinet. He was happy for them. Somebody around here should be having some fun. Because in a minute, he was going to have to walk upstairs and have a conversation with his niece that would be about as far from fun as a funeral.

He finished the lukewarm coffee he'd poured earlier, took one last glance around the sparkling kitchen, opened the window a crack, then made his way upstairs. He stopped outside Mia's bedroom. No loud music, but he heard her talking. That was odd. She didn't spend a lot of time on her cell phone. Didn't have many friends, at least not ones she was too eager to hang out with. There were a couple girls from her class that she'd talked about, but she pretty much kept to herself.

"Mia?" Matt knocked and waited until she yelled for him to come in. He didn't do the usual head around the door first thing, because he'd probably chicken out and put this off. Instead, he stepped into her room like he meant business.

Mia sat cross-legged on her bed, holding her phone to her ear. "What?"

"Need to talk." He pushed his hands into the pockets of his jeans and rocked back on the balls of his feet.

"I gotta go," Mia said to whoever was on the other end of the call. "See ya tomorrow."

She clicked off and put the phone down. A smile slid across her mouth, but she covered it quickly.

Matt raised a brow. "Who was that?"

"None of your business."

"Ah. The Cooper kid."

Her face turned three different shades of red. "I said none of your business."

He grinned, swallowed rising emotion, and lowered himself onto the edge of her bed. "Is he a good kid?"

"How would I know? I guess so." She shrugged and stretched over her legs.

"Well, you're a pretty good judge of character, and you don't let too many people get close, so I'm going to go with your instincts on this one."

"We're just friends, Uncle Matt."

"Good." He smiled. "I'm glad you have a friend."

"Me too." She fiddled with her phone. "Which is kinda weird. Because I never thought I wanted one. But . . . I don't know. I guess it's better than talking to Liz all the time, huh?"

"I guess." Interesting. "You talk to her a lot?"

"More than I thought I would, that's for sure. She's actually pretty cool, don't you think?"

"Sure." He'd leave it at that. "So it's okay then, having her next door?"

"It's cool. I text her when you're at work sometimes. Sometimes I go over. You said I should bug her instead of your folks, right?"

"Right. Well. That's good." No way was he going to get baited into discussing Elizabeth right now.

"What's up with her and her sister though?" Mia narrowed her eyes. "I mean, she gets all weird around her. Like the other day at Wyldewood when we walked in on them fighting, and at the old folks' home last week. Like she's jealous of her or something? I don't know why. Lynette seems nice, but . . ." Mia shrugged. "It's dumb, right?"

"I suppose sometimes siblings don't always get along. Your mom and I have had our share of disagreements."

"But my mom's also a junkie, which probably has something to do with that." She scanned her phone and put it down again. "Whatever. I'm glad Liz is there when you're working." She snorted and shot him a grin. "Never thought I'd say that."

Matt smiled. His decision was easy, seeing her so much happier. "About that. Me working nights. I've been thinking. I might quit that job."

Mia squished back against her many multi-colored pillows and scrunched her nose. "Why? I thought you needed the money."

"Well." He pressed a hand to the back of his neck. This wasn't meant to be part of the conversation. "Um, so my mom's parents, your great-grandparents?"

"The ones that lived here?"

"Yeah. So. My grandfather's family was well-off. So he had a lot of money. They set up trust funds for your mom and I when we were little, and . . ."

"Trust funds? Like, you're loaded?" Mia's eyes shone with new revelation.

"I don't know. I never touched it."

"Why not? Are you crazy? Oh, wait . . ."

"Shut it." He chucked a stray cushion at her. "I just wasn't into all that. The money, the status, being a trust fund kid. My parents tried to talk me into using the money for college or for traveling. But I wanted to make my own way."

"Dumb. So now you're gonna take it?"

"May as well." Matt wound his thumbs together. "It would help. I have a loan I need to pay off. And keeping you fed and clothed ain't no walk in the park, right?"

"Right. On account of all those juicy steaks I make you buy for me." She hesitated, her forehead pinching. "So does my mom have one too? This trust fund thing?"

Matt sighed. Okay . . . "She did, but my folks . . . when she started using, after it was clear she was an addict and refusing treatment, they went to court and denied her access."

"Can they do that?"

"They did." He shrugged, not clear on the details. "I think the judge was a friend."

"She would have probably shot it all up her arm anyways."

"I'm sure that's what they were afraid of. Anyway." He ran a finger around the collar of his shirt. "If I take the money, I'm not going to spend it all on a yacht or anything, so don't get any ideas."

She bounced a little on the bed. "You could buy me a car. You know my birthday's coming up. My *sixteenth* birthday." Her grin was infectious, and he couldn't help smiling.

"I guess you should probably get your learner's permit in that case."

"Are you serious?" She narrowed her eyes, that distrust creeping in. He longed for the day when it wouldn't be there.

"I think you can get your learner's, yeah. But I'm not buying you a car. I'll help you out a little when the time comes, but you should earn that on your own."

"How? I don't have that kind of money!"

Her incredulous look was almost too much. He let out a chuckle. "You're babysitting, right? And maybe Mrs. McIntyre will hire you on once you're done working off what you owe her for the garden. How long has it been now?"

"Too long."

"Okay. Well . . . we can talk more about that later." He liked this, just shooting the breeze, without the tension. "So your grandparents decided to abandon us in favor of a romantic getaway this evening."

"Gross." Mia screwed up her nose. "But kinda cool. Where'd they go?"

"The Wauwinet." Matt grinned. "I wondered if you wanted to go out with your lame uncle for pizza tonight? You can ask Cooper to come along if you want. You know, your friend."

A sly look inched into her eyes. "I'll ask my friend if you ask yours."

Dang, she was good. Heat raced up the back of his neck. "I don't know what you're talking about."

"Do too. I see the way you look at Liz when you think nobody's watching. I think you'd like to be more than friends."

Seriously? At this rate he'd never move on to the reason he came in here. "I'm not asking Elizabeth out for pizza."

"Chicken."

He gaped. Well, that was so not true. And all she could say was no. "Nuh-uh. Give me that phone." He scanned her contacts for

Elizabeth's number and punched it in before he lost his nerve. "Hi. No, it's me. Hijacked her phone. So, what are you doing tonight?"

A moment later Matt handed Mia her phone back. "There. Your turn."

She slapped a hand to her forehead. "You know what? I'm helping with the twins tonight! I totally forgot. Oh dear. Well, I guess you and Miss Carlisle have a date, huh?"

Matt stared at his niece in disbelief. "You set me up."

She shrugged and gave her head a toss. "You deserved it. And lighten up. You might even have fun."

"You're something else, you know that?"

"Yup. And so are you."

Oh, man. Matt sighed and studied the floor a moment. Time to get on with it. He steadied his breathing, looked back at Mia. She stared back at him through questioning eyes. "I need to ask you something, but I don't want you to freak out. I want you to be honest."

The wall went up almost at once. He could see that old defiance creeping in. "I didn't do anything. Whatever anyone is accusing me of."

Hostility laced with a bit of desperation covered her words and pulled his stomach into a knot. "It's nothing like that." He pressed his palms onto his knees, stared at the faded floorboards, then faced her again. "Mia, have you ever . . . um, hurt yourself?"

She inched backward. "What do you mean hurt myself? Like fell down and hit my head or something?"

"No. Not like that. Like . . . intentionally." He sucked in air and said the awful word. "Cutting."

Her eyes widened, just enough to tip him off. "Of course not." Moisture pooled on her lashes, and she swiped a hand across her face. "Why would you ask me something so stupid?"

Matt exhaled and prayed for the right words. "Because I know you've been through a lot, and I just—"

"I said no! You don't believe me?"

"I'm just saying that I want you to know I'm here for you, Mia. You can talk to me. About anything. Even that Cooper kid." He tried out a grin, but she still looked miserable.

"I'm not doing anything," she whispered, lower lip trembling. "I can't even believe you would ask me this." Her eyes didn't meet his.

Ask to see her arms.

The thought jarred him. Because what if . . . No. He couldn't do that. Wouldn't. He knew she wasn't being honest with him. But if he pushed her, she was too unpredictable. She had run away before, back in Boston. He couldn't risk her running now, getting on the ferry and disappearing on the mainland.

"Are you telling me the truth?"

"I swear! You're just like everyone else, aren't you? Nobody believes anything I say. Ever."

"Mia, that's not—"

"Whatever. Just stop. Leave me alone."

"I'm not done." He raked his hands through his hair and waited until she looked up, her glare scathing. "I think it might be a good idea for you to talk to someone, about your feelings. About everything you went through with your mom."

"A shrink?" She spat the word at him, anger flashing again. "No freaking way! I'm not crazy!"

"I'm not saying you're crazy." He fisted his hands and swallowed acid. "But you've been through more than most kids your age. I'd like you to see this therapist. I talked to her yesterday, she's real nice. I think it would help. The nightmares aren't going away, Mia . . . come on, when's the last time either of us got a full night's sleep, huh?"

"I'm so sorry to be such a burden to you."

"Yeah, you should be." He tapped her on the knee and smiled, hoping to chase off a bit of her dark mood. "Listen, kid, if you don't know by now, I'm on your side. For better or worse, I'm not going anywhere. And that means I'm going to do everything in my power to make your life the best it can be. If that means dragging you to therapy appointments, I'm down. And I'm not above using you getting your learner's permit as bribery."

"What the—? Oh my gosh, you are such a jerk!" She ground out the words through gritted teeth.

Yeah, he could live with that. "Do we have a deal?" He held out his hand and wondered if anything he'd said had sunk in. Only God knew.

"Not like I have a choice." She smacked his hand away.

"Unless you want to get rides from me and Elizabeth for the foreseeable future. There's always the bus too."

"Okay, fine. But I don't have to like it. And I kind of hate you right now." She reached for her cellphone and fiddled with it.

He stood up. Conversation over.

twenty-five

Liz brushed her hair a final time, applied a little lipstick, and studied her appearance in the mirror. Since the alarm had been installed, she'd been sleeping better. The shadows under her eyes weren't quite so dark. She hadn't woken from a nightmare in a few days. She still didn't feel completely safe, but you couldn't have everything.

Her cell phone sat on the dresser. Lately, her gut churned every time it buzzed. Laurence wasn't quitting. He kept texting, leaving voice mails. Baiting her.

She'd almost ignored the call from earlier, thinking it was him again. Then she saw Mia's number and picked up. Funny how the surly teen had somehow managed to work her way into Liz's life. But they shared common ground, although Mia didn't know it.

Liz understood her fears, her struggles to be liked and accepted, even understood her nightmares. And to her surprise, she'd actually come to care for the girl. Not so long ago, she wouldn't have given her a second glance. Would have written her off as trouble and steered clear. She wouldn't have looked beyond the makeup and the fashion choices and the attitude. Wouldn't have seen the talented young woman hiding beneath it all, just waiting for someone to unlock the chains that held her prisoner.

Liz still had a few chains of her own clanging along behind her.

She pressed her palms down on her dresser and blew out a breath. "What am I doing?" Times like these she missed the dogs. At least she could talk to them without coming off as crazy. What had she been thinking, agreeing to go out for pizza with Matthew? He'd said Mia was going to ask her friend Chris Cooper to come along. But wouldn't that make it a date? A double date?

Is that was this was? Oh, Lordy. And hadn't she just told the man she wasn't about to go out with anyone or get into another relationship? He'd seemed to understand. So maybe this really was only a couple of friends chaperoning the kids and enjoying some pizza together.

She threw on a gray cashmere sweater over her white blouse and skinny jeans. Heels or no heels? Or maybe boots. It was cold enough. A moment later she'd grabbed her purse and jacket and pulled on leather gloves. Liz locked up, took a final deep breath, and walked across the courtyard to the main house. As she was about to head up the back steps, the door opened and Matthew appeared, jangling a set of keys.

"Right on time." He hopped down the steps, looking sharp in a thick navy cable-knit, skinny jeans, and brown Oxfords, a faded leather jacket slung over one arm. "We can take my Jeep, unless you wanted to drive." His smile was a tad too cheery.

"No, I figured you would." Liz stepped back a bit and caught a snatch of woodsy cologne. "Where are the kids?"

"Ah." He gave a half-smile, a feeble laugh tagging behind. "Funny thing."

"Don't even tell me." Liz gripped the strap of her purse.

Matthew held up a hand with a look of chagrin. "She's babysitting. Said she forgot."

Liz stared. Opened her mouth to speak and shut it again. "You'd better be kidding."

"Sorry. No. It's uh . . . just the two of us."

"Or not." Liz turned on her heel and he caught her by the hand.

"See, I figured that'd be your reaction. But listen. You have to eat. So do I. We can go get a pizza together, Elizabeth. I promise not to propose until dessert."

She almost smiled. "This was a total set-up?" Of course it was. And she was no longer having warm and fuzzy thoughts about Mia Stone.

"So it would seem. Sorry about that." He chucked his keys from one hand to the other. "If you're up for it, I could really use the company. It was kind of a rough afternoon."

Liz assessed the unease on his face, the worry lines on his forehead, and the slight hint of hope in his eyes. "I could use the company too." She tossed him a small smile and headed toward his Jeep.

Later that evening, surrounded by amazing aromas, she was pleased she'd agreed. "I can't remember the last time I had pizza." Liz looked at the large pan of cheesy goodness just placed in front of them, wanting to dive right in.

Matthew served her two slices. "No pizza in New York?"

"Oh, of course. Very good pizza. But I never ate it. We usually hit the high-end restaurants. You know, the kind where food is art and the servings are small and . . ." Liz smiled at the look on his face. "You have no idea what I'm talking about."

"It's been a few years since I ate in a fancy restaurant." He waggled a brow and took a big bite, mozzarella dripping off the pizza onto his chin. "But this has to be better. Right?"

"Definitely." She enjoyed a few bites in companionable silence. "Did you like living in New York?"

Did she? Good question. "I thought I did. I really enjoyed my job at the beginning. But it was high pressure. The company I worked for dealt with a lot of massively wealthy clients. I was always terrified I'd be the one to make the mistake that would bring the whole place crashing down."

"That's no way to live is it?" His question was gentle, not judging, and garnered a smile.

"I suppose not. I did like the hum of the city though. But now that I'm here, I think there's something to be said for peace and quiet and the sound of the sea. Laurence always called me an island girl."

"Your ex?"

"That would be him." She thought about the cellphone in her purse and wondered how many messages she'd see by the time the night was over.

"Heard from him lately?"

Liz wrestled with telling the truth as he poured more wine into their glasses. "He's been pretty relentless. I haven't talked to him, but the thing is . . . he's got something of mine I want back." Her head screamed at her to stop. "I mean, money I invested with him. I'd like to get that cash back. It's a significant amount."

"That won't be easy. Can you go to court?"

She shook her head. "It sounds simple enough, but no. Trust me, he's not a man you want to cross."

"I'm sorry." His sincere words wrapped around her and made her feel a little better.

"I'll figure it out." The cozy restaurant was half empty. Most were this time of year. Her mother always bemoaned the winter. Too boring; all the fun people were back on the mainland. But her father relished it, holing up for hours in his studio, creating his masterpieces.

Mom would leave sometimes. Travel off on her own someplace. Or maybe she wasn't alone. That wasn't out of the question, given what they knew now.

"You okay?" Matthew studied her in concern. "You disappeared for a second there."

Liz pushed off the past and took a sip of the rich cabernet he'd ordered. "I was thinking things are never as they seem. Not really."

He helped himself to the Caesar salad and offered the wooden bowl to her. "How do you mean?"

Liz swallowed sorrow that still came when she thought of the past summer's events. "I always envisioned my parents as the ultimate happy couple, you know? I mean, they had their issues, but they always seemed so content together. Then when I was about twelve, I guess, everything changed."

"They weren't so happy anymore?" His clear gaze made her want to tell him the whole story. So she did. Beginning with her father's slow descent into alcoholism, her mother's untimely death, ending with the revelations last summer had brought.

The wine was finished, the pizza long gone, and the salad bowl scraped clean. And her soul bared. Liz sat back and dabbed her lips with a napkin. "So there you have it. My ideal family wasn't so idyllic after all. Shocked?"

"Not especially." Matthew spun his glass, running a finger around the rim. "I'm not sure any family is perfect, Elizabeth. I'm sorry your mother had an affair though, sorry you found out the way you did."

They had found their mother's diary this past summer, and the revelations it held had changed all of them. But in a way, she realized having to deal with the past had also brought her siblings closer together. "It's strange," she mused. "As jaded as I am, as unhappy as I knew she was in her last years, I never went there. Never thought she would cheat on my father. And I certainly wouldn't have imagined it would be with a man like Anthony Cooper."

"It must have been awful for all of you."

"Yes. Nick. Lynnie especially, blocking it all out for so long. But we have to move on, don't we? No amount of moping will change the past."

"I guess that's true." He released a sigh and shook his head. "Speaking of the Coopers, I think Mia might be interested in being more than friends with the Cooper boy. Nick's cousin. Chris? I'm not sure I'm ready for this part of the parenting package."

Liz laughed at his anxious expression. "I did pick up on that. He tends to hang outside the gallery right around the time Mia heads out. I'm sure he's a good kid. I don't know him personally, of course. But I can talk to Nick if you like. Put out a few feelers."

He widened his eyes. "Only if you can do it on the sly. Mia already hates my guts at the moment. Finding out I was snooping would just seal the deal."

"She does not *hate your guts*, Matthew. She's a teenager with issues. It's not going to be like riding the teacups with her."

"No. More like The Tower of Terror." He ran a hand down his face. "So I talked to her. Today. About the cutting."

Their waiter chose that moment to interrupt, so they ordered coffee, no dessert. Liz sat forward. "What did she say?"

"Denied it. She was pretty hostile, like she couldn't believe I'd even ask such a thing."

"Did you ask to see her arms?"

He sat back with a pained expression. "Thought about it. But I couldn't bring myself to do it."

Liz nodded and took a moment to consider her reply. "But you think she is. I can see it all over your face."

"Yeah. I think she is. But I did get her to agree to see somebody. Well, I kind of bribed her." He chuckled and fell silent as their coffee arrived.

"This I can't wait to hear." Liz stirred sweetener into her coffee and passed on the cream.

"I told her she could get her learner's if she agreed to see a therapist." He tugged at his collar with a grim smile. "It wasn't one of my finer moments."

"Hey, if it worked." Liz shrugged. In her old world, a little bribery now and again got the job done. "I've been thinking about going back to counseling myself. Seems I still have some unresolved issues."

He smiled, no judgment. "Maybe I should sign up too."

They shared a laugh and Liz finished her coffee. "I have to admit, your niece has grown on me. I think she's got a good heart. Once she figures out how to deal with her pain in other ways, I have a feeling she'll be all right."

"She does seem to be resilient, I'll give her that." He paid the bill and stood. "There. That wasn't too painful was it?"

Liz smiled as he helped her on with her jacket. No, it hadn't been painful at all. Now she needed to figure out if that was a problem.

Outside the air was cool but not unbearable. She stopped when they reached his Jeep, the parking-lot illuminated in silver light. "Full moon." She looked up and felt a smile tug at the corners of her mouth, remembering the way her dad and Ryan would drag out the big telescope on nights like these. "Look at all those stars. Did you ever wonder . . ." She shoved her hands in the pockets of her jacket and cut off her words.

"Wonder what?" He leaned against the vehicle and watched her in that quiet way of his that unnerved her slightly. Whether it was the wine or the pizza or pure recklessness, she joined him, pressed her back against the window of the Jeep, so close their shoulders touched.

"How they all got there. The stars. The moon. All the planets."

"Hmm." He shifted slightly and turned toward her. "Always figured God put them there."

"Ah." Liz leaned back and watched the twinkling lights in the sky. "My sister would say the same. She's one of the faithful. So is our brother Ryan. He's a pastor, over in Africa at the moment."

"And you?"

"If you're asking whether I believe in God,"—she turned toward him, her face suddenly warm—"I'd say probably. Part of me does believe in a Creator who made the heavens and the earth. It's comforting to think we're not all here by some random explosion. The other part of me thinks that if there is some higher being responsible for all this, he took the day off a long time ago and never came back."

"That's fair." He shrugged, a sad sort of smile toying with his lips. "Can't say I haven't thought the same over the last year. It's hard sometimes, holding on to faith."

"But you do. Don't you? Why?"

His smile broadened. "I guess I need something to believe in."

Liz nodded. A cold wind came out of nowhere and blew her hair around her face. He raised a hand, as if to push it away from her eyes, then must have thought the better of it, and shoved it in his jacket pocket instead. "Feel like taking a walk on the beach?"

"At night? In November?"

"We have natural light, it's not real cold." Matthew shrugged. "I can't think of a better time."

twenty-six

Matt was kicking himself. Suggesting a moonlit walk on the beach with Elizabeth Carlisle was about the stupidest thing he'd ever done. But here they were, walking in silence with only the crashing waves for company.

"I saw your mom out walking the other morning." She looked over at him. "Still here, huh?"

Matt let go a sigh. "Still here. Could be for a long time. Turns out my dad has retired. In a manner of speaking."

"Really?"

He gave in to impulse and relayed the story. "It infuriates me. He's so smart in so many ways, yet he's clueless when it comes to respecting women."

Elizabeth looked across the dark ocean. "To be honest, I had heard a few things when I was at Harvard."

He clenched his jaw and hoped she wouldn't elaborate. "I'm sorry."

"Don't be." She gave his arm a quick squeeze. "His behavior has nothing to do with you. But perhaps this is his wake up call, you know? Maybe it was what he needed."

"Maybe. Seems to be. He's certainly more pleasant to be around. They both are. And Mia's been spending more time with them, so I guess that's good."

"You see? There's always a silver lining."

Yeah, he guessed there was. "How are the wedding plans going?" He'd put them back on neutral territory.

"They're going." She laughed. "Not sure where, but they're definitely going." She kicked at a piece of driftwood and sent it flying. "I will say that the extra crew David hired is doing a great job. The living room has been rewired and they're laying new floor this week. If I hold my breath and think good thoughts, maybe find a little fairy dust, we might be ready by Christmas."

"What about the kitchen? You'll need that up and running for the wedding won't you?"

"Absolutely. And I don't know if it will be. So there's that." Moonlight accentuated her pained look, and he felt her stress.

"Are you sure there's no other venue?"

"Oh, there are. Believe me, I called around. But Gray insists on having the wedding at Wyldewood. I don't think Tori really cares, but for some reason, my dear brother has gone all sentimental and I can't change his mind."

"Well, let me know if you need an extra hand. I'm pretty good with a paintbrush."

"I bet you are." She laughed. "Do you paint? I mean, like Mia and my dad?"

Matt inhaled salty air. "Not exactly. I used to."

"Sounds like a story."

The interest in her voice turned his head. He stopped walking, lost in memory for a moment. He hadn't realized he was still holding onto it. Still carrying around the pain of that season in his life. "It's a long one. And not terribly pretty."

"You don't need to tell me." She picked up her pace again, and Matt caught up with her.

"It's fine. I mean, it's not a secret or anything. Well, Mia doesn't know, but . . ." He sighed again, events crowding his mind like they happened yesterday. Elizabeth stood still, held his gaze, and offered a small smile.

"Before he was hired at Harvard, my father taught at a college outside of Boston, in the town where I grew up. All through high school, I knew I wanted to be an artist. I was good. Won all kinds of awards. My dad didn't share my enthusiasm for art. Actually, he discouraged me at every turn."

"Why?"

"Who knows. The gist of it was that he didn't think becoming an artist was a worthy calling. We fought all the time. We've never had a great relationship. My mother says it's because we're both too stubborn, and she's probably right. Anyway, I hoped to go to art school when I graduated high school. The Royal Academy of Arts. In London."

"That was a lofty goal. I'm sure there were good schools closer to home."

"Oh, there were. Rhode Island. California. New York. But I wanted London. And my father wanted medical school."

"Medical school?" Confusion narrowed her eyes. "For an artistic student? That seems a stretch."

"Not really." Matt ground the top of his shoe into the sand. "I was one of those geeky kids all the other kids make fun of. Academically gifted. I could have been a doctor or a lawyer or a mathematician if

I'd wanted. But all I wanted to do was draw and paint and capture the world in the way only I could." Okay, he was getting carried away. He shot her an apologetic smile. "But you don't always get what you want."

"What happened?"

"Oh, you know, life." He started walking and she fell into step beside him. "The first big thing was my father announced that he was going to become a Harvard professor. So we were moving. They'd already found our new home, nice and close to the university."

"In your last year of high school?"

"Yup. I think he figured getting me away from the influences at my old school and into a new routine would chase off the crazy. I refused to switch schools and lived with my buddy Pat's family during the week. And I applied to the Academy anyway. I had my mother's ear. And she had her parents' money. She didn't like the thought of London, but she wanted me happy. If I'm honest, I have to wonder if she took my side simply to annoy my father."

"Sounds like my mother." Elizabeth laughed. "Still, it couldn't have been easy."

"No, but I was determined I was getting out. I'd start my real life in London. In the midst of all the letters, application forms, and arguments, my sister started a downward spiral. Hanging with the wrong crowd, drinking, drugs. And then she got pregnant."

"Perfect timing," she said in a soft voice.

Matt clenched his jaw. "Hardly. She was a few months away from her sixteenth birthday. My parents were beyond furious. There were a lot of crazy fights. Scenes I wish I hadn't witnessed. Rachel got the brunt of it, but I tried to stick up for her." He steadied his breathing, trying to put the pieces of the past in the right order. "As it turns out, there's a lot of stuff I didn't know."

"Such as?"

"My parents tried to get Rachel to put the baby up for adoption. They just told me that. They would have sent her away, anywhere she wanted, to get help, start over. She refused all their offers and eventually moved out of the house. I always thought they'd kicked her out. It's what she told me, and I guess I was so angry at them for the way they'd treated her. You'd think having a baby was as good as murder the way they carried on. So. My future was not exactly on their radar that year."

"You never went to London?"

"I never went. I graduated high school and spent most of my spare time helping Rachel with Mia. I worked whatever jobs I could get, went to a community college, and decided if I couldn't become a full-time artist, I'd teach."

"Where was Rachel living if your folks kicked her out?"

"With the O'Donohues." Matt smiled. "Pat's family. They're pretty much saints. Once I was out on my own and making enough to get my own place, Rach and Mia lived with me for a while. It was hard. My sister was a sporadic user, and when she was high I was scared for Mia. She'd quit and go to rehab and be all repentant, but the demon always dug its claws in again."

Elizabeth pushed hair off her face and glanced his way. "What do you think will happen now that she's out?"

He'd been trying not to think about it. Trying to put off talking to Mia again about going to visit her mom. "She has to stay clean right now. She gets tested every week. Honestly, I don't know. I hope she can kick it for good, but time will tell."

"Yes, it will. You know, my brother Gray was an addict. He got help, went to rehab, and so far, he seems to be doing well. There are success stories out there."

Matt wasn't so sure, but had to hope. "We'll see." He made a slow turn, heading them back in the direction of the car. "So, I wanted to ask. Mia's birthday is coming up. In a few weeks actually. Right before Thanksgiving. I'd like to do something for her, but I'm stumped."

"Ah." Elizabeth nodded, her eyes fixed on the path ahead. "Her sixteenth. You can't go overboard; she'd hate that."

"I know. A surprise party is probably out."

"Who does she hang out with at school?"

He should know this. What kind of parent didn't know who his kid's friends were?

But he wasn't a parent.

"Aside from the Cooper kid, I have no clue. There might be one or two girls, but truthfully, I don't know. She never has anyone over. Her teachers say she's kind of a loner."

Elizabeth nodded. "Have you asked her how things are at school? Are those girls still giving her trouble?"

"I asked, and she says everything is fine. That's her standard answer."

"Well." They headed up the walkway toward his Jeep. "I'm a bit preoccupied with wedding planning, but let me think about the birthday a bit. I'll toss some ideas around."

"Thanks." Matt studied her face in the moonlight. It was impossible to deny the attraction he felt for this woman. Impossible to deny that he wanted to protect her. To make her feel safe again. Maybe even loved. "You're a good person, Elizabeth Carlisle."

Her eyes flared a moment, then she laughed and tossed her head, almost shy. It was adorably cute. "I wouldn't go that far. You don't know me that well yet."

"Right. That take-no-prisoners-tough-cookie side you claim you have. I'm not seeing it."

She veered her gaze and he wondered if he'd upset her. Or annoyed her. Then her eyes met his again and they were filled with something new. Something he hadn't seen in them before. "Do you really believe people can change, Matthew?" Her voice caught on the wind, turning the question into a whisper. She shivered and he stepped closer.

"I do. I think if a person really wants a different life, anything's possible. With enough faith."

She gave a half-nod and lowered her head. "I want . . ."

His heart gave an unexpected lurch, and he placed two fingers under her trembling chin, tipping her face toward him. "What do you want, Elizabeth?"

She didn't answer right away. Just stared, silent tears painting fine silver lines over her cheeks. "I want to feel whole again. To feel like I'm worth something. I want to sleep without the lights on. I'm so tired of being afraid all the time."

Matt's eyes stung, every word piercing him. It wasn't fair, this kind of pain. What kind of person could do this? Leave such lasting scars and haunting sorrow? He sighed and slipped his arms around her, pulling her close. She resisted at first, but then she sank against him, her muffled sob getting lost in his jacket. He inhaled salty, damp air and simply held her and waited through the silence.

"I'm sorry." She looked up at last, her sad smile slaying him. "I don't usually fall apart like that. It's just . . . you just . . ."

"It's okay." Somehow his hands found their way to her face, his thumbs brushing tears off her cheeks. "Sometimes you need a good cry, huh?"

"I suppose." She stared back at him, silent a moment. "I want to start trusting again."

He nodded, wanting to kiss her fears away. Wishing it were that simple. But if there was one thing he'd figured out the last few weeks, it was that Elizabeth Carlisle was anything but simple. And he needed to be gentle. And patient. "I know I said it before, but you can trust me."

"I already do." Her smile appeared like a glimpse of sun after a storm. He wondered if she really had any idea how beautiful she was. Or how attracted he was to her.

"Good." Matt dropped his hands and fished for his keys. "Now let's get you home so you can work on that full night's sleep. Have you tried counting goats?"

"Goats?" She laughed as she rounded the vehicle and got in on the passenger side. "Don't you mean sheep?"

"Nah. Sheep are so boring." He started the engine and got them on the road again. "They just stand there and blink and bleat. Goats dance."

"Dance?" Her laughter got a little louder and ran around the Jeep's warm interior. "They do not."

"Oh, they absolutely do. I'll show you sometime."

"How? Do you know any goats?"

"As a matter of fact, I do."

"Well, now you have to introduce me."

He laughed and shot her a side look. "Maybe I will."

They were home before he wanted to be. But he parked the Jeep and walked her to her door, even though she insisted she was fine.

"Thanks for a fun evening." She disarmed the alarm and turned in the doorway. "I'm glad I said yes."

"That makes two of us. I feel much better than I did this afternoon."

"Me too." A smile came and went. She didn't move.

He raised a brow. His heart picked up a little as she closed the gap between them, took hold of his hands and leaned up to graze the side of his cheek with her lips. She pulled back before he could think about responding. "Goodnight, Matthew."

Matt swallowed, smiled, and gently brushed a strand of blond hair behind her ear, his hand brushing her cheek. "Goodnight, Elizabeth." Oh, he didn't have this kind of willpower. Everything in him wanted to pull her against him and kiss her. But it was too soon.

He blew out a breath and shot her a wink. "Go dream of goats."

He could still hear her laughter as he crossed the courtyard and opened the back door.

twenty-seven

MIA
Letters to Dad

Hi Dad,

Uncle Matt knows. About the cutting. Yesterday he flat out asked me if I did. I have no clue why, except I think I dropped a stupid razor blade in the bathroom the last time. He was yelling at me to get downstairs for dinner, and I guess I rushed out, because I couldn't find it later. He must have found it. I'm so mad and scared and mostly just mad. I lied. And I feel even worse about that. He doesn't deserve that. But if I told him the truth?? I have no clue what he'd do. I know I should trust him. I want to trust him. But I don't know if I want to stop. He's out right now, running. He does that a lot. Crazy man. So I cut again. Just a little bit. Hardly any blood. But it made me feel better. And I made sure to clean up.

Oh, Uncle Matt also wants me to see a shrink. Well, therapist, he said. Same thing in my mind. And I don't have a choice, because I want to get my learner's and he said I have to go. So that'll be fun. I don't know what I'm supposed to say if they ask me about it either.

My mom's been calling my cell phone the last few days. I don't know how she got my number. Probably from Uncle Pat. I haven't answered. I don't know if I want to talk to her, you know? I mean, part of me does. Really does. I miss her. She's my mom. And when she's not using, she's awesome. Well, when she wasn't sticking up for that creepo. We had some good times. But so much went on. I don't know. I don't want to talk to her right now. It hurts. I'm scared that I'm going to have to though. That they're gonna make me go visit her. Maybe even go back to live with her.

But in other news, so there's this dude. Chris. He started school here the same time as me. His family moved over because his uncle's dying and his parents are helping out . . . anyway. He's like, well, if you saw him you'd think he was a model for Vineyard Vines or something. Total prep whose family probably has more money than God. Except he's not like the other rich kids I've met. He's actually nice. He listens to me. For some reason he seems to like me. And I kind of like him, but I'd never tell him to his face. I've never had a boyfriend, and I'm not sure I want one. Guys are only out for one thing. But Chris seems like he's for real. I want to trust him. We're hanging out some, but not like dating or anything. It's cool. I know the other girls hate that he's paying me any attention, because they think I'm white trash or something. I don't actually care what they think.

Things with the grandparents are better. They may not be so bad after all. At least they're talking to me like I'm not some alien now. And they're not fighting nearly as much. I think they still hate my mom. She probably gave them good reason. I bet she was a junkie even before she had me. It's a wonder I came out normal. I guess they'd probably know a lot of stuff about my mom that I don't. I wonder if they know you. I don't know what they'd say if I asked. I don't have the nerve yet. And if they told me who you were, well, I don't even know what I'd do with that.

Would you want to know me?

———————

Matt pulled into a parking space outside the gallery on Thursday afternoon and cut the engine. He sank back against the seat with a shuddering yawn. He was a bit early picking Mia up, but he'd come straight from his last class. There was no point in going home first. His cell buzzed from the pocket of his jeans and he fished it out. Scanned the number and grinned. "Hey, dude."

"Matt, my man!" Pat O'Donohue's baritone boomed down the line, followed by the familiar chuckle Matt missed more than he'd admit to. "How're you surviving over there? Winter set in yet?"

"It's coming." Now in the first week of November, the air was definitely cold and snow was in the forecast. "How's everything with you?"

"Oh, the same. School, church, work. Kids are growing like weeds, keeping Kathleen on her toes, you know."

Matt didn't know, but if raising grade schoolers was worse than a high schooler, he'd empathize. "You guys should come for a visit sometime. Mia would love to see you."

"Yeah. Maybe in the summer, huh? When we can beach it. Actually, we were thinking, ya know, you guys could maybe come here. For Thanksgiving."

"Oh." Matt rubbed his jaw and watched an elderly couple cross the street. "Well. My folks are still here. I'm not sure they're heading back to Boston anytime soon. Dad was looking at real estate the other day. I tell you that?"

"No way." Pat gave a long whistle. "And here you thought you'd escape on Nantucket, huh?"

"Tell me about it." Matt laughed. His life was so nuts that laughter was the only response. But having his folks around seemed to be helping. Mia had been doing well. Until their conversation on Saturday, which ended in disaster. She was still ignoring him.

"So listen . . ." Pat's sigh made Matt sit up a bit. "I was hoping you'd think about Thanksgiving, because Rachel . . . well, she really wants to see Mia. I told her I'd talk to you."

Matt stifled the word he wanted to say and bit his lip. "I told you the last time we talked, Mia's not ready. I won't force her."

"You don't have a choice, man. She's talked to the social worker. Her parole officer. They're all on her side. She's talking about getting a court order if you keep refusing. No clue whether she can, but . . ."

"All right, all right." Matt shut his eyes and battled nausea. Why now? He fought the urge to start the car and drive away, call and ask if Liz could give Mia a ride. "I'll talk to Mia."

"I can do it if you want."

"No. You've done enough." Matt regretted the sharp words at once. "Look, I know you're just trying to help. But Mia . . . she's doing good now, you know?"

"So is Rachel. Which you'd see for yourself if you came over once in a while. She just wants to see her daughter. It's the right thing to do."

"Is it?" Matt clenched his fingers around the steering wheel. He'd thought he had a blind spot when it came to his sister, but Pat was worse. He'd been surprised when Rachel had run off with Giovanni, because he'd always figured she and Pat would end up together somehow, but Pat met Kathleen soon after Rach left and the rest was history.

"So you'll come?" Pat was always too pushy for his own good.

"I said I'll talk to her. That's all I can say for now." Matt stared in his rearview mirror as Chris Cooper's gangly figure came into view. He watched the kid peer through the window of the gallery, wave, then disappear through the door. Huh.

"Matt, are you still there?"

"Still here." He craned his neck to see through the gallery window, but there was a painting in the way. The door opened again and Mia came out, Cooper following. They headed up the street, away from him. "I gotta go, Pat." He clicked off and jumped out of the Jeep. "Hey!" He hollered at them, but they either didn't hear or ignored his yell. Matt jogged up the sidewalk and yelled again. This time the kids stopped and turned around.

"What?" Mia put her hands on her hips, staring at him like he had two heads.

Matt walked up to them, a little out of breath. "Where are you going? I'm here to pick you up."

"Why?" Mia's look grew more intense. Her hair was longer, and the pink streaks had disappeared sometime on Sunday, replaced by a softer brown color he quite liked. She'd toned down the makeup, and her chunky boots had disappeared a few weeks back, replaced by sneakers mostly, sometimes black flats if Evy had her working up front in the gallery.

The Cooper kid had been coming around lately, a few nights a week, for 'homework'. Matt made them sit in the kitchen, much to Mia's chagrin, but he had the backing of his parents on that one, and she didn't get far with her arguments.

"Um, Mia. Doctor's appointment?" If this was her attempt at getting out of seeing the therapist, she had another thing coming.

Mia sighed. "On Friday. Today is Thursday."

And that would be correct. "Huh." He pulled up the zip of his leather jacket and found a smile. "I guess it is."

Mia tipped her head slightly to study him. "Are you okay, Uncle Matt?"

"I'm fine." He made a quick recovery and cleared his throat. "Where are you headed?"

"Just going to The Juice Bar, sir." Cooper stepped forward with a reassuring smile. "I'll drop her home in time for dinner, if that's okay?"

Matt's brain suddenly turned to scrambled eggs. "You're driving?" Did he know that? How old was this boy? Should he ask to see the kid's license? "Can I see your license?"

"Uncle Matt!" Mia glared.

He raised his hands with a grin as the kid was already fishing for his wallet. "Kidding." But, not. He gave his head a shake. "Okay, don't be too late. I need to talk to you tonight."

"What now?" Mia narrowed her eyes and shifted the strap of her backpack to her left shoulder. The plaid scarf around her neck blew in the breeze. That old distrust flared again and hit him in the gut.

"Nothing. It can wait." He shoved his hands in his pockets and nodded. "Go. Have fun."

Mia turned too fast and walked off. She probably thought he was going to interrogate her again. But he'd followed through after their discussion on Saturday. When he picked her up, tomorrow, Friday, they were heading to the therapist's office for her first appointment. Crap, he hoped it wouldn't blow up in his face.

He kicked at a few stray leaves and walked back to his Jeep. Wondered if it might snow tonight as predicted. The first snowfall was always the best. Matt hesitated with a backward glance toward the gallery. He hadn't talked to Elizabeth since Saturday night. He should at least go in and say hi.

She'd shocked the heck out of him with that peck on the cheek. What was that about? She didn't seem the overly affectionate type, and it had come out of left field. Not that he was complaining but . . . had it been her way of saying she'd be open to being more than friends? Or had it simply been a friendly gesture, a hey, thanks, I had a nice time? Matt sighed and shook his head. Women. This was exactly why he steered clear of long-term relationships. But Elizabeth Carlisle had somehow opened the door to his heart and practically moved in the minute he'd met her. And he wasn't sure what to do about it.

A man stood in front of the gallery window, staring at a painting. Well dressed, a black wool coat, unbuttoned, over a gray suit. When Matt looked closer, it seemed more like the guy was staring beyond the painting. Staring at the desk where Elizabeth stood talking to a female customer.

Staring at Elizabeth.

Matt stepped closer. "Intriguing scene, isn't it?"

The stranger made a slow pivot, settling a steely gaze on Matt. Something in the guy's guarded expression immediately put him on edge.

"It's one of Lynette Carlisle's, isn't it? Are you a fan?" He spoke with a slightly British accent.

Matt nodded, carefully shifting his gaze to where Elizabeth was still talking. "Miss Carlisle is very talented. But I can't afford her prices."

The man smiled and ran a hand over short blond hair. "Quite. Do you know the family?"

"Not really." Matt registered the niggling feeling that was sending red flags up in every direction.

"She has a sister, doesn't she? Older. Lives here on the island?"

"Couldn't tell ya." Matt shrugged, a knot twisting in his stomach. "Are you going in?" He motioned toward the door and the man back-pedaled.

"Not today. Good evening." He turned on the heel of smart black loafers and walked away, whistling an eerie tune that sent a shiver up Matt's spine. He yanked the door open and stepped inside the warm gallery.

twenty-eight

The last customer was on the way out and Elizabeth motioned for him to flip the sign on the door to closed. He did so. And turned the lock before he had second thoughts.

"Why did you lock the door?" She pushed papers together and put them away in a drawer.

"Habit, I guess." He shrugged it off and tried to appear nonchalant. "Evy here?"

"Nope, she already left. So did Mia. It's just me."

Matt tried to quell the hammering of his heart. Tried not to think about the scenario that might have taken place if he hadn't been outside. "Yeah, I saw Mia. I got my days mixed up and came to pick her up."

"I wondered why you were here." She pulled on her jacket and leveled her gaze.

Should he share his suspicions with her? He had to. If it were true . . . "Um, so there was a guy outside a minute ago." He tugged his jaw. She was busy closing down the computer and locking drawers on the desk.

"Anyone you know?" She slung her purse over her shoulder and scanned the room. "I'm going to organize a patron's night. Did I tell you that?"

"No, I don't think so." Matt tried to smile, because the excitement in her eyes required it.

"I talked to Evy today. She thinks it's a fantastic idea. Says she hasn't done one in a while. We'll have a special showing of our best artists, have them here to mingle with the clients, wine and cheese, perhaps a string quartet for background music or soft jazz. Which do you think?" She walked to the door, keys jangling.

"Don't know." He stepped around her to get to the door first, unlocked it, and pushed it open, scanning the street.

"Matthew?" Elizabeth stepped outside and pulled the zip on her jacket.

"What?"

"I asked what you're looking for. You're acting weird."

"Sorry." He watched his breath curl in the cold night air. The temperature had dropped since the weekend. He could be totally off base. The guy could have been anyone. He didn't want to freak her out for no reason. "You, um, want to get a bite to eat?"

She pulled on gloves and shook her head. "I'd love to, but I'm going over to Wyldewood to check on the progress and join the family for dinner." A frown crossed her face. "Apparently there's been a hold up with the electrical work. At this rate, I'm having serious doubts about the viability of a New Year's Eve wedding. You're welcome to tag along if you like. I'm sure there will be plenty of food. Oh, and I had a thought about Mia's birthday I wanted to tell you about."

"Okay. Sounds like a plan." He grinned and tabled his worrying thoughts for now. "I'll follow you."

———————

Liz finished her last bite of chicken and watched Matthew from across the noisy kitchen table. Lynette was over at Nick's. David and Josslyn were coaxing the twins to finish their food and the two little scamps were not having it. Trying to have adult conversation amidst the din was nearly impossible. Not that Matthew had much to say. He'd been distracted from the moment he'd stepped into the gallery, and she didn't have the slightest idea why. Except . . .

Perhaps it had been a mistake giving into impulse on Saturday night. She wasn't sure why she'd done that. Kissed him on the cheek. Didn't know what had possessed her. And she couldn't exactly take it back now.

He helped her clear and put the dishes in the dishwasher while the twins were taken upstairs. Once the kitchen was clean, she made coffee. "Come on, I want to walk through the house. See how far they've gotten."

Matthew took his mug and followed as she went through the back door of the new addition, through the large new laundry room, and into what would be Wyldewood's new kitchen.

"Hey, this looks great." He spun around with an appreciative smile. Liz nodded. It did. The new appliances were all out of their boxes, ready to be installed. The big butcher block working space in the middle of the room was impressive, and a new long window looked out over the ocean.

"David thinks we'll manage with a chef and one or two helpers in the kitchen. Then we'll need wait-staff, two at least. I suppose we'll see how things go once we open." She crossed the room to the new sinks and turned the tap. Water splashed out and made her smile. "Ah. Running water. That's encouraging."

They wandered through into another spacious room. "And this is the dining room," she told him. It was a wide, bright room, with windows running across the length of the room, allowing guests an ocean view while they ate. A new patio, still under construction, would give the option of al fresco dining during the summer months. "Well, the floors are done at least. And those beams look good. Sconces are up." They'd chosen simple Colonial double brass candles, in keeping with the original look of the house. The walls had been painted a light beige, the hardwood newly buffed and varnished. She glanced upward to the wooden beams that stretched across the ceiling. "But no overhead lights yet."

Matthew took a slow walk around the darkened room. "How many tables do you aim to put in here?"

"We'll need at least ten. Round. David's got a few selected, we just need to decide what we want to go with and place the order. And chairs too."

"Is this where you're planning to have the wedding reception?"

Liz felt the knot in her stomach tighten. She'd have Gray to thank when she ended up in the hospital with an ulcer. "That's the plan."

"If they don't get the lights up in time, you can string lighting across the beams." He pointed upward with a sweeping motion. "Like Christmas lights or small round bulbs?"

"Yes, I was thinking that too." A crash came from somewhere in the house and Liz jumped. He was beside her in an instant. Almost shielding her from whatever harm he imagined coming their way.

"It was probably just a shutter banging." She tried to laugh, but the look on his face was worrisome. "Okay, what is up with you? You've been acting strangely since you came into the gallery this afternoon."

He did that thing where he pushed his fingers through his hair. Probably a nervous habit, but it was an attractive one. And the smile that followed intensified the butterflies already flying around her stomach. "Have I?"

"Yes. You have. Any particular reason?"

Matthew cleared his throat and gave a shrug. He moved away from her to the door on the other side of the room that led to the living room. "This looks nice."

Evading the question. He was good at that. Liz swallowed frustration and followed after him. "Oh." It did indeed. Two new leather couches were positioned in front of the large fireplace. Lounge chairs sat by the windows for reading or relaxing. The old faded rugs were gone, new colorful creations in their place. No curtains yet. The rods were up on two windows, the rest piled in one corner of the room. Her eyes settled on the spot to the left of the fireplace where their old tattered sofa had sat.

"Come on, Elizabeth. Get your nose out of that book and join us!" A flash of memory startled her.

Mom sat on the sofa, surrounded by all of them, reading from the tattered book of fairy tales they'd all loved so much at various stages of their lives. Even as they got older, story time was something they still enjoyed, mostly because of the funny voices Mom made. Sometimes if the mood struck him, Dad would join in, and the show would become even more theatrical. Lynnie, still small enough to sit on Mom's lap, Gray and Ryan on either side of her, and David sprawled on the floor with a book of his own, pretending not to listen. Liz preferred to perch on the window seat, away from them. She was halfway through Gone with the Wind, *determined to finish this week. She shook her head and went back to her reading.*

"Well, suit yourself," Mom sighed. "But remember, you might miss out on a whole lot of life if you insist on seeing it from the sidelines."

Suddenly Liz needed to sit.

"You all right?" Matthew lowered himself beside her.

"I was just remembering what it was like before. When we were kids. My mother used to read to all of us in here." Unwanted tears burned. "It's all so different. It just hit me all of a sudden." She sniffed and shot him a sheepish smile. "How is it possible to miss someone who's been gone so long?" The old grandfather clock at the far side of the room ticked out time in a tune she could sing in her sleep.

Matthew nodded and rubbed her back in gentle circular motion. "I'm not sure there's a right answer to that. I think we always miss the ones we love, no matter how long it's been."

"I suppose so." She felt the pang of loneliness pinch a forgotten longing in her soul. "Sometimes I wish I'd done things differently. Been more a part of the family. I was always off doing my own thing. Thinking I didn't need them. And I can't get that time back."

"No. But you can make the most of what you have now. Can't you?"

Liz met his eyes, grateful for his perspective. "You're right." She laughed. "Though if I change too much, my siblings might wonder what I'm smoking."

His low chuckle warmed her, but the wariness in his eyes remained. "I should ask you something. But I don't want to scare you."

"Scare me? You just did." She sat back a little, her heart picking up speed. "Is this about that stupid peck on the cheek the other night? Because I have no idea why I did that, and honestly, if you thought I—"

"Elizabeth." He slipped his hands around the side of her face, his expression too serious. "It's not that."

"Then what?"

He rested his forehead against hers a moment. Being so close, feeling the warmth of his touch, his lips mere inches from hers . . . all she had to do was lean in a little. Meet his lips with hers. If she dared.

New feelings unfurled like a budding rose, opening to the sun after hiding from a summer storm. Her hands moved of their own accord, sliding up the softness of his wool sweater, tentatively brushing over his face, her fingers finding their way into his thick hair.

"Eliza—"

"Just . . . kiss me." She cut off his groan with her mouth, waiting, hoping he would respond even as his lips made contact with hers. Gently at first, as though afraid she'd pull back in realization of this colossal mistake, and when she didn't, he pulled her closer, ran his hands over her hair, and kissed her with more passion than she'd expected from this quiet man who'd somehow managed to turn her life inside out in such a short space of time.

At last, he loosened his embrace and leaned back a little, his breathing heavy, eyes bright. Liz steadied her own ragged breathing in a shaky smile. Unspoken words sat between them. The corners of his mouth turned upward as he ran the back of his hand down her face.

"I wasn't expecting that." His voice trembled ever so slightly.

"Should I apologize?"

"No. Of course not." His smile faltered. "Unless you're having second thoughts."

She rolled her eyes. "No."

A low rumble came from his chest. "You are full of surprises, Elizabeth."

"Well." She sat back against the couch, her hand in his, their fingers intertwined. "Of course, now I'll have to figure out exactly why I did it." She started up at the ceiling with a happy smile. "Though at the moment I can't say I care."

He leaned back and laughed, bringing her fingers to his lips. "Is this going to be a one-off thing or do we get to do it again sometime?"

"I don't know." She turned her head to meet his shining eyes. "I haven't decided yet." A small part of her was cowering in the corner, telling her she'd just opened Pandora's box. Because she'd let him in. Let him see inside her soul. After she'd vowed never to let anyone get that close again.

"You're thinking." He ran a finger down her nose and she shivered.

"I am." Moisture wet her lashes, but she smiled anyway. "I'm not sure I should share my thoughts though."

"Mmm." He wrapped an arm around her and she leaned against him, hearing his heart steady against his chest, reminding her that this was safe. He wasn't going to hurt her. "You're thinking you can't handle this. Being with someone who doesn't want a thing from you. Who only wants to see you smile, know that you're happy and that you feel safe. And you're not completely sure I could be that person. And you're also not sure you deserve that kind of good."

Liz bit her lip and placed a hand on his chest. For a long moment, she didn't move. Stayed in that moment where the world stood still, nightmares didn't exist, and all the past mistakes she'd ever made disintegrated like dust. "I don't know if I do."

He brushed her hair back and placed a kiss on her temple. "Will you let me convince you otherwise?"

"I think if anyone can, it might be you." She closed her eyes as he brushed tears off her face, leaned in and claimed her mouth in a sweet kiss that made no demands, only offered hope, and perhaps, if she'd allow it, a chance to heal. "I'm terrified of this," she admitted on a half-laugh.

"I know you are." Matthew sat up and pulled her with him, taking her hands in his. "The truth? I've been attracted to you from the moment we met. But I didn't want to push you. I knew you weren't ready. So you call the shots here. If you want to explore the idea of a relationship, I'm all for it. If you need more time, that's fine too. I'll wait."

"What if I'm never ready?"

His sad expression tugged at her heart. "That would be my great loss."

She sniffed back tears and studied the serious face staring back at her. "Are you actually this nice all the time?"

"Nah." He nuzzled her nose and gave a chuckle. "Not at six in the morning. And I turn into a bit of a bear after midnight."

"Ah. Then the night shift must be loads of fun for you."

"Right. Well, actually, I quit."

"You did?" This was new. "Why?"

He got to his feet with a low groan. "Long story. I will tell you, but . . . we should probably get back before they come looking for us, huh?"

She couldn't help laughing at his worried look. "Believe me, they're all wrapped up in bath and bedtime stories. It takes forever to put those two down for the night. And I want to tell you my ideas. For Mia's birthday."

"Okay, Miss Carlisle." Matthew bowed toward the door. "Walk me out and talk on the way. And then, if you're done here, I'll escort you home."

He drove behind her all the way back from Wyldewood, constantly checking his rearview, convinced every car was following them. But when she made the turn into their driveway, none of the other cars slowed or stopped. They all kept driving.

Matt parked, still debating whether to share his strange encounter that afternoon. He watched her exit her vehicle, her smile visible even from here, and his heart clenched. Why chase that off?

She deserved a good night's sleep without worrying about her ex lurking in the bushes. Matt would worry about that for her.

She didn't approach him as he stepped onto the driveway. Just skipped up her steps, unlocked the door, and he heard her disarming the system as she stepped inside. Then she appeared again and gave a wave.

He tipped his head with a smile.

She tossed him a smile in return and disappeared. He heard the click of the locks and the faint beeping of the alarm being set. Slowly he let out his breath and glanced around the darkened driveway. Yes, they definitely needed a dog.

It was a little after ten when he moved through the kitchen, not sure if anyone would be awake. As he passed the living room he saw his parents, still up, playing a game of Scrabble at the gaming table.

"Hey." He wandered into the room, exhaustion hitting hard.

"How was your dinner?" Mom smiled brightly as he sank onto the couch.

"It was good." He smothered a yawn. "What'd you guys have?"

Dad stretched his arms and turned his head this way and that, joints cracking. "Your mother made coq au vin. And it was exceptional."

"Exceptional." Matt whistled and smiled at his mother's blush. "Way to go, Ma. Mia got home, right?"

"She did." His mother took off her reading glass and nodded. "Her nice friend joined us for dinner."

"Oh, really?" Matt sat up a bit. "Sorry I missed that."

Mom waved a hand. "Not to worry. I'm sure there will be another opportunity. Such a lovely boy. How was Elizabeth?"

He felt the back of his neck heat, sat up and leaned over his knees. "Fine." Dad's chuckle made him look up in a hurry. "What?"

"Nothing. I just remember you doing that a lot whenever you had a new girl you were interested in."

"Doing what?" Matt frowned. And since when had his father ever paid that much attention?

"That." Dad pointed. "You'd lean over your knees and let out that sigh that sits somewhere between frustration and elation."

"Gimme me a break." Matt grinned just the same.

"Oh, I remember that too!" Mom nodded. "Matthew, are you and Elizabeth . . ."

"NO. Drop it." He did his best to look annoyed, and his parents shared a smile. "Now look, Mia's birthday is just around the corner and I've got an idea. But I'm going to need your help. Are you interested?"

twenty-nine

Liz ate a quick breakfast and got ready for work. How did it get to be Friday already? Before going to bed last night, she'd made a long list of all the potential guests she'd invite to the gallery event. She hoped Evy would have time today to sit down and make a firm plan with her. They could put a date on the calendar and start looking at invitations. Speaking of invitations, she needed to make sure Gray and Victoria had sent theirs out like she'd told them to. To wait another week was cutting it too close.

Well, she supposed it was a good thing she had so many things going on. She needed the distraction. Because she was no longer obsessing over Laurence. She was thinking about Matthew Stone. And that amazing kiss.

The memory warmed her face, and she banished the thought. She'd definitely allowed herself to get carried away. Got caught up in memories of the past, felt vulnerable, and he'd been comforting and . . . oh, who was she kidding? She was attracted to him, plain and simple. But that didn't mean it was wise to jump into a relationship with him. Tempting, yes. Wise, no.

And she definitely wouldn't be jumping into bed with him. That part of her life was one she was trying to forget. She lived with regret, but wouldn't be making that mistake again. Still, the more she learned about Matthew, the safer she felt around him. Weird as it was, she didn't think he held any expectations when it came to what he wanted from their relationship. She thought . . . that all he wanted was to see her happy. And that was almost unbelievable.

She pulled on her coat and gloves, checked her bag one more time, made sure she hadn't forgotten her laptop or phone, and headed out the door.

And speak of the devil.

Matthew leaned against his Jeep dressed in dark jeans and a baggy sweater, his hair rumpled and his jaw sporting stubble. He sipped from a large Red Sox mug and nodded as she headed his way. "Morning, Elizabeth."

"Matthew. Aren't you going to be late for work? You're usually long gone by now."

"No classes today, so I decided not to go in. How'd you sleep?"

"Actually, quite well." She glanced at the gray sky and shivered. Snow was forecast for the weekend. "You look like you could use a few more hours."

"Yeah. Well, Mia was up a couple times last night. I think she's worried about the doctor's appointment this afternoon."

Liz nodded. She'd almost forgotten. "Will you let me know how that goes? I really should get going. I have to open this morning. Evy's coming in later."

"Sure." He drained his mug and moved to set it on the window ledge of the garage behind his vehicle. "I'm headed to the bank myself, so I'll follow you."

"Okay. If you want. Have a good day." She sent him a smile, got into her car and started the engine. Miraculously, it turned over right away. The old thing could be fussy in colder weather. Was Matthew still acting weird? Or was she overreacting and on edge? Hopefully he didn't think she'd been rude. She didn't mean to be. She just didn't know what to do about him yet.

And by lunchtime, when the bell on the door tinkled as Lynette breezed into the gallery, she wasn't any closer to a solution.

"Darling!" Evy rushed to Lynette at once, presenting her with the double air kiss Liz was familiar with by now. If Mia had been here she'd have rolled her eyes. And Matthew would have laughed. Okay, seriously? She really needed to stop thinking about the man.

"Hey, Liz." Lynnie left Evy to return to her two customers and hovered near the desk.

Liz jotted a note on the file she was working on and took off her reading glasses. "Lynnie. What brings you by?"

Lynnie scrunched up her nose the way she did when something confused her. "You sent me a text this morning. Asked me to pop in if I got a chance. You had something you wanted to discuss?"

Liz gave her head a shake and sighed. She clearly hadn't consumed enough coffee today. "Right. Well. Yes." She rounded the desk and walked her sister around the gallery, sharing her ideas for the patron's night. "We thought you'd get this wall here. You'll have some new pieces to show by then, won't you?"

"Do I really have to come?" Lynette fidgeted with her bangles, looking like she was still in Africa in her long, gaily patterned skirt and simple peasant blouse and boots.

"Yes, you really have to come." Liz sighed in frustration. "That's the whole point. It's a meet and greet."

"Ugh. Early new year? I'll probably have some new paintings by then. But things might be busy, with the wedding and everything . . . Nick's dad." Lynette's eyes filled and she looked away.

"Oh. Lynnie, I'm sorry." Liz wished Evy would hurry up and join them. She wasn't much good at this comforting big sister stuff. "I'm sure it'll work out." She patted Lynette's shoulder.

"The man is dying, Liz. How is that *going to work out?*"

"I didn't mean . . . I just meant . . . If you don't have new stuff don't worry about it. We can display some of your older pieces. And Dad's."

"Right. Yeah. That's good. I don't want the pressure. Honestly. He could go any day now." She pulled her fingers through her long hair. "I need Nick to take time off. He's overworked and super stressed. But I think he's avoiding being home for longer than he has to. You know?"

Liz didn't know, but she nodded anyway and watched her sister fumble in her large straw bag for some Kleenex. "Do you want to get some lunch, Shortstop?"

She may as well have asked her if she wanted to swim around the island. Lynette gaped and swallowed a giggle. "What's gotten into you?"

Liz scowled. "What? I thought it'd be nice to have lunch with my sister who's been gone for six weeks. If you'd rather not—"

"Oh, don't have a cow. I'd love to have lunch. We can go to the Longshoreman! I haven't seen Jed yet."

"Really?" A greasy burger was not exactly the lunch she'd had in mind. But Lynnie was all excited now, so she nodded and tried to look enthused. "We're off to lunch, Evy," she called. "Be back in an hour."

Evy waved a manicured hand, her silver bracelets jangling. "Take two if you want, for coming in early."

Liz managed a tight smile and squelched rejecting that idea. But honestly. A two-hour lunch at the Longshoreman with Lynette? Heaven help her.

Jed Hagerman practically flew over the bar at the sight of her sister. He enveloped Lynette in a huge bear hug that went on a few moments too long, ushered them to a booth, and took too much time wiping down the scratched tabletop. Liz summoned every bit of strength she possessed not to tell the guy to get lost.

They sat, ordered food and drinks, and fell into awkward silence. "That boyfriend of yours should put a ring on your finger," Liz said, tipping her head toward the bar. "Otherwise your bartender friend over there might beat him to the punch."

Lynette exploded into peals of laughter. "Jed? Liz, seriously?"

"What? He's been in love with you since high school. It's no secret."

"No, it's just his way. Jed knows how I feel. He's a good friend."

"If you say so." She fiddled with a cork coaster, same stamped-on design they'd used for years. She remembered coming in here with friends when she was home from college. Nothing about the dark, damp bar had changed. "So Nick's not coping well, hmm?"

Lynette shook her head with a forlorn expression. "I'm hoping he'll be okay. I think part of him still held out hope for a miracle cure or something. But Anthony's liver functions are low this week. His kidneys are shutting down. It won't be long. And Nick needs to find a way to deal with the inevitable."

"Death can be cruel."

"Yes, it can," Lynette agreed. They both knew that truth too well. Liz's eyes began to burn. What was with all this emotion lately? Last night she'd found herself in tears during a television commercial.

She scanned her phone for something to do. She kept it on because she wanted to be reachable, but every time a call or text came through, she dreaded seeing Laurence's name. He'd been quiet the last couple days though.

"Dad seems happy," Lynette said. "I can't believe he's painting again."

"Right?" Liz silently thanked her sister for changing the subject. "It's almost like he's back to his old self when he's holding a paintbrush. It was such a great idea for Matthew to bring the kids in. I think they all get so much out of it. And Mia loves Dad, although she'd never admit it of course. But she lights up when she's in that room. The change in her is crazy. Just like when she's with the twins. It's like she finally allows herself to be happy. Matthew's always so worried about her. I think she's going to be all right though, I really do."

Jed brought their food himself and hung around until Liz finally glared at him and he shuffled off. She poured a bit of vinaigrette on her salad and looked across the table to see Lynette grinning at her over the top of a monstrous cheeseburger.

"Why are you looking at me like that? And you have ketchup on your chin." She handed her a wad of napkins and grabbed her bottle of Perrier, wishing she'd ordered wine.

Lynette wound a few fries into a blob of ketchup and made an annoying humming sound. Liz cleared her throat. "Lynette, don't make me smack you in public."

"You'd never smack me anyway. You only did that once, and Cecily made you do all the dishes the rest of the week."

"You were a six-year-old brat who came into my room, tried on my best dresses, and spilled perfume all over the place. You deserved that smack."

Her sister shrugged and went back to work on her burger. "I always wanted to be like you," she said after a while, luminous eyes glowing under the hanging lantern. "You were my big sister. I idolized you. Didn't you know that?"

Oh, for goodness sake. Liz sniffed, tears forming before she could do a thing about it. "Don't be silly."

Lynette arched a brow and took another bite of her burger. "I'm not being silly, I'm being honest. I hated that you didn't like me."

"Lynnie." Okay, she was really going to lose it. Were they actually going to have this conversation here, in the seediest bar on Nantucket, with Hagerman leering at them from across the counter? "I never hated you. Never."

"Oh my gosh, don't cry about it. Want some fries?" Her sister had a knack for changing tack at the strangest of times.

Liz smiled and nodded. "Thanks. But really, I never hated you. I might have found you annoying, but . . ."

Lynette leaned in a little, serious. "Do you know how I was always afraid to speak my mind? Afraid of what people might think of me?"

"Yes." Liz swallowed the lump in her throat, not sure she liked this direction either.

"Well, I'm not afraid anymore." She smiled like it was the simplest thing in the world. "We're given clarity of thought and the ability to speak truth in love for a purpose. It took a while for that to sink in, but it finally did. So here's what I know. For whatever reason, you've always been jealous of me. I don't know whether it was because I was the baby or you thought I got extra attention or what, and I honestly don't care. What I do care about is the relationship we have going forward. We're sisters, and that's never going to change, but I'd like us to be friends too. Do you think that would be possible?"

Ho. Ly. Cow. Liz scrunched a paper napkin and waited until she trusted speech. "I'm sorry," she whispered. "I know I was horrible to you. I was a terrible sister. You have every right to hate me."

"Liz." Lynette reached across the table and grabbed her hand. "Stop that. Of course I don't hate you. I never did. I couldn't. I love you. That's what I'm trying to tell you. I want us to move on from all that."

Liz nodded, her mouth dry, unable to form words. She didn't deserve this. Whatever it was.

Grace. The word floated into her mind on a whisper.

Yes, that's exactly what it was.

Grace. The power of forgiveness and the gift of healing.

"Thank you for that, Lynnie." She wiped her eyes and smiled. "And yes, I'd like us to be friends. I say it's high time."

"Done." Lynette gave Liz's hand another squeeze and let go. "Now spill it. I want to know exactly how long you've been in love with Matthew Stone. Does he know?"

"What?" Liz sputtered through her straw. Fizz shot up her nose and made her cough. "I am not in love with Matthew Stone!"

"Oh, come on." Lynette laughed. "It's written all over your face."

"That African sun has addled your brain, sister."

Lynette wagged a finger. "I know what I see when you talk about him. And his niece. Think you've got a bit of a soft spot for her too, don't you? Come on Liz, honestly, who am I going to tell?"

"Um, the entire world? You're the worst at keeping secrets!"

"That's not true. I knew about Mom and Mr. Cooper for ages and I never said a word."

"You were blocking it out!" Liz didn't bother keeping her voice down. The place was empty. "You couldn't remember that they had an affair for years. That doesn't count."

"Okay, fine." Lynette rolled her eyes. "But I'm right about this. Aren't I?"

"Lynnie . . ." Liz gave a long exhale. She may as well. She let go a little tension, gave up good sense, and proceeded to tell her sister everything.

thirty

DRAKE

She's here again. The gifted one. When I saw her in the doorway of the dayroom, looking around, looking half afraid of being kicked out, I thought they were all coming. But the newspaper in my lap says it's Saturday. And those kids don't come on Saturday. So I don't know why she's here. Don't suppose it matters much.

"Hey, Mr. Carlisle." She stands in front of my perch in the window seat. A nice sunny spot where the warmth wakes my tired bones.

"Hey yourself."

"It's Mia. Remember?"

"Mia. How could I forget?" I smile and she smirks. She knows better by now. Smart as a whip, this one. But I see a restlessness in her eyes today, churning like a stormy sea. Like she's carrying something too heavy but doesn't have a place to put it down.

"Are you going to stay?" I ask because she's rocking back and forth, like she might bolt at any moment. And I'd rather she didn't.

"Okay." She pushes her hair behind her ears, revealing too many piercings to count. Glory, what kids do to themselves these days. Though I suppose if I had the luxury of youth again, I might consider an earring.

"Your hair is different." I don't know why I say this. What was it like before?

"Yeah. Got rid of the pink. Going back to my natural color."

"Suits you."

"Thanks." She fumbles in a backpack and pulls out a couple of sketchpads and pencils. Hands one to me. "Wanna just draw?"

I give a slow nod and take an HB pencil from her hand. "That sounds delightful."

She makes herself at home beside me. We draw for a while. I don't know how long. Time means nothing to me these days. Could be minutes, could be an hour. Every now and then she sniffs and wipes her nose with the sleeve of her sweatshirt. But she doesn't speak.

A memory sparks; a young kid, maybe about her age, sitting at the piano, playing until he couldn't anymore and had to stop. Had to give those overwhelming feelings their freedom. Another one, the girl with long blond hair and blue eyes, she would join me in the upstairs studio, her face all tight, secrets hidden so deep I knew I'd never pry them from her. But secrets were always welcome in that sacred space. And so we'd paint in silence until the tears came.

Losing the emotion to the art.

That's what I called it. Finding that place within, digging as deep as necessary until all that pain surfaces.

The great release was always worth the suffering.

"Shade, there." I point to the part of the tree she's missed, and she mutters something under her breath. The trembling in her hand tells me all I need to know. She's getting close. "What are those, sun showers?"

"Sunflowers." She sniffs again and puts her pencil down. Her sigh is weighted and when she finally looks at me, I see all she's trying so hard to stuff down. "My mother loves sunflowers."

And we're there.

Her slender shoulders start to shake and she gulps down a sob.

I take her sketchpad and mine and place them and the pencils on the seat beside me. Then I put my arm around her and she leans against my chest. I pat her shoulder and can't think of a thing to say, but maybe that's okay.

"You know how sometimes life just sucks no matter what you do?" Her voice gets lost in my sweater and the words aren't clear, but I nod anyhow.

"Sure."

"I finally talked to my mom this morning. And she was nice. And now . . ." She lifts her head and stares at me. She doesn't have to say another word.

"You're scared."

––––––––

Mia got off the bus at the stop closest to their house, shivered in the cold, and shoved her hands in her coat pockets. She'd forgotten her gloves. Left the house in a hurry so she could get to the nursing home, hadn't told them where she was going.

Uncle Matt had come into her room around nine that morning, phone in hand. Said she had to talk to her mom, they didn't have a choice. The social worker was there with her mother. The look on his face said it all. It wasn't fair how they were being intimidated, but what could she do?

Mom made the same old promises, and Mia had listened and half-heartedly agreed. She couldn't really remember now what she'd said. Her brain was still mush from that dumb therapist's appointment yesterday. Which hadn't been all bad.

Uncle Matt was right. The lady had been nice. Said Mia could call her by her first name if she wanted. Christa. They talked some about her mom. What were the worst things about growing up with an addict? What were the best things about her mom? Stupid stuff like that. Christa asked if Mia ever intentionally hurt herself, and she hadn't known what to say. So she'd stayed quiet. Christa said anything Mia told her would be kept between them—unless she was having thoughts of suicide. Then she'd be obligated to share that information.

Mia didn't want to kill herself.

She'd thought about it. Once or twice, before they moved back to Boston. But not anymore. Christa talked about cutting. About how it was an addiction. No duh. She suggested that if it was something Mia struggled with, to try to find something to do instead that would take her mind off the need to cut. Asked her if she liked to sing or dance or draw. Mia admitted that art was her passion and Christa's eyes lit. "Do that then. Do that until you can't think of anything else except the creation in front of you."

So this morning, after that phone call, she'd hopped on the bus and gone to see Drake. That's how she thought of him, though she'd never call him anything but Mr. Carlisle. It had helped some, but she still felt like running upstairs to the bathroom, cutting. Maybe she'd go over to Wyldewood and play with the kids or see if the dogs needed to go for a walk. Or maybe . . .

"Excuse me?"

A man she didn't recognize approached from the other side of the road as she was about to turn into their driveway. Maybe a tourist. But they didn't get many in November. "You lost?"

"I think so." He smiled and Mia stiffened. Dude gave her the creeps. He looked like some movie star, almost too good-looking. And he had an accent, British maybe. "Actually I'm looking for a friend's house. I thought it was around here somewhere. Elizabeth Carlisle?"

Mia felt the first few flakes of snow fall on her face. A Jeep crested the hill. Uncle Matt. "Never heard of her."

"Oh. That's a shame. I suppose I'm completely turned around. I'll keep looking then. Thank you." He strolled off in the opposite direction. Mia's heart pounded as she jogged toward the house. She waited by the garage while her uncle parked and got out.

"Did you see that dude? Blond hair, really creepy looking? He was hanging around here when I got off the bus and—"

Uncle Matt reached her in several strides and put his hands on her shoulders. "Slow down. Take a breath." She did and he exhaled. "First off, where the heck did you go? I've been looking all over the island for you!"

Mia stared at her sneakers, then met his frantic gaze. "I went to see Mr. Carlisle."

"You what?" Confusion skirted his brow.

"To draw. I just needed to . . . never mind. Did you see that guy though?"

"What guy?"

"Oh my gosh." She sucked her teeth. "Are you deaf? I said there was this guy hanging around the bushes over there. He asked if I knew where Liz lived. I'm pretty sure he knew already though."

Uncle Matt's eyes got big and he glanced all around. "What did this guy look like?"

"Blond. Creepy. I already told you."

"Did he have an accent?"

"Yeah. Like British or something. You know him?"

"No." He shook his head, his eyes telling her more than he probably meant to.

"What do you know, Uncle Matt?"

"Nothing for you to worry about." He fished out his phone. "Go in the house and lock the door."

"What?"

"On second thought, get in the car. Your grandparents are out." He held the phone up to his ear. "Come on, pick up. Hey, it's me. Call me as soon as you get this message. Please."

"Did you just call Liz?" Mia couldn't stop a grin. Sure she was freaked, but this was way too intriguing.

"Did this guy say anything else?" They got in the car and he gunned the engine. "You're sure he asked for Elizabeth?"

"Yes. He said he was a bit lost and looking for a friend's house. Then he asked if I knew Elizabeth Carlisle."

He let go a word she'd never heard him use before.

"Dude."

He flashed her a look as they pulled onto the main road. "Shut it."

Mia snorted. "Well, this is fun." She clicked her belt into place and slapped her hands on her knees. "Where are we going?"

"I don't have a clue," he muttered.

Mia nodded. "Good plan."

"Was Elizabeth working today? Is she at the gallery?" They were heading toward town, so Mia hoped so. Otherwise Uncle Matt was gonna have a coronary.

"I don't know. I can't remember. Maybe?"

"Think, Mia! Was she working or not?"

She clenched her jaw and stared out the window. "Sure. I think so."

He drummed his fingers on the steering wheel and shot her a side look. "Are you okay?"

"It's not the first time you've yelled at me."

He gave a brief chuckle. "Sorry for yelling. But that's not what I meant. Do you want to talk about your mom?"

"What's to talk about? We'll go see her over Thanksgiving like you said, because we have to, then we'll see that nothing has changed. We'll come back here and life goes on."

His phone buzzed and he grabbed it at once. "Thank God." He pressed the button and pulled over to the side of the road. Of course. Mia sighed and reached for her own phone, pretending to scan it so it wouldn't be totally obvious she was listening to his every word.

"You're at the gallery? Okay. At noon?" Uncle Matt glanced at his watch. "No, don't leave. We're on the way there now. What? Oh, me and Mia. What? Yeah, that thing we talked about. Thought we could do it this afternoon. Yeah?" His smile was goofy and Mia snorted. "All right. See you soon."

"Oh man." She couldn't hold in a giggle as he pulled back onto the road.

"What's so funny?"

"You. You're so totally crazy about that chick."

"Mia." He sighed then fell silent.

"Well. I didn't say that was a bad thing. Geez. So what's with the dude?"

Uncle Matt scratched his head and slowed at a set of lights. "I think it's her ex."

Okay, that wasn't good. "Does she know he's here?"

"I doubt it. Listen, Mia . . ." He hesitated as they approached Main. "From what Elizabeth has told me, this is not a nice guy. I'm not sure what he wants, and I don't want to scare her. So just . . . go along with this afternoon and don't say anything to her. I need to talk to her, and I will, just not yet."

"You're so weird."

"Yeah, I've heard that a few times." They parked near the gallery and got out. Uncle Matt grabbed her hand. "Hey. Are you sure you're okay? Because you didn't say much after your appointment last night, and I worry."

Mia tried to smile, but really, she just wanted to cry. She felt like that a lot lately and she hated it. "I'm fine. Leave it." She pulled her hand away and walked into the gallery. Grown-ups were too bizarre. Maybe she'd call Chris and see if he wanted to tag along on this super exciting adventure they were apparently going on.

The four of them had lunch in town. Uncle Matt was surprisingly chill around Chris, thank goodness. And she kept her mouth shut, though it was hard because, honestly, if some creep was after Liz, didn't she have a right to know that? But Uncle Matt would handle it. Thursday night made more sense now. He'd been wide awake when he'd come into her room after her nightmare. Hadn't even gotten into sweats and the t-shirt he usually slept in. And at three in the morning that was a little odd. When she settled down and pretended to be asleep, she'd seen him standing at her window for a long time. Later, when she'd gotten up to go to the bathroom, she saw the light on in his Jeep. And he was sitting in it.

She smothered a smile and finished her veggie wrap. He was something special all right.

"So, I thought we'd go for a drive." Uncle Matt pulled on gloves as they headed back to the Jeep.

"Drive where?" Mia finished her coke. "I have homework."

He stared. "You'd rather do homework than hang out with me?" His hand went to his heart and he staggered back.

"Come on, Mia. A little fresh air won't hurt you." Liz held out a set of keys. "You and Chris can take my car and drive behind us. How about that?"

"Can I drive?" she asked. It was worth a shot.

"No!" They all said it, even Chris.

Mia shrugged. "What?"

"Your learner's test is next week. After that, sure." Chris took the keys from Liz and gave Mia a wink that set her cheeks on fire. Good grief.

They followed Uncle Matt and Liz through town and out into what Mia liked to call cow country. "Where is he going?" Chris wanted to know. "And how sweet is this car? Gotta be from the '60's, right?"

"It's about to fall apart," Mia grumbled. "We'll probably get stuck on the side of the road."

"Ever the optimist." He grinned and adjusted the air vents. "Not much heat coming out of there." He fiddled with a few knobs and eventually gave up. Mia listened to the radio and tried not to think about the creep who might be staking out their house this very moment.

"So are you going to tell me what happened with your mom?" Chris finally asked. "Your text said you talked to her, but that was it."

Mia chewed on a thumbnail, stopped, and shoved her hands under her legs. Another habit she was trying to break. "Basically, she was all apologetic. Wished she could see me more. Says she's got a new job someplace. I can't remember what, but I doubt it's anything fun. I have to go to Boston for Thanksgiving."

"You have to?" He rammed fingers through his blond hair. "What if you don't want to?"

Mia shrugged, her eyes stinging. "I don't want to. But Uncle Matt says it's better to go voluntarily than have DCF jumping down his throat."

"But doesn't he have custody of you?"

"Yeah. But"—She scratched her arm—"my mom could contest it if she got mad. It's just better this way, I guess. It sucks."

"Sorry." He sighed and turned the music down a bit. "Maybe it won't be so bad."

"Maybe." But it would be. There was no maybe about it.

"Looks like we're going in here." Chris hit the turn signal and took a slow right down a long dirt road. Brown fields stretched out on either side of them. In a far off pasture, brown and white cows grazed. Leftover corn stalks waved in the breeze, and a few more flakes of snow dusted the windshield. "Do you know this place?"

"Rusty's farm." Mia grinned. "He's one of my uncle's buddies. We came here once when we first moved over. His wife made the best blueberry pie ever. If you like pie."

Chris's brows shot skyward. "Oh man. I hope there's pie. I love pie."

Mia laughed and zipped up her jacket as he parked and cut the engine. "I think you just like food in general."

"Well, that's true."

They trudged over to where Uncle Matt and Liz waited. Rusty approached from around the barn with a big wave.

"What's up, pilgrims?" He was a big dude with a red beard that took over half his face. Mia figured the red hair was why he was called Rusty, but she'd never ask. "Whoa, now!" He leaned over and looked her up and down. "Weren't you just five last time you were here?"

She shook her head and tried not to smile, but he made it impossible. "I was fifteen. Same age as I am now."

"Well, I reckon so then, but I hear you have a birthday coming up."

Mia glanced at Uncle Matt. He was grinning like an idiot. And Liz looked a little too happy. Chris appeared to be the only normal one in this crew. "It's next Saturday."

"Yep. That's what I hear." Rusty stuck his thumbs under the straps of his denim overalls and tipped his head toward the barn. "Come on over here. Got something you might like."

"Um . . ." Mia scrunched her nose. "I'm not much into cows. Or horses."

His belly laugh carried on the wind behind him. Uncle Matt prodded her shoulder. "Go on."

"This is the dumbest day." She looked over her shoulder at Chris. He shrugged and followed her into the barn. At least it was warm inside. And it didn't stink too bad. They walked past a row of stalls until Rusty reached a door at the far side of the structure.

"My office." He opened the door with a gentle click and motioned for Mia to go in.

She heard the whimpering first. Tiny yips and yaps filled the warm room.

"Puppies," she whispered, staring at the large wood enclosure against the wall. A golden retriever lay inside it, six puppies crawling all around her. "Oh my gosh."

Uncle Matt put a hand on her shoulder. "Cute, huh?"

Rusty beckoned her over. "They're six weeks today. Come get a closer look."

"They're adorable." Mia leaned over and smiled at the big dog eyeing her carefully. "Hey, mama. I'm just saying hi to your babies. I won't hurt you."

"Oh, Blossom knows that. She's a sweetheart. Did a good job with these little fellas. Four girls and two boys. You see the ribbons?"

"Yeah." Each pup had a thin blue or red ribbon around its neck. Mia crouched and put a hand into the box. The pups immediately crowded around, checking her out.

"So which one do you want?" Rusty asked.

"All of them." Mia giggled and patted the little girl closest to her hand.

Uncle Matt crouched beside her and patted one of the boys. "I definitely don't want six dogs," he said quietly. "But I think one would be great."

Mia turned and saw his smile. "Are you serious?" Her heart gave a little kick.

He arched a brow. "If you are. This would be your dog. Your responsibility."

She blinked hard, trying to comprehend what was happening. "I can have a puppy?"

He shrugged and picked up one of the pups. "I couldn't figure out what to get you. Then I ran into Rusty at the hardware store. It seemed like a good idea." The pup licked his nose and he chuckled, put it back with the others, and met her gaze. "What do you think?"

Don't cry, don't cry, don't cry.

Mia nodded, rubbed a hand across her nose, and rested her head against his shoulder. Uncle Matt leaned his head against hers and they sat quiet for a long moment. "I don't know anything about puppies." Her voice came out all muffled.

"I bought a few books." Uncle Matt's nose was a little red, but she could tell he was happy. They stood, and Liz and Chris came closer.

"It was more like ten. I was there. It was a bit embarrassing, actually." Liz laughed.

Mia grinned at her uncle, her heart about to burst out of her chest. "That's Uncle Matt. OTT all the way."

"Go big or go home," he quipped.

"Puppies are just like kids," Rusty put in, his big face beaming. "Feed and water 'em, give 'em a whole lot of love and a bit of discipline and you're good to go."

Mia studied the puppies again. "I don't know how to choose."

"Ah. Well, you just get on in there," Rusty took her hand, helped her step over the side of the box, and she sat cross-legged, surrounded by puppies. "Now you wait and see which one you click with."

Mia let the puppies crawl over her, ran her hands over their soft fur, smiled at Chris, and knew this was the best day of her life.

"We'll leave you to pick." Uncle Matt took Liz's hand. "We have another appointment in the back field."

Mia smiled. He was such a goof, but right then she didn't care. "Thanks, Uncle Matt."

He nodded, his eyes about to spill over any second. "Happy Birthday, kid."

thirty-one

"That was the sweetest thing I've ever seen." Liz scanned the photos on her iPhone as they left the barn.

"Did you see her face when she finally realized what was happening?" Matthew hopped a little as he walked, his face glowing. If she wasn't already in love with him, she might be now.

"I got video too. I think she was a bit overwhelmed."

"Well, they won't be ready to leave for another few weeks. Which is pretty good timing, with Christmas break coming up. We'll have to figure something out during the day once school starts back up."

"Maybe your parents will move in with you forever." Liz shot him a playful grin and he scowled.

"Please, no. But they've agreed to help while they're here. Funny, but I think I'm going to miss them when they do leave. I think they're learning to relax."

"See. Things are looking up all around, aren't they?"

Matthew's smile seemed a little shaky. "Well. Look over there." He brightened, led her toward a white wooden fence, and pointed. Liz let out a little shriek.

"Goats?" There were about seven of them, some black, some white, frolicking in the field, butting heads, and making weird noises. "You weren't kidding."

"I never kid. Pun intended." He pulled himself up onto the fence and flashed a grin. "Watch."

One goat started it. Like someone flipped a switch, he jumped high into the air. Landed, bounced up and down, and leaped again. And then another joined in. And then another. Frolicking around the field in an almost choreographed display.

Dancing goats.

It was the silliest, most amazing thing Liz had ever seen.

"They really are dancing." She snapped a few photos and found him watching her with a satisfied smile.

"You should see your face right now." He hopped off the fence and stood beside her.

Liz rolled her eyes and smothered a groan. "Okay, whatever They're cute."

"They are." He trailed his fingers over her forehead. "I think you're pretty cute too."

"Matthew . . ." She leaned into him. Let him pull her closer and allowed herself the luxury of being held. When she met his eyes, he wore that serious expression again. Liz let him go and stepped back. "Are you going to tell me what's wrong, or do you want me to continue to think up a thousand worst-case scenarios, none of which make the slightest bit of sense."

He scratched his jaw, pulled at the zip of his jacket, and sighed. "I think your ex is on the island."

He might as well have poured a bucket of ice water over her head. Of all the things he could have said, she hadn't expected this. She wound her gloved hands together and studied his face for any clues that might help her form an appropriate response. But there were none. "What makes you say that?"

"I . . . do you have a picture of him?"

Liz flipped through the photos on her phone, her hands shaking so badly she thought she'd drop it. "Here." She held the screen toward Matthew and watched him lose a little color.

"Yeah. That's him."

She took steadying breaths, half tempted to scan the area to make sure Laurence wasn't lurking in the distance. "Where did you see him?"

"Outside the gallery the other day. And then this morning . . ." He looked away and she grabbed his hand.

"This morning, what? Matthew, you have to tell me!"

He faced her with an anguished expression. "He was outside our house. Mia saw him when she got off the bus. He asked if she knew where you lived."

"Oh no." Liz let out a long breath and blinked tears. "She didn't tell him?"

"No. She didn't. Said he creeped her out." He wrapped his arms around her, and somehow gave her the calm she needed. "Can you get a restraining order?"

"He hasn't done anything. He's got every right to be here. Until he actually hurts me . . ."

"That won't happen." Matthew pulled back and shook his head. "Not on my watch."

Oh, how she wanted to believe that. But Laurence wanted something from her. She didn't know what yet, but it had to be big or he wouldn't be here. Well, she wanted something from him too. So maybe . . .

"I won't hide from him." She shoved her hands in the pockets of her coat and set her jaw. "I won't be afraid of him. Not anymore."

"Elizabeth, you need to be careful. Guys like that . . . if anything happened to you . . ."

"I'll be fine. I'll call him and see what he wants. I'll meet him in a public place." And get those pictures back somehow. Whatever it took.

Matthew shook his head, not convinced.

Fear found its way in again, said she'd never be free of the past. Not really. And here she was trying so hard to move on.

Matthew insisted she stay for dinner at their place. Liz didn't argue. She enjoyed Phyllis's company and steered clear of Harrison. Later, while Mia and Matthew were showing them pictures of the puppies, she sat in the living room and fired up her laptop. It was time to put some things to rest.

She'd check Facebook first. She barely used it—didn't like posting her business for the world to see, and people kept adding her to groups. But she remembered a while back she'd popped into a group created by some girls from her old school. She scanned her list, found it, and clicked over. Still in use, filled with photos from days gone by along with weddings, babies, boyfriends . . . yeah, no thanks. She gaped at the old photos. They all looked so young. Innocent. She looked almost happy. Of course. It had been taken in the art studio. Before she'd made the biggest mistake of her life.

Her fingers paused over the keys. Nausea burned. Could she do this?

'Hey all! Anyone know where Howarth ended up? Just curious.'

She typed the words quickly, before she lost her nerve. Left the page and opened her messages. Nothing unusual. Except . . . one new one from a girl she didn't recognize. She squinted at the name. Alannah Grimes. Something made her click on the message.

'Dear Elizabeth, you don't know me, and I'm sorry to reach out through Facebook of all places. But you have an unlisted number and I'm not sure where you live now. I'm writing because we have something in common. For the past year and a half, I've been involved with Laurence Broadhurst. Yes, before you broke up. (Sorry). He told me he was single. I found out about you through a friend. I was with him the day you came to the apartment to get your things. Threre weeks ago I called 911. He broke my arm, shattered my jaw, and attempted to rape me. I managed to get away and get to my phone. He was released on bail. From what I've heard, you've seen that side of him too. My lawyer has your name, and I'm sure you'll be hearing from her soon. We're hoping you'll testify at the trial. If Laurence tries to contact you and convince you not to, please stay strong. We need men like him behind bars. Personally, I'd like to see him dead, but I'll take a jail sentence. Here's my number. Please call me.'

"Elizabeth?" Matthew stood a few feet away, concern in his eyes.

She was so stunned she could barely speak. "Read this."

He sat beside her and she waited while he read the message.

Matthew let out a low whistle and took her shaking hand. "Wow. That's something."

"Now we know why he's here." A shuddering sigh escaped. "I'm sure he wants to convince me not to testify."

"Which you absolutely have to do," Matthew said firmly. "You know that, right?"

Did she?

She leaned against the cushions of the couch and closed her eyes. "I used to think about it all the time. Taking him on in court.

Watching him try to lie his way out of it. I never actually believed it would happen. And I'm still not sure. He has a lot of friends in high places."

"But now there's a police report. Evidence." He rubbed the top of her hand in gentle circular motions.

"I'm so scared," she whispered. "I don't know if I can do this."

"What if this is the closure you need? So you can finally get on with your life? Don't you think you deserve that?"

"I don't know what I deserve." She stared at him through wet eyes.

"Oh, Elizabeth." His smile was sad as he leaned in and kissed her softly. "You deserve every good thing. And I can't wait for the moment you finally begin to believe that."

They joined Mia and his parents, played a few rounds of Scrabble, then Matthew walked her home, made sure she put her alarm on. He'd tried to convince her to stay the night with them, but she'd refused. She couldn't give in to fear.

A few minutes later he was back. Insisted on sleeping on her couch. Said his parents were okay with it, they'd call if Mia woke up. So there she was, curled up under the covers, her personal security guard in the next room. But she couldn't calm her pounding heart. If she testified, there was no telling what Laurence would do with those photographs. And if she didn't testify . . . could she really live with herself?

And how could she explain that decision to Matthew or her siblings? Of course, she could just tell the truth—if she weren't so utterly petrified of what they would all think.

Just as she was starting to doze off, her phone buzzed. She grabbed it off her bedside table and scanned the screen. A Facebook notification from her school group.

'Hey, Liz. Sorry to be the bearer of bad news, but Howarth died two years ago. Cancer.'

She shut her phone off and took deep, calming breaths.

He was gone. Perhaps she should be sad, but she wasn't. All she felt was relief.

One demon down. One to go.

Maybe exorcizing the past was possible after all.

If she were brave enough.

thirty-two

None of them wanted her to meet with Laurence. David was vehemently opposed. Matthew didn't have to say a word. But Liz couldn't bear the thought of Laurence approaching Mia again. Or Lynette. Or Evy. Eventually she convinced them that this was something she had to do, but she agreed to do it on their terms. So she made the call, and he agreed to come back to the island on Saturday.

Liz hadn't really slept all week. She arranged to meet him in a coffee shop. David sat in a booth on the other side of the room, out of sight. Matthew sat in his Jeep in the parking lot. Liz ordered coffee and stirred her spoon around the dark liquid so vigorously it splashed over the side.

Eventually, Laurence appeared, slid into the seat opposite her, and actually smiled. Not a hair out of place, nothing on his face to indicate the trouble he was in. "Hello, Lizzie."

"Laurence." She took a sip of the hot beverage and summoned every ounce of calm.

"You're looking very lovely. Island life suits you."

"I know why you're here." She put her cup down and met his eyes. She'd almost expected to be sucked in again. To be drawn by that magnetic force that had attracted her to him in the first place. But all she felt was contempt.

"Ridiculous business." He waved a hand, his thin smile showing a smidge of uncertainty.

"Laurence. You put that girl in the hospital."

"So she claims. You weren't there, Elizabeth. You don't know what actually happened."

"Oh, I can guess." She clenched her fists and blinked, tears too close. "She fell. Tripped. Water on the floor. Heel broke. I can think up a thousand excuses. I've used them all."

"Let's just cut to the chase, shall we?" He reached into his jacket pocket and pulled out an envelope. Placed it on the table in front of him, his eyes cold. "You won't testify."

Her chest rose and fell while she measured his words and her response. "I don't want you harassing that girl. I know you're not allowed near her. If you do anything stupid, they'll lock you up for sure."

He leaned back, two fingers pressing down on the envelope. "Your concern for me is touching, Lizzie."

Something shifted in his eyes. She had to be careful. "I'm afraid the case won't amount to much anyway." She smiled. "You'll work your magic and make it all go away. Won't you?"

"Well, it is one of my talents." He pushed the envelope toward her. "Friends in high places and all that. So. You can have these back, since they seem to mean so much to you. And a little something for your trouble."

Liz steeled herself against the urge to grab the envelope and run. Instead, she nodded, lifted the flap, and looked inside. The photos were there. Along with a check. She inhaled and slowly let out her breath. "I don't want your money."

"It's yours anyway." He played with the gray cashmere scarf around his neck. "And you're right. Even with your testimony, I doubt they'll convict me. Alannah has . . . issues. But I knew you'd see reason, Lizzie. You always do."

"Don't come here again." She worked to keep her voice level. To hide her fear. "Don't contact me or any of my family. I want you gone from my life, Laurence. Like you never existed."

He studied her for a long moment, then flashed the smile she'd come to fear. "I've got much better things to do with my time, darling. I'm so glad we had this little chat, but I really must go. I'm flying out in half an hour. You're welcome to come and watch the plane take off if you like."

"Just go, Laurence." She shook her head as he stood and tried to reach for her hand. "Just go."

She watched him bang out the door and blinked moisture. Saw David studying her across the room. Heard the chatter of the patrons around her, carrying on with their normal lives, enjoying a normal day. What she wouldn't give to feel normal again.

She'd come so close. With Matthew. And her family. Their relationship was better than ever. She felt closer to all her siblings, even Gray, who was still driving her crazy. But what she was about to do could well blow all of that out of the water. Because they'd see her for who she really was.

Unreliable. Untrustworthy. Weak.

It was too late for second thoughts. And Liz knew one thing for sure.

She wouldn't be testifying at that trial.

Matt packed the last of his clothes into his carry-on and zipped it up. They were catching the afternoon ferry to Hyannis, and Patrick was meeting them, driving them to Boston. Tomorrow they'd see Rachel. She was coming to Pat's for Thanksgiving, and he'd see how the rest of the weekend would go from there. Mia was nervous and he hated that. Hated all of this.

Matt shot his head up at the knock on his door, surprised to see his father standing there.

"May I come in?" Dad looked a little wary, like he wouldn't be welcomed.

Matt shrugged, put his case on the floor, and tried a smile. "Sure."

Dad walked across the rug and stood in front of the window that faced the ocean. Let out a long sigh then turned, holding out a white envelope. "Would you please give this to your sister?"

Matt swallowed and moved in slow motion. Took the envelope from his father and lowered himself onto the edge of the bed. "What is it?"

Dad found the chair in the corner of the room and sat, hands on his knees. Behind the black frames, his eyes grew moist. He cleared his throat. "A letter. An apology. I'd like to give it in person, but she won't see us. What do you think the chances she'll change her mind are?"

Slim to none. Matt shrugged. "No idea. But it's worth a shot."

"Yes, well." He sniffed and folded his hands in his lap. "I owe you an apology as well. I know I was too hard on you growing up. I should never have pushed my hopes for you so hard. Should have let you go to art school. It's what you were meant to do. I'm sorry I didn't see that our relationship was more important than getting my way."

"Wow." The word popped out and Matt couldn't take it back.

"And I know what you must think of me, of my behavior toward those young women." He blanched and studied his shoes for a moment. "I've apologized to each of them. To your mother. And I am trying to change. I hope you can believe that."

The room grew warm as the winter sun shone through the windowpanes, reaching toward him like a gentle prod.

Forgiveness. Grace. Mercy. All those things he said he believed in, stood for. When it came down to it, Matt knew he'd failed. Knew he'd held onto his anger. Anger he really didn't have a right to. Because he'd made his own mistakes. He'd been self-righteous and stubborn. It had kept him from forgiving his father for so many things. Even now, when his parents were clearly trying to make amends, he'd held himself at arm's length, pride preventing him from giving them the simplest gift of all.

He paced the room, heart heavy as he processed the past, finally coming to that place where the road parted. He could continue down the path of the familiar or step over onto a new path. One that might lead to a very different future. For all of them.

"I'm sorry too." He made a slow turn and walked to where his father sat. "I've held onto all of this for far too long. And life's too short for that." He held out a hand. "I forgive you, Dad. I know you've always wanted the best for me. My life worked out the way it was meant to. I'm happy. So what say we move on?"

Dad stood with a grunt and clasped Matt's hand in his. "I would like that, son. Very much." They didn't hug. But the smile his father gave him felt as good as one.

"This doesn't mean I'm over everything." Matt had to be honest. "That could take a while."

"Rome wasn't built in a day."

Matt grinned. It was such a typical Dad-ism. "You would know."

His father laughed. "I was thinking, maybe in the summer we can get out on the water, hmm? I'm not much of a sailor, but I'd love to learn."

"I think we can do that." Matt nodded. "I'd like that a lot."

He and Mia sat on the couch in Pat's living room, the day after Thanksgiving, the whole brood filling every available space as they watched the game, cheering and booing and talking over the sportscasters. Mia was drawing in her sketchbook like her life depended on it. And suddenly the crowded room was the last place Matt wanted to be.

He tapped his niece on the shoulder. "I'm going to the kitchen for some ice cream."

She looked up, her eyes filled with that familiar fear he'd so hoped was long gone. But it had returned the moment she'd seen her mother that morning. And Matt didn't know how to get rid of it. "Want some? Think there's still some chocolate left."

Mia nodded, held her sketchbook to her chest and shuffled behind him to the kitchen. Patrick's mom and Kathleen were doing the last of the dishes.

"We came for ice cream." Matt tried to sound bright but heard the strain in his voice. They all knew this had been difficult for Mia. For him too. Rachel had tried too hard. Forcing conversation. Asking Mia too many questions. She'd suggested lunch tomorrow at her apartment. So she could show Mia where she was living and how nice it was. Matt wanted to give his sister the benefit of the doubt, but history stood in the way. She'd taken the letter from Dad though. Probably hoping there was money in it. He prayed there wasn't.

"Plenty left, we'll leave you to it." Trish kissed him on the cheek as she and her daughter-in-law left the room. Matt sank into a chair at the table, suddenly exhausted.

Mia put down her sketchpad. "I guess I'll get the ice cream then."

A few moments later they were eating out of the carton because she couldn't find any clean bowls. Matt wasn't even hungry, but needed something to do.

"You still mad at Liz?" Mia asked.

He studied the clock on the wall and put his spoon down on a paper towel. "I don't understand why she won't testify. It's the right thing to do." Ever since she'd stupidly met with the man, her mind was made up. She wouldn't do it, and no amount of arguing would sway her.

"She's probably scared." Mia scraped what was left out of the carton and into her mouth. "I would be."

"Yeah." He put his hands behind his head. Of course she was scared. He knew that. "I guess that's it. She said he didn't threaten her, but he must have. It doesn't make sense."

"Whatever. He'll probably get off anyway." Mia pushed hair behind her ears and met his eyes. "So. Are you going to tell me to go see my mom tomorrow?"

Oh, boy. Matt tried to smile but didn't have it in him. "Do you want to go?"

She shrugged in that nonchalant manner that hid her true feelings. "I sort of do. Is that weird?"

"Mia." He sighed and splayed his hands on the table. "She's your mom. If you want to go over there, that's your decision. I'm not going to tell you what to do."

"She seemed different, though, right? Like she was before? When she wasn't using."

That was true. Rachel looked good. Too thin, but then she always had been. And she did seem more at peace. He'd scrutinized her carefully and been satisfied with what he'd seen. For now. "She's definitely not using. So there's that." He fiddled with his phone and wished Elizabeth were here. She'd know what to say.

"I'll just go for lunch, like we talked about. Then we can go see that movie if you want."

"Sounds good. Make sure your phone is charged." He could insist on going with her, and he wanted to, but that probably wouldn't be fair to Mia or Rachel. He put his head in his hands and wished his gut wasn't churning like he could hurl any moment.

"Uncle Matt?"

"Yeah." He looked up and swallowed the tightness in his throat.

Mia's smile twisted his heart inside out. "It'll be okay."

He wasn't so sure. But he couldn't be there for her every second, much as he wanted to be. He could easily talk her out of going. But this was her journey. And at some point, he needed to trust that she would find the right path.

thirty-three

Mia got off the T on Saturday and checked the directions her mom texted her that morning. She walked a few blocks south and found the apartment building easily enough. Uncle Matt was hanging back at the house with Uncle Pat. At first, she wasn't sure he'd let her come by herself, but when he'd asked if she wanted him to come, she'd hesitated. Part of her wanted him there, but it had been tense enough between them on the first day. She'd get a better read on how her mom was really doing without Uncle Matt hovering, waiting for his sister to slip up. So she'd come alone.

Her cell buzzed just as she was about to enter. She stepped back and fished it from her coat pocket. Chris.

"Hey."

"Hey." He sounded weird.

"What's up?"

"My uncle died. Around two this morning."

"Oh man." Mia leaned against the wall and shut her eyes. "You okay?"

"I guess. It's just busy around here today. Lots of people coming and going. Discussing funeral arrangements and all."

"How's Nick?"

His sigh said not good. "You know. He'll be okay. Lynnie hasn't left his side. She's holding him together I think."

"That's good." She had so many questions she wanted to ask. Namely, did this mean he'd be going back to New York. But now wasn't the time. "Well, hang in there. I'll see you when I get back on Sunday."

"Can't wait." She could imagine his grin and wished she hadn't fallen so hard.

"I gotta go. Talk to you soon. Tell everyone I'm sorry." She hung up quick before she said something stupid. Like, love you. Because she wasn't sure if she did. But she might.

Ridiculous.

Mia stared at the door of the apartment building, took a breath, and went inside. It was warm and smelled like curry and meatloaf and turkey. Gross. She walked two flights of stairs and found the apartment. Unzipped her coat, bit the side of her cheek, and forced herself to knock. It would be okay. That's what she'd told Uncle Matt. That's what she had to believe.

Mom flung open the door and grabbed her. "Mia!" She pulled her against her thin frame and hugged her too hard. She smelled like fast food and cigarettes. And nothing like home. "You came! I'm so glad."

Mia stepped back too quickly. "I said I would." She glanced around the dimly lit apartment.

"Come on in. Take your coat off. Let me show you around." She took Mia's coat and hung it on a hook on the wall. Mia slipped out of her boots, glad she'd worn thick socks, because the wood floor was cold.

There wasn't much to see. The living room was boxy with a beat-up couch and two recliners, and a TV. A scratched coffee table held an overflowing ashtray, a couple of Dunkin Donuts cups, and a beer bottle. Mia's heart clenched. Mom chatted away as two cats jumped off the bed in the small room beside an even smaller bathroom. Mia side-stepped the animals. She hated cats.

"Let's go to the kitchen and get you something to eat, huh?" Mom still held her hand. Her grip was tight and she looked so happy. "Is your uncle feeding you properly? He wasn't much of a cook as I recall."

Mia managed to pry her hand away. "Uncle Matt cooks great."

Mom gave a little sniff and tossed her head. Her hair was too dark and made her skin look pale, like she was sick or something. "Well. Once you come home, we'll fatten you up."

"I'm fine." And I'm not coming home. She bit that back and trailed her mother into a tiny kitchen. "What the—?" Mia felt the room closing in. Hands closing around her throat. She couldn't breathe. Couldn't think. And thought she might pass out.

Joe Giovanni sat at the kitchen table. Looking like he owned the place. "Hey, kid. Surprise." The glint in his dark eyes made Mia's blood run cold.

Her mother went to stand behind his chair and put her hands on his shoulders. "I didn't want to tell you yesterday because I knew Matt would freak out. But Joe and I got back together. Isn't that great?"

No, no, no. Mia pushed trembling hands through her hair, her throat dry.

"Aren't you going to say anything, kid?" Joe tugged at his t-shirt and got to his feet. He was already wasted. She recognized the slur and the sway. "Come on, it hasn't been that long. Give your old man a hug."

Every muscle in her body went rigid, and she recoiled from his outstretched hand. "Don't touch me."

"Mia, don't start that crap again." Mom sighed with the look Mia was too familiar with.

Joe raised his hands and backed off, his grin leering. "Don't be coming in here with that attitude. Nobody needs that the day after Thanksgiving." He cursed and sat again, glaring at her mother. "Told you nothing would change. Living with that brother of yours, she'll have me arrested before you can say jack squat."

"Joe, please . . ." Mom wound her hands together and shot Mia a scared look.

"Ah, shut up," Joe barked. "Get me a beer. What time are we eating? I'm starved."

"I have to go to the bathroom." Mia turned and fled the room. Locked herself in the small bathroom, leaned over the toilet, and threw up. Then she perched on the edge of the tub and pulled her phone from her jeans, thankful she hadn't left it in her coat. Her hands shook so bad she could barely punch in Uncle Matt's number.

It rang through to his voicemail. Unbelievable! Mia swore and smacked the side of the tub. She couldn't call Chris, that wasn't fair. She took a trembling breath and pressed another button.

"Mia? What's up?" Liz picked up right away, and Mia's eyes filled.

"He . . . he's here . . . and I don't know what to do." Her words tumbled out through tears.

"Mia." Liz's calm, take-charge tone fell over her. "Take a breath, sweetie. Where are you?"

"At my mom's. In the bathroom." Her breath hitched, and she worked to steady her breathing.

"At your mom's? Okay. Is your uncle there?"

"No. Just my mom. And Joe. They're in the kitchen."

"Joe? Your stepfather?"

"Uh huh." Tears slipped down her cheeks. "I didn't know he was here. I didn't . . . I can't get hold of Uncle Matt. I don't know what to do."

Liz muttered something that Mia didn't catch. "Mia, listen to me. You can leave. Say you don't feel well. Just go. Do you know how to get back to where you're staying?"

"Yeah. I took the T here." Mia rubbed a hand across her face. "What if he follows me?"

"I don't think he will, hon. But stay close to other people. Go now, walk as fast as you can, and call me back when you're out of there. I'm going to try to get hold of your uncle. Okay?"

"I'm scared."

"I know you are." Liz sounded like she might be crying too. "But you can do this. You can be brave. You are brave, Mia Stone. Trust me on that."

"Okay." She washed her face and walked back to the living room. She slipped on her boots and grabbed her jacket.

"What are you doing?" Mom stood in the doorway of the kitchen, cigarette in hand. "We're about to eat. I'm gonna order pizza."

"I don't feel good." Mia pushed her hands through the sleeves of her coat as quickly as she could. "I have to go."

Joe appeared and shook his bald head with a groan. "Really, Mia?"

Somehow she met his eyes. "I don't have to stay. Neither of you can make me. I don't have to be around you one minute more. And if you come after me, I will call the cops."

"Oh, for the love, Mia! Stop with the drama. You haven't changed a bit." Mom blew smoke, her lips curled in disgust.

"Yeah, that's right." Joe laughed. "You run away like a scared little rabbit. See if we care. All your lies about me don't mean squat, kid."

"They're not lies." Mia set her jaw and opened the door. "You know what you did. And so does she." She slammed the door as hard as she could, called Liz back, and didn't stop running until she got on the T and the doors slid closed.

———————

Matt finally left Mia's room, his heart shattered. Why her first call hadn't come through, he didn't know. When Elizabeth had called to let him know what was happening, he'd run out of Pat's house so fast a car almost hit him as he raced across the street. He ran the five blocks toward the T stop, lungs burning. When he saw Mia trudging up the steps, he wanted to fall to his knees and cry with relief. She fell against him with an anguished sob and said the words he thought he'd never hear. "Take me home. I just want to go home. Back to Nantucket."

Pat drove them back to Hyannis and they'd caught the last ferry. Now it was after midnight, but he knew he wouldn't sleep a wink.

"How is she?" Mom placed a warm mug in his hands as he entered the kitchen. The smell of cocoa was comforting.

"I doubt she'll be asleep long." He sat numbly, sipped and put the mug down. Elizabeth reached for his trembling hand.

"Rachel called while you were on your way back." Dad took off his glasses, wiped his eyes, put them back on again. "I'm afraid she thinks the sonofagun walks on water."

"I don't know what's going to happen to her," Mom said shakily. "She still sounds so unstable."

"I don't give a crap." Matt's voice came out hoarse. "Until she can put her daughter first, we're done. She can take me to court if she wants." But she wouldn't. He knew that. Sorrow thickened the room. Dad nodded. Mom wiped tears and hid a yawn. He suddenly felt enormously grateful for their presence. "You both look exhausted.

Go to bed." They didn't argue. Matt finished his cocoa, then he and Elizabeth sat in the living room. He held her for a long time. Couldn't find the words he wanted, wasn't sure they were necessary anyway.

After a while, she sat up, studied him through sad eyes, and let out a long breath. "I need to tell you something."

———————

Liz knew what she had to do the moment she'd seen Mia get off the ferry that night. The girl was wrecked. Shaken and scared, and Liz knew exactly how she felt. And she didn't want anyone to ever feel like that. Not if she could help it.

Alannah's lawyer had called twice that week. Liz told her both times she wasn't going to change her mind. Two more girls from Laurence's past had come forward. The case seemed pretty cut and dried in her opinion. They didn't really need her. But now . . .

She retrieved the envelope from her purse, sat beside Matthew on the couch. In the next few moments, everything would change. "I know you've been angry with me since I said I didn't want to testify. And while you haven't said it, I know you're wondering what Laurence could possibly have on me that would lead me to make that decision."

"So he does." Matthew leaned forward and let out a breath. "Have something on you." It wasn't a question.

She steeled herself against the hurt in his eyes and went on before she lost her nerve. "When I was fourteen, I went to boarding school. I was happy there, and I did well. But in my senior year, something happened. And it changed my life."

She managed, somehow, without tears, to tell him her story. Told him how she'd believed, at seventeen, she'd found the man of her dreams. The man who convinced her that it was okay for her, a minor, to pose while he took photographs of her. "Soon I was posing with nothing on at all. The first time he touched me, I thought it was exciting. Doing something I knew was wrong, yet I convinced myself it was right. Afterward, I felt used. Dirty. And he made me promise I'd never tell a soul. He talked about how we'd run away together after I graduated. How he loved me." A bitter laugh scratched her throat. "It went on that whole year. I'm lucky I didn't get pregnant. When I finally came to my senses and realized he was just using me, it was too late. And then my mother died." She finished her tale, put the pictures on the couch between them, and met Matthew's silent gaze. "And I never told a soul."

"So now you know. I'm no different than a prostitute, really. The things I let him do. Things I let Laurence do. I never fought back. Never said no." Tears crested her cheeks and burned her eyes. "It's all come back to haunt me. I have no doubt Laurence made copies of these. He's not that stupid. If I testify, I don't know what he'll do. But I don't care anymore. I don't care what anyone thinks of me. I know this may change things between us. But I just want to do the right thing." She couldn't look at him. So she stood and walked on trembling legs to the window and looked through the darkness. Soft light from a far off ship shone in the distance. And she wished she were on it.

"Elizabeth."

She made a slow turn.

Matthew held the pictures in his hands. Slowly he ripped them in half, and then again, until tiny shreds fell to the floor between them. "Those pictures? This isn't who you are. This was never who you are." He cupped her face in his warm hands. "You are so much more than that, Elizabeth. What those men did to you was wrong. The way you felt about yourself was wrong. But you don't have to feel that way anymore. I don't ever want you to feel that way again."

Surely he didn't mean it. "You don't know what you're saying."

"Oh, yes I do." He ran his hands over her hair, his eyes locked on her. "I might be exhausted and wrecked, but I know exactly what I'm saying. I love you, Elizabeth. And nothing you can tell me about your past is going to change that."

"I don't know what to say," she whispered.

He drew her close and rested his forehead against hers. "Say you love me too."

"I do." She wound her arms around his neck and smiled through tears. "I absolutely do."

He took her mouth in a purposeful kiss that shattered all her doubts and fears and sent new hope coursing through her veins. Liz kissed him back without reservation. Without shame. Knowing, perhaps for the first time in her life, that she was truly loved.

Unconditionally.

"Uncle Matt!" A loud wail tore them apart at once.

Mia stood in the doorway, holding her arm, a blood-soaked towel wrapped around it. Mia's face went very white, and then she crumpled to the ground.

thirty-four

Mia opened her eyes, her throat thick. She had a really bad headache. She couldn't remember much of last night, and she'd slept most of the day. Must be Sunday. They were giving her something for the pain. Being in hospital sucked, but it was probably the best place for her. For now. Until she didn't feel crazy anymore.

"You're awake!" Chris's anxious face came into focus.

"What are you doing here?" She studied the white gauze bandages on her arm, and her eyes filled. She hadn't been going to cut at all. But when she woke from a nightmare, thought about Joe Giovanni and what he could still do to her, the fear was too intense. And she'd gone too deep.

"Hey, kiddo." Uncle Matt leaned over the other side of the bed and kissed her forehead.

Mia gave a weak smile. "You look like crap."

His grin popped out. "Yeah, well. No sleep will do that to a guy."

"Do Grandma and Grandpa know?" They'd write her off for real this time.

"They've been here all night. I sent them home a little while ago." He rubbed his jaw with a tired smile. "They said to tell you they love you. They'll come back this afternoon."

"Oh." Mia scrunched her eyes, emotion threatening to explode. She was vaguely aware that Chris was holding her hand. "They said that? Really?"

"Really."

Over the top of Chris's head, she saw Liz standing in the corner of the room. Talking to some guy who looked like . . . Mia's breath hitched and she gave Chris a shove. "Dude, move, I can't see. Is that . . . oh my gosh." Her voice turned into a high pitched squeak as Gray Carlisle turned and smiled at her. "I'm gonna pass out."

Chris and Uncle Matt laughed as Liz and her brother approached her bed.

"So, we'll, ah, go get some coffee." Uncle Matt sent Chris a pointed look, and they left the room in a hurry.

Mia stared at Liz, and then at Gray, and finally found her voice. "What the actual heck, Liz! I'm wearing a hospital gown!"

"I've worn a few of those myself. It's a better look on you." Gray perched on the edge of her bed and flashed a grin. "So, you're Mia. I've heard a lot about you."

"I'll bet." She scowled at Liz. She was so dead. But Liz looked as happy as Rusty's stupid goats. And she actually leaned over and kissed her cheek.

"Don't ever do anything like that ever again, you hear me?"

Mia grinned and rolled her eyes. "I'll do my best."

Gray flicked a strand of blond hair away from his eyes. "So I hear you're helping plan me a wedding."

"Liz has done most of it. She's pretty awesome." Ugh. Why'd she say that? Mia looked away fast, but Liz laughed and touched her arm.

"You're pretty awesome yourself, kiddo. You know that?"

Mia sighed and blinked tears. Great. Now she was going to cry in front of Gray Carlisle. "I'm not awesome. Just stupid."

"Hey." Gray cleared his throat and she met his gaze, still finding it hard to believe he was sitting beside her. "You've had a rough go. I know what that's like. You probably know my sordid story. Drugs, alcohol."

"Yeah." Mia knew. It had been all over the news. "But you're good now, right?"

"Clean and sober." Gray nodded. "But it took a while. Still, with the right help and support, you can kick addiction in the a—I mean . . . second chances are possible." He smiled a little sheepishly, and Mia couldn't stop a grin.

"I know all about second chances," Liz put in, her eyes wet again. "And I've definitely made my share of mistakes."

"You?" Mia found that hard to believe. Liz was pretty much perfect as far as she was concerned. Well. Except for the crazy ex-boyfriend bit.

Liz nodded and glanced at her brother. "Yes, Mia. Me." Then she sat back a bit, sighed, and told them a story Mia wouldn't soon forget.

One month later.

Mia perched on the back porch, under a blanket, writing in her journal as Lucy, her new puppy, peed on all the trees.

Dear Dad,

I've decided this will be my last letter to you. A lot's happened since I last wrote. Some bad stuff. Some good stuff too. Maybe I'll get to tell you about it someday. Or maybe I won't. I don't care that much anymore. Whoever you are, if you're out there, we'll find each other if we're meant to. Because life has a way of working out. I've learned that lesson the hard way, but you know what? I wouldn't change a thing.

And I'm going to be okay.

I'm not cutting anymore. I'm trying really hard, and for the most part, I feel better. Not so scared, though I still sleep with the light on. Christa, my therapist, says it'll take time, and not to be so hard on myself.

So, that's where I'm at. Letting go of the past. And I guess that means letting go of you.

Or at least the dream of who I hoped you were. I always thought it sucked that I didn't have a dad. But I don't think that anymore. I have Uncle Matt.

So, I guess this is goodbye for now. I wish you all the good things.

Love, Mia.

She closed her journal with a smile. Christmas a few days away now, snow covered the ground and made everything look pretty, like the land sparkled with diamonds. She wondered if the little pup found it too cold though. Maybe they should get her some booties. Though she'd probably chew them up.

The past few weeks had been hard. She'd missed some school because of everything she'd had going on. But she was glad to have things out in the open now. Glad they could talk about her past and her cutting and how she didn't have to be afraid anymore.

The back door squeaked open. "Lunch is ready." Liz sat beside her, huddled in a down winter jacket. "Is she almost done?"

"I think so. C'mon, Lucy!" The pup turned her head and barked, then buried her nose in the snow, throwing it every which way. Mia and Liz laughed.

"Gray and Tori are flying in tomorrow. Can't wait for you to meet Tess."

"Me either." Mia smiled at the mention of Gray's little girl. They'd chatted over Facetime a couple of times. Well, as much as you could chat with a toddler. Gray called her all the time. Checking up on her. They'd talked a lot over the couple days he'd been here. About fear and addiction and how not to give in to the power it held. He'd given her his number. Sometimes she'd just stare at his name in her contacts, hardly daring to believe it. She called him sometimes, when she felt afraid. And he always made her laugh. "You think everything is going to be ready for the wedding?"

Liz slipped her arm through hers and gave a shrug. "I'm praying so."

"Things must be really behind schedule."

"Hey, now. Am I not allowed to pray?"

Mia laughed a little. "Well. I pray every time I see my mom's number come up. Sometimes it helps."

"Mothers aren't always perfect, Mia," Liz said softly. "And that's hard."

"I talk to her sometimes. Christa thinks it's a good idea. I guess it is. I don't know for sure if she'll really change, but I can't stay mad forever."

"No, you can't," Liz agreed. They stood, let Lucy in first, and stopped in the outside hall to take off their boots and jackets. "Heard from Chris?"

Mia blew on her hands to warm them. "Yeah. He says New York sucks. But he's applying for a summer job at the yacht club. So he'll be on Nantucket by Memorial Day if he gets it."

"That's awesome. And what about you? What are your plans for the summer?"

"I don't know for sure. Evy wants me to work at the gallery. Even said something about giving me my own show sometime. As if. But my grandparents want to take me to Europe."

"Europe? That sounds exciting."

"It'd be in June. Then we'd be back for the rest of summer. So Chris . . ." Mia dried Lucy with a towel and grinned. "Well. We'd still get most of the summer together. They said I'd get to visit the Louvre. I can't imagine seeing all those paintings in person. Uncle Matt might come too. He hasn't decided yet."

"I know. I'm trying to convince him to put his photographs together for a show. I think he wants to use the trip as an excuse not to."

That was true. Uncle Matt had spent all his free time lately taking photographs. Of birds and whatever wildlife he could find. The ones of people were good. He'd captured the twins playing in the snow. Even shot a few of Mia and Drake painting together. She had one of those framed on the wall of the new art studio upstairs that Uncle Matt and her grandparents fixed up for her. Another birthday surprise. She went up there now whenever she could. And lost her emotion to the art. But out of all the photographs he'd taken over the last few weeks, she liked the ones of Liz the best.

To Liz's great relief, their brother Ryan and his small son Isaiah flew in from Africa just in time for Christmas, after a twenty-four-hour delay that had them all on pins and needles. Gray had misplaced his normally calm composure, and Liz had had to talk him down off more than one ledge this week. Mia was getting pretty good at that too. They made an interesting pair, but every time she saw them together, Liz couldn't stop a smile.

The snow stopped two days before New Year's Eve. The last nail on the floorboards went in. Tables and chairs and linens were set. Lights were strung, the music ready. Flowers were delivered and set, perfectly in place, and the dining room looked spectacular. Evy had jumped in to help with the decorating, and Liz couldn't have managed without her.

All the guests arrived as scheduled, safely sequestered in the new guestrooms upstairs.

Now the day had finally arrived. Liz sat beside Matthew at the front of the living room, ten rows of chairs on either side behind them, every seat filled. The processional music began to play and Liz watched Lynette walk hand in hand with Tess, the grinning three-year-old looking like an angel in an ankle-length white dress, burgundy velvet ribbon around her waist, white patent leathers skipping a little as she tried to pick up the pace. She held a basket of white rose petals and scattered them as she went. Two attendants followed, and then the music changed.

Tori processed down the red carpet between the chairs to a piano instrumental Gray had written for her, and Liz held her breath. She caught Cecily dabbing her eyes already as she held tightly to Dad's arm.

Liz felt as though she'd been wiping tears all day. Mia grinned at her from where she sat beside Josslyn, helping with the twins while David stood with Nick up front.

Gray looked every inch the star that he was. His three-piece dark blue suit was perfect, and he'd shaved at last and cut his hair. Nerves apparently gone, she'd never seen him so happy. And so clearly head over heels in love with his bride. Her brother caught her eye and tipped his head with his classic grin. "Thank you," he mouthed.

And she was crying again.

"Welcome." Ryan smiled at them all, bible in hand, Isaiah holding the rings beside him. "It is my distinct honor to welcome you to Wyldewood this afternoon, as we celebrate the marriage of Grayson John Carlisle and Victoria Michelle Montgomery. And if I may say so, as the brother of the groom, it's about dang time."

———

Liz slipped out of the dining room after dessert, before the speeches started. She wasn't sure why. She just needed a moment. She stood in the deserted living room, closed her eyes, and allowed all the memories in again. They'd missed Mom today. Lynnie especially, but Gray most of all. Yet somehow, Liz knew she was with them in spirit.

Diana Carlisle never missed a celebration.

Having Dad here with them made the day even more special. They weren't sure what emotions seeing his old home might evoke, if any at all, but he'd strolled through the rooms earlier, whistling a tune they recognized as an old song he used to play incessantly, one that he and their mother would often dance to.

When they reached the living room, he'd stopped before the fireplace and gazed up at the family portrait he'd painted so many years ago. Liz remembered sitting for it, how they'd all grumbled but gone along because it was a surprise for their mother. She and David had corralled their younger brothers, put a dress on Lynette despite her protests, and made sure they were all neat and spit-shined. Liz had been fourteen, about to leave for boarding school at the end of that summer.

"There we are then." Dad had stared at the painting for some time, and then stared at her, his eyes bright. "We're a good bunch, aren't we Bizzy-Lizzy?"

Liz wiped her eyes and filed the memory away with all the other good ones.

"Hello, gorgeous." She jumped as Matthew's arms came around her waist and he nuzzled her neck. "That was quite a wedding. Congratulations."

She made a slow turn in his arms and admired him not for the first time that day. She'd never seen him in a suit, and he wore it well. The way he'd stared at her when he'd first arrived made her stomach flip. In her opinion, he was the best looking man in the room. But then she was slightly biased.

"Thank you for all your help the last couple weeks. Especially with everything going on with Mia. She's been such a help too."

His face lit with the smile she was getting very comfortable with. "It gave her something else to focus on. And you know she loves Gray."

"That she does." Liz laughed.

He tucked a loose curl behind her ear and gave a low whistle. "Did I tell you how amazing you look today?"

She smoothed down her green satin dress with a smile. "Yes, but you can tell me again."

His eyes crinkled. "What are you thinking about out here all alone, Elizabeth?"

She leaned into his embrace once more. "A few things. How lucky I am. How much I love my family. How I'll never take that for granted again. And . . . that no matter what happens with the court case next week, it'll be okay. I'll be okay."

"You will." He nodded. "And I'll be right there with you. It'll be over before you know it. And then we'll come home."

"Home." She smiled at the realization. "I haven't thought of Nantucket as home for a long time. But now it's the only place home could be. Funny, isn't it? I think I've finally figured out where I belong."

"I think you have too." He touched the top of her nose with his. "What else?"

"Oh, you know." Laughter bubbled upward as she basked in his smile and the sparkle in his eyes. "I was thinking this whole wedding thing might not be so bad after all."

"What a coincidence." Matthew grinned, kissed her full on the lips and his smile broadened. "I was thinking the exact same thing."

thank you!

Each time I come to this point in a book's production, I choke a little. Because how do you adequately thank so many people in such a wee space when there really aren't enough words in the world to express my heart . . . but I must try anyway.

First of all, my long-suffering family. I think they're all used to this routine by now, and my two kids are fortunately long out of the house, so no longer have to suffer burned dinners, no dinner, takeout dinner . . . so the real thanks must go to my husband, who still graciously puts up with all the craziness, and steps in to make dinner more times than I can count, and that is why we're both still alive, really. And he insists that I model all my male heroes after him. Well. Why wouldn't I?

Sarah, Randy, Annabel, and baby who will have a name and a face at the time of this book's release—your unwavering support of my writing means more than I can say. My 'Annabel days' make up for any stress-inducing days, and I'm so grateful to be her Mimi, and can't wait to meet our next bundle of joy! You are truly amazing parents and I'm so proud of you both.

Chris and Deni – your artistic talent still blows me away. I love that we get to be fellow storytellers together. It's an incredible privilege, and I've so enjoyed listening to your music mature right along with you over the years. We are always looking forward to the next thing from The Western Den! Your beautiful souls inspire me, and we can't wait to watch your marriage unfold, with all the joys that married life will bring.

Rachelle Gardner, my agent, my friend—what an honor it is to be able to say that. I can always count on you to give me the straight talk, encourage and lift me up, and remind me that things aren't as bad as all that on those days when I'm fully convinced they are. None of this would be possible without your support and belief that I have a place in publishing! I am so beyond grateful to have you as my cheering section and partner on this often crazy journey!

So many friends to thank and I'm always afraid of leaving someone out . . . yikes!

Mick Silva, for taking on the editing of this novel, and making it even better. It's always a pleasure to work with you and learn from you. Yvonne Parks at pearcreative.ca for coming alongside me on another project and knocking it out of the park with such a beautiful cover, wow! Rel Mollet for all your encouragement and hard work on my behalf, I am so fortunate to have you on my team, (and we can all thank her for keeping my scattered brain organized). So many writing friends who truly get me and stay with me and talk me down from all the ledges – Beth Vogt, well you're just an angel, that's all there is to say. Jennifer Major, ditto, our chats and enthusiasm have helped me keep going more times than I can count. All my ACFW friends, I'm so glad we're all in this together. Katie Ganshert, Rachel Linden, Lindsay Harrel, and so many others. I love that we're strapped onto the same rollercoaster and enjoying the ride, even with all the ups and downs!

My Dad and Vivian, you're always there to lend support and cheer me on, and I'm so grateful for that! Thank you! LeeAnne, my BFF, I don't know what I'd do without you. Probably just lay on the couch and cry. My sister, Pam, I can always count on you to be there for me, and I still marvel that that miracle. All my family far flung across the globe, I love you all.

And finally to my wonderful readers . . . thank you, thank you, thank you. For every email. For every shout out on social media, for everything you do to help boost my books and get them into the hands of more readers. You allow me to continue to write, and your support is something I definitely could not do without. So thank you and I hope I continue to give you stories you love.

Until next time!

About the Author

Catherine West is an award-winning author of contemporary women's fiction. When she's not at the computer working on her next story, you can find her taking her border collie for long walks or reading books by her favorite authors. She and her husband reside in Bermuda, and have two adult children and one beautiful granddaughter. Visit her online at catherinejwest.com.

You can connect with Catherine on social media:

CatherineJWest

@cathwestwrites

@cathwest

The Things We Knew

MEET THE CARLISLE FAMILY!

As their father's failing health and financial concerns bring the Carlisle siblings home, secrets surface that will either restore their shattered relationships or separate the siblings forever.

www.catherinejwest.com

CATHERINE WEST

where hope begins

A Novel

Where Hope Begins

SOMETIMES WE'RE ALLOWED TO GLIMPSE THE
BEAUTY FROM WITHIN THE BROKENNESS . . .

"*Where Hope Begins* will take you breath, and quite possibly
your heart."

–Patti Callahan Henry, *New York Times* bestselling author.

www.catherinejwest.com